THIS IS NOT THE END

JESSE JORDAN

THIS IS NOT THE END

JESSE JORDAN

MEDALLION

Medallion Press, Inc.
Printed in USA

Published 2016 by Medallion Press, Inc.,
4222 Meridian Pkwy, Suite 110, Aurora, IL 60504

The MEDALLION PRESS LOGO
is a registered trademark of Medallion Press, Inc.

Names, characters, places, and incidents are the products of the author's imagination or are used fictionally. Any resemblance to actual events, locales, or persons, living or dead, is entirely coincidental.

Cataloging-in-Publication Data is on file with the Library of Congress

Typeset in Adobe Garamond Pro
Printed in the United States of America
ISBN # 978-194254632-0

10 9 8 7 6 5 4 3 2 1
First Edition

Ricki, Ben, Charlie.
To the three of you.
Clink.

"What . . . ?"

—Abraham

1. In the Beginning

The world was asleep.

Two thirty-five on a Tuesday morning and Stone Grove, Illinois, barely registered a heartbeat. A couple cars, a few dogs barking to each other across the distance, and the sound of Route 83 transporting irregular speeders just outside town. Clusters of dark homes sat interspersed with those which maintained the pulsing eyes of overnight TV.

All of this was visible from the catwalk atop the town's only working water tower, a fat-bodied marshmallow in desperate need of a paint job, chipped white paint giving way to giant used-to-be-true-blue letters: ST N G VE. The tower sat upon a latticework of triangled steel legs and ladders, set dead in the center of the town's public-works yard, just behind the city hall/police station building.

And there, on that catwalk, in an old gray hoodie and ill-fitting blue jeans, sat a baby-faced boy with unkempt, double-cowlicked brown hair. James Salley, who'd slipped through a small hole in the public-works fence as he had so many times before, sat on the Stone Grove water-tower catwalk on the morning of his sixteenth birthday, willing himself to stand and jump.

What James actually felt at that moment, though, was his resolve slipping. He'd snuck out so certain, made his way through the sleeping town with rage pulling him on. It was wonderful. The sucking sadness that had filled his brain so long was replaced for a moment, pushed out by this beautiful rage.

Go. Get out of here. Do it. They'll all see and they'll . . .

And he'd pulled on his clothes and rushed out quick and quiet and headed for the water tower to end it. Oh, god, the sweet rush; the very thought of an end was the strongest tonic he'd ever felt.

But now, sitting up here, James searched for that rage, that righteousness of purpose, and found nothing. Anxiety grew through his body like vines, spreading the realization—*You're not gonna do it.*

Shut up!

James squeezed his eyes tight and replayed the events of that day, rebuilding the shame, testing the sharpness of it against his skin.

Nick Schroeder.

Colin O'Connor.

There were others there. Lots of them.

But those two lived in his mind like real life right now—after school, blinking into the afternoon sun, the tug on his backpack.

"Let me see your drawings, Jimmy."

"How come you never let us see your drawings, Jimmy?" Nick stepped directly in front of him.

James stopped, awkward and unsure.

Nick's neck muscles torqued like steel cables as he tilted his head. "Slow down, Jimmy. Where ya headed?"

"Look—"

"Why don't you come to wrestling practice with us?"

James didn't even answer. Eyes down, willing the moment to hurry up and hurt and end, he just shook his head.

"Who knows, Jimmy? Maybe you'd be good at it."

Colin answered with that big laugh, that outdoor Midwest laugh.

Nick rolled his head the other way on his thick neck and smiled. "I could show you some moves."

"Could you just leave me alone, man?" It took extraordinary effort to mumble those seven words, and as they were out, James tried to push past—and then it all happened, too quick for him to dissect.

Pressure on the back of his head as his right leg swept out in front of him, and then he was on his side. A few wood chips from the playground pressed between the blacktop and his ribs, and he tried to wriggle away.

Nick's grip mocked the effort. "See, this is called a basket cradle." His other arm scooped up James's left knee until it was almost touching James's face. Nick threw his leg over his and rolled him over, pinning his back with both legs.

Tears built as James wriggled, more helpless than he'd ever felt.

"See, from here it's an easy pin. It's also real good for a pink belly."

"Pink belly!" Colin shrieked as he dropped to the tangle of limbs, pulling back James's shirt to reveal his soft, dimpled belly.

James kicked. His grunts were uneven and came out with desperate squeaks intermingled, but nothing changed.

"Pink belly, pink belly, pink belly." Colin giggled, licking both his palms and rubbing them together.

Slap.

Slap.

"Stop!" James saw Gail and Maria and Jess and LaMarcus, and some were laughing and some looked like they didn't want to be watching this, and he couldn't decide which was worse as the tears started to pour over his face.

Slap.

Slap.

Slap, slap, slap, slap, slap, slap.

James tried to tell them to stop. He tried to curse them with the worst words he knew. But nothing would come. Instead, he began to sob, and the crying seized his breathing, and his belly burned.

Colin stopped and stood up, wearing a defensive smile. "Oh my god, dude, I barely got you. You're fine."

Nick released the hold and rolled up to his feet in one athletic movement. "It's okay, man. Jimmy's sensitive. He's an artist." He laughed, but no one joined in.

He pinched James's stomach hard. "Got that soft pink piggy belly."

James pulled his shirt down and noticed Jess walking off, along with a few others, though he couldn't see who. Nick turned to say something to them, and in the instant he was ignored, James scrambled up, dragging his backpack, and ran. Behind him, Nick shouted something, but mercifully it was lost in the wind and pulse buffeting his ears.

James remembered that feeling of running, tears cooling on his cheeks, stomach on fire, and he stood up on the water-tower catwalk. He leaned against the railing, feeling it press against his sternum. He leaned out over the edge. *Push out. Up and out.*

James wondered how they'd talk about it at school. He wondered if they'd blame Nick. The idea had seemed like an attack before—an offensive act after so much defense. But now, as he thought about the actual effects, it seemed more like admitting defeat. His suicide wouldn't destroy or haunt Nick Schroeder. *Who knows what Nick would feel?* Furthermore, he didn't particularly care.

Would they see it as confirmation? He was weak: of course he quit; of course he chickened out.

James leaned out farther and concentrated on the ground. He saw himself leaping forward, tipping headfirst. An instant of falling, the ground screaming at him. And then . . . the smash. The crack? What would it be like when he and the concrete collided? He imagined the thunderclap shockwave of it through his whole self.

It was impossible to deny how terrified he was.

I could do it! I'm not scared.

Who are you trying to convince?

James let out his breath, and the last of his energy went with it—the last of this self-deception. The fog cleared, and the realization sat there, staring at him: *You're not gonna jump. You were never really gonna jump.*

Nothing was going to happen. Nothing was going to change. James could see Nick at him again tomorrow. He could see a thousand more lunches eaten alone, a thousand more nights spent in his room, cut off.

James Salley stood on the catwalk of the Stone Grove water tower overlooking the sleeping town, and he saw the rest of his life laid out before him.

And he began to cry.

2. The Ordinary World

James looked down at the plate and the piece of paper whose edge was pinned beneath it. On the plate sat three orange Danish, no longer hot from the oven. James's mom always made him orange Danish[1] on his birthday, though in the past she'd managed to deliver the pastry personally every time.

The letter read:

Hey, Lovie,[2]

Dad and I both had to work early this morning. Enjoy your Danish! Give me a call later and let me know where you want to go for your birthday dinner.

Love you and Happy Birthday from Mom and Dad!

(Oh, and Dad said to remind you that soccer sign-ups are this weekend.)

Love you.

James put one Danish in his mouth as he headed for the

---

1 Orange Danish, for those unfortunate few who've never experienced them, are cinnamon rolls covered in orange-flavored icing. Pillsbury makes a fine version.

2 James's middle name (it's a long story). Within the last few years James had asked his mom to refrain from using that particular sobriquet unless she was positive that no one was around.

laundry room. It was just as he'd suspected—barely luke-warm, the icing already congealing.

James kicked around the laundry room for a while as he ate, picking up shirts and casting them aside. This step always slowed the process; such is the torture of the chubby, the bulky, the thick—the *husky*, as Mom liked to say. There are so many ways any shirt can be wrong; so few in which it can be right.

James settled on a loose, long-sleeve T-shirt and returned to the kitchen to eat another Danish and stare at the news on the kitchen TV. It washed over him, the same old stories,[3] but failed to penetrate. James replayed last night, wondering now in the bright clarity of morning how close he'd really been. And he replayed the afternoon before with Nick. But now, more than the helplessness and the pain, it was the shame that stung. He could feel new fear being born as he saw himself crying, saw all those eyes on him.

Dread. That was what hit big. Dread to go there, to see any of them.

Was this dread really that different from his regular dread, though? His daily dread? *Most likely,* he figured, *they'll just ignore me like always.*

James grabbed the last Danish and slipped his back-pack on. He pushed his feet into sneakers and almost sorta smiled. How many times had he cursed his ostra-cism, pleaded with God for it to end? And here he was, so used to it that it'd become a source of comfort. It was a blan-ket, and he wrapped it around himself now for protection.

---

3 That island in the Pacific that disappeared, the tallies from the Great Drought last summer, updates on the fallout from the India-Pakistan nuke skirmish, etc.

James scanned the note once more. He crumpled it and tossed it in the garbage, and stepped out the back door.

His parents were around less and less these days. Both climbing and, it appeared to James, terrified that if they stopped for a moment they'd be fired—maybe publicly shamed and put out as well. At least that was how they acted. It seemed things were going well. A few promotions, a few raises. They both drove nicer cars and looked at bigger houses a lot and talked about moving, but that was about it. To James, life didn't seem much different from back when they treated work like it was just a job.

And the soccer thing. Jesus Christ. At what point exactly did my weight become his business? I'm actually pretty average. Okay, sure, maybe I have a little too much baby fat still, but it's not like I'm . . .

James thought of those peers of his who had, in the last couple years, grown into sleek missiles of coiled muscle. He still had a soft belly, and his chest was flabbier than he would have liked. He did not, however, have tits. This was an important distinction. Ken Lakatos had tits. Ken was a massive, black-haired awkward kid, and the folds of his chest were a source of constant glee among the boys of George Washington High School. So much so that James, who was in the same gym class, would watch Ken out of the corner of his eye, waiting for the moment Ken removed his shirt in order to remove his own, knowing that whatever ridicule was about to be unleashed on Ken would draw any possible attention away from him. Still, James considered himself far from obese; more importantly, he didn't recall asking for his father's help with the issue.

Across the street loomed The Eights, the stretch of four-story, redbrick apartment buildings that ran along the south side of the train tracks.[4] James crossed the parking lot and cut between two of The Eights, to where the makeshift track entrance was. Stone Grove, you see, was perfectly bisected by the train tracks. Two parallel steel tracks sitting on rows of wooden teeth, themselves raised

---

4 **The Composite Story of The Eights, as Passed to James by General Consensus—** The Eights was the second-largest building complex in Stone Grove. The largest was the abandoned ChocoMalt factory, and these two were intrinsically tied to each other in the mind of the town.

ChocoMalt was started in the 1930s and was soon the second-largest chocolate malted milk producer in the US, behind Ovaltine. In the 1960s, they built their new central factory here in Stone Grove, and in a matter of years, it *was* the town. The president of ChocoMalt, Gary Gilmore, donated a lot of the money to build the high school (which is how it got the unfortunate original moniker of Gary Gilmore High School, which was changed in 1983 after a town-wide vote), and the company was almost completely responsible for the modernization of the town hall/police and fire complex. By the 1970s, just about everyone worked for ChocoMalt, and no major civic decisions were undertaken without Mr. Gilmore's insight (okay). In fact, a few times ChocoMalt even paid their taxes early simply because they knew the town was low on funds.

Then, as often happened in the 1980s, everything turned to hot garbage. It had been noticeable for a while, and even as the town and ChocoMalt tried to show the world a brave and happy face, they continued to hemorrhage. Until, in 1987, two years after Mr. Gilmore's death from an opiate overdose that was written up as a slip in the shower when his son convinced the police it would be in everyone's best interest if this was handled with some decorum, the company finally shuttered its doors. An apocalyptic portion of the town was out of work. The factory, which took up nearly one-tenth of the real estate in town, sat empty and quickly became a petri dish of dares and ghost stories and Satanists and gangbangers and smoking weed/tripping/rolling/etc.

Now, at about the same time, the City of Chicago finally accepted the fact that perhaps stacking the impoverished in thirty-story slums was not the best idea, and so they began to tear down the projects (Cabrini Green, Henry Horner Homes, Robert Taylor Homes, etc.), relocating families into the south and west sides of the city but also into mixed-income properties they were building in the outlying suburbs. Stone Grove had no idea how to function without ChocoMalt's input and attorneys, no idea even what it was they wanted (except, of course, for it to be the 1970s again). So, in 1991, a private developer, in concert with the Chicago Housing Authority, paid a one-time fee for the right to build mixed-income complexes along the tracks off Madison Avenue. Section 8 residents moved in, and the remaining apartments slowly filled with others moving west. The demographics of the town changed. The old residents talked about how the town used to smell like chocolate, as if they were remembering some Oz-like make-believe world, though it seemed what they really meant was that the town used to be all-white and all-middle-class and all-employed (regardless of skill set) and the world generally didn't used to be such a scary place.

on gray-and-white stones, which dipped away to each side, forming little embankments. At the lowest points of these embankments, guarding both flanks of the tracks, were six-foot-tall chain-link fences that, if they scratched you, seemed to instantly convey a subtle itching and burning, a feeling that lockjaw and infection were imminent.

Main Street and Orange Street, being the main north/south thoroughfares, offered breaks in the fences and the freedom to cross, and this arrangement seemed to work fine for all those blessed with automobiles. For kids, though, bolt cutters were visas. A few years earlier, the police made a concerted effort to repair and arrest, but the futility of it soon became so obvious that even the higher-ups understood. After that a kind of unspoken truce was made: *We'll let you keep the access points, but don't be a dick and cut them every five feet.* The citizenry, for the most part, obliged.

James arrived at the farthest east access hole in The Eights as he did every morning, but just as he was about to duck through, he noticed the freight train. Lost in his recriminations of Dad, James hadn't heard the train until it was close, only fifty feet or so to his left and on the far tracks. For a moment he considered going for it, just sprinting across the rocks and over the tracks. He could probably make it, too. *Probably.*

He pictured himself running, saw the rocks slipping loose underneath, becoming a conveyor belt, his foot comically shooting out behind him as he falls on the tracks. His head connects with the steel with the grotesque crack of skull meeting metal, and then he just lies there.

His heart picked up, beating with ancient animal purpose as he watched the James in his mind prone on the rail and tried to pull him back to consciousness: He flips open punch-drunk eyes just in time to see the razor-hammer wheel meet the track where his head lies, where it offers no resistance as it bursts.

James shook his head just as the train made it to him and continued past.

He hated the trains. Hated the horns, the screech of brakes, the mind-blanking rumbling roar. But more than anything, James hated how constant they seemed; unable to stop or turn, unfazed by all of us, just unrelenting metal monsters.

This feeling was worse than it had once been. Last February, on a crisp Tuesday morning when everything was covered in a night's worth of heavy, fresh snow, James walked this same path toward school, his mind on post-sleep autopilot, feet following a muscle-memory route, until the moment he ducked through the hole in the fence, when he realized something was very wrong. Cops and firefighters gathered around the tracks about thirty yards to the west, and at the base of the decline, pressed up against the fence, was a body. There was a dark cloth over it, but the wind kept blowing up large enough segments to see a crumpled shape beneath, as if some giant had merely picked up a person, squeezed out everything that made them real, and then dropped the lifeless collection of bones and slack muscle on the ground. One bare foot poked out the entire time, facing James.

It wasn't until later that day at school that he finally learned what'd happened. Some drunk lady (apparently well known locally for her habitual presence at area bars and occasional explosions of passion and effrontery) was walking home around five in the morning when she—either accidentally or on purpose—ended up on the same track as a cross-country freight. James still saw her in his mind, especially when it snowed, and he found variations on the foot sneaking into his drawings occasionally, as if her corpse was a germ which had entered through his eye and infected his mind.

James blinked away the vision and leaned back against the fence. And just as he did—at the exact moment his back touched the chain links—he noticed a black SUV in the parking lot across from him.

It was nothing special. Just a truck. Still, there was something about it.

Even though the parking lot was only half full, the SUV was parked all the way over at the east end, so that no other car was within fifty feet of it.

James hiked up the strap on his shoulder and considered the vehicle.

Below the level of the tracks, James watched between the bottom of the cars and the rails, so that he could see the SUV both underneath and between the cars of the train. Through this flipbook vision, James began to feel something was, well . . . off. It was a Cadillac Escalade, and at first he figured it was parked off by itself because the owner was paranoid about damages or maybe having some early-morning affair. But then James noticed the white exhaust drifting away—and then he saw him.

Seated behind the wheel was a single man in dark clothes. It looked like he had blond hair. James couldn't make out his face because there was something in front of it, something black and boxy. James leaned away from the fence and realized it was a camera—and it was pointed directly at him.

He's probably just filming the train.

The train? Who films trains?

Well, whatta you think? You think he's filming you?

I don't know. It's weird.

If he's a pervert, then he's making the lamest kiddie porn ever.

James could not dislodge the feeling that the blond man was watching him. He looked to the left and saw the end of the train coming around the trees, maybe two or three hundred yards off. He took a few steps in that direction before looking back to the Escalade. It really seemed like the camera followed him. James felt that ugly, little-kid fear tighten his scrotum, and he shook his head because he was being silly. He checked left—the end of the train was a hundred yards away and picking up speed. When he looked back, the man in the Escalade seemed to have noticed it too.

The blond man turned back toward James as he

tossed the camera aside. James couldn't distinguish his face from that distance, but then the man was turning, one arm slung across the seat next to him, and the Escalade backed up.

The panic built. *This is silly.* Still, James checked the end of the train, willing it to speed up, speed up, speed up, and just get past already.

Fifty yards.

Twenty-five. The blond man put the Escalade in drive and started off through the parking lot as James sidestepped toward the last car.

Ten yards.

Five. Two. One. And then it was past, its fat backward engine announcing its retreat as James rushed up the embankment until he was standing on the tracks. The black Escalade reached the end of the parking lot and turned right. By the time it occurred to James to get the license plate, the street was empty.

James skid-slipped down the embankment until he was standing against the other fence. He watched the intersection where the Escalade disappeared and wondered why he felt like he'd just missed something terribly important, something big and scary and very, very bad. He headed off to school along the tracks, all the while searching the streets to his right for a glimpse of the automobile.

As he replayed the image of the blond man with the camera, James trudged slowly over the rocks. Along the tracks, past Main Street and three other access holes leaking children, he saw that thin, light face over and over, until he found himself at the hole in the fence that led to the back fields of George Washington High School.

Ducking through the hole, James noticed Nick Schroeder and a small group of beauties and ogres standing off to the right amongst the ruins of the community center playground.[5] He immediately doubled his pace, disappearing into the river of kids as he locked his gaze straight ahead (while keeping track of the group in his periphery). He sped across the soccer field toward the back of the school.

This is probably as good a time as any to explain something about James.

Nobody likes him.

It may sound harsh, but it's true. You wouldn't like him if you knew him. And oddly enough, you wouldn't quite be able to articulate why. No one could. "Just something about him." That's what people always said. James had, in fact, come to grips with this aspect of his interaction with the outside world in the last few years. He always said the wrong thing at the exact wrong time, always smiled when he should have frowned. It was like everyone in the world was dancing to a song he couldn't hear. People

---

5 LaMarcus Daniels, Gail Asbury, Maria Montero, Jess Gerber, and Lucas Astrauskas—introductions to follow later, as necessary.

often found they felt a bit anxious or slightly depressed whenever he was near. Some people—the very sensitive— would even feel a little nauseated.

While almost everyone seemed to find James's presence unpleasant, it had an especially profound effect on Nicholas Allan Schroeder. Nick is a difficult child to describe, regardless of the objectivity of the narrator. At times he seems such a cliché that it's difficult to believe he's real. It's also difficult to believe he exists in total ignorance of his clichéness. Do people like Nick watch *The Karate Kid* and identify with Johnny?

Still, Nick was real, and he was tall and strong, and he did have blond hair (though not as blond as Johnny's), and he was the point guard and captain of the basketball team as well as a wrestler over whom the varsity coaches were already drooling.[6]

Nick had a physical reaction to James. Simply seeing James caused the muscles of his back to tense, his teeth to grind. Nick hated the way he felt around James, and being sixteen, he expressed this by beating the crap out of him, by tipping over his lunch tray and tripping him. At this point their interactions were routine for both of them.

At the edge of the blacktop, James snuck a look back to find Nick and his group heading toward him, though seemingly still unaware of (or unconcerned with) his

---

6 Of course, it's only fair to mention that Nick was the youngest of five brothers, known throughout town for their unyielding toughness and occasional cruelty. Kevin, John, Pat, and Steve Schroeder ranged from 19 to 24 years of age, and between them they had served two years in juvenile detention facilities, 17 months in county jail, and had a combined 6–2 MMA record. They considered Nick soft, and so made a concerted effort to harden him, as if he were being hazed into his own family. So who knows? Maybe if Nick had been born into a different family, he'd be a completely different boy. Sadly, though, he was not, and the reactionary bundle of defensive rage known as Nick Schroeder was what the world got.

presence. James made his way around the building, steeling himself with two deep breaths before he rounded the corner to the front of the school.

A large, concrete apron sat before the front doors like a wagging tongue. Little knots of students stood wasting time, separated from each other by only a few feet geographically but by an invisible line of absolute truth socially.

The dance never changes for kids like James: *Don't engage the groups. Don't court rejection and mockery. But don't sit out there alone either. Predators always look for prey that's been detached from the herd.*

James edged along the wall until he was a few feet from a congregation of popular juniors. Far enough away that they'd probably just ignore him but close enough that, to an uninterested glance, he may appear part of the group. He heard snatches of their conversation: girls they were chasing and debating, a fight that may or may not have happened, and a tale of a five-on-one ass-whipping that was most likely apocryphal. Still, it was another reminder to James of the life he was not leading. The boyfriends and girlfriends and friendship and arguments and drama, the sexual adventures—hell, even just kissing—the intimacy and betrayal of teenage life, happening all around him, without him. It was impossible to not feel stunted in his small and lonely world. It was impossible to not arrive at the obvious conclusion—*Something's wrong with me.*

"Nick," Colin O'Connor shouted, and James looked up to see Nick and Gail come around the side of the building with LaMarcus and Jess trailing. James, torn between the urge to watch Jess's beautiful citrus legs and the need to avoid Nick's attention, settled on the safe alternative and eased farther behind the juniors.

The bell rang and James, waiting until Nick and most of the others had made their way in, hitched up his bag and turned to walk inside. As he did, though, he saw the blinds on the nearest window snap shut. It was just some random classroom. Just blinds closing. But it happened so suddenly, and he wasn't sure, but he could've sworn there'd been eyes there. Like someone was watching him.

3. George Washington High School Gets a New Librarian

Mrs. Windermere was clueless. Everyone knew it, and frankly she could give a damn. She was sixty-two years old and probably should have stopped teaching when she was fifty-two. She no longer had any patience. She no longer cared. In fact, she no longer liked any kids except the really nice and exceptional ones (and if that's the case, then you just don't like kids). Her white-and-gray curly hair was almost as unkempt as her clothes, as if she didn't feel her job deserved even the niceties of grooming anymore. She was the very definition of burnt-out; she was also James's first-hour geometry teacher.

James sat in his seat, devouring a battle between Wolverine and Sabretooth as random clusters of students trickled into the classroom. The second bell, which announced the beginning of classes, had not yet rung, and while most students liked to cut it close, milking as much hallway social time as possible, James always felt he was more likely to be left alone once in class.

He smelled her before he saw her, and a Pavlovian smile inched across his face as he looked up from the X-Men to see Dorian walk in talking to Jess, both with their arms crossed over the books pressed tightly to their breasts, pictures of youth and purity and all that *Sweet Valley High* folklore. That smell of Dorian's—shea butter, vanilla, and Sweet Pea[7]—it was an obsession. It barely had to tickle the teensiest bit of his nose and his body woke up and his heart beat with a terrible/wonderful fear, a roller-coaster fear: slowly climbing up, up, up.

Jess peeled off, and Dorian looked over and caught James's smile and nod. She smiled back and waved, and Mrs. Windermere chewed on the end of her mechanical pencil, stumped by what she felt was a particularly difficult crossword clue,[8] fighting the urge to Google it. Dorian was one of the only people (though if we exclude family, she would be the only person) who was outwardly nice to James. He could tell he bothered her sometimes too, but since the Incident last year, she'd been nothing but kind; and Dorian's kindness was no small thing.

Dorian Delaney was one of the most popular girls in school, and the fact that she not only didn't shun James but was actively nice to him would be social seppuku for anyone else. Dorian, though, could pull it off. She was pretty and smart and funny, and the teachers liked her as much as the students did. The janitors, if polled, probably had nice things to say about her. People tended to

---

7 James was rightly embarrassed about this. While at the mall, he had made his way into Bath and Body Works more than once, sampling different lotions and body splashes until he nailed the smell. He will never tell anyone this.

8 16 Down—*Deer Hunter* Director (6 Letters)

describe her as adorable and beautiful and talented, and they hoped their daughters turned out like her.

A big part of this, of course, was a result of her singing. She was the closest thing George Washington High School had to a celebrity, having sung the national anthem at a NASCAR race, a minor-league hockey game, and a pro soccer game at Soldier Field, not to mention singing "O Holy Night" on the local NBC *Christmas Eve Gala* program two years prior. She'd been operatically trained since she was just a bit more than a baby, practiced every day after school and on the weekends, and sometimes even missed school to perform. Everyone was pretty sure that someday she'd be famous, and you don't risk alienating that just because she's nice to the weird kid who gives everyone the creeps.

James watched Dorian. She was so beautiful it hurt. Pale white skin like a shook sheet coming to rest on a clean bed. The straight, light-red hair that hung just below her shoulders was the same color as her freckles; and the freckles, which were everywhere, grew darkest over the bridge of her nose and across her cheeks. James once told her it looked like the mask Robin wore, but she didn't smile. Thin and meticulous, she'd always been one of the shortest girls in her class so that she gave off the impression of being breakable.

The tan speaker box up in the corner of the room emitted an electric scratch and burped to life, followed by a whisper of feedback and Dean Worthington clearing his throat. "Good morning, students and faculty. Handling the announcements today will be student council secretary Mitch Toller."

Sssht. Silence.

Then the pop of the feed returning and the shuffle/crinkle of paper. "Uh, good morning," Mitch Toller began. "The, uh, the freshmen girls' volleyball team traveled to Huntington to take on the perennial power Wildcats. Great passing and communication led to a . . . to a . . . twenty-five-to-sixteen victory." Ssht—pop. "Go, Cardinals. The varsity girls didn't fare as well, losing a tense game that was much closer than its twenty-five-to-two score." Paper shuffling. A cough, a throat cleared. "Hey, everybody, if you haven't . . . heard, Camera Club is more than just . . . taking pictures. Also, you, uh, you don't even have to have your own camera. Come by Room 813 today after school to check it out. Br-bring a friend." Shuffle, shuffle.

James reached into his bag and pulled out his sketchbook.

"And finally, school librarian Mrs. Hauser will be away for the remainder of . . . of the year. There will be an inter-interim, uh, librarian. Please introduce yourself to Mr. Moon when you see him in the library, and give him a big Washington welcome. Uh, okay, that's it for announcements. Thank you, and have a great day."

James wasn't surprised. Mrs. Hauser probably had cancer or something. She always looked sick, but that could've just been from sitting in the library with her Diet Cokes all day.

Mrs. Windermere took attendance as James opened his sketchpad, which was in fact his only possession of any real psychic value to him. James drew. He drew well and often, and when he did, he forgot about the world around him or he twisted it into his own creation: a world where he wasn't ignored and stomped and floating alone. He opened his mind and let everything pour onto these pages.

James began to draw. He wasn't even paying attention, just half listening to Mrs. Windermere and sneaking looks at Jess's legs and the side of Dorian's neck as his pen moved across the page. It wasn't until the bell rang that he looked down and noticed what he'd been drawing: the black Escalade.

Lunch, like gym and before and after school, could be a dangerous time. It allowed for gatherings and groupthink and kangaroo courts, and it was for these reasons that James attempted to remove himself from the entire exercise. He sat mostly alone, though nobody could sit completely alone, as there simply wasn't enough real estate in the cafeteria for the physical manifestation of ostracization. Most of the outcasts sat clustered at the two tables farthest from the windows. And castes existed even within this motley gathering of losers—second-and-third-level misfits—so that some people managed to be rejected by multiple groups of descending popularity each day. James avoided most of that, though. For some reason, the other pariahs tended to ignore him.

James stacked his french fries in overlapping rows on the dry, rectangular pizza sitting on his yellow tray, and he was sad. He was profoundly sad. While he was often bullied and ignored, and while he rarely (if ever) felt that other people wanted to connect with him in any way, what he experienced now was a crippling sadness. James pictured himself diving off that catwalk last night, and the falling felt like flying. It all felt like relief.

He wondered if he'd go back tonight. He wondered how many nights he'd have to go back until he wasn't too scared.

James noticed the heat of imminent tears and took a massive bite of fry-pizza, and as he did, as he looked up and began to masticate the antisocial mouthful, he saw a man watching him.

There. He'd been right there, at the doors, leaning against the door frame and looking at James. A tall, thin man with light-brown hair graying at the temples, watching him with a small, soft smile. But he was gone. James shook his head and looked again. No one. But he could've sworn he saw him.

He could've sworn.

As often happens with humans, when James's brain was given time to ruminate, it worked itself into a very excited state. The day progressed, and the image of the man's smiling face returned again and again to James's mind, along with those blinds snapping closed when school started. *Those eyes. There had been eyes there. His eyes? And that Escalade . . . ?*

Seventh hour. Art. The class toiled on wood carvings, half of the students bent intently over their work, while the other half giggled and gossiped. James tried to concentrate, but he couldn't help but watch Jess from the edges of his eyes. Jess sat with Gail, Maria, and Katie and laughed louder than anyone, repeating mildly amusing phrases as if they were comedy gold.

To James, though, she looked sad. She looked sad and scared to show she was sad, using her howling glee like a shield. James watched, transfixed, because it seemed so obvious to him. How could the others not notice?

"I know! I wanna lock myself in the bathroom with Oreos, but then I'll just be doing cardio until midnight!"

The others laughed along with her, and as she turned back to Maria, she saw him. Her eyes screamed like someone caught, and for an instant, her loud mask slipped aside. It was like James could see *inside* of her. Just for an instant. And what shone through was fear and wretched sadness. Jess seemed to reset herself, and the glimpse disappeared and she was staring at James, who had to look away. Those eyes—he saw them still in his mind, full of rebuke, as if he'd done something reprehensible. He didn't look up at her again throughout the period. He just kept his head down and focused on his project.

Everyone had selected a plank of wood and, using chisels and soldering irons, proceeded to create an image of their choosing. A few peace signs and crucifixes were under way as well as the requisite butterflies, flowers, and footballs. James's plank was a relief of Batman that used three different levels of wood depth. For the last two classes, he'd worked on nothing but the cape, which was caught by the wind, billowing off Batman's left shoulder.

Mr. Gere, the art teacher, moved quickly by James's work space with an offhand "Nice, James."[9] The other students, too, would stop by and look at the piece and smile and marvel. James's art, he'd noted long ago, didn't have the same effect on people that he did. When they finally did look up, though, when they tore their gazes from whatever he was working on and looked up to him, their smiles inevitably faltered. Then he'd be left with some mumbled, monosyllabic compliment and their backs.

James finished a large swath of cape that he'd been working with the soldering iron and set the tool back in its aluminum tray before massaging the cramp gripping his hand. The muscles in the webbing between his thumb and forefinger felt like they were being bisected by a hot, dull knife. He kneaded the pain with the thumb and knuckle of his left hand and leaned back in his chair. He

---

9 Mr. Gere was only a so-so teacher; obviously more interested in his own fledgling art career (painting famous war photographs, such as *General Nguyen Ngoc Loan Executing a Viet Cong Prisoner in Saigon*, on large mirrors) than the education of his students. Still, he encouraged James when he was working on something challenging and was honest when James made crap. Plus, he'd been the one who showed James *Guernica* and explained the historical context and symbolism of it, at which point *Guernica* became James's favorite painting ever. (He even had a big print of it on his bedroom wall.) But for the most part, Mr. Gere was only ever half present (not to mention he always smelled like patchouli, chemicals, and armpit).

blew out a deep breath and looked around—and there it was.

Just outside the window behind Mr. Gere's desk, sitting in the morning drop-off zone, was the black Escalade. He couldn't see the driver this time, as the vehicle had its passenger side to him and offered only the dismissal of tinted windows.

James stood, and just then, the brake lights announced the Escalade's shift into drive. James made for the window, bumping desks and chairs and trailing shouts and grunts. The Escalade erupted from its position, speeding out of the parking lot and then to the right, again denying James a look at the license plate. James stood at the window, his face pressed to the pane long after the vehicle disappeared, and for the first time, he was positive something was very, very wrong. Liquid-ice fear spread through his stomach and pressed his lungs tight.

"Mr. Salley," Mr. Gere said, "is something the matter?"

The final bell released them.

James dumped his books in his locker, put his head down, and made for the exit at the back of the school.

Before he reached it, though, Nick and Colin and LaMarcus erupted from the main-hall boys' bathroom like guided cannonballs in a cloud of shouts and laughter, trailing the noises of mischief wrought within. All three were puffed up and riled with that hunting-party look of theirs.

James froze. *This is the worst—the absolute worst—time to run into them.* He turned to make for the other exit but, in doing so, smacked into the torso of a man standing there, almost falling—*A fall! At a time like this? Might as well wear a bell*—and looked up to see the man from earlier smiling down at him out of two light-blue eyes. Though, he noticed, the eyes weren't the same. In the right eye, the pupil was much more open than in the other eye, a dark circle ringed by a thin river of blue.

"Are you alright?"

"Yeah," James said, finding it hard to look away from those eyes, even though he knew he should check on Nick's confederacy. When he finally did manage to look away, sure enough, there they were. They'd seen him. "Uh, I gotta go."

"My name is Mr. Moon." He extended a sinuous left hand.

James shook it with absent politeness—*Quite a grip you got there, man*—and mumbled, "James." He was about to step around the new librarian when his periphery was filled up all of a sudden: Nick and Colin on one side and LaMarcus on the other.[10]

"Jimmy," Colin said, almost stepping between James and Mr. Moon. "Jimmy, Jimmy."

"You walkin'?" Nick said, his smile pure extortion.[11]

James tried to say something about having to stay

---

10 LaMarcus would later often feel a nauseating wave of shame when he thought of how they'd tortured that weird kid in high school. He often thought of tracking him down, of reaching out and saying how sorry he was. Unfortunately, LaMarcus never became the kind of man who acted on thoughts like that.

11 FLASH: *Early last summer—Nick sitting on the small of my back, fingers under my chin, cranking—Laughter, glimpses of Jess and sky and trees—"Camel clutch!"—Helpless, terrified—Pops in my spine, scary bad pressure, screaming, crying, that face upside down.*

late, but his usually reliable trove of lies returned nothing. He stood there frozen, mouth open, watching Nick's eyes beat him up in advance.

"Nicholas, is it?" Mr. Moon's words were clipped, like they'd been made in a factory.

Nick looked up at Mr. Moon. "James and I are having a conversation. You boys run along." Mr. Moon retained his friendly countenance, but Nick's nose crinkled and he got this look on his face like he was trying to place a memory.

LaMarcus said, "Nick?"

"C'mon," Nick said, and in a single motion he was gone, striding down the hall to the front doors with Colin and LaMarcus fighting to catch up without appearing to.

James watched this scene with mounting unease. *This is not right. The whole way Nick just reacted, that's not . . . not . . .*

"Well, James, I think you'll be fine walking home now." Mr. Moon's cheeks pulled back into a running-for-office smile, and he once again proffered his hand.

James shook it in dumb compliance. *What was I just thinking about?*

"It was nice meeting you." And with that, Mr. Moon turned sharply and strode away, his heels beating out a military march.

James watched him go, and when the new librarian turned the corner, he realized he was standing alone in the hallway.

4. Enter Antichrist

Mom called not long after he got home to tell him the whole sales/PR/marketing team was going to stay late to do a run-through on the entire company's presentation at the sales conference in New York that weekend and she, as the project leader—and what a huge opportunity that was—really, really should stay, but she'd leave if he wanted her to.

James told her it was fine and he understood.

She said, "Thanks, Lovie,"[12] and told him they'd do something big that weekend.

Approximately ten minutes later, Mom called back to tell him it turned out Dad had a great networking opportunity[13] he'd put off for the birthday dinner, but if they were moving the dinner to the weekend, then he guessed he'd go. She told James to just go ahead and use

---

12 James knew she still used it as an endearment, and he didn't have the heart to tell her just how much he disliked it. Lovie, his middle name, was a family callback. Mom had been super close with her sister, Shannon, who James never knew because she died of Leukemia when she was 12. Shannon used to call things and people she was affectionate about *lovie*. It was a word that worked its way into the sisters' relationship and became shorthand. James could tell how proud Mom was to have passed it along, how hard she tried to keep it going, but he didn't care. It was embarrassing and he hated it.

13 The CFO was taking a handful of managers to the Cubs game.

the credit card in the kitchen drawer to order pizza, which is exactly what he did.

James told himself he should work on his comic book or maybe go for a run like he kept telling himself he was going to start doing. By eight o'clock that night, however, all he'd done was eaten three-quarters of a pepperoni-and-mushroom pizza and a bowl of chocolate ice cream, drank three Cokes, reread half an Avengers trade paperback,[14] and watched part of a documentary on HBO about the disappearance of five hundred people in a cult in Colorado.

James considered sneaking one of Dad's Budweisers from the fridge, still thinking the thoughts of earlier in the day, of slurping down a couple beers and a bunch of booze from the liquor cabinet for courage and heading back to the water tower to do it right this time. But he had to admit the thought had lost its charge. He felt better. He always felt better after a night like this. Food without judgment and comic books and movies—they were his salve.

Instead, James lifted one of the Marlboro Lights from the carton Mom kept in cryofreeze in the bulk freezer in the garage. He went out to the front, where he rocked on the porch swing with the Kree-Skrull War blocking out the world, sneaking tiny drags.

He'd been outside for exactly six minutes and twelve seconds when he heard it.

A distant, high-low squeak drifted through the neighborhood, and James instinctively cupped the cigarette

---

14 *The Kree-Skrull War*

behind the swing to hide it. He stopped the porch swing with a toe to the ground. *What is that?* The squeak was repetitive and rhythmic, and it seemed to be growing louder, closer. The breeze died; the neighborhood felt still as a child's hiding place, other than the squeak. Nine thirty on a suburban weeknight—the leaves tussle, cars are tucked into driveways and garages, and random house lights tell the stories of who's up and what they're doing.

The squeak grew, and James noticed a pattern in it, a sort of cycling repetition. Squeak-*squeak* . . . squeak-*squeak* . . . squeak-*squeak*. Then, in the distance, a few blocks down, James caught sight of what appeared to be a man on a larger-than-usual bicycle. It seemed the squeak accompanied the downstrokes of the pedals, though he could see the man only as he passed through the yellow circles of light the street lamps threw on the asphalt below.

It wasn't until the man reached his block that James recognized him.

It was Mr. Moon.

The bicycle he rode was indeed larger than normal, an old, battleship-gray monster that looked like the prototype. And atop it sat Mr. Moon, still in his dress pants, shirt, and sweater vest, though he'd abandoned the sport coat and rolled up his sleeves.

It tickled James's brain all wrong, that this man should be out on his prehistoric bicycle so late at night and in this dead neighborhood. *What if he sees me?* James imagined him stopping to chat and felt a strong urge to dive into the bushes. Then he remembered the cigarette, and he wondered if something could be made of it even though he wasn't presently at school. He thought about going inside, but Mr. Moon was almost to his house, and a sudden movement seemed more likely to draw his attention. So instead, James just sank into the porch swing and sat very, very still.

The bicycle squeak-*squeaked* up to the walkway in front of James's house and stopped. Mr. Moon swung his left leg off the contraption with the agility of a ballet dancer. Bracing it along the curb by the kickstand, he looked up at James and smiled.

James found himself smiling back. He had no idea why; he didn't feel like smiling, but the muscles of his face pulled his mouth into a welcoming grin anyway.

"Happy birthday, James," Mr. Moon said as he made his way toward the porch in long, even strides.

James's first thought was simple—*Run inside and slam the door.* But he didn't. Couldn't? It was as if he was slipping in and out of a dream, one where his legs refused to recognize the orders of his brain. *Dude, who is this guy? Why is he here? How does he know it's my birthday? What the hell, man? Get up. Move, moron!*

But James didn't move, and Mr. Moon—the interim school librarian, let's not forget—ascended the steps. His smile did not falter or fade. It was a wide, powerful smile, showing teeth and calling back to some old, old memories lodged in the minds of all humans, of returning friends who the tribe had once thought lost. It was warming and comforting, and it was oddly paralyzing.

Mr. Moon walked to the top step and leaned against one of the posts, easy as could be. "You don't have to be afraid, James. Believe me."

Those last two words came at James with the sincerity of an old dog's gaze, and he felt himself relax a little. "Uh, Mr. Moon—"

"Ezra."

"What?" James said.

"Ezra. My name is Ezra Moon, and as we're gonna be friends, you can call me Ezra."

"Okay, Ezra—"

"I don't want you to perform fellatio on me, James."

There were a few seconds of silence, and then James nodded. *That's good.*

"Nor do I want to perform fellatio on you. I don't want to penetrate or fondle you. Also, I don't want to videotape you masturbating, and I don't want you to urinate or defecate on me or to spank or hold me or for either of us to do anything to each other that would be, in any way, sexually gratifying to either of us. I am not a pedophile, a pederast, a kidnapper, a murderer, or a pervert. Does that pretty much clear up what was, I believe, your main concern?"

James's earlier smile had morphed halfway into confusion before locking up, and what remained was simian: brows down and in, mouth slightly agape.

Ezra continued, "So again I say, happy birthday, James."

"How do you know it's my birthday?"

"Oh, I know a lot of things." He crossed his arms and looked skyward, as if accessing some long-dormant part of his memory. "I know your family has missed your birthday. I know you want to draw comic books when you grow up. And I know it was you who threw a rock through the Schroeders' living room window last summer."

The warm summer-night air seemed to freeze on the back of James's neck. He looked away from Ezra and searched up and down the street. *Nothing. Just us.*

"I know about Dorian. And I know where you were last night. I daresay I know what you were considering doing as well."

James's mind moved in slow motion, like all his thoughts were trying to ascend through a lake of sap. He stared at Ezra, saying nothing.

"You agree, right, James, there's no way I could know these things?"

A single nod.

"Good. That'll make things easier. There's nothing I hate like arguments in the face of overwhelming logic. There are two reasons I know more than is possible about you. The first is simply that more is possible than you comprehend. The second is that we've been keeping track of you for a very long time, because you are a very special boy. I'm sorry—young man. A very special young man. You must excuse a certain amount of unintentional condescension from those of us who are very old. In any case, what I was beginning to say is that I've been watching you. And I've been waiting for this day, when I could finally meet you and begin."

James managed to unlock his throat. "Begin?"

"Yes, begin! That's what this is. A beginning. We are about to embark on the—*The!*—single greatest adventure anyone has ever known." Ezra took a great breath, straightened up, and stepped forward. "James, do you want to know who you really are?"

"Are you with the Escalades?" James said.

A monstrous breeze rushed through the neighborhood, bending branches, and for the first time, Ezra's face hit a sharp note. James felt for an instant as if he'd just come awake, and some part of his brain screamed to get the hell out of there.

"James? James."

James looked up to see Ezra's face, the hand of the captain once more. *What was I just thinking?*

"What Escalades, James?"

"There was an Escalade this morning, by the tracks, and I thought the guy was watching me. Then, later, I saw another one."

"Hm. Well, that is unfortunate. I'd hoped we were uniquely aware of you."

"What do you mean?"

"I only mean that this is unfortunate. It means they're aware of you, at least as a possibility. Hopefully as no more than that."

"Who?"

"Who? Oh, I think that's a question for another time. For now, let's just say they are suspicious that you may be someone important, but they're not sure. I'm sure they have a large pool of boys they're watching. You're just one of many."

"Many what? What does that mean?"

Ezra stepped closer to James, moving like pouring water until he was kneeling in front of him, eye to eye and unblinking. "You, James, are the most important person to have ever been born. You are the person who will change this place—this planet—*this world*. I tell you, James, you can't even imagine it. Not yet."

James realized he could no longer feel his feet. It was as if he were melting into the evening from the bottom up. His head filled with warmth and disintegrated, and all at once he couldn't identify himself as a being at all. He was the screen onto which Ezra projected his thoughts.

"You, James, are the One. You're the War Bringer." Ezra leaned into the pregnant silence.

James did not react.

"Or, to use this region's name for it, you, James, are the Antichrist."

The words ricocheted and replayed through James's brain: *You, James, are the Antichrist.*

"For lack of a better term, that is."

And it was at this exact moment the forgotten cigarette burned down to his fingers. While he yelped and dropped it, the pain defibrillated James out of his intense focus on Ezra. *What are you doing out here with this psycho?*

Then James was standing, and his sudden movement sent the swing bouncing off the siding.

Ezra observed him, his head cocked as if this eruption elicited nothing but curiosity.

"What . . . what's the matter with you?" James said, his voice cracking as he sidestepped toward the front door, his back pressed firmly to the siding. "Psycho! I'm calling the cops!" James's hand flailed behind him before locating the handle.

Ezra's face remained an open greeting, and his patient half smile followed as James put a clumsy shoulder into the door, burst inside, and then slammed it behind himself.

One breath.

Two.

The Antichrist? James ran to the kitchen. He pulled the chef's knife from its wooden slab, knocking that over in the process and sending knives clat-tat-tattering into the sink as he rushed back to the door with the knife before him.

As he reached the entryway, he turned the knife handle over in his palm. He slipped his feet from his gym shoes and tiptoed the last few feet, until he was able to look out the center windowpane of the old wooden door.

Nothing.

Even the wind left, now weakly brushing the lawns without conviction.

Where'd he go? There's no way he could be gone already.

James pressed his face to the cold glass and looked up and down the block, but there was nothing.

James lay in bed and replayed the conversation in his head, wondering which bits he'd invented and which had really happened. The community bulletin channel scrolled mutely across the small TV on his dresser, saving the room from total darkness.

How did he know that stuff?

An hour ago, James had stood in the kitchen and locked the back door, his hand clutching the phone. He'd dialed 91 . . . and stopped. He was trying to get the narrative straight, but it jumped from place to place, now reviving the squeak of Mr. Moon's bicycle, now the Schroeders' living room window collapsing inward, the glass seeming to chase the brick into the house, now the dial tone, now Ezra's calm—*Loving? Was it loving?*—smile.

Half an hour ago he was in bed and the room was black, and he heard his parents come home separately, only ten or so minutes apart, and some little boy inside of him wanted to fling off the covers and run to them and tell them what had happened. But he didn't. *How did he know about the Schroeders' window? How did he know about Dorian?*

And so he stayed in bed and didn't say a word, and

when Mom came in, he shut his eyes and pretended to be asleep. As she closed the door, he felt his eyes get hot and wet because he had never, in all his life, felt this alone.

The image played in his mind like he was sitting in the front row of a movie theater. Over and over. Mr. Moon's mouth opening into what was almost a smile— *An*—his tongue against his top teeth—*ti*—and his lips pushing forward as if preparing to kiss—*christ*. Over and over, over and over.

Then, sometime between 1:33:40 and 1:34:05 in the morning, while the image of Mr. Moon forming that final three-syllable word continued to run, James Salley fell into a deep, deep sleep.

It's night. Cold. Winter. I can see my breath. I'm on a stage—sitting at the back, lined up with old men . . . looking at me, smiling, nodding, mouthing words I can't understand what you're saying . . . I'm sorry, I can't—and at the front of the stage is a single microphone. Beyond it—oh my god, the crowd. It's like the ocean, so massive I can't see the edges of it; it just seems to go on and on forever, disappearing into the night. A blue light surrounds us on stage. In the moving searchlights, I see brick and asphalt and metal and even the clouds above. The light turns into spotty particles in the clouds—but then a spotlight swings past my

face—blindingly bright.

I'm me, but I'm not. I'm a different sort of me—older, maybe? Before I can investigate, I hear the crowd SCRRREEEEAAAM. I look to see the seated men standing now, applauding now, waving me up to the microphone now, and as I stand, the crowd erupts. They are noise. This impossible rumbling, it sounds like a metal giant eating a highway. I can feel the sound inside—it's like being hit with a hammer made of air. I've never been so aware of my body. With every step, my toes flex against socks, shoes, stage. Foot to calf to knee, knee to thigh to hip.

Back straight, chest out. I feel myself accepting the adoration. Part of me—outside of me—knows it should embarrass me, but it doesn't. I take the last few steps to the microphone and see the faces in the front, eyes wide and wet, mouths working at calls and shouts that drown in the noise. I can feel it all. This is the real me. This is the version of me I was always meant to be. I place my hands on the podium and close my eyes, and they scream for me.

I am.

5. The Possibilities of the Violin

James came out of sleep slowly, as if emerging from a warm bath—which is an appropriate simile, as the T-shirt and boxers he'd worn to bed, along with his pillow and sheets, were soaked.

James was out of the bathroom after a quick pee/brush/deodorize dance, forgoing his usual morning ritual. The dream sat center stage. *It was just so real. Never—I mean, I could feel the air. I could smell cigarettes and truck engines.* He looked down to see mismatched socks. Absorbed as he was in the dream, James barely noticed as his body mechanically pulled on clothes. His legs took over responsibility, transferring him down the stairs and into the kitchen. His hands set up a bowl of Honey Nut Cheerios, but all the while, he was on that stage. Standing there: strong and beloved. The man he'd always wanted to be. *God, what a feeling!*

Second period: American history with Ms. Adderley,[15] who stood at the front of the bright classroom without any books or notes, already a good fifteen minutes into this lesson about Vietnam. James's attention drifted in and out as he drew the face of a young girl in his notebook, her round features animated by her amazement. She'd been in the front row, there, in the dream, watching him as he approached the podium.

"But they'd been warned so many times, and so many times nothing had happened. The Tet Offensive was in many ways a case of the boy who cried—"

There was a pop as the PA came alive and Dean Worthington gently cleared his throat to soften the interruption. "Pardon me. Would James Salley please report to the library?"

Faces turned to him.

"James Salley to the library. Thank you."

"Ooooooooooo . . ."

Whatta you mean, "Ooooooooooo"? Who gets called to the library?

"Enough," Ms. Adderley said, cutting off the class with that final syllable.

James flipped his sketchbook closed and left the class with everyone's gaze tight on him; it did not feel like the dream.

What are you doing? James stopped in the middle of

---

15 Ms. Adderley was a student favorite. She was the kind of teacher who talked about things that weren't in the textbook. She was one of only two black teachers at the school, and she was super pretty and athletic (she'd played volleyball at a D-II college in Wisconsin). Being young and funny helped too, but her lack of condescension was probably her best trait.

the empty hallway. *Mr. Moon is in the library. He had the office call you. He wants you there.*

James spent the next ninety-six seconds standing right there. He was sure he should run out of the building or go to the office or call Mom and Dad or something. He was sure he should do pretty much anything except go down to the library.

But you still haven't told anyone.

Like a wind-up toy released, James jumped from dead-still to charging toward his locker. Upon arriving, he spun the combo lock open and flung his bag inside. *Fine. Go see Mr. Moon. But just to tell him to stay away from you.* James slammed the command home with each movement, grabbing one of his gym socks and dropping the lock inside before slamming the locker and stowing the makeshift weapon in his back pocket.[16]

James made his way to the library in long, no-fooling-around steps, clenching and unclenching his fists, ready, envisioning the confrontation, watching himself flinging the doors open and telling Mr. Moon what's-what.

When he reached the library, however, his hand slipped off the handle so that he walked right into the door. The failed entrance poured cold oatmeal over his fervor, and before he knew it, he was standing in the open doorway.

Mr. Moon smiled and nodded, beckoning James to follow as he excused himself from a table of students.

---

16 He'd learned this last year when Ileana Soto fought Rachel Kusamanoff out in the tennis courts. Rachel, having a good fifty pounds and five inches on Ileana, came into the fight pretty confident. That confidence (along with the orbital bone of her left eye) was shattered when Ileana faked a left hook and, with her right hand, swung a black tube sock with a combo lock in the toes. The crack sounded just like when a train runs over a piece of wood on the tracks.

Mr. Moon's office was buried in the far right corner. He left the door open, and James reached back and wrapped his right hand in the tail end of the sock as he followed.

The office was bland as a cubicle. It felt unlived-in. The three wooden walls were unadorned but for a few decaying READ posters,[17] and behind the desk was a stone wall painted the gray of eternity.

Mr. Moon sat behind a metal-and-pressed-wood desk, leaning forward, his fingers steepled. He nodded in the direction of the kids he'd been talking to. "I don't know how people do this job every day. Those children are very stupid. It's extremely frustrating."

James looked over to see two freshman boys laughing in hysterical silence, pointing at something in a textbook as the girl seated at the end of the table rolled her eyes while simultaneously ignoring them.

"Uh, okay, look," James began. He stared at Mr. Moon's chest, at the sky-blue shirt and the pastel-yellow tie, because he found he had trouble ordering his thoughts when he looked the man in his mismatched eyes. His right hand held the sock tight, the muscles in his shoulder twitching as if they wanted to yank the weapon free. "I don't know what that was last night or why . . . why you said what you did—or even how you coulda known stuff. I'm not saying you were, you know, right about all of it— or any of it—but, look, that stuff you said is crazy. I'm not even, I mean, I'm Catholic. My mom's really Catholic and

---

17 Michael J. Fox, George Burns, Michael Keaton

I'm sorta Catholic, so I can't—not that it even is, you know?"

"I'm sorry, do I know what?"

"Just stay away from me, okay?" It came out in a sort of screamed whisper.

James let his eyes drift up, but Mr. Moon retained a countenance of perfect relaxation, and this lack of any sort of reaction pushed James back into the red. "Look, you psycho, I'll call the cops! I'll tell 'em you're a pervert and you're stalking me and saying crazy shit! Okay? You'll get, you'll get . . . fired!" His hands shook. His knees rebelled against standing, but still he gripped the sock, and still he held Mr. Moon's gaze.

Mr. Moon's face finally lost its vacational jocularity. He pressed his lips together and leaned forward. "Okay. Okay, James. I'll tell you what. I can see you're upset, I can, but if you'll just sit down"—and here he stifled James's urgent response with one hand, palm out—"and hear what I have to say, then I promise I will leave you alone. Alright?"

James shifted his feet, measuring Mr. Moon and scouting glances around him: a small potted plant on one of the shelves, a timeworn mini fridge in the far corner. He looked at the students in the library and determined he could get their attention if an emergency necessitated. So without another word, he sat in the '70s-era, wood-and-fabric rolling chair across from Mr. Moon.

"Excellent. Thank you, James." Mr. Moon scooted his chair over to the mini fridge and returned with two cans of Coca-Cola. "May I also say I'm very impressed with your bravery? Whether you believe me or not, I can understand what you must be going through. How scary this must be. And yet here you are, like a man, holding that modern mace you've improvised there and ready to change your whole life, to brain a school librarian, if you deem it necessary."

"I'm not scared, Mr. Moon."

"Please, James, call me Ezra. Regardless, all I was saying was that it's impressive you're not shrinking from the situation or depending on supposed authority figures and rules of conduct." He slid one of the Cokes to James, who didn't touch it. "So here's to you." And with that, he tapped the top twice, cracked the tab, and loudly drank half the can, finishing with a satisfied, commercial-worthy "Aaaahhhh."

"So, as I said yesterday, my name is Ezra Moon, and you are the Antichrist—Ah, ah, ah, now you said you'd let me speak, so if you don't mind, I'll get through a rather large swath of information, and then we'll double back to address any questions you may have. Sound good? Okay. As I was saying, you are the *Antichrist*." Ezra said the word with earnest finger quotes beside his cheeks. "Now, that in itself is misleading. You are not the opposite of the man humans call Jesus Christ, nor are you his sworn enemy. In fact, you have nothing to do with him whatsoever. You are, however, the human emissary of the forces of a being humans usually—in a gross misunderstanding—refer to as Satan but who I think would be more accurately labeled by one of his other monikers: the Adversary . . . I'm sorry? Of course, um, an emissary is like a standard bearer. The Adversary can't be here, so you represent him.

"Where was I? Oh, yes, the whole thing is all muddled. Heaven and hell, Jesus and the devil, all wrong. As such, calling you the Antichrist is technically inaccurate, but the job description is very much the same. Ah, sorry, little joke. No, I don't suppose this is helping very much. I can see by the look in your eyes that I've done nothing to dispel your confusion or fear. Allow me to start again.

"There is another world. Not another planet, you understand, but a whole other realm, another . . . place, that touches your own. And in this place a war has been simmering for millennia. Humans, from their earliest days, crawling out of caves, have caught glimpses of this world in their dreams and prayers and revelries, and they have assigned a thousand names to it: heaven, hell, Aaru, Neraka, Tartarus, Tian, Jannah, et cetera, et cetera. The specifics, however, don't really matter. What matters are the basic truths, the things which your people have gotten right. There will be a war—the War to end all wars—fought by the beings of our realm, but here, on Earth. And there will be a human champion who begins it.

"For longer than any human could imagine, we have known this, and we have waited. One born here will release the Adversary and the two armies will mass, and then all will cross over and the War will begin. Right here.

"That, James, is you. You are the one who will free the great Adversary, who will raise a human army to fight alongside us. You will be the greatest man the world has ever seen. People will follow you; they will love you." Ezra's eyes were wide and wild, but his smile somehow remained encouraging. He leaned toward James, waiting.

It was quiet for a long time, except for the muffled library conversations outside.

Finally, James said, "But . . . I'm nobody. I mean, I'm no one special. It's not like my dad is Satan or anything. My dad's name is *Josh*."

"Why in the world should it matter who your father is?"

"I don't know. It always does in stories."

"Well, not in this one."

"Okay, let's pretend I don't think you're crazy. Let's say all that stuff is true, okay? Let's say you're right and I'm supposed to do those things."

Ezra nodded.

"Well, two problems I can think of right off the bat. One: *No*. How 'bout that? And two: You have the wrong person. I'm not somebody people follow. I'm not some—"

"Are you familiar with the violin, James?"

"What?"

"Are you familiar with the violin?"

"I don't . . . I don't play it if that's what you mean."

"What I mean is have you ever heard anyone play the violin poorly?"

James nodded.

"Well, then you know it is an awful, awful thing. Horrible to endure. A screeching violin is an abomination, a desecration of a beautiful thing. It will turn the most loving parent into a frustrated, angry mess."

"Okay . . ."

"Now, have you ever heard the violin played by a master?"

James's head rocked from side to side.

Ezra's smile grew into something indecent and triumphant. He leaned back in his seat and closed his eyes. "It is the most beautiful thing in the world. The paintings of Rembrandt, the *chilaquiles* made in the kitchen of Señora Ana Dos Santos of Guadalajara, Mike Tyson's mid-'80s fights, Kurosawa, even Joel Robuchon's La Truffe Noire—they are nothing when compared to a single violin played perfectly. Here—"

And with that one word, the room disappeared and James was in a lake of darkness, drifting, as if free from all his senses. He felt the initial moment of panic melt away. A memory of floating in warm salt water came to him, the sun on his face, his body sure and held.

Then the music started. It was . . . He couldn't find words for it. Each note trembled, like every perfect note was made up of a chorus of a thousand others. As one note ended, it slid effortlessly into the next. For some reason, the music made James feel a warm sadness, as if the world were much larger than he'd ever imagined, yet he was not diminished by that feeling. The tempo increased and the music became louder in his head, and he remembered being a little boy and watching his mother cry after a fight with his father. They'd been arguing, and then Dad got louder and louder and Mom retreated, and finally Dad finished with a closing flourish, grabbed his coat, and was out the door. Then Mom sat on one of the kitchen chairs and started to cry in big, ugly spasms. He remembered seeing it—so low to the ground, how young must he have been? And it was as if this music was made for that moment, written for that memory, for the feeling of helplessly watching your mother cry—and then it changed again, and the music was hopeful and flitting, like questions, and the relief made James's eyes wet, even as his body relaxed further, and he could swear he was drinking the music. It felt wonderful and optimistic, and it ended with a soft sigh like someone's gentle breath against your lips.

And then he was back. James grabbed the arms of the chair, as if he'd just fallen into it, but he was as stationary as could be. The office looked different to him now, somehow fake or flimsy, like a movie set. But as he gathered himself, he saw that everything was as it should be: the mini fridge, the lighting, the kids out in the library, Ezra's warm smile.

The air cooled James's face, and he realized his cheeks were lined with tears. He looked away and wiped roughly with the back of his sleeve, embarrassed and bewildered all at once. But when he looked back at Ezra, the librarian waved it off; just another secret between old friends.

"That's you," he said as he opened James's Coca-Cola for him and set it back down. "You're a violin. You've just never learned how to play yourself. Think. You *are* that powerful. If what I say is true—and it is, believe me—then you will be a man all men will want to follow. So that means the effect you have on others—the power over them—must be extraordinarily strong, no? That's what I mean when I say you're a violin. When you're in tune and playing well, you have an amazing influence over others—influence that will grow to heights you can't believe. Not yet.

"But right now you're not in tune, and you're being played with clumsy directionless rips. Do you understand? You're sad. You're insecure. You're unsure and petty and frightened. So others, when they come into contact with you—that's what they feel. Haven't you always wondered about this? You must have. 'Why does everyone dislike me?' Well, James, because you make them feel bad. When they are near you, they feel horrible—sad and scared and angry. Alone. Just like you feel, only more so. Some—the sensitive who are easily affected, easily led—the Jacques Louis Davids, as I call them—never mind, never mind—they experience it more strongly than others."

James sensed a longing he was unable to define. An obsessive track within was grabbing hold of Ezra's words because, as absolutely crazy as it all was, it somehow felt right. *It could all be true. It could be.*

Ezra finished his Coca-Cola and moved on to James's. "You have to admit I've shown you some pretty good tricks. I know things no one could, I played you a violin concerto from 1849,[18] and I explained the great mystery of your life. And all I ask in return is that you do one thing for me."

James waited, but Ezra said nothing.

"What?"

"Try. That's it. Just try. Try to be the man you really are. You can go now, James. I'll leave you alone. But at some point today, I want you to walk up to someone and envision yourself as a great, strong man and see them as a follower. Do you hear me? A follower. Someone who loves you. Someone who adores you. I want you to see them as such and simply . . . talk to them. That's it. Just once. Play yourself with confidence and joy and see what happens. If nothing changes, then I'm gone. I won't be here tomorrow. You will never see me again. Deal?"

James was busy swimming upstream through the memories of every cross look, every angry barb and accidental slight. He saw his mom pulling away from a hug quickly, saw Dorian when she thanked him, saw Nick's eyes alive with hate and disgust and fear—*It was fear, wasn't it?*—and from below these heavy, deep waters, he said, "Deal."

Deal.

18 In 1849, the Hungarian violin prodigy Joseph Joachim (b.1831, d.1907) was eighteen years old and living in Weimar, Germany. He was already world-renowned for his virtuosity and, in fact, had been trained by Mendelssohn himself. One night, in late November of that year, Joseph met a man near a downtown hotel. The man recognized the violinist, and the two began talking music. Before long, they were having drinks. They drank and sang with a group of beer-hall regulars until late into the night. Then, at roughly two o'clock that morning, the stranger produced a violin and convinced Joseph to play. What followed—what James had just heard—was possibly the most beautiful violin performance ever. Joseph Joachim played the second movement of Mendelssohn's violin concerto in a mostly empty beer hall in front of the owners, a local drunk named Dirk, two prostitutes, a Prussian officer, and the stranger.

A minute later, James was out in the hallway, his feet carrying him back to American history class. As he reached the end of the main hall, though, he didn't turn left to return. He stopped. To the outside world at that moment, he looked only like a stoned kid contemplating the floor—eyes vacant, mouth just slightly open. Inside, he was spinning. The protocols which he'd been taught—both by parents and school, through curricula hidden and exposed—screamed that he needed to tell someone about all of this *right now*, but those protocols battled every natural impulse of his personal being.

The soft fip-fap of shoes on tile brought his gaze up. Jess Gerber walked toward him, her dishwater-blonde hair piled high and little ringlets falling and framing her face. He watched the way her breasts pressed against her red-and-white cheer sweater, watched her perfect golden legs from the short-short skirt to the impossibly white gym shoes, and realized—*Oh no!*—he was staring. Caught!

He looked down at his own feet, at the ground hiding there, hoping to avoid the meeting, but he couldn't help it, couldn't stop himself. As he heard her draw even, he snuck his gaze up.

"What're you looking at?" The question made it apparent there was no correct response. The only right answer was to not be looking, to have the courtesy to not even exist. James dropped his gaze and mumbled a denial/apology.

But then, in that moment as she moved past him, James remembered what Ezra had said. He remembered the version of himself in the dream. He remembered that feeling of for once not being the mirror reflecting anxiety and shame again and again but of being complete and full and real.

"Hey, Jess." James turned to face her. He pulled his shoulders back and felt his own weight, there, held by the earth.

Jess whirled around, her head whipping over her shoulder to lead the move like a spinning figure skater. When she saw him, though, her entire countenance changed. It was as if she'd expected to see dog shit, and there, instead, was the purebred itself. She looked confused. That deep, deep confusion that's scary to get lost in. Her eyes widened, betraying a bit of her panic.

James said, "I just wanted to tell you that you look real good today. Hot, y'know? You look hot."

And then it happened.

She giggled. There's no other word for it, because that is exactly—to the very definition—what it was. Jess giggled, and her hands came together in front of her stomach and then apart, the left to her hip and the right through her hair. "Thanks," she said, infusing the word itself with the giggle, and then she was off again. At the end of the hall, before she disappeared around the corner, she craned to see him and gave him a crooked little smile, as if he'd surprised her with an extravagant and naughty gift.

James didn't move. He just stood there in the hallway of George Washington High School, his smile on pause. *What's happening?*

5½. Interlude: Eliza & Erik

James Salley, unlike most sixteen-year-olds, knew exactly what he wanted to do with his life. Perhaps those ambitions would shift, but at the time of these incidents, he was wholly invested in the singular goal of one day writing and drawing his own comic book.

It used to be that his ambition manifested only in loose-leaf universes of sketches and scraps filled with ideas for stories which invariably failed to mature beyond that initial point. Then, a few weeks after his fifteenth birthday, he took the Metra to the Harold Washington Library downtown to see Ben Ishii, a young, Japanese-American, LA-based artist who was speaking. Ishii was one of the fastest-rising stars in comics, especially since his six-issue Lobo story arc—Blind, Deaf, Dumb World—and his own new title, *Long-Dead Ladies*.

James had never been so moved by anyone's words before. Downstairs, in a small, dim auditorium with fifty or so other people, James listened as this slight man in bright-yellow-and-red-mod attire spoke in his delicate, worked English about the path to making comic books: "Do not talk about doing. Just do . . . Drawing and story-telling are muscles; you must work them, like athletes lift weights . . . Tell stories you want to read . . . What excites you? . . . Either work or quit."

James left that day with his mind aflame. Immediately, he began to catalogue the story ideas he had; he began to draw with a purpose. He knew he wasn't a great artist, and he doubted he'd ever be as good as the really special ones, but he thought he could be good enough. And while before he'd always been waiting until he was good enough, Ishii had convinced him the only way to ever be good enough was to start now.

Then, one night, while he was drawing a Mohawked girl with double-Ds strapped into a teeny-tiny biki-ni swinging a massive battle-axe, an idea—The Idea—popped into his head, pouring as if it were something fully formed that he was only catching. He worked from 9:42 that night until 3:14 in the morning—notes and sketches and scratched-out-rewritten details until the story started to move and breathe on its own—and then he wrote this down:

Eliza and Erik are U.S. soldiers (really good ones, like Green Berets or Navy SEALS or something). They're both chosen— no, signed up (and chosen)—to be part of this super-soldier project, like some modern Captain America thing. So the day they sign up (they don't know each other yet), they meet all the other great soldiers. Erik meets a guy named Sam White. (Eliza's full name is Eliza Anne Sable and Erik's is Erik Thomas Fuller). Erik and Sam become friends right away. They have the same sense of humor and initially are going through the phases of the program together.

The program is a mixture of drugs (steroids, human-growth hormones, new-age amphetamines for focus, and some other top-secret drug to increase brain function and strength and speed), along with nanotechnology (little computers and stuff inserted to increase blood flow, hearing, eyesight and decrease exhaustion and pain receptors).

Erik never talks to Eliza, but Sam falls in love with her at first sight. He keeps after her, even though she keeps rejecting him (but the rejections are getting warmer—she can't help it. Sam is awesome—think Han Solo).

So eventually, as different people react to the program differently, they begin to be separated into subgroups. Eliza and Sam, who have reacted the best to everything, are sent off together with the doctors and trainers. Over the next few months, they work together and become superhuman together. Faster, stronger, smarter. She begins to see what kind of man he is, and so she begins to admire and respect him, and then she falls in love with him. They live, for a little bit, in a perfect sort of Utopia of their own, just training and spending time with each other and boning like crazy. They're pushing each other as they advance to never-before-seen heights of human ability.

After a while, though, Sam starts getting distracted and distant. See, Eliza loves the new powers. She revels in them. But they worry Sam. He knows they've reached levels of strength, speed, and internal data computation that are just impossible for human beings. He wants to know more, so he starts to sneak out at night. It's easy to get past THEIR security (to uncover THEIR secrets), because THEY made him specifically to be able to do things like that. He starts to find out things that bother him, references to "failed" subjects and stuff like that. Soldiers whose bodies "refused the treatment." But he doesn't know what happened to the "failed" soldiers. Did they just wash out? Get sent home or back to their regular assignments?

Then he finds Erik.

Erik's file tells the story of a new reaction to the drugs. "Exponential growth/new side effects." His strength and speed grew crazy fast, way faster than the others', but he had weird side effects. "Headaches, blurred vision, hearing problems." Also, the brain drugs didn't seem to be increasing him, just sort of keeping everything level. THEY upped the dosage. "Cognitive problems, blindness, petit mal seizures." But the muscles, the flesh—it was something unheard of. His muscles grew huge and flexible. His skin became hard as leather (then harder), and his features seemed to flatten out. MRIs of his brain showed decreased activity. The same day he ran a 100-yard dash in eight seconds, he also bench-pressed 850 pounds. He reverted. His brain grew dim. THEY fit him with nano-implants to replace his eyes and ears, which were useless by this point, and THEY kept feeding him the stuff.

By the time Sam finds him, he's no longer the joking, red-haired soldier he became friends with just a year ago. He's a monster. He has the mind of a child, but he remembers his friend Sam. He has robot eyes and ears and he's the strongest, fastest man to ever live on planet Earth. Sam looks at his friend and starts to cry. THEY tortured him—killed him, really—and Sam decides then and there that he's done. He goes back and tells Eliza all of it. He tells her he loves her more than anything and wants her to come with him—it would kill him to leave her—but he's done. He has to go and has to take Erik with him. Eliza kisses him and says, "Yes, of course, yes."

Apparently, though, THEY have more eyes and ears than even Eliza and Sam know, because THEY have found out about their prize weapons' plan to escape. The night before the scheduled breakout, THEY come for them. Eliza and Sam and Erik will all be taken and split up, probably at underground bases on different sides of the country, and brainwashed (wiped?) so that they'll just do their duty and shut up.

Sam breaks free and attacks the soldiers. He calls to Eliza to get Erik, which she runs and does, herself killing and disabling a few soldiers as she goes. She gets Erik, and the two of them fight their way back to Sam, but Sam has been overtaken. As they get there, they see an unconscious Sam being loaded onto a helicopter and taken away. They scream and try to stop it, but it's gone, and then the rest of the soldiers attack.

But they're no match, not for Eliza's skill and blind rage,

nor for Erik's otherworldly abilities. They fight through them, destroying the base in the process, and find themselves alone in the woods of the Northwest on a cold, gray, rainy morning.

So begins the story of Eliza and Erik, rogue government experiments obsessed with finding out who did this to them while they fight to elude detection and capture. Most of all, though, they want to find Sam. Where is Sam?

He called the comic *Fearless*. Not *The Fearless Duo* or *The Fearless Team* or *Fearless Force* or anything else. Just *Fearless*. It'd come to him while he was riding home from a doctor's appointment with Mom, sitting in the passenger seat looking out the window at an afternoon sky, a storm coming in, turning the gold sky a dark iridescent violet. The sun outlined the dark clouds moving in, and James thought . . . *Fearless* . . . and within those two syllables was a gut-and-nuts feeling of a whole way of life, a philosophy as clear as a slap. Some people are fearless. Eliza is fearless because of her pride in her own abilities and because of her rage. Her need for revenge barely covers up her own unconscious death wish, that if she can't be with Sam, then she doesn't want to live. Erik, on the other hand, is fearless because of his love for his friends—the only good thing left in his world. He would do anything for them.

James fantasized inside and outside of the comic. He longed to live in the simplicity of Erik, to have a clear reason for being, a comrade, or sometimes just to touch Eliza. The lines of her breasts, her legs; he loved them differently every time he drew them. (Though he was still completely unable to draw Eliza's face. He kept trying, and while some sketches seemed okay, none really felt like Eliza. He tried to just let it go, but he couldn't ignore what a lie it was to get her wrong. So he kept trying.)

What's it like to not be afraid all the time? What's it like to be sure?

But that was it. Just fantasies. He was stuck. He had the origin, had the look and the characters, but he needed that first story. Ishii had said (emphatically) that so many first-time writers make the same mistake: no story. Comic books are so much about origin—so much about prelude—that writers got lost in it. They submit backstory, just like James had, all ready for the story to begin and . . . nothing. James knew he needed a story—a great story—to start with, and from there, within that story, he'd weave their origin.

Knowing and having, however, are very different things. James had the backstory; in fact, the longer he had it, the more it grew. As he read and reread it, the characters grew history and depth. Eliza was a rich girl from Philadelphia whose parents disowned her when she joined the military, Erik had been a closeted homosexual, Eliza once almost killed another girl in a fight when she was younger, Erik was afraid of the dark now, and on and on. But still, James did not have the story. What he had were plans—and fantasies, of course; he had them too.

His fantasies outside of the comic were simple. The book is discovered and he is given carte blanche.

The youngest artist/writer in Marvel (or DC; that's fine too) history. *Fearless* comes out and the comic community goes mad. How could someone this young be this good? How could he be so insightful? How could his characters be so fully realized, so expertly imagined? He pictured himself sitting in that same auditorium in the Harold Washington Library, only this time he's up on the stage. He pictured the adoring fans who drove from all over the Midwest to see him. People crowd into the space, whispering and pointing. They look from the comic to James, then down and back again. "How can it be?"

Then they all come by—Nick and Ileana and Colin and LaMarcus and Jess and all of their friends, Ms. Adderley and Mr. Gere and Mom and Dad—they all come. The whole town comes, one by one, and they see *Fearless*, and they see him. They finally get it. They can see him now. And then Dorian comes, and as she flips through the comic, she starts to cry because she can see the characters for who they really are, and she wipes away the tears and smiles, and—making a little joke of it—she asks James to sign her copy. And he does, and he's not sure what he writes, but he writes something great and cool, and she looks at him—sees him—like she's supposed to.

5. The Possibilities of the Violin (rejoin)

The next day was a Friday—the first toxic-hot morning since last summer—and it felt to James that it should be a monumental day. But it wasn't. It was an odd day, made more so by its conventionality.

Is something going to happen now?

James felt like he was existing in two places at once. There was the James walking to school, going through the halls, eating lunch, and sitting in class. But that James was empty. It was as if he'd sent a copy of himself. The other James had retreated to a dark room inside to be alone and think. And that's what he did, though it seemed to go nowhere. Every course of thought led to the same logical conclusion: *It's true.* But whatever part of him graded the answers refused to accept that, and so he was sent back to redo the problem once more.

He avoided Ezra that day, though how intentional that was, it's hard to say. Twice—the only times that he remembered Ezra's words in an opportune moment—he tried the trick from the day before.[19] *Just like Ezra said.* He pictured himself as that man from the stage—*No, not "that man." Me. It's me*—pictured himself as happy and confident, and he smiled.[20] And while it did work both times, it took quite a lot of effort. It was difficult to hold on to happiness and confidence, though it did seem to be getting easier the more he did it.

The final bell rang at 2:50. James would've sworn he'd only been in the building an hour or so, but he grabbed his bag and merged into the highway of exiting children all the same.

A black Escalade turned left onto Wisconsin Avenue just as James stepped out the front doors, and for the first time in hours, he snapped back into the present. *It's probably just a normal Escalade. The world's full of them.*

Or, it could be THEM.

Though who THEY were, James had no idea.

He took the bus home anyway. It seemed somehow safer than walking, being in the cocoon of the bus, under

---

19 He couldn't help but think of it as a trick. James, like most people, tended to treat the opinions of those who disliked him as rock-solid insight.

20 The first time he smiled at Ileana Soto, which he would have never had the courage to do outside of his current fugue state. Ileana looked over at Ceasar (Almedina, who she'd been seeing for the last month or so), and when she was sure he wasn't looking, she smiled back.

The other smile was directed at a blonde freshman that James didn't know. He was pretty sure her name was Rachel or Raquel or something. She reacted to his smile by giggling and rushing off toward her friends. James wondered what she'd say when she got there.

the purview of institutions and adults, under School District 77 and Russ the bus driver.[21]

When James got off the bus, he fully expected to see another Escalade, but the street was empty except for a decade-old Chevy picking up some girl he didn't know. The quiet, tree-lined street seemed to mock his paranoia as he walked home or, rather, as he began to walk. He found it impossible to stop checking. *(What's that? What's that sound? What if one of the Escalades came around the corner right now?)* He couldn't shake the feeling that someone was watching him, and so his walk became a trot, trot to jog, and then a full sprint down the last half block and up the front stairs. He slammed the door behind himself and looked out at the world, full now of horrors he'd never even imagined.

---

21 Though tangential to this tale, Russell Lawrence Zoller, it bears noting, has stories enough to fill his own book. What the children on the bus and the parents loading and unloading them never saw was the smattering of tattoos that hid beneath his clothes: illustrations that called back to his time with Special Forces, specifically 1st Special Forces Operational Detachment-Delta (Delta Force) by way of the 75th Ranger Regiment. After an unfortunate series of events at the end of his active career (possible PTSD-related late-onset mood disorder, as well as blossoming addictions to alcohol and Vicodin) resulted in a quiet discharge, he began a wandering sort of period, working first for a private security contractor, then training Garamba National Park rangers in the Democratic Republic of Congo for their war against poachers, followed by a stint working as a glorified bodyguard for a Greek billionaire, and then the teensiest little stretch doing transport security for some multinational interests smuggling heroin out of Afghanistan.

Now, here he was back in his hometown of Stone Grove, taking care of his ill mother at the end of her life; just watching the wheels go 'round. He spent most of his time, when he wasn't caring for her, drinking at Moon's Pub, trying to figure out where he was supposed to go from here. He'd started driving the buses a couple months ago, and he liked it just fine. He found it calming and thought of it as a sort of vacation from himself. Every vacation, though, is temporary by definition, and in almost six months his mother will be dead, and two months after that he'll be gone. In fact, exactly one year after this day when James decides to take the bus, Russ the bus driver will be in bed with an assistant to the president of the Deutsche Bundesbank, embroiled in a plot to make counterfeit Euros.

6. The Homunculus

Gray dirt—is it dirt? Gray sand? Small hills in the distance swaying in the fog. Smog? It's wet and shimmering and, and I'm in some kind of valley, the same everywhere, as if I'm surrounded by photocopies. No, not everywhere. There, up ahead . . . dark, and I'm moving towards it. Not walking. Like I'm being pulled. As I get closer I notice the ground sloping in—and I see it. It's a hole—no, no, not a hole—a Pit. Like a wound in the ground. No edges—the ground just flows into it. Even before I can see down, I know it's deep. It's still pulling me, like it's got its own gravity. How big is it? How deep?

Scrape-thump. Scraaaape-thump. Scrape-thump.

I see his head first, and I try to run away but something's holding me there. He's coming up from the Pit, so that I see him a bit at a time. His head is bald—huge—bigger than any I've ever seen. Tiny eyes, close to the nose, which is bent down so far I can't see the nostrils—oh, god! His arms and chest! His arms are the size of a normal man's waist, and his chest is like the front of a car. He's naked and fat, and his skin glistens as if wet. He drips as he clears the top of the Pit and stands there. His feet grip the ground like a bird's, but it seems to flow around the talons. He's got to be thirteen or fourteen feet tall, and his hands—those monstrous fingers tapering to a point, spotted with something . . . meat? His hands hang at my eye level, and though some part of me is screaming to turn and run, I stand where I am and watch this thing breathe.

His little, dark mouth opens. "I am Leviathan. I am waiting for you."

"What?"

"I am Leviathan. I am waiting for the One."

"Am I . . . ?"

"I am to allow no one but the One to enter. I am Leviathan, and I am waiting for you."

"Why?"

"I do not understand your question."

For a second, I can't think how to continue. "Who told you that I was the One?"

"I do not understand. You are the One. I am Leviathan."

"Yes, okay, I get that you're Leviathan. How do you know that I'm the One?"

He's confused. Not annoyed or angry, though; just confused. Patient. "I know you are the One because you are the One. I am Leviathan, and I am to allow only the One to enter. I stop all others. You are allowed to enter. You are the One."

"Okay, uh, nobody told you I was the One, so . . . how about, do you remember when you were told that you were supposed to guard this place and only let me—I mean, the One—in?"

"I do not understand."

"When did you get your orders?"

"What is when?"

"What is when?"

"Yes."

"When. Not now. Some other time. Y'know, if not now, then when?"

"I am now."

I stare at this monster. The liquid doesn't seem to dry on him, as if it is him. I'm not afraid anymore, just aggravated. It feels like I'm trying to argue with the wind.

Suddenly, he turns. He's amazingly quick for his mass, and his feet chew up the ground as he walks. "Here," he says, and I'm standing next to him. "I am Leviathan, and you are the One. I am to allow the One passage, and the One is to descend these steps."

I look down, and for an instant, I think my heart has hardened in my chest. I can't breathe. It's like standing at the edge of space and looking down at your house. We're at the edge of the Pit, and now I can see it's at least two or three football fields across. There, at my feet, is a small ledge, which leads to a thin, vertical staircase. It rings the Pit as it descends. It has no railing, no visible support of any kind, except for the side of the Pit.

"If you do not descend, then you are not the One," the giant says, and I look up at him. "If you are not the One, then you cannot descend. If the One cannot descend, then I *serve no purpose. I am not Leviathan."*

I look down again. The steps eventually disappear into darkness. Swallowed. The word repeats in my head.

"I am Leviathan," he says, "and you must descend the steps."

James became aware that he was awake at 3:54 a.m. The dream remained vivid in his mind, even down to the mildew-and-blood-iron smell of the giant. He lay in bed and watched the dream as it replayed, losing clarity each time. Then, sometime around 4:30, the dream receded enough that he became conscious of himself, awake in his dark room.

The room looked different. For a moment he saw it as if it were already a memory. He could see himself looking back as an older man, and in that moment, an illusion of security which he'd never even realized existed was gone, and he recognized that this was just a room. It was like a thousand others and held no intrinsic value. It would appear in his memories as the chrysalis of his adolescence, but that's only because it happened to be his room. He could've had any of a thousand other rooms and the feelings would've been exactly the same.

This realization felt somehow profound to James. It seemed to hint at something else—some greater, more valuable understanding just out of his reach—but the more he thought about it, the thinner the threads became. Within a few minutes, the thought had lost its potency and drifted into memory itself. A few minutes after that, he was asleep again.

Days melted. James chased sleep at night, unable to slow his mind, and filled the days with clipped naps, from which he awoke like a guard on duty. Snippets of the dream replayed: thin, stone steps descending and circling, disappearing into darkness. Real-life vertigo.

Time passed in such a blur that at one point, James just sort of noticed he was at school. Apparently, another week had started. Apparently, it was Tuesday already.

James and Ezra saw each other in the halls and at lunch, but while they made eye contact and one or the other occasionally nodded, neither made any further attempt at communication.

One thought repeated in James's head as the days piled up: *If I accept what he says, then what?*

What now?

Dorian Delaney lived in the complete opposite direction of James. Every day, when school ended, James would watch as she walked away, bouncing and energetic. Often she was lost in a cloud of other girls, individuals reporting back to the group with the day's reconnaissance. What was learned about this guy or that couple, which teacher was a bitch, which one was a freak, who said who was a slut, what said slut said in response, et cetera, et cetera. Of course, the group allowed that all nations protected their own personal sensitive data; no confessions were required. James watched them with fascination.

Dorian enjoyed the group—that was obvious—but she didn't seem as needy of it, or as scared of it, as the rest of them did. If a natural group didn't form quickly and organically, she didn't wait forever or go off looking for companionship. She would simply cut off her waiting with a decisive flip of her hair and walk home alone.

James had been waiting for just such an opportunity, and that Friday his chance arose. It was a true end-of-the-school-year kind of day, hot and humid and sun-wrapped, but with the singular charity of a strong, cool breeze. It felt like the first day of summer, and in many ways, this day would be the beginning of James's summer.

As soon as she began to stroll home, he made after her. White shoes, pale skin, abbreviated jean shorts, white sleeveless blouse—he trailed with purpose, throwing in a few seconds of jogging every couple of yards, careful not to run.

James caught up to her by the end of the block with an offhand, "Hey, Dorian." He'd rehearsed a story about an errand that necessitated his walking this direction, but since Dorian didn't question it—she just smiled and asked how he was—he let it go.

"Good," he said. "Good. You?"

"I'm awesome."

"Awesome?"

"Practice was cancelled this afternoon. I seriously can't

tell you the last time I just, like, had a whole afternoon to myself to do whatever I want." Her red hair was pulled back from her bright face in a tight ponytail that bobbed with each step. It was beautiful, and James felt his adoration growing each time it bounced. He was happy; doubly happy that she was happy. "You know what I think I'm gonna do?"

"What?"

"Nothing." She smiled to herself, enjoying some private triumph. "I'm gonna lay out in the backyard and tan. Then I'm gonna make lemonade and cook a pizza and just sit in front of the TV."

"That's wonderful," he said, feeling the awkward formality of it even as it left his mouth.

Dorian half smiled and checked him out of the corner of her eye. "Yeah," she said.

He had to speak. Every nanosecond he allowed to pass was just another filled only with his awkwardness, his missteps. It was imperative that he move the conversation. *Say something.* But nothing came to him, and so they walked in silence for another half block and she sipped from her water bottle[22] as if covering for him like an actor who's forgotten his lines, until a thought finally floated to the surface.

"I, uh, when I was heading to English today," James

---

22 Even Dorian's water bottle, if you believe it, held weight and meaning in James's conception of her. It was a gray bottle with a worn, black-and-yellow bumblebee on it, along with the words *The Hair Bee.* That was the salon in town where Dorian got her hair done. To James it was a phantasmagoria of incalculable female power and sex. Dorian loved it there; loved sitting among the girls and women, perms cooking, nails buffing, scissors clipping as stories and laughter fought for audible supremacy. James walked by when a route took him near, and looked in as surreptitiously as possible, but the pure feminine gigantosaurus-dynamism of the place was just slightly more terrifying than appealing, so he kept his distance.

began, "I heard this girl—she's a junior, I think. April, I think. A tall, like, dark-haired girl . . ."

"Yeah, I know her. What about her?" Dorian's look was equal parts expectant and pensive.

"She said she was in Mr. Llewellyn's class today—she was wearing a short dress thing I guess, and she said he knocked a pen off his desk on purpose and then, when he leaned over to pick it up, he tried to look up her skirt."

"Oh my god, he's such a perv!" In her affronted agitation, she seemed to turn toward James and speed up at the same time. At once she launched into a diatribe about Mr. Llewellyn, and as she walked, her lips animated each word and her hands held the ideas out in front of James before shoving them aside. He peeped the muscles of her calf as she moved a half step ahead, and followed the leg up. "No one knows, 'cause maybe he was doing pervy stuff forever. But like ten years ago, he had this student—I think she was Japanese or Chinese or something—she was a real quiet girl, I guess. But he had her stay after school—not like a trouble thing, just like an extra-credit smart-girl thing, and I don't think he raped her but he definitely did something. I mean, she agreed to it, you know? He, like, fingered her or made her give him a blow job or something. Anyway, I guess it kept going on and became like a regular thing. But she wrote about it in her diary and her mom found it and confronted her and called the cops. So Mr. Llewellyn got arrested and put on suspension, but the girl stole her diary back and burnt it and refused to say anything, so the cops had to let him go. Her parents moved her away, and the school had to take him back. So now he's, like, more careful about it, but he's still a total perv."[23]

James could watch her talk until he died. Even when it was gossip, it never felt bitter or malicious, more like a child showing you all the cool features of their new toy. James wondered if one day she'd be a writer. He could see that: Dorian and him lost in their own worlds, sitting at back-to-back desks. He fantasized about bringing her coffee and rubbing her neck as she looked over her stories. (Though, admittedly, the fantasy then progressed to passionate, back-scratching Cinemax-level sex.)

Dorian had moved on to talking about Gail Asbury, who she said was purposefully pressing her tits together and bending over in front of Mr. Llewellyn, hoping that

---

[23] The actual incident being referred to happened thirteen years earlier. The student in question was, in fact, Korean. Mr. Llewellyn failed her after repeatedly warning her about absences and missed assignments. She cried and pleaded and even screamed at him a little and kicked a desk over, but Mr. Llewellyn refused to reverse his decision. The student in question had a solid panic attack on the way home, because failing science would get her grounded, which would mean she wouldn't get to go to Tampa with her best friend's family. So when she got home she crushed up and snorted some of her brother's asthma medication and proceeded to write a fake diary entry for an anonymous girl, claiming that Mr. Llewellyn had asked this girl to stay after school, at which point he kissed her and felt her breasts and put his finger inside her.

She left the diary pages in the first-floor girls' bathroom the next day, and when they were discovered, the school went crazy. Mr. Llewellyn was taken away by the police and the counselors were seeing kids one after the other, trying to ascertain whose diary this was and if perhaps there were others.

Of course, the defining characteristic of most teenagers is their inability to keep a secret, and so it wasn't long before the diary's author shared hers with the aforementioned best friend, who in turn told someone who told someone, and within 24 hours Mr. Llewellyn was back in the bosom of his home and the student was expelled. Charges were of course never filed against Mr. Llewellyn, nor were they filed against the girl, though the newspaper ran stories about the whole affair and how the girl was in counseling now and attending an all-girls Catholic school, and six months later the family moved to Iowa.

Still, every school has the perv teacher. The teacher that all the students agree is a creep. Usually they're just socially inept, awkward fellas and gals, but sometimes, of course, they are actual creepazoids. Mr. Llewellyn was the former. He held eye contact a bit too long and had sinus problems that often caused him to breathe through his mouth in a lascivious manner. Then there was the combover. God, will these men never realize the effect those combovers have?

teasing would lead to positive feelings, ipso ergo facto, a better biology grade. James watched her speak and found himself gripped in his belly by an urge to love and protect this girl, and in this swell of concern he said, "So, how are things?"

There could be no mistaking his meaning, not with that inflection, not with his glimpse alighting over the thin scars on her wrists.

Dorian's face went around the world in an instant—pause, confusion, realization, shame, annoyance, stone. James knew immediately that it had been a catastrophic misstep.

"I'm fine, James."

"Right. I mean, obviously." He said nothing the rest of the block. The earlier, uncomfortable silence was back, but on steroids. He wanted to tell her he'd only said it out of a sense of concern, because he wanted to take care of her, but he could already sense the change. He remembered a drawing of mitosis on a chalkboard; from one into two. The connection was severed, and there was no way to bring it back.

"I'm gonna stop in here," she said, gesturing to the J&J Food Mart. "I'll see you."

Dorian peeled off before he could say anything. "See ya," he called to her back.

Stupid, stupid, stupid! She obviously doesn't want to talk about it. James let his feet carry him to the end of the block before he turned left, starting the large circle home. *She doesn't want to talk about it or remember it, and when you bring it up, you become a reminder of it. You become the symbol of the bad thing.*

That's it, isn't it? James realized—in an avalanche of intuition that he couldn't quite follow—that this was the way things worked in life. He had saved her, hadn't he? *But that doesn't matter. Not anymore. The initial thankfulness gives way to shame, and that same person who saved us becomes repellent to us.*

James's breath stopped. The very idea was frightening enough to be paralytic, and he swore that moment he would never mention the Incident again.

James turned left again, walking parallel to the train tracks along the road, and several blocks ahead he thought he saw—

6½. Interlude—The Incident²⁴

24 James was just discovering the works of Harvey Pekar and Art Spiegelman and Will Eisner and Chris Ware when the Incident—as he refers to it—happened. This all had the effect on him that one would expect with any young artist. He thought that perhaps instead of drawing superheroes and planet-swallowing alien hordes, he would be a cartoonist who chronicled the drama and beauty of real life. It was in this spirit that he created the attached cartoon.

But as much as he wanted to feel fulfilled by it, the experience left him hungry. No one can choose what cranks their gears, and the rooting of his drawing in his own life seemed somehow to diminish and cheapen both.

The next day he was working on a new supervillian: a mutated, genius silverback gorilla who could speak like a human but who commanded all of monkeyhood and longed for the extinction of man and primate dominion.

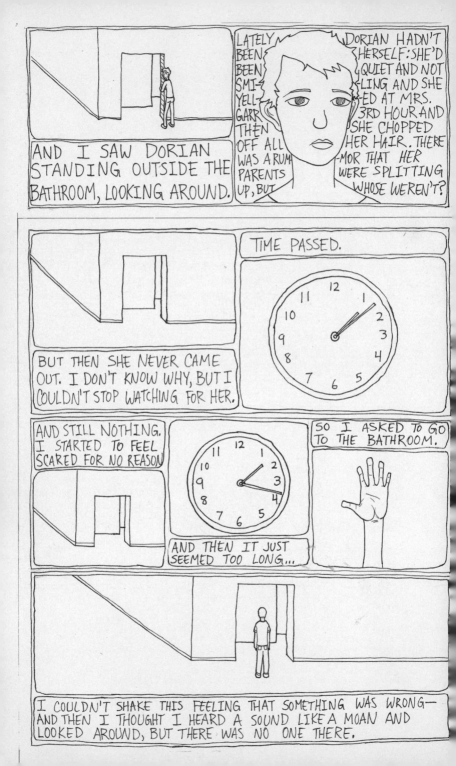

25 James never finished the last frame of the comic. He felt as if there should be some revelation, some moment of wisdom there. But, unfortunately, he had nothing. He reached no realization—and so had no ending.

6. The Homunculus (rejoin)

—another black Escalade. James had begun to mellow out about the appearances of the black Escalades, as most turned out to be manned by moms and businessmen and guys who popped the collars on their polo shirts. This one was parked two blocks up, on the right side of the road, and though James had no reason to believe there was anything special about it, he felt his Spidey-sense tingling. *No lights, no exhaust; it's definitely off.* James couldn't see anyone sitting in the vehicle, but he felt certain that someone was.

As he crossed the next street, he slowed, and all at once he knew he did not want to walk by that Escalade. It was a feeling he couldn't explain—or rather, a certainty he couldn't explain. He looked to his right and saw a small hole cut into the fence about ten yards up and sighed. *What anorexic midget cuts a hole that small?*

James realized two things at the same instant: he had stopped walking, and he could hear an engine close behind. He turned, and it was as if a balloon of cold fear popped in his belly. A black Escalade sat there, maybe ten feet behind him, turned sideways and blocking the road. He felt his blood surge through his veins in thick, painful waves, and that's when he heard the screaming engine to his right. James turned barely in time to see a third Escalade come flying around the corner, brakes squealing as the wheels turned and the black monster skidded to a stop, its right side only a foot or two from James.

Run.

The side doors flew open, and two men were out in a flash. One a tall, blond reed of focused movement, the other a muscular man with a brown flattop. They both rushed for him, reaching to grab him, and as they did their shoulders bumped, momentarily sending each slightly off course.

Run!

James turned and immediately felt a pull. *Backpack!* He let his arms go slack, the backpack slipped free, and he sprang forward. Behind him he heard the two men fall together, and his shoes scraped across asphalt as he ran for the opening in the fence. He heard them regaining their feet and starting after him, but he couldn't look back, sure they'd be only a foot behind him and closing.

Time and distance stretched—each step was a hundred yards and a solid hour—then he was at the fence, scrambling through the hole, throwing himself through, and the edges of the chain-link cut into his left shoulder and elbow, his right thigh. James was up again and running, his feet fighting for grip on the loose rocks around the tracks. He scrambled over the tracks to the decline on the other side before looking back. The Escalades that had been in front of and behind him were already driving away, while the one from which the two men had jumped remained. Flattop was climbing back into the passenger seat, but the blond man just stood there at the hole in the fence, holding the backpack at his side and staring at James.

The blond man took off his sunglasses to reveal thin eyes whose light-blue irises barely stood out from the whites. His look was clinical, as if James was a specimen under glass. "Are you him?"

James turned and ran. He ran with furious purpose, and twice on the way home, he hid in bushes and behind cars as he heard the approach of vehicles.

James ran inside the house and spun on his heel, slamming the front door with two hands and all his weight. He flipped the knob lock, jammed home the dead bolt, and ran up to his room. He shoved that door shut and locked it as well. Hands up, barely breathing, James backed away as if they were right behind him, as if the door could burst open any second and the blond man would come rushing in. His hands shook, and his breath felt ragged in his throat.

Help.

Hot, itchy pre-tears filled his eyes, and he wished for someone—for help. What amazed him in that moment, though, was that it wasn't Mom or Dad or even the police that he longed to see. It was Ezra.

Three sharp knocks sounded off the door, and James's breath stopped. His feet moved up and down automatically, but he went nowhere. He spun, searching, though whether he was looking for a weapon or an escape route, he couldn't say. He pictured the blond man and his cohorts on the other side of the door, their ears pressed to the wood, listening, and he clapped his hand over his mouth to quiet his breathing.

Get out of here. The window.

They'll have someone down there!

Climb down to the living room!

What? Why?

What are you doing? Call the police!

But just as James tore into his pocket to get at his phone—

"It's okay, James. It's me."

Ezra. James couldn't believe it. *How . . . ?* But he didn't think; he snapped the lock free and swung the door open to find Ezra standing in his hallway, balancing a plate of chocolate chip cookies and two glasses of milk.

"May I come in?"

James moved out of his way without a word, and Ezra buzzed into the room.

How . . . ?

"Now," Ezra said, "why did you want to see me?"

"How did you know that I wanted to see you?"

Ezra looked up, as if searching for the right words. "In time, questions like those will be obvious, but right now they may take more time than the answer is worth. Plus, it doesn't answer my question to you. So for now let's just say you're putting out waves and I'm tuned to the frequency. Does that make sense?"

"No."

Ezra smiled and it felt to James like a pat on the back. "It's good to be honest. People who pretend to understand things they don't just to avoid looking stupid often end up looking stupid at the worst possible moment. But don't worry; in time this will all make sense." Ezra took two cookies and a glass of milk for himself, placing the rest on the bedside table. He sat at James's desk, careful to set the plate and glass where it wouldn't disturb any of James's work.

James stood with his back to the wall. He looked at Ezra, half illuminated by the weak desk lamp. A part of James wanted to rush across the room and throw his arms around Ezra, and while he was pretty sure Ezra would hold him, some other part knew it wouldn't satisfy the urge. As if Ezra's hugs would be like a copy of an original.

Ezra had a cookie only inches from his mouth when James said, "Those guys tried to grab me."

Ezra stopped. "The men in the Escalades?" James nodded, and Ezra set down his cookie. "Tell me everything."

James told him what had happened, and for once, Ezra's cool deserted him. He stood and made as if to pace but settled by the window, his hands massaging each other as he looked out at the late afternoon. He asked for details, slowing James down twice as the story touched on the blond man.

When Ezra turned back, his comforting smile had returned. Ezra went back for the cookies he'd left on the desk and pushed the rest toward James. "Eat, James. I have a lot to tell you, and everything goes down better with cookies and milk."

James and Ezra each took a bite of cookie, though James wasn't hungry at all.

"Hm, dry," Ezra said. He dunked the remaining cookie in his glass of milk. "Easily remedied." When Ezra had finished both cookies, he clapped the crumbs from his hands and stood, looking down at James. "The men who attempted to abduct you this afternoon are part of a Roman Catholic cabal, hundreds of years old and backed—at least financially—by the Vatican." He paused, perhaps expecting some sort of reaction, but James remained quiet. James waited, tense and listening, and Ezra smiled, laying his hand on James's shoulder. "You're going to do very well, James."

Ezra once again sat at the desk, crossing his legs. He spoke slowly. "Everything's backwards in this world. The sooner you realize that, the clearer your perceptions will become. For instance, this little event tonight. Now, it would seem that Catholics would be the natural enemy of the"—Ezra air-quotes—"*Antichrist*, right?"

James nodded. He found that he couldn't keep his gaze from rounding on the window. *What's out there? What's coming? What was that sound?*

"But that's wrong," Ezra continued. "According to their books, the Antichrist is supposed to shepherd in the great end—the Rapture, the battle between heaven and hell, and the return of Jesus Christ to Earth. This is what they want. The Antichrist, in other words, is the rain that brings the rainbow. The thing is, a small cabal of Roman Catholics long ago had a different interpretation of their role in the Apocalypse. Some mixture of perverse humanism and to-the-letter Christian duty. This cabal—and this goes back to the late 1400s, you understand—they believe it's their duty to keep the End at bay until they've converted the whole world. Do you see? The conclusion they've come to is that it's every Christian's duty not just to proselytize but to convert *everyone*. The Apocalypse is sort of like the final tally, and it's their job to have everyone on the right side of the line by the time Dad gets home. I'm sorry, do you mind?" Ezra reached over and plucked another cookie from the plate. "It's just that you haven't even finished yours and, well, anyway . . . where was I? Ah, yes, who knows how many false Antichrists they've killed in their history—?"

James's eyes went wide, and his fists closed around the blanket. That word[26] vibrated every minuscule tissue of his body. His mind recoiled, and he felt a childish urge to close his eyes, cover his ears, and scream. And then, in

---

26 Killed killed killed killed killed killed killed killed killed killed killed killed killed killed killed killed killed

an instant that was over so fast he felt as if he'd missed it, James's unlived life passed by. Dates and college and being a father and family vacations on Florida beaches with sandwiches in Tupperware while kids raged against the surf and being old and looking back and gone.

"It's okay, James." Ezra caught his eye. "It'll be alright. I promise.

"I don't know how they found you. They're a closely guarded organization. I've heard that they believe in a mystical numerology, using some kind of mathematical soothsaying to reveal things which they take as divine messages. They apparently believe math is some form of communication with"—again the air quotes—"*God.*"

"But I'm getting off on a tangent. Like I said before, you're going to be just fine. This is not that big of a deal. They're on to you? Fine. We'll just get you some protection." Ezra looked around the room and, apparently not finding what he was looking for, said, "Pardon me, James, but I believe I saw a potted plant in the hallway. Was it real?"

"What?"

"Is the plant real? Is the soil it sits in actual ground?"

"Uh . . ." James felt unable to access the information Ezra wanted. His mind was drowning in the blond man, in a group of grown-ups who wanted to kill him, and he found it almost impossible to breach the surface back to this room, this now. " . . . yeah."

"Wonderful. Would you please go and get me a handful of the soil?"

James didn't move.

"Now, please."

James stood like a somnambulist and walked out.

Ezra called after him. "You must steel yourself, James. You must marshal all that you have within. In time it will all be necessary."

James heard him crunch down on another cookie and speak through his mouthful. "Do you know what stands in your way? Fear. Fear is the mind-killer, as a great man[27] once said.[28] You need to address your fear, to address those things which create the fear."

James walked in thinking, *Those things which create the fear? Oh, you mean THE PEOPLE WHO WANT TO KILL ME! How's that, you asshole?* He held a fistful of soil out to Ezra.

"Ah, thank you. Right here, if you will." Ezra took the dirt without looking at it. "This anti-Antichrist cabal, for instance. Terrifying, right?"

James nodded. *They want to kill you.*

"Well, maybe not so. What do we know of them? We know they made a concerted effort today to abduct an unguarded, unarmed, unsuspecting sixteen-year-old boy and failed. We know they are a secret society that passes their secrets down with their genes, cousins marrying cousins, half-sisters and half-brothers, like a royal family. And what does that tell us? Inbreeding. Which means they are working against a stacked genetic deck. I

---

27 Frank Herbert b.1920, d.1986.

28 Bene Gesserit Litany Against Fear: "I must not fear. Fear is the mind-killer. Fear is the little-death that brings total obliteration. I will face my fear. I will permit it to pass over me and through me. And when it has gone past I will turn the inner eye to see its path. Where the fear has gone there will be nothing. Only I will remain."

would wager a good many of their number are—to put it kindly—unduly challenged in the development of their mental capacities. And finally, I think we can say with certainty that their original goal has been corrupted. You see, the Vatican knows about them. The Vatican is very much like any government, and as such it has intelligence operations—like the CIA, for instance. You run rebels here, you back a dictator there, finance a guerilla war or two, but always while maintaining deniability. The Vatican, as I've said, operates in much the same way. Who knows? This cabal could be right. Or this one. Or that one. Support each one at a distance, but keep them close enough to jump on board at a moment's notice.

"So, the Vatican has been financing them from the beginning, and this anti-Antichrist cabal lives big and fat, and they hunt potential Antichrists. They no longer proselytize or try to convert anyone. If you want my opinion, I think they've grown to like their status, their lives. I think 100 percent be damned, they just want to keep the Apocalypse at bay. Or maybe at this point they're simply acting out of habit. Either way, you'll be able to navigate them without the slightest problem once you begin to accept and master your gifts. And until then, as I said, we'll just get you a little protection.

"Spit, please." Ezra held out the handful of dirt, and James looked at it without moving. "Spit, James."

James decided—and it happened in that single instant—that he was too tired to question and fight anymore.

I believe. And as the decision struck him, it felt as though he descended into a warm bath; his tension broke, and the weight was lessened. James leaned forward and spit in the dirt. The spit was light brown from the cookies and milk. "Sorry."

"Perfectly alright, James. Again, please."

James spat twice more at Ezra's insistence, until the clump was sufficiently muddied.

Ezra pressed his hands together, and the muscles and tendons of his fingers and forearms jumped and flexed as he squeezed harder and harder. Then he released, and in the open palm of his left hand was a tightly packed ball of mud. Ezra kept his hand where it was, bringing his face down to it. He opened his mouth and exhaled onto the mud, which seemed to shudder.

Then he spoke, whispering to it. "Dii-iiink . . . Dii-iiink . . ."

Ezra straightened up and held his hand out so that it was between the two of them. James watched.

The ball of mud . . . shuddered.

James's first instinct was to back away, but he didn't. He stood and tightened his fists and told himself not to be scared. However, what he saw next did scare him. It is a singular experience and one experienced by very few in the history of this Earth—James saw the impossible.

The ball of mud shook, was still, and then opened like a flower. But it wasn't a flower; it was a man. A tiny man made of mud, and as if he'd been lying on his back curled in a ball, he unfolded, his arms and legs unfurling until he lay spread in Ezra's palm like the Vitruvian Man. Then he did something truly amazing: he stretched. It was such a human gesture, and it reminded James of the way babies stretched when first awoken. The little mud man finished his stretch and sat up, looking around, and when he saw Ezra it was as if his whole body sagged.

"What?" the little man said, and James was amazed at the voice, so loud and clear. "What am I doing here?"

"Hello, Dink," Ezra said with his customary smile.

"Hurry, Asmodis." The little man turned fully now, setting his feet and planting his fists firmly on his hips. He looked up at Ezra's beaming visage. "Spit it out, or I'm gone."

"Dink, I'm afraid that your singular services are once again needed."

"No, okay? No. I'm too busy."

This can't be real. This isn't happening.

"Whatever it is this time," Dink said, "it doesn't matter. Okay? Just no. Plus, you're supposed to be looking for the One, but every time I see you, you're just hanging around and you got some—" The little man froze as he caught James in his periphery.

Oh, crap.

Dink turned to face James, and if possible, his shoulders pulled back farther. "Who am I looking at, Asmodis?"

James's voice came out weak. "Why does he keep calling you that?"

Ezra chuckled and set Dink on the bed, where he continued to stare up at James. "Don't worry; that's just what I'm called in the place where I'm from. And to answer your question," he said to Dink, drawing the little man's attention up to him, "this is James Salley." Ezra paused, clearly enjoying the moment. "He is the One."

The little mud man's entire body reacted to these words. His shoulders tightened, and his knees flexed, as if he were preparing to leap at James. But instead, he snapped his ankles together and brought his left fist up to his chest in a single, crisp motion. "Honor," the little man said. "I am Kesin of the Army of Morning Star, though everyone calls me Dink." He nodded once.

James immediately knew two things: Dink was a warrior, and things like honor were important to him. He didn't know how he knew these things, but he was sure that if he didn't answer honestly and earnestly, then something would forever be missing between them.

"Hello, Dink. I'm James. I'm . . . Ezra, who you call Asmodis—he told me that I'm the One, sort of." James shifted under Dink's gaze but didn't look away. "To be totally honest . . . I'm pretty freaked out right now."

"The Antichrist hunters have been after him," Ezra said, a small smile on his face.

Dink looked from James to Ezra and then back again. "I'll watch over him."

"You must be ready at all times, Dink."

"I've pledged to watch over him, which means I will,"

Dink said without looking at Ezra. "Don't talk to me like I'm an asshole."

"As you can see, James, Dink is not the most charming of acquaintances, but he is our most fearsome warrior. He'll keep you safe. If—"

"Thank you," James said, jamming it between Ezra's words. "Thank you, Dink."

Dink nodded without taking his little, dark eyes from James's.

"As I was saying, if you need Dink, all you have to do is call him."

James stood up. He felt a sense of ceremony for which he had no training or natural inclination. James gave a nod to match Dink's and reached out a hand.

The little man took hold of the tip of James's middle finger with both hands and shook. "I'll be ready," Dink said. Then he looked to Ezra. "I'll tell the others the time is at hand, Asmodis." And with that, the life was instantly extinguished from his eyes. The expression went from his face and his small form folded up once more, until again he resembled a small oval of hard dirt, though one packed impossibly tight. Ezra picked it up and handed it to James.

God, it's so light. It looked so heavy when . . . when it was Dink.

"Keep that with you at all times," Ezra said. James looked at it, unsure of what he should do now. Eventually he placed it on the top of his bedside table with the same care with which one would lay a child in its cradle. "Soon you will need no such protection. You, James, will be the greatest power this world has ever known."

Here we go.

But Ezra seemed to read James's exhaustion and exasperation and did not go on. "I think that's enough for tonight."

James looked out his bedroom window to see the red of summer dusk giving way to the deep-ocean dark blue of night. A breeze blew the trees back and forth, back and forth, and their leaves and branches clicked and swished. *It's all really gonna happen.*

"Who're the others?" James said, turning away from the window.

"Pardon me?"

"Dink said he was gonna tell the others. Who did he mean?"

The instant Ezra smiled, James knew the question wasn't about to be answered. "It's a very long story and one that should be told with the time and respect it deserves. Tonight is not the time. You've had a long day. Tomorrow. Tomorrow I'll tell you everything. For now, though, get some sleep."

Fifteen minutes after Ezra had gone, James remained seated on his bed.

The room was different. No doubt about that. The corners buzzed with energy, as if every inanimate object had been imbued with power and foreboding. It was bigger and smaller all at once. James looked at the dirt on his bedside table. *You know what you saw.* A part of him felt that he should be frightened by what he'd just seen, should be upset, but what he really felt was relief. Some things are true, and whatever part of your body or soul or brain it is that responds to truth, it recognizes it when it's near. That part rang out strong and straight as he spoke with Dink, as he looked in the little man's "eyes." *He'll protect me.*

But beyond that, James was stuck.

The Great Battle. That's what he said. The One, the Antichrist, the Great Battle. James got up and walked little circles across his room. *The Great Battle. The Great Battle? You know this; you know this. Think.* James collapsed on the bed with a great, impatient huff. *The Antichrist, the Great Battle, Apocalypse, Armageddon. What's the story? Armageddon, Apocalypse, battle, war, Satan, Great Battle, the Apocalypse, rivers of blood, Moon turns . . . What the hell is the—?*

And then it hit him, and James was out of his bed. He left the dirt/homunculus and made his way downstairs to the living room. The image had flashed through his mind only moments before. He saw the small bookcase by the couch, and on it—along with unread copies of *A Tale of Two Cities* and *Moby Dick* and *Ulysses*—was the Bible. As he plucked it from the shelf, he wondered how many times he'd seen it without ever really registering the fact.

Then he was back in his room, stretched out on the bed, lying on his belly, and flipping through the book until he found it.

The Book of Revelation.

James left his light off as night took the room, reading only by the illumination of his desk lamp. He didn't want Mom coming in when she got home and asking questions about his newfound spiritual curiosity.

The moonless sky battled the streetlights as a few spare birds and bugs called out. James's room was silent otherwise, save for the occasional sound of a flimsy page being flipped. The book was hard to read, and often James had to go back and read passages two and three times.

As far as James could make out, the story was told by John. He knew John was one of the apostles.[29] It said that Jesus appeared to him—like an angel or something, so this was obviously after Jesus was dead—and he showed John a vision of the end of the world.

The way James read it, there was a scroll that Jesus took, and he opened the seven seals on the scroll, and each time he opened one, a different thing happened. Opening some of the first ones released the Four Horsemen of the Apocalypse. He knew about the four horsemen because Duane Duncan had done a report on them last year in history class.[30] The first horseman rides a white horse and gets a crown, and James thought he remembered that he was supposed to represent plague or something. The second horseman rides a red horse and takes peace from

---

29 John, Mark, Luke, Paul, Judas . . . that's it. James could think of five apostles.

30 And even though it was by far the coolest report that anyone had done, Ms. Adderley (who also teaches world history) made him do a different report because she said that the four horsemen were not historical figures. Duane's mom got really pissed, and she got a bunch of other holy-rolling parents on board, and they made a big thing about the school being anti-Christian and keeping God out and religious persecution. In the end, the administration made Ms. Adderley pass it. She gave him a C–.

the Earth, so he represents war. Then the third horseman comes riding a black horse and carrying scales, and James was pretty sure he was famine. Finally, the last horseman arrives. He rides a pale horse—not a white one, but a kind of sickly green/eggshell sort of thing—and he brings death.

So Jesus keeps opening the seals, and there are earthquakes and stuff, and James figured it was about to all go kablooey, but when Jesus opens the seventh seal it just brings out seven angels blowing trumpets, and then the same sort of thing happens again. But when these angels blow their trumpets, everything goes to epic shit. The sky and the oceans and the trees and everything—it all just dies. Locusts swarm the world, and an army begins a slaughter like nothing ever seen before. Humans into the auger. And then Satan arrives. There are dragons—multiple dragons—fighting alongside Satan, and there's a war, but it's really vague as to what happens.

Then there're these bowls. James began to feel lost at this point. There are angels, and they're holding bowls—seven of them—and they're pouring them out, which makes even more terrible things happen. Water turns to blood, and the sun burns the land, and everything is total darkness. *Preparations are made for the Great Battle*—preparations are made for the Great Battle—the Final Battle. But then Babylon—*Babylon? Where's Babylon? Are we supposed to go to Babylon? Are we Babylon?*—is destroyed and everybody praises God, and there's no battle . . . It's already over. The Beast and the False Prophet are thrown into the Lake of Fire, and Satan is imprisoned. But wait, Satan breaks free, so they start the war again—but no, it's over. Just like that. Satan is cast into the Lake of Fire. Everyone is judged, and Earth becomes heaven. New heaven.

James finished the Book of Revelation and flipped right back to the beginning. So John is alone on this island, and Jesus appears to him, and then John writes seven letters to seven churches . . .

James went on like that deep into the night, trying to chip away the two-thousand-year divide to get at the ideas within. He read the book over and over, and each time he saw in his mind's eye as the Lamb laid waste to the Beast and the Dragon. *Is that all?* James had trouble arranging his main concern into a coherent thought, but what it boiled down to was this: Had he been chosen only to be the Washington Generals?

And though he'd wondered earlier in the night if he'd be able to sleep with the dirt corpse of Dink next to him, even while he contemplated the Whore of Babylon and the Dragon from the Sea, his body finally revolted. The day had simply been too long, the strain too much. Unbidden, James's eyes closed and he slumped against the Bible and slept like a dead man.

7. A Brief History of Fighting

It was still dark when James woke. He couldn't remember his dream, only a sense of pressure and panic. The flat, digital clock on his dresser read 4:13. There was no reason to be up, but James knew there would be no returning to sleep. He lay in bed, his eyes open and his body bristling. The only illumination was a shadow of red from the clock and the edges of the streetlight.

He looked to his right, where he could just barely make out the small ball of dirt. *Dink*. A dog began to bark, off in the night, at least a couple blocks away, and something about the bark reached James like a bat's sonar screams, and all at once he was aware of the distance between the dog and himself, and of the world outside altogether. In his mind he could see it, deserted, just before the town wakes up, and the impulse took hold of him.

James swung his feet off the bed, and a few moments later, he'd pulled on a pair of shorts. Without turning on the light, he grabbed a hoodie and stuffed his feet into his gym shoes. He paused for an instant before sliding the small ball of dirt into his pocket, and then he was out, in the hallway and tiptoeing down the stairs. He unlocked the back door, and as he stepped outside, it felt as if he were stepping out of his own skin. The air was cool, and the night had a liquid purple hue that was unfamiliar to him.

He went to the garage and noiselessly removed his bike, walking it down the drive. He was at a trot by the bottom, jumping on and pumping the pedals all in one motion. The way was flat, and though James could've coasted, his legs wanted to work. Every thirty seconds or so, he stood for a few rotations just to get more torque. The wind in his face felt five degrees cooler, and in the dark, each quiet house was a private bedroom.

James rode in the opposite direction of school, taking Jackson Street west to Gilmore Street. He didn't know where he was going, but the ride didn't feel directionless. At each intersection, he felt a strong pull one way or the other.

Once, when he was younger, James had seen an empty boat come untied on the Chicago River when his family was visiting the city. It was one of those tourist boats, a sky-blue-and-white dart of a boat, and as the men on the shores screamed at each other and ran across the bridges, the boat just floated down the river, unconcerned. James didn't know why the image came to his mind just then, but it tightened the knot in his stomach.

On Gilmore Street he became aware of the overgrown

trees and abandoned train tracks. This was the small, two-track offshoot that ran to and from the ChocoMalt factory.[31] It used to carry train cars loaded with malt powder and malted chocolate balls and nuts and bars, and now it just lay there like an outgrown child's toy in the backyard. The grass was weeds. And in another minute, he cleared the line of trees and the old factory sat before him like God's tank. Football fields of red brick laid on their sides and stacked and filled with so many broken windows—more than you'd ever want to count. Row after row after row. Even on the upper floors, flung rocks had found the brittle glass and blasted it. This mass of forced openness—of uncovered should-be windows— felt almost indecent, like an open fly.

James squeezed the brakes, and his tires skidded and kicked up microparticles of dirt and road. Then he stood, his legs posted on each side of the bike as he stared up at the monstrous building. *This is a special place.* James could feel—in his gut, in the place where you know you

---

31 **The Story of Stone Grove/ChocoMalt/the Eights as Told by the United States Census**—As much as the citizens of Stone Grove seemed to enjoy the narrative of the closing of the ChocoMalt factory decimating the town, followed by the oozing land-dealers sneaking in clumps of Section 8 housing, befouling the once-pure town with elements of urban rot and crime, the US Census Bureau tells a different tale. While it is true that the demographics have changed, it would appear that the rest of the damage has been largely imaginary and hysterical. The 1970 census reported Stone Grove's population as 95 percent white/non-Hispanic, with the African American population at .004 percent and the Hispanic population at .019 percent. As of the last census, Stone Grove's white/non-Hispanic population was 71 percent, while African American citizens comprised 4.1 percent of the total population and the Hispanic population came in around 17 percent.

Here's the rub, though. The crime rate is 135.6 (per 100,000) which is both well below the national average and roughly where it was when ChocoMalt was still operating. The schools are all well (if not exceptionally) rated; George Washington (formerly Gary Gilmore) High School, for example, is ranked No. 56 in Illinois, which is just slightly higher than the year the factory closed. Seventy-five percent of Stone Grove's workforce now hold white-collar jobs. There's also the fact that, in spite of all of its civic generosity, in spite of being the town's benefactor through some rough times, at its height the ChocoMalt factory only actually employed around 300 people, many of whom were not residents of Stone Grove.

Nobody likes this story, though. It lacks drama.

love your mom—that this was more than a building. *This place is a thing.* The thought didn't make total logical sense to him, but he knew it was right. The way a rabbi sees a temple, the way a teacher sees a school, that was what James sensed in the dilapidated factory: weight, importance, sacrality.

He felt an urge that'd never before touched him: he wanted to go in.

Going into the ChocoMalt factory was a common dare/brag in Stone Grove, as well as a familiar source for cautionary tales. Of the factory, James had heard four main things:

1) Satan worshippers hang out there. They do animal sacrifices and stuff, and they're all crazy and if they catch you there, they could do anything. Colin claimed that a friend of one of his older brothers had his ear cut off as a warning to stay away. Dorian said she heard that the Satanists raped a guy in the butt just to scare everyone else away.

2) Gangbangers hang out there. This is where they do their initiations.[32] The factory is their turf, and if you show up, they will seriously mess you up. Maybe kill you, though there's no way anyone would find a body.

3) It's a deadly condemned building. You could just be walking and the entire floor could collapse, and you'd fall—maybe just onto the floor below, but maybe through that too, maybe onto some machinery. James heard one kid almost died when he opened a door and

---

32 The year before, James learned (read: overheard a conversation) that when guys get initiated into a gang they get beat in, but when girls get initiated they get to choose if they want to get beat in or have sex with all the guys in the gang. He heard Ileana's friend Lala say that her cousin in Cicero went with the sex option, but that the guys never respect you if you do that, and if she ever gets in she's gonna get beat in.

walked through it and there was just nothing there. It was an elevator shaft, and the kid fell into it. Luckily, it was full of water, so he didn't die, but he lost a leg.

4) The cops are always watching it. If you go in at all, they'll bust you. You'll be in there, and they'll just come out of nowhere. They know the place like the back of their hands, so there's no way you can get away.

James rode around the factory until he was by the back.[33] There was a small window frame with only a few shards pointing to the center. James laid his bike in the grass/weeds and walked over. He looked around, but everything was dark and still. He stood in the tall grass and put his hands on the stone windowsill, feeling a bit of grime and harmless glass under his palms. Then he leaned forward, until his head and chest were actually inside the factory.

There was very little he could make out. He could tell that the room he was looking into was long and tall, like a steel ballroom. The space directly in front of him appeared open, and at the far, far end was a mass that looked like some kind of manufacturing equipment. James remembered the lighter in his pocket and dug it out. It caught on the second attempt, and weak orange illumination filled the area directly around him. To his right he saw the main wall. It'd originally been white or gray, but now it was the color of snow by the side of the road, streaked with stains and covered with graffiti. A few signs, like the upside-down pitchfork and the crown and

---

33 On the east side, by the large parking lot and the dilapidated water tower.

the five-pointed star, James recognized as gang tags, but most of it was indecipherable. He did see a pentagram, though, and a spot where, in big black letters, it said: THE PIGS WILLLLLLLL PAY!!!

James turned to look at the rest of the room, bringing the light around. It was like one of those postapocalyptic wastelands in the movies: barren but not empty. He moved the lighter slowly to the left. It didn't shed enough light for him to see the machinery across the way, just a twenty- or twenty-five-foot arc. The floor was covered with cigarette butts and shards of glass and what looked like rust shavings. He noticed a broken desk and a filing cabinet without any drawers, and then as his arm swept past his own face, he saw something. Directly across from him, a ways off but not quite to the mechanical graveyard on the other side, was a . . . a shape. He squinted into the darkness, but while his ocular system was unable to clarify what it was, some part of James was certain—*It's a man*. Standing there, unmoving, watching him. James immediately became aware of the sound of his own breathing, the way he must look with the little flame held before him.

Then something moved. There was a shuffle and a clatter and James leapt back, dropping the lighter. He fell on his ass in the weeds and scrambled up, two factions of his mind arguing about whether that had been a man, whether it had moved, what had actually happened. But all of that was only background noise. The operating system ran without words as he was on his bike and moving in a single motion. He replayed what he'd seen—didn't believe what he thought he'd seen—but pedaled furiously nonetheless, checking behind him as he went, sure that someone would be there when he looked back. But there was nothing.

James rode south as the glow of the sun began to edge over the earth. He rode as fast as he could, until the burn made its way from his calves to his thighs, from his chest to his biceps and wrists, and then he rode over the hill and down to Haley Pond, where he collapsed on the grass.

The air hurt as it became his breath. James sprawled on his back and watched the sky turn orange-blue and yellow-purple. As he lay there next to the water, though, what he felt swelling through him wasn't the fear that had propelled him from the factory. Nor was it the fear which he'd felt so much lately. It was anger. A shamed anger pointing directly in. His anger was a blade, and he sank it into his solar plexus. Tired of being suffocated by it, of being afraid, he hated that part of himself, hollered at it to do better, to work, to *keep up*, like one would a gimpy leg or a weak back. He begged and implored and threatened, but the only feeling that turned into words was *I hate you*.

He thought of Ezra's words, of his promises, and he realized that his entire life had been about fear. His inter-action with every person, his hiding of his own joys and loves and sadnesses, his timidity with strangers and bul-lies and the whole goddamn world. Even the moments in which he'd thought himself brave, he realized, the times he'd let bits of himself out, they were only pleas. It was him begging for someone—anyone—to notice him.

James stood up. The first light refracted off the dew, and Haley Pond sat before him like green glass. James felt the sudden urge to strip off his clothes and dive into it, to disrupt the perfect, splendid beauty of undisturbed water and to splash around and feel himself submersed in it. It was a powerful, cellular urge, and James even began to pull his hoodie over his head. But then he stopped. He looked around at the few houses which sat near Haley Pond. *They could be up already.* Some mom looking out her kitchen window at this weird boy. Or worse, someone he knew. The thought stopped him dead, and he pulled the hoodie back on.

Should be heading back anyway. Have to meet Ezra.

Of course, Ezra didn't say where we're meeting. James pushed his bike up to the street and threw a leg over it, but just then he heard a noise and stopped. It was soft noise, a wheel in need of oil, an oscillating squeak-*squeak.*

Ezra and James sat in The Omelet Shack, in a booth next to a window which claimed to seat four but would have been awfully tight. Single servings of butter and jam lay in a bowl between them as they slurped coffee. James had already eaten[34] and his plate held scraps in the center of the table.

Ezra let out a deep breath, taking his coffee in both

---

34 And though he'd been sure he wouldn't be able to eat, James took down a bacon-and-cheese omelet with the hashbrowns cooked inside, two pieces of buttered toast, and two sausage links.

hands. "It's hard to know where to begin."

In the pause that followed, over the sounds of scraping chairs and silverware clinking plates, James said, "I read Revelations last night."

Ezra smiled. "Good. I guess that's as good a place as any. And what did you think?"

"Whatta you mean what did I think? I read it. I know what happens."

"Really?" Ezra smiled and tipped the cup to his lips. "Because I don't."

"But . . . it says that Jesus opens the seals—seven seals—and then everything gets all . . . the four horsemen are the first—"

"I know what the Revelation says, James. I've read it. Though it has been quite a while." Ezra pulled a quick sip and set the cup aside. "Let's start with this, before we move on to anything else. There is no Jesus. At least not in the sense you mean or the sense that Christians view things.

"I wasn't in the area at the time, but the impression I got from those who were was that this Jesus fellow was a revolutionary—a pioneer of nonviolent rebellion. A serious guy. One of those people who run wholly on their own internal moral compass—which is rare, James. You may not realize that yet, but it's rare as hell. He, uh, he challenged the rabbis, the temples; he challenged the Romans; and, as you might expect, all of them were pretty happy when he finally got crucified. You have to understand, though, everyone and anyone who pissed off the

Romans was getting crucified in those days. You couldn't swing a Jew crucified for sedition without hitting a Jew about to be crucified for sedition. But there was something about this Jesus, something special, and the stories about him grew. As far as I can tell, he never said he was the Messiah, never came back from the dead, nothing. But people were looking for a Messiah and he got cast. That's it. He in no way plays in to the events currently unfolding. He is not of our realm."

The waitress, a beautiful girl who James had a hard time looking away from, with her two-tone hair and too-baggy skirt and too-tight top, swooped by, refilling Ezra's cup and pouring James's to the brim.

"Our realm," Ezra continued, "was made before yours. I'm not sure *realm* is the right word here, but I think it's probably the closest. You see, ours was made first and then yours, and the two have always been somewhat connected. Or rather, wholly and completely connected but in unseen ways. In a sense, we are your dreams and you are ours. We are your ghosts and vice versa.

"Now, as I said, for the most part we are each ignorant of the other. The difference is that we know you exist, and the opposite is not true. And so when we catch glimpses of your leavings or your traces, we see them for what they are. On the other hand, when you catch bits of us in the ether, you tend to assign it to wherever your personal belief dictates. This is the Voice of God, this is a poltergeist, this is artistic inspiration, et cetera, et cetera."

Ezra emptied a third of his coffee in a single gulp.

"I always think of it like an antenna. Artists and mystics and what have you—they tend to have the best antennas, but they also tend to be the most irrational, emotional, and predisposed to their own prejudices and ardent beliefs. So, now, let us look at John, the author of the Revelation. Now, this John was not the apostle of Jesus. That guy, from what I've heard, was a total schmuck.[35] No, this John was a true mystic and a real steel-in-the-back believer in the tenets of Christianity. This was in about 100 AD. He was always proselytizing, always preaching, and often falling into a religious ecstasy, wailing, thrashing, speaking in tongues, all that stuff. In other words, he was about 60 to 70 percent crazy. He was one of those religious folks who most of us cross the street to avoid. However, he did have an extraordinarily strong antenna. He most definitely picked up things from our realm. There can be no doubting that.

"After a couple years of telling everyone that they weren't pious enough and rousing the local rabble, the powers that be got sick of old crazy John, and they exiled him to the Isle of Patmos. There he found the solitude agreed with him, and—I bet—cleared away enough noise that he was really able to focus on what was coming through that old antenna of his. So he sat down and he wrote the story of his Revelation. But here's the thing: the antenna doesn't work like that. I've yet to find a human who could see or hear or feel clear, uninterrupted

---

35 According to Ezra, the apostle John was commonly referred to as John the Know-It-All, John the Suck-Up, and John the Shitstain—roughly translated from the original Aramaic.

impressions of Taloon. No, what it's like is—"

"Taloon?"

Ezra was frozen for a moment; the interruption had caught him off guard. "Yes, Taloon. That is . . . well, that's what we call our world. I'll get to that. Shortly, shortly. Let me just, ah, where was I?"

"People don't get, like, complete things from your place, from Taloon."

"Yes, thank you. Ah, excuse me, miss." Ezra waved over the beauty. "My friend here has let his coffee go cold. Would you mind dumping this and bringing him a new one? Thank you."

James felt a momentary embarrassment at being babied in front of this girl, but the feeling was quickly overtaken, because Ezra was off and talking again.

"Yes, see, that's why I compare it to an antenna. The way impressions from our world are received is very much like listening to a radio station that you can't quite get, or perhaps like having the receiver set halfway between two stations. You get a couple words here, maybe a sentence there, a half word, a bit of a description, then silence and silence and more silence, then a blurp and a beep and two words that couldn't possibly be what you thought they were.

"Do you see what I'm saying, James? Old John on his island, he got some things from our world: the seals, the coming war, the Beast, and Michael. He got all that, but he assigned it the prejudices of his existence. He inserted Jesus, he made the Archangel Michael a good guy—a hero—and he wrote the ending he wanted."

"How do you know?" James said, with far too much intensity for The Omelet Shack, and exactly at the same time that their waitress walked up and set his cup down. She gave him that look he'd seen so many times: brows scrunched, lip curled—*What a weirdo.*

Damn it, James thought as the cold hooks of shame sank into his gut. *Go away!* It was immediate. The sensation was so intense, as if the thought itself was electricity flowing from him to her. He felt it land in her, felt her shrink and back away. *It was like she heard me.*

He turned back to Ezra, whose face beamed with that proud-papa smile, and he remembered where he was. "How do you know he didn't see the ending?"

"Because no one does, James. No one knows how it's going to shake out, not in your world or ours. No, Old John simply saw the state of our world, which includes this prophecy. The prophecy itself, though, doesn't say who will win, only that there will be war. Great and horrible war." The thought didn't seem to bother Ezra nearly as much as James felt it should. Ezra just slurped his coffee and looked out the window as if picturing the conflict there in Stone Grove.

James gave him his moment; he turned and saw the waitress watching through one of the little portholes in the swinging kitchen doors, and when he did, she ducked out of sight.

"This is just the way humans work," Ezra continued.

"They fill in the gaps with the information they have. Incomplete pictures make them anxious. Questions without answers enrage them. You see? Old John wasn't lying. He didn't think he was making things up. He thought he was just filling in the parts of the message that got lost. The antennas, they're imperfect—and all different. Dante, for example, was very strong. His Inferno, as he called it, I wonder if you know what that was based on."

The dream—a burp of fear-recognition scorched every synapse. "The Pit."

"Exactly. He's obviously seen it or, or felt it or something. He saw this place, the descent into the terrifying abyss, and those trapped within, and he naturally thought, *Hell*. But we know what it really is. A prison. Still, the picture is incomplete, so he fills in the rest himself. He fills Hell with local politicians, Florentines who have disappointed him, and while some of them definitely deserve to be in Hell if it exists, the list is a little Italy heavy.[36] He has Brutus and Cassius—those are the guys who killed Julius Caesar—he has them in the bottom level of Hell, because they destroyed some idea he has of a unified Italy. Ach, it's all"— Ezra threw both hands up as if waving away a fly—"but

---

36 Ezra's case: The thirteenth-century politician Count Ugolino is in the Ninth Circle (Antenora) along with Archbishop Ruggieri, both of them condemned due to their acts of betrayal. The Count sentenced there because of a life of political and military betrayal, including working a side deal with Archbishop Ruggieri to get Ugolino's nephew (with whom he was sharing power) exiled. The Archbishop was placed in the Ninth Circle because he then screwed Ugolino on the deal, turned the public against him, and had the Count, along with his two sons and two grandsons, arrested and locked in a tower, at which point the door was nailed shut, the key literally thrown in a river, and the Count and his family left to starve to death. There were whispers of cannibalism to survive, though in the end it didn't matter. All perished.

Dante has placed them together in the Inferno, the Count gnawing on the back of the Archbishop's head for eternity. The Archbishop having been the worse betrayer(?), and the Count driven on always by his rage. Now, bad guys? No doubt. But do their political double-dealings (and an admittedly cruel quintuple homicide) really compare with the betrayals of mankind perpetrated by Ashurnasirpal II or Caligula or Qin Shi Huang?

that's what I mean. It's all . . . half true. And the worst of it is the artists. They're a thousand times worse than the crazies and the generals and the prophets. Old John on Pathos and Dante there, they figure they got the truth of it, so then they set about framing it in a good story. I mean, come on, the Revelation, that's a story. Seven seals, seven bowls, seven trumpets. And, if I may add a little literary criticism here, it's a bit heavy-handed about the power and the victory and all that. I think the lady doth protest too much, you know. 'I am the Alpha and the Omega'? Come on. And that ending? Awful. Okay, everyone's in Heaven, Satan's destroyed—what, he's back? What, there are more people to kill? That hundred-pound hail after the fifteenth earthquake didn't do it? Really? More judging? That's a storyteller trying to frighten you into behaving, trying to convince you of the power of his hero. If I give you any advice that you heed, James, let it be this: do not trust stories. Stories can be very dangerous. Always ask why someone is telling you this story, because often when someone is telling you a story, their ultimate goal is to take a part of their mind and slyly sneak it into your mind. You think it's entertainment, but it's actually infestation. Remember that."

"Uh, so . . . sorry . . . so what's the real story, then?"

"Yes, the real story. Well, as I've heard it . . ." Ezra pushed his empty mug away and married his fingers. "In the beginning, there was the Creator."

"God?"

"Ah, I think not. That word has a bit too much baggage here for what I mean. Let's just say, the Creator.

"So in the beginning there was the Creator. Now, you understand, when I say *the beginning*, I mean only our beginning. Where the Creator was before this, what it was doing, what other worlds it may have made?" An easy shrug. "No one knows. But in our beginning, the Creator made our realm—Taloon. It was like a blank sheet of paper. The Creator made this world in massive strokes, and it lacked for detail or design. It was . . . unfinished. Then the Creator made two great beings, called Metatron and Morning Star. They were special, James. Brilliant and beautiful, with the eyes of poets and the hearts of warriors. The Creator told Metatron and Morning Star that they were free to make this world as they saw fit, and so the two of them set about the work together. They were closer than any two beings have ever been or will ever be, their love a heart-and-muscle bond of sibling and lover and parent all melded into one.

"The Creator watched as its two creations molded Taloon. They made mountains and forests and fields of flowers, and Morning Star made the Moon and Metatron made the Sea, and together they made the tower in which they dwelt.

"As time went on, the two of them became more and more comfortable in their roles as builders of the mind, and they worked to shape Taloon into a place where they could live and be happy forever. Then the Creator began to make more beings to dwell in the realm. It made Leviathan[37] and Bahamut next, and though they were both great and horrible, they could not shape Taloon the way that Metatron and Morning Star could, and—much more importantly—they did not know the Creator. Only Its first two creations were allowed to know It, to bask in Its warmth. The Creator next made those like me. It made more and more of us, until we fully populated the world It had made. But like Leviathan and Bahamut before us, we did not know the Creator, only what the two great ones told us. Once, Morning Star described the Creator to me by saying, 'I don't think of the Creator as a being or a thing; the Creator is an Is. You don't have conversations with the Creator, nor do you give or take anything from the Creator. The Creator creates. It is all It does.' That is, of course, why I shoo away the notion of 'God.' This is not a kindly old man with a white beard sitting in the clouds and watching over us. I think of the Creator more like an automaton with a single function. For all we know, some old race created It and set It loose upon . . . upon whatever plane this little narrative of ours is playing out.

"Anyway," Ezra continued, "we lived that way for a while. Taloon was taking shape, but it was still very much like a dream. Though the rest of us weren't as powerful, en masse we could affect the world too, almost accidentally, through the things we experienced and came to believe. So the more that came to dwell there, the harder it became for the perceptions of Metatron and Morning Star

---

37 James felt his heart falter—the literal skipping of a beat—at the mention of the monster's name. He was terrified that Ezra would describe him, that it would be verified beyond a doubt—but he longed for it, too. His dreams were an eclipse begging to be stared at.

to fashion it. And though the land remained unfinished, the Creator no longer attended to it. Metatron and Morning Star, too, began to neglect the molding of the world. They began to hold long discussions, away from all of us, and would tell us only that the Creator was away, presumably creating other worlds. We began, slowly, to become aware of your realm, to see its logical cosmos composing itself as we lay in the Great Field of Dreaming."

Ezra drank from an empty mug for a moment before realizing. He smiled without moving his mouth and set it down. "Morning Star finally came to us all and said that the Creator was gone. That was it. Poof, just gone. Morning Star said we must accept this and move on. We were crushed, but Morning Star tried to rally us, telling us that this was a good thing, that we should embrace the independence of our destiny. Metatron was furious. Metatron said we couldn't be sure that the Creator was gone, and even if It was, then it was our duty to discover what we'd done to anger the Creator, to bring It back. If we had to beg, then we would beg. If we had to wait, then wait we would. The fault lay with us.

"The two of them began to fight. It was . . . awful. No, that doesn't do it justice. They fought like wounded animals, like deranged lovers, and as their anger and irrationality took hold, the world around us responded likewise. They were its masters, and it bent before their fury. Taloon became a nightmarescape. It was not uncommon at that time for day to turn to night, for the Sea to turn black or the Moon to blink out. You would wake to find that you were somewhere else or that all of a sudden you were standing in the sky with your head pointing toward the ground. And when we would hear them . . . noises of hatred between two who'd so loved each other, who'd watched over us . . . oh, how we trembled."

Ezra closed his eyes for a moment, and James saw an entire storm cross his face. "I really don't know how long this period lasted," Ezra said. "Time was just another piece of our realm that their anger and fear warped. It was like water. Now flowing, now stopped, now dripping, now half plugged and spraying wildly in several directions at once. I do know that Metatron came and spoke with us often, as did Morning Star. Metatron would say that Morning Star had forsaken the Creator, as had so many of us, and that we must reform our ways if we wished for the Creator's return. Morning Star was heartbroken and said often that we must release the Creator in our hearts and move on. Morning Star said there were much worse truths to accept than this one. And, as should be expected in any situation like this, minds were split and factions formed. I saw more sense in what Morning Star said and so aligned myself likewise. There were less of us, though. Many less. Most believed Metatron and clung to that hope.

"Then, after an especially horrific fight between the two, when the sky cracked open and the air filled with insects—"

"Coffee?" It was a different girl, squat and friendly-faced.

James pushed his cup toward her without a thought.

"No, I—oh, what the hell," Ezra said. "Sure."

She filled both cups before quickly retreating. James saw her shrug as she reached the kitchen, where their previous waitress crouched, waiting for a report.

"So as I was saying . . . after the, uh, after the fight, Morning Star sent word that everyone should gather at the tower, that there was something to tell all of us. What Morning Star was going to say, though, we never learned. As soon as Morning Star's invitation went out, Metatron, along with some of his followers, bound and took Morning Star. They set out from there, a war party. We were . . . so unprepared for any of it. We were taken unawares. Only a very few of us were able to elude capture.

"Metatron made a prison in the Sea, which I believe you've seen. Morning Star and the others were taken there and held. Morning Star was bound in a . . . a prison within the prison, a cell that fit only one . . . held firm by seven seals. Now, these are exactly what they sound like, nothing more. They are seven unbreakable seals, which can be opened only by the utterance of Morning Star's true name. That was how Metatron was able to do the binding."

James felt the muscles in his arms twitch and tense, felt short hairs at the top of his spine prickle. "What do you mean, true name?"

"The Creator gave Metatron and Morning Star true names. Names that only they knew. Names which they called each other by. None of us knew this, you understand. No one knew until after it was done. Meta-tron told us of the secret names and how the only ones who knew Morning Star's true name were the Creator and himself. And, to ensure that he could never be bound in the same way, Metatron gave up his public name, taking the true name that the Creator had given him: Mikhael.

"From that day forward, he was Mikhael. He returned to his tower, and those who dwelt at the base of the tower said that Mikhael could be heard praying and begging at all hours of each day. Mikhael's tears turned to ice and his wails to fire, and he beat his fists, and deep fissures showed in the walls and windows of the tower. Mikhael exhorted the Creator to return, pleading the case that he'd been faithful, that he had bound Morning Star; but there was no response. Or, at least, for a very long time there was no response. After a very, very long time, the tower grew quiet. There were those who wondered if Mikhael had died, but the flame continued to burn in his tower, and the deep, wet sighs of his breath could be heard by any who came near to his sanctuary. Some of Mikhael's follow-ers were brave enough to approach the tower and call out, begging for Mikhael to come down, but he did nothing. He was silence.

"Then, after a long, long time, Mikhael emerged from the tower. He was not the same Mikhael who went in. His eyes focused far off, like he couldn't even see any of us. And he didn't seem tortured by the rift with Morning Star or the Creator's absence or anything. He was . . . serene.

"Mikhael called to everyone to come and listen at the edge of the Sea, so that everyone—including those in the Pit—could truly listen. Then he told us what had happened.

"He told us that the Creator had returned to him after his long wait in the tower. The Creator returned and said that Taloon had become wicked and weak and that It had created Its new world—your world, James—so that we may prove ourselves. That's the only reason your world even exists. The Creator designed this world solely as a test, and when we were truly ready, one would be born to this other world, and that one will come to Taloon and release Morning Star. The door between our two worlds will swing open, and the battle will be fought on Earth. If Mikhael and all of his followers defeat us, defeat the wicked masses, then the Creator will return."

"And if we defeat them?"

Ezra smiled and sipped his coffee. "Then we'll be free."

"So all this time, you've all just been waiting for . . ."

"The One. Yes."

"And that's me?"

A nod.

"And I'm supposed to go to Taloon and release Morning Star, and then . . ."

"And then there will be war."

"What'll happen to all of us?"

"Us? Who's us? You and me? Morning Star and Dink and the rest? The people of Earth?"

"What'll happen to Earth?"

"I don't know."

James was about to protest, but Ezra pushed through.

"Truly, I don't. The battle will happen here, and it will be massive. There will be . . . devastation, but beyond that . . . who knows? The humans will choose sides. I know that. But what part they'll play—you'll play—in the War, I can't say. Maybe when it's over, our worlds will merge. Maybe we'll all come to dwell here and Taloon will just blow away. Maybe Taloon will become the paradise it was always meant to be.

"All I really know is that you are the difference. You're what we have that they don't. You can release Morning Star. You can rally humans like no one else who's ever lived. You can shape this world. What else you can do, there's just no telling."

"But you know it'll be terrible, right? I mean, it's a war, so tons of people will die. That's what you want me to do. You want me to *start a war.*"

"No, James, that's what's going to happen. It's not that I want you to do anything. This War is coming. Both of our worlds are begging for it. And, yes, people will die. But is that all that matters? Is that the only factor?" Ezra pushed his cup aside and leaned close to James. "Have you learned about World War II in school?"

James nodded.

"Then you know that war was an undeniably terrible thing, and you also know the world is undeniably a better place for it." And then Ezra's smile was serene, as though he were discussing nothing more taxing than a Sunday stroll. "This War must happen, James. The most that we can hope to do is shape it."

For an instant, James felt a mindless calm settle over him. He was nowhere and no one. His mind was empty, and he felt his purpose like an arrow that'd been shot by another and was in flight. It was a pure and serene feeling, though as soon as it came, it was gone.

James went to the bathroom and peed, and when he came back, Ezra had paid the bill and was in the act of dropping a few dollars on the table.

"How are you feeling?"

James's lips parted for a moment before meeting once again. *How do you feel? How do you feel?* "Tired."

Ezra smiled and placed a long, bony hand on James's shoulder. "You're quite amazing. I wonder how I would have responded to all of this if I were in your shoes. Not nearly so well, I think."

James took a sucker from the jar by the register and pushed his way through the glass double doors, with Ezra following.

"Where are you off to?" Ezra asked.

James responded immediately. "I gotta go to school."

Ezra plucked his antique bicycle from the wall and clucked his tongue. "This is something you really must learn, James. You don't *have* to do anything. You are free. Think about that. Roll it around in your head. You. Are. Free. Today, instead of going to school, you could steal a car and drive to California. If you don't do that, it's because you've chosen not to. This is something people never seem to understand. And you need to understand it more than anyone."

"Why?"

"Because you're powerful, James. Being the Antichrist doesn't have to be a bad thing."

"Please don't call me that."

"Ah, sorry. Just a shorthand. All I mean is that you don't have to do things out of some sense of fear or duty. You have to grab hold of your life. You're a god amongst men. Do you understand?"

James pulled his own bike from the rack, thinking how far off Ezra was. *If you could do anything, if you really were a god among men, you wouldn't run off. You'd change the world around you, the people and places you already know, the ones you have to adjust to. Let them adjust to me. Try that for a while.* "Okay, but I got a lot to think about, so I might as well just go. I mean, if you need a place to be left alone with your thoughts, where better than school?"

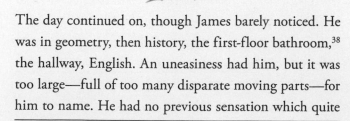

The day continued on, though James barely noticed. He was in geometry, then history, the first-floor bathroom,[38] the hallway, English. An uneasiness had him, but it was too large—full of too many disparate moving parts—for him to name. He had no previous sensation which quite

---

38 Anxiety always went straight to James's stomach.

compared. It was as if fear, excitement, anger, and sadness were being blended within him, screaming by, each in turn, overwhelming the weak and untested emotional defense of the teenage mind.

Why me?

He wondered at the new way people were looking at him, the ways he was becoming able to change that—and he replayed the story Ezra had told at breakfast, and he didn't want to do what Ezra asked—or demanded—and yet he did—oh, god, how much he did! To be that man, to be great. Great!

James was in class[39] and that indefinable feeling[40] was back and[41] growing[42]. It was a sort of jittery-jacked-icky-all-over weight. Gross energy flowed from his heart like psychostatic electricity, and his mouth created extra saliva. He felt the urge to run, to burn off this excess.

The bell to end the day was an alarm clock pulling James from a night of sleep. He gathered his stuff and walked out the back doors in the midst of a sea of kids. His feet carried him along at a pace to match everyone else's. *You are the One. You're going to free Morning Star (how?) and gather people together (how?) and lead them (again, how?) and, and, and you're going to fight to, to . . .* It sounded ridiculous, even when he was saying it only in his head.

The girl directly in front of James stopped hard, and before he knew what was happening, he walked up her

39 But he couldn't focus, not on the class or his own crisis. There was no clarity to be had.

40 His consciousness refused to stay on one course.

41 Thoughts interrupted thoughts interrupted thoughts.

42 As if his mind was not his own.

heel and into her back.

"Ow! What the *hellllluh*?" The girl whirled around like a fighting ballerina: one leg up, both hands out and ready, her face a mask of disgust and affront and thousands of years of Germanic and British genetics. James recognized her immediately: Gail Asbury.[43] She recognized him, too, and it did not soften her reaction.

And there was Nick. James had heard something about Nick and Jess breaking up and how Nick and Gail were hooking up now, but it'd been white noise and hadn't actually sunk in until this very moment. Colin and LaMarcus stood off to one side, lazy smiles drawn on their faces. Their eyes said it all: Oh, good. Entertainment.

"What's your problem?" James had wondered recently if he could change the way Nick saw him as well. He'd kept meaning to try, but each time the opportunity arose, he chickened out. Now, with Nick pressing in on him, he knew it was too late. All he felt was fear. He saw Nick's top lip pull back just slightly, like he was disgusted, like he'd just smelled something turning to pure rot, and he thought, *No, that's not right. It's not just fear.*

Nick grabbed James's shirt in two fistfuls, and James felt the crowd around them growing. "I said, what the fuck is your problem, retard?"

"Get off me!" It happened before James had time to examine the action or its repercussions. Both hands came

43 Gail had gone to school with all of them since fifth grade, existing in the middle ground of nonpopular nonpariahs. However, in the summer between eighth grade and freshmen year, Gail underwent major changes. To quote Colin O'Connor: "I shit you not, man, her tits musta grown three sizes. Just wait 'til you see her." She also became a blonde and eschewed the cute and innocent outfits which her mother had previously picked out, instead building a wardrobe of short, tight, low, and high. The social vacancy momentarily left by Dorian's suicide attempt was filled by Gail with military efficiency.

up and shot straight out. He felt his palms dig into Nick's chest and drive him back, saw Nick's arms reaching for purchase, saw how he would have fallen had Colin and LaMarcus not been there. For a second Nick's eyes were wide and uncomprehending, and then they were animated by the wild fury of embarrassment. He took a step toward James but was corralled by LaMarcus.

"Fight in the courts!" Colin bellowed, steering Nick away.

The crowd continued to swell, and a furious energy of shouts and jeers closed around James, propelling him. He walked to the courts in the wake of Nick and Gail and Colin, catching glimpses of Jess and Ileana and even Ken Lakatos. Nick looked back to make sure James was following, and what was actually happening finally hit him: he was going to fight Nick. *Oh no, no, no! No, this was a mistake. Didn't mean to push him, he—maybe I could just run. Seriously, right now. Just run. People will think you're a—who gives a shit what people will think? They all hate you anyway. Not anymore. He's gonna kick every scrap of your ass. Not anymore. You know he's gonna kick your ass. Remember last summer, when he pinned your arms down with his knees and slapped you until your cheeks looked like strawberries? Yes. The Camel Clutch? Yes. Remember when he gave you that wedgie on the Fullers' front lawn and he pulled it until you started crying? Yes. Remember hiding the underwear in the garbage and how it hurt to wipe for like a week?*

Yes.

James didn't know what he was going to do, but he

knew he wasn't going to run. The crowd grew as word of the fight spread. The mass of students crossed the blacktop until they reached the tennis courts, where all afterschool fights took place. Two courts, side by side, both missing their nets, and all of it surrounded by twelve-foot-high chain-link fence.

Fights at the courts had a natural time limit. As soon as any concerned adult noticed the unnatural mob of adolescents, the police would not be far behind.[44] Fights were fast and sloppy and usually ended without any real damage done to either party, outside of embarrassment if one failed to acquit oneself honorably. Then, whenever the cops or the teachers did arrive, the mob disbanded instantaneously. The courts had four exits and sat at the intersection of two streets (not to mention the blacktop back toward the school) and the tracks nearby. If you got caught, then it was really more because of poor cardio or a lack of will.

James squeezed through the entrance into the courts along with a couple older girls and a red-haired kid with apocalyptic acne and a bloodthirsty grin. Nick was waiting. He'd already made it to the center of the closest court and turned to face James. The crowd pushed in, desperate for the best view but trying to create at least some small circle in which the battle might take place.

James breathed in and was amazed—lilac. He could smell the lilac bushes down the street. He could smell watermelon bubblegum and the press of students around

---

44 More than one student-turned-pugilist had employed the grab-and-wait (or lay-and-pray) tactic, wherein the goal is to grab your opponent and hold them until the inevitable arrival of the police.

him, many still unaccustomed to the notion of regular washings. James looked at Nick and felt his mind flush with focus. He saw that Nick had a quarter-sized cluster of razor burn on the side of his neck; he saw that he was bouncing from foot to foot, that the middle finger on his right hand was shaking, and that beads of sweat dappled the left side of his forehead.

James felt hands on his shoulder blades guiding him toward Nick, and when he was a foot or two away, the touch disappeared and the way behind James was swallowed up by eager, bouncing bodies. The circle was alive, expanding here, dipping back there, and holding Nick and James inside of it like a belly.

James's entire body felt as if, for the first time in his life, it was at his disposal. He was aware of the feeling of his shorts against the backs of his thighs, of the socks and rubber soles between the balls of his feet and the blacktop, of the muscles that nature had strung across his back. And close up now, James saw it. He looked at Nick—*in Nick*—and in his eyes, he saw unbridled fear. Fear run wild. He saw fear as far back as Nick himself and saw that, like water, it'd been boiled and frozen into many forms, but it was always fear.

Gail's warning siren screech tore through the air. "Fuck him up, Niiiick!"

Like a starting gun, it released them. Nick pulled back his right fist, so James dove into Nick's belly— "Oooomph"—and the two of them hit the ground on their sides. The screaming went up in volume and timbre, and as James wondered, *What do I do? What do I do? What do I do?* he felt Nick's hands slip inside his guard and find his throat.

The pain was intense and immediate. Nick's thumbs pressed on James's Adam's apple and the artery beside it. James's neck crushed, blood stopped, black dots pop-popping already; and then his feet were coming up, knees high, until they were between the boys. James kicked out, feeling his shoes catch against the soft matter of belly and groin, and the fingers relaxed enough for him to wriggle free and roll away.

They both got to their feet with arms flailing defensively, eyes searching, until they found they were a good six feet from each other. Nick held his balls with his left hand. He opened his mouth as if to speak, but before any sound came out James was charging, and in this charge was all of their relationship, from childhood to this moment—all the hateful looks, all the times spit was dribbled and sucked up to taunt, all the shoulder bumps in the hallways, all the "faggots" and "retards" and "spazzes," all the pitiless hatred for Nick that James had wrapped tightly in his arms and held back. And though he was screaming a warrior's bloody release in his mind, outwardly James was silent.

Nick cocked his right fist and shifted his weight to his back foot. James had obviously never been in a fight, rushing in like that, presenting his chin. Nick exuded the confidence of veteran know-how as he measured James's approach. A slight dip of his shoulder showed his intention to bob to the right, out of James's path, and bash James's exposed face with a right cross at the same time. The moment was interminable for both boys, though for the crowd it was less than an instant, only part of the disorderly, random fighting.

James saw Nick's fist at the last possible point, realizing his error, and in his mind he screamed, *No!*

And the fist froze. It caught dead in the air only inches from Nick's own ear, and James threw his punch with everything he ever wanted to do or say to Nick. He saw Nick's eyes, dull and confused, searching upward toward the paralyzed fist. He saw his own punch connect at the tip of Nick's jaw, and it was like a switch turned off. Nick's eyes rolled topside as his knees went, and he crumpled to the ground, folding over his own legs, his head bouncing off the blacktop with an apathetic smack.

"Oooooooohhhhhhh." The sound moved over and through them like a strong wind. The crowd a choir of disbelief now, and then a voice, "Oh, shit!" and there were shouts and shrieks and laughs and claps and hoots.

The fight was over, sudden and without narrative arc. Surprise and relief like pure sunshine happiness warmed James. He felt hands slapping his back—he saw Gail looking at him with a mingling of disgust and wariness, as one would look at a skunk in their backyard—and he saw Nick, lying there, unmoving, his left foot underneath him, his right splayed out straight.

The terror was unmistakable. *He's really hurt. Oh no, no, no.* Whether it was a fear that he'd get in trouble or a fear for Nick's well-being, James didn't investigate. He knew only that he needed Nick to move, to wake up. Now.

LaMarcus bent down by Nick and shook him. "Nick."

Nick's eyes opened, though they appeared to be looking at two objects simultaneously, one close and one very far. "My hand. It's stuck."

LaMarcus pulled Nick up to his feet, supporting his weight easily. "Okay, man, cops'll be here soon." They began to walk, though Nick's feet were able to successfully participate only every few steps. Colin walked behind them, and when Gail paused, as if considering whether she wanted to follow, Jess ran up and took Nick's other arm, at which point Gail made up her mind and hurried after them. The crowd grew loose, taking extra-special care to give the vanquished party a wide berth, and James thought he didn't understand anything about girls. Not a goddamn thing.

Woop-woop!

Children squealed, dashing in all directions. A few yelled, "Cops!" but most just ran. James stood dead-still on the spot where he'd knocked Nick Schroeder out and watched them go. He watched the freshmen sprint in genuine panic, watched Nick and Colin ladderwalk away to the west, watched Maria and Katie scramble into a bush to hide, watched kids whooping and laughing as they ran.

A strong, firm hand pressed his arm. He followed the arm up to the face of Ken Lakatos. "Go," he said. "Run."

The cops walked in yelling for everyone to stay exactly where they were, and James was gone, sprinting past a portly, mustachioed cop, who offered a perfunctory "Stop."

He looked back to see a few kids sheeped in a corner, suffering their first interrogation. No one gave chase, and those who had run now slowed to ambles, drifting away with eyes back, waving to James, swinging fists through the air, knocking out their own invisible enemies.

8. How to Open Up a Human Being and Look Inside

Mom left mushroom chicken and wild rice on a small plate inside a glass dish in the oven, as she had book club and it was one of Dad's prescheduled late nights of work. James watched the news as he ate, though he couldn't follow any of it.[45] He could barely concentrate on the act of shoveling food into his mouth. His mind went again and again to the feeling of the rock of his coiled fist meeting the wobbly hinge of jaw. He replayed the fight over and over like *SportsCenter* and felt the rush again and again and saw the kids waving and heard them hollering. He saw Nick's fist freeze, saw the locked arm, the terrified look on his face, and he felt something oddly like shame mingling with the triumph.

James also remembered a thought which had been born earlier in the day as he sat in Ms. Adderley's class. She'd been talking about General Westmoreland's failed plan to create a war of attrition against North Vietnam,

---

45 Half a story about an Illinois senator pushing to have Russia's lack of diplomatic contact with the United States officially recognized as an act of aggression tantamount to troop mobilization, followed by a story about a fundamentalist faction in Africa pulling drive-bys on teen girls in driver's education courses.

with large-scale bombing drawing them into massive battles, and how it didn't work because the North knew that it was a guerilla army and refused to change their tactics, no matter how much Westmoreland baited them. James had forgotten all about this because of the fight, but it came rushing back now. The sense of urgency in class—*You need to know these things. You need to learn these things.* He figured he should learn all he could about what great generals had done in the past but also—remembering how Ezra said if the War started right now the other side's numbers would be way superior—how a smaller fighting force attacked a larger one.

James powered up the laptop in the living room, and from the kitchen he grabbed a notepad, a pen, and a glass of chocolate milk.

As James navigated to Wikipedia, he drew a line down the middle of the yellow, lined paper. At the top, to the left of the line, he wrote, *Generals to Research*, with a line under it. On the other side of the center line he wrote, *Military Tactics*, with a line under it, under which he wrote, *Guerilla Warfare*.

His hands hovered over the keys. He didn't want to research Westmoreland; that guy sounded like a real dumbass. But he remembered something else Ms. Adderley said and began to type. Earlier in the year, she'd spent a whole day on how the story we've all been told about George Washington is a cartoon obscuring the portrait of an amazing man. She talked about what a hard and smart general he was, as well as how everyone who knew him respected and was drawn to him.

This was exactly what James was looking for.

However, after two readings of Washington's Wikipedia entry, the only thing James had added to his *Military Tactics* column was *Good Communication*.

James pivoted, jumping hyperlinks from Washington to other generals, building a solid research list. Thirty minutes later, the left side of the notepad read, *General Washington, Alexander the Great, Napoleon, Julius Caesar, Hannibal, Genghis Khan, Edwin Rommel, George Patton, Sun Tzu, Belisarius, Robert E. Lee, Generalissimo, Shogun, Winston Churchill.*

James spent the next two hours and fifteen minutes jumping from page to page, with intermittent breaks to pee and make more chocolate milk. The yellow notepad remained beside him, though he failed to write anything else.

There seemed to be little to learn from any of them that had practical applications. Make your enemy think you have superior numbers, or if possible, actually have superior numbers; attack in unexpected ways; earn the esteem and loyalty of your troops; never give up, unless you have to, then give up graciously; be a bastard. It seemed at first as though there was something close by in all this researching, something just on the other side of what he was reading, but soon he was only clicking through, clicking through, clicking through.

Anxiety burned into exhaustion, and though he

wasn't aware he was doing it, James slowly laid his head on the desk and let his eyes close as the Wikipedia page for Ashikaga Takauji glowed before him.

I'm descending. I look up and see that monster, Leviathan, watching me, his nightmare face piercing the circle of sky above. I'm not walking—am I? It feels like I'm floating down, down, down this giant circle. The walls are dark, and they seem to shimmer and move, and behind them a scrap of light appears and disappears, blinks once here, then there, then gone. Down, down, down. It feels like forever, and . . . god, it's cold . . . getting colder, hadn't noticed until now, until it's already so cold.

Light. Here. Through the wall, through the shimmer. It's . . . giving off light. What . . . It's gold and softly glowing, shaped like a teardrop, maybe the size of an overstuffed backpack. It looks like a genie's lamp. I lean in, 'cause I can barely make it out, like the silhouette of someone showering—oh my god! There are thousands of them! Millions! I back away, turning now, descending farther. They're everywhere. Behind these weird, warbly walls like an infestation, and, oh man oh man oh man oh man oh . . . there's something horrible about them, something trapped and vicious and screaming in pain. Ten million cockroaches pouring out of the walls of your house.

Down, down, down, trying not to look, but there they

are, and I think they've noticed me. They're, they're . . . shaking, rattling . . . screaming energy of so, so many, like prisoners reaching through the bars, screaming, and I know that at any moment it's going to give. The walls will shatter, will melt, and these things will swarm, will eat me, and I try to run, but it's so slow, and a noise is growing, a buzzing like the whispers of the whole school. But with something under it, higher, like screams. I can't help it—I'm looking at the golden teardrops as I pass by and they shake like angry fists, and each one seems to recognize me, to press against the shimmering wall, pleading, moaning louder, dying to a whimper as I pass . . .

And then he was awake, soaked with sweat. Again. Even in the safety of consciousness and familiar surroundings, the dream felt awful: full of divinity and accusation. James had no interest in returning to that place or sleeping at all. The muscles of his neck and back were rock; his jaw quivered. He pushed himself up and made a round of the room, turning on each light as he came to it. He turned on the TV and charged through the channels until he found an infomercial for a collection of old Dean Martin Roasts on DVD, and then he let the modern appliances do what they do best: chase away the products of the mind. He stripped and showered and brushed his teeth, but even the bathroom light bulbs' implacable realism could not dissolve the terror of that descent, of the clamoring behind those walls.

James took one of Mom's cigarettes and went out to the front porch to drink a chocolate breakfast shake as he waited for the sun to please, please come up; and when it did, it felt like he'd been granted a stay.

Now all I have to do is never fall asleep again.

On Monday, the first thing James saw when he entered school along with a crush of his classmates was the handmade sign with removable, cardboard numbers that hung, low-slung, in front of the main doors to the gym:

Only 3 Days of School Left!!!

James put his head down and dissolved into the crowd. Locker, pee, first-hour geometry. He saw glances and the backs of hands, whispers directed around him, and one kid who just out-and-out pointed. James ducked into class and took out his sketchbook. Eyes down, he started to work.

"Hey."

James's head snapped up, and he saw Dorian already in her seat, smiling. (Her eyes: *You didn't look for me.*)

He jammed the sketchbook back into his bag. "Hey."

"Guess I missed some excitement on Friday."

"Yeah . . . I don't know."

Leaning across her desk now. "Did you really knock him out?"

He nodded, looked around, everyone pretending not to listen.

"I suppose he had that coming."

"Yeah, I guess."

She started to say something else but stopped, smile gone, sitting back in her seat. She nodded with a single, tiny head raise toward the door.

"Mr. Salley?"

James turned to see Ms. Vargas, the dean's secretary, standing in the doorway, holding a clipboard as if it were a holy scroll. She addressed the question to Mrs. Windermere, who nodded over to him, her eyes all there-he-is-if-you-want-him disinterest. All faces followed.

"The dean would like to see you," Ms. Vargas added, taking a single step back into the hall, waiting.

James stood, shrugging his bag over his shoulder, and walked to the door. Just before he reached it, though—

"Hey." Ceasar Almedina leaned out from his front-row chair, his fist outstretched toward James. "That's a clean hook, man."

The class spit up a menagerie of tsks and ooohs and laughter, followed by Mrs. Windermere's lackadaisical, "Mr. Almedina."

James just smiled and bumped Ceasar's fist before following the secretary out of the room and down the hall. Then into the egg-yolk outer office—past Nick sitting in one of the two black-pleather chairs reserved for kids who're in trouble—and into the main office, where Mr. Worthington sat behind his desk. He was a big man, like a linebacker gone soft, with a reddish bulb of a nose.

He made the universal hand gesture for James to sit and looked down at the papers before him, shuffled and set them aside. Then, looking up at James once more, his eyes somber and disappointed, he shook his head. "I suppose you know that you and Mr. Schroeder are in quite a bit of trouble."

James hadn't even thought of this, not with everything going on. *Trouble? Oh, right.* The images of the call home, suspension, Mom and Dad yelling at him, grounded, it all sprayed across his mind in an instant, and then he was almost up out of his chair, leaning forward.

"No, you can't—"

"I'm sorry?" *Challenged, insulted. Good job, genius, you pissed him off.*

"I mean, what, what did Nick say?"

"Mr. Schroeder told me about the fight you two had on school grounds Friday afternoon."

Bullshit.

Bullshit?

Bullshit.

James didn't know how he knew it—though he was learning to trust that little tuning fork inside—but as soon as the words were out of Mr. Worthington's mouth, James knew they were a lie. Nick stonewalled. Shouldn't be much of a surprise, not like he'd want to broadcast what happened; but it was something else too. James got a sense all of a sudden that Nick wouldn't have said a word anyway. He sensed a steel rod of rules holding Nick up, and one of those was that cops and teachers and deans got nothing.

Mr. Worthington continued to stare down his nose at James in the too-big seat. James felt him holding his bluff, felt him ready to rejoice inside when James inevitably broke and revealed all, begging for leniency, a much easier child to manipulate than that hunk of rock sitting out there, and as he saw those things, the entirety of William Worthington, high school dean, opened up before James. He saw the man's path: a better teacher than an administrator, wonderful with the students, kind and supportive, everyone's favorite. Pressure from other teachers and administrators ("But you'd make such a good administrator") as well as from home ("If you went into administration, we could save more for Kelly's college and finally move out of this place") pushed him into this role, which he'd never grown to love as he had teaching. Then the marriage ended, and even if he wanted to go back to it now, he couldn't; the alimony was prohibitive. Earlier then, earlier, back to college, majoring in education and theater, a ham, well liked by the ladies, a change for him, because high school had been such a nightmare, his open, sensitive nature and interest in the arts assigned him as such a natural victim, corralled by shoves—"Do something, fag. C'mon."—so often the butt of the joke, followed by the wedgie, the unseen shove in the hallway—

—and James knew what to do.

"Could I ask you a favor, Mr. Worthington?"

"You're not really in any position."

"I know."

A pause. Mr. Worthington shifted, a bit annoyed that James hadn't cracked open as he'd planned.

"Okay, then. What is it?"

"Could we just forget about this?"

The pause was longer this time. Mr. Worthington tilted his head—two cartoon blinks—and looked at James as if he'd just suggested that his desk was made of marshmallows. "Could we . . . ?"

"Just forget that it happened."

"This isn't just . . . this is very serious—"

"Look, Mr. Worthington, I'm not gonna say that there was a fight on Friday. I heard there was one, but by the time I got out there, the police had chased everyone away. Okay?"

Those big blinks again. He had no idea what was happening.

"So you could dig into this and go asking around and all that; I know you could. I'm asking you not to." James leaned forward until he was almost touching the desk, and he looked as far into Mr. Worthington's eyes as he could. "I know that you know what it's like. He—Nick, he's made my life hell. He's waited for me outside so that when I leave school, my stomach's all spasmy—Will he be there? What will it be today? Charley horse? Nurples? A group shoving? Face full of wood chips? Once, he got me in a headlock and noogied me until my scalp bled. I've—" James felt the tears coming, couldn't stop them, stopped trying. "I've been so scared for so long. Do you know what that's like?"

Tears appeared floating atop Mr. Worthington's bottom lids, but he did a better job of holding them there.

James could feel the tracks already turning cold on his cheeks. "So I'm not saying I did, but what if last Friday I finally said enough, finally stood up to him? What if we went to the courts and we did fight?" He couldn't keep the smile from the corner of his mouth, but he knew it didn't matter, knew it would play. "And what if I hit him once, square on the chin, and knocked him out? Can't you understand what that would mean? Freedom, y'know, from fear and . . . and all that."

Mr. Worthington's gaze shifted to Nick on the big, black-pleather chair, and then back to James.

"Don't you wish," James said quietly, as if they were coconspirators, "that you had stood up to them? That you'd been able to feel that?"

Mr. Worthington stood up and turned his back to James, facing the window. He coughed. He took off his glasses and rubbed his face and stood for a while that way before settling them back over his ears and heaving a great breath. He turned back to James. "You will tell me if you hear who was in that fight on Friday?"

James nodded, hoping it got his gratitude across. "I will."

"Tell Mr. Schroeder he can leave as well. At the moment, I don't think I want to . . ." A headshake—James could tell he was remembering the monster of his youth and wondered what his name was. "Make sure I don't see you in here again, Mr. Salley."

"You won't," James said, backing toward the door. "Thanks." And then he was out. He closed the door behind himself and, a moment later, heard the blinds snap shut. Ms. Vargas's taunting grin went slack as James went by without a word. He walked out the door and stood before Nick, who looked up, his whole body giving off a miasma of fear and revulsion.

For a few moments, they just stared at each other. Nick looked smaller to James now. He remained seated while James stood, and it seemed to James that there was a question of who would finally speak. Looking down, James saw Nick's knuckles, scraped and split, dried blood not quite gone to scab.

Nick pulled his hands back. "What?"

"Worthington says we're free to go."

"Whatever." Then he's up and off.

"Wait." Nick stopped. He turned, slowly, eyes wide again. "What happened to your knuckles?" James felt the words come out like a command, and he knew Nick would answer.

Nick changed his fingers into fists and inspected the

damage. "Colin told my brothers what happened. They worked me all weekend, said I'm supposed to fight you again." He looked up and James saw it: he was terrified.

It took James two steps to cover the ground between them. He wanted to slap him. He wanted to spit in his face. *You fucking coward! You were so happy to torture me, to, to, to—so happy to fight when the outcome was certain, and now—look at you; you're terrified—you're scared. How's it feel, asshole?*

James put his finger in Nick's chest, hard. "You listen to me. You and me are done. You got it? Done. You stay away from me, and I'll stay away from you. You tell your brothers the dean said if we fight again, he'll expel you. Do you understand?"

Nick's eyes went into rapid blink, mouth working furiously on nothing. One nod. Two.

James felt a sensation sorta-kinda like pity crawling up and said, "Go away."

Nick turned and almost ran down the hall before disappearing around the corner.

The high had worn off. James now felt a mild sickness at the eyes turning toward him, the electrocharged air, the whispers. The final bell reminded him of being released from a punishment. Bag over the shoulder, through the classroom door, he wondered if he'd be the first person out of the building.

"James!" From back down the hall, no mistaking the voice.

James stopped and turned and waited for Dorian to catch up.

"Hey," she said, turning left.

Without a thought, James followed, away from the back doors from which he usually exited.

"So are you gonna tell me what happened?" They reached the front doors before the mob made the main hall. Again Dorian turned, without a word or question, toward her own home.

James followed. "It just . . . sorta happened. It was an accident."

Dorian reached her hand around her head and pulled that explosion of red hair across her neck so that it dangled on the other side. It was the single most beautiful gesture he'd ever seen. Done and over already but replaying in his mind. Elbow out—the soft, freckled white of the underside of her arm—the hand swinging across the face, a circle, her tiny fingers under the hair, pulling it taut, just around the neck and then down, down, so she could look at him without its rude presence.

"How exactly is punching someone in the face an accident?"

"Not that. That—I mean, the fight was an accident. I didn't want to fight him."

Her little fist shot out and hit James lightly on the

elbow. "Not even a little?"

James smiled and they walked on, letting their eyes take in sights they'd seen a thousand times.

"I wish I'd been there. I would have loved to see you . . . anyway, I had a thing."

"What?"

"Oh, nothing. It's . . . um, you know NPR?"

"Yeah," James said, thinking of the bored British and whispered Midwestern voices he heard when driving with his father.

"Well, they . . . It's silly, but they did this . . . thing on me, like a small interview thing, and then, y'know, I sang."

"Oh my god, that's amazing. Dorian, that's awesome. Wait. So I missed it? Why didn't you say—?"

"No, I just recorded it Friday. They're not playing it until this weekend. Saturday, I think."

"You think?"

"No, it's Saturday." Cheeks red, tight smirk, she checked him out of the corner of her eye. "Like 10:45 in the morning."

"That's so cool. I'm gonna make sure I hear it. I'm gonna make sure I'm listening."

She tried to keep it small, but the smile took over her whole face. "Thanks."

"Of course. I can't wait."

Another pause. James and Dorian walked, and he was aware of the sound of his gym shoes on the sidewalk and the sweat at the small of his back, and he couldn't understand why he felt so naked and vulnerable after he said things he meant, but he could see why some people never did. Life must be so much easier with jokes and primping and chest-puffing.

The compassionate breeze turned his brow sweat to cold water as they continued past the J&J and the elementary school. James felt the urge to say so much. He wanted to talk to her but found himself completely without content. His eyes implored the side of her neck and looked away from her answering smile. His mouth hung half open as if about to speak, but he said nothing as they passed the last few houses.

As they reached Dorian's house, James noticed her mom standing next to their idling Volvo. She was a stringy, porcelain thing, just like Dorian, but with a Scandinavian's untouched blonde hair. Where Dorian looked fragile, though, her mom felt sharp and unyielding. Something in the pulled-back shoulders, in the tight line of her mouth.

"Practice," Dorian said when she saw her mom.

"Right."

That damn silence again.

"Okay," Dorian said, "I'll talk to you later, James."

Then she turned to go, and suddenly the courage was there. Something about the way she said his name, maybe. Who knows?

"You're beautiful."

Dorian stopped. She looked back over her shoulder—disbelief?—a smile! Small but there. "What?"

"Nothing." *No, no, go on, go on.* He pressed ahead. "It's just, I always wanted to say that and I never have." And then the embarrassment was simply too much. He turned and went—*Escape! Run away! No! Don't run!* For an instant he pictured himself actually running away, and though he didn't think it possible, it increased the embarrassment, so instead he just walked hard and fast, like that group of old ladies he saw frantically stomping past the house on Sunday mornings.

He heard Dorian's mom—"Who was that, Dory?"—but he didn't hear her response.

9. End of (School) Days

A glass of orange juice devoured in two gulps, a bowl of Honey Nut Cheerios while watching the morning news,[46] another note from Mom, and then James was out the door.

James had never felt so untethered. Walk, SUV (*not Them*), school, people—his mind vacillated between an intense focus on the moment and a complete absence from his surroundings. Thoughts of the Pit and Taloon were cut off by the PTSD-intensity-level replays of what he'd said to Dorian, which was interrupted by his dreams and *What was that with Dean Worthington?* That one was overtaken by the sight of Jess and Nick back together and making out by her locker,[47] just as ruminations on Ezra's words about made-up rules were impeded by Dorian's sudden appearance in the hallway, at which point he dove into the faculty bathroom. The part of his

---

46 Two of those new-Messiah cults got into a firefight in Jerusalem, there was a mass suicide in Argentina, trees in the Black Forest were mysteriously rotting, and a representative from Kansas died of what appeared to be spontaneous combustion.

47 Nick wouldn't let her go this time, wouldn't be flippant or cool. He'd realized that he only really felt happy and at ease around her, and he began to create long, detailed fantasies about the two of them leaving town together (getting him out of that goddamned house), maybe even dropping out of school and just taking off. He wasn't sure what they'd do (and he hadn't discussed any of this with her), but he knew he was going to love her completely and hold on to her so tight that she could never, ever get away.

mind which harbored hope that she could feel for him what he felt for her had risen up (*Good for you!*) and gotten its one big shining moment, but now it was grounded. In class, pretending to be engrossed, feeling her eyes; head up, robot smile, back down. Good.

Ezra had James called down to the library at lunch, where he had sandwiches from the Italian deli and bottles of Cherry Coke set out for both of them. He congratulated James on his "first successful foray into combat" and asked him if he had any questions from what they'd discussed the morning before.

James said he did not.

James did, of course. He had millions of questions. Questions Ezra couldn't answer or wouldn't; questions he was afraid to have answered; questions so profound he lacked the vocabulary to ask them. He wanted to know everything they knew about the supposed War, and how they could be so sure what the Creator would do, and what would happen if he just ran away, and a lot more things.

So, no, James told him, no questions now. But he'd let Ezra know when he did.

Ezra seemed to not want the lunch to end, prodding James with little questions about his dreams and what specifically he'd heard or seen, and finally he outright asked if James knew Morning Star's true name yet. James, his mouth full of salami, capicola, bread, and cheese, just shook his head. He'd assumed Ezra knew how and when he was supposed to learn the name. Ezra's ignorance about how this was all going to proceed was apparently not the act James had supposed the morning before.

They both left the lunch with an uncomfortable uncertainty nesting in their heads, each disappointed by every aspect of the lunch except the sandwiches and the Cherry Cokes.

Then, after the final bell, as James slumped toward the back doors, he saw three freshmen wrestling a smaller freshman into a locker. At first he stopped, thinking he should say something, but then he noticed the kid in the locker laughing as he was stuffed in, kicking awkwardly out at his friends. It reminded James of the shimmering behind the walls of his dream, and as he turned back to the door and grabbed the handle, it happened. Just as his hand touched the warm corrugated metal of the door and the sunlight flashed into his eyes, he had it.

9½. Interlude: Eliza & Erik—First Issue

James ran home. The ecstasy of the breakthrough propelled him, and he thought of nothing but the idea as he ran, feeling no burn or resistance, only fluidity and speed.

After all this time, he finally had it. And it had come to him complete, fully formed, this story unfolding like a flower in his mind, so natural, as if there was no other way it could happen. He stormed into the house and climbed the little mountain of stairs, pulling himself on the rail even as he bounded up and forward. Into the room and straight to his desk, where he sat down and expelled the story for the debut of *Fearless* like it was an organic excretion.

Eliza and Erik have escaped their initial capture with only one piece of information: a sheet of paper with two sets of co-ordinates on it. One set of coordinates is the base where they were held. They do not know what the other is. But we don't know any of this at the beginning. The issue starts off with a big house—not like a mansion, but more like a big North-east family house/cottage. See, it's night, and we're in Maine. There's the house by the edge of a cliff, beautiful, overlooking the ocean (on a cliff), but it has to be really creepy Maine, too. (Think about the images you get when you read Ste-phen King—that Maine!) Dark, fog, etc. We see the house, and it looks like a totally normal house, but then the images get closer (bunch of frames, closer, closer, like zooming in) and you can see like laser fences and hidden artillery and all that. Then we see the sheet of paper with the coordinates and Eliza holding it, along with binoculars, and Erik's with her (maybe they're coming in on a boat, or maybe further down the cliff) and the coordinates for this place are circled in red, and she tells Erik, "Yeah, this is definitely the place."

"Just looks like a house."

"That's what it's supposed to look like."

So then they try to sneak in, but at some point they miss a trip wire or sensor or something and the alarms go off and all the soldiers come and they have to fight their way through this house, which, just like Eliza said, is waaaaay more than a house. Below the ground is a massive laboratory complex, and they have to fight their way into and through it. Final-ly there's a final door—a major like steel vault door—and somehow Eliza gets them through it (need to think of some-thing really cool for that—she has to use her smarts mostly for this task, like a puzzle, code-breaker kind of thing). In-side they find a small nothing sort of room. It's all steel, with no—what are those things called—rivets? There's a steel column about waist-high, and on it there's a big glass (bulletproof) case. Inside is something that looks like one of those gold teardrop things from the dream. And behind it, standing like a teacher, is an old, frail (Japanese?) scientist.

The scientist says, "That was very impressive. Who are you?" Eliza asks him what this place is and where's Sam, but he just sort of tilts his head. "I'll tell you what, you tell me who you are and I'll tell you what I know." Eliza says she could just have Erik rip his arms off and he says yes, and then I'd be dead, and you'd know nothing. Fine—Eliza gives him a short version of what happened to them (the outline, basic origin story, give details bit by bit later). Then the scientist says that the two of them—Eliza and Erik—have become very famous and that the government is looking everywhere for them. He says that Sam is not here (Eliza starts to freak out), but he says they have come to the right place. He says this program is a sister program to Project: Awaken, which was theirs. He's acting like a parent, and he says it's inhuman what they did to them. He says that what they need to find and take back Sam is right here, in this room.

Then the scientist goes over to the pedestal and presses a button, and the glass slides back. He reaches in and picks up the gold teardrop, and immediately Eliza and Erik freeze. It's like their brains are filled with wet sand. The thing pulses light and energy and heat.

"Amazing, isn't it?" the scientist says. "It's alien. We don't know from where or when, though. We've been studying it, and the only thing we've been able to ascertain so far is that whoever holds it can control the minds and bodies of others." Then he makes Erik dance, and it terrifies Erik that he can't stop himself and he starts to cry and Eliza screams at the scientist. He compliments her revealing little outfit and has her pull the zipper down a little to show more cleavage.

Then he says, "Enough play, I suppose. They'll be quite pleased with me for taking care of this problem all by myself. Might even get some extra funding next year." He says that they'll want Erik for further testing and studies but that Eliza is not needed. Then Erik walks over and puts his hands around Eliza's throat—he's screaming and sobbing, she's telling him to stop, arms pinned at her side—and then he starts to choke her. He resists some and there are bits of words she can get out. Her face is turning purple and she says, "s'okay . . . not you . . . don't . . . blame . . . y'self . . . love y—" Erik screams and somehow pulls his hands apart (his will momentarily destroys the thing's power), and the scientist's eyes get big and scared, but before he can do a thing Erik has leapt across the room, and in one fluid motion he grabs the scientist by the throat and breaks his neck.

Eliza tries to yell, "No!" but it barely comes out. She rubs at her throat as the alien thing clatters to the floor, and she scampers across the room to the scientist. "We needed to question him." Erik says sorry as she lifts the scientist's head. He is barely alive, gasping his last breaths.

"Give me something!" she screams, and the scientist whispers something. Don't know what. Maybe the name of the main bad guy, like the general in charge or maybe where they should check next. Then he dies.

THIS IS NOT THE END

Erik says sorry again, and she goes to him and hugs him and says he never has to say sorry and that he saved them both and she's so proud of him. Then he's like, "What now?" and Eliza goes, "They take Sam, we take from them." She picks up the lamp/golden teardrop thing and says, "And we burn the rest."

The end of the issue is them walking away, along the cliff, as the cottage burns in the night behind them.

James put the manuscript aside and pulled up a fresh piece of drawing paper. He wanted to get the image of the burning cottage down before he lost it. But just as his pen touched the heavy, threaded paper, a thought stopped him—*This will never happen. You'll never make this comic.* That life—the dream of that life—was not his future anymore.

The sensation activated a memory: Nick punching him in the stomach earlier this year, the immediate emptying of all his body's energy, along with his will and breath—he'd never known a thought could do the same. *This will never happen.*

Why? Why couldn't it happen? Ezra says you're gonna be this superpowerful sorta leader, so, so why can't you . . . ?

The pen clattered onto the desk, and the paper, marred by a single black line, was dimpled, plop by plop.

Something which James felt as if he'd known for a while, something which had been hiding in the back of his brain, where he didn't want to look, stepped out into the light. This War would be his everything.

9. End of (School) Days (rejoin)

The sign read, **Only [1] Days of School Left!!!**

George Washington High School was a pulsing heart of joyful anticipation that day, noise and smell and motion all wordlessly communicating the group's barely contained exuberance. The teachers hid smiles and whispered to each other; they laughed louder and barely watched the students who walked below their gazes. You could feel that they were already somewhere else. They had plans. Maybe a barbeque at one of their houses or drinks and hors d'oeuvres at Senor Salsa's Hacienda. Sighs and laughs and margaritas and God-am-I-glad-to-be-rid-of-that-class-I-thought-they'd-kill-me and Oh-that-Gail-what-a-little . . .

The kids were racehorses bucking against the starting gate. They gyrated on their seats, leaning forward, eyes to the clock, then to whoever was talking loudest, out the window (blue-blue sky on a perfect 84-degree day), and around and around. Their legs shook, feet tapped, gym shoes trying to dig through asbestos[48] floors. They were like runners at the starting block, tense with anticipation. There would be no lessons today. Only anxious fun, waiting for that glorious moment: final bell, rushing out into warmth and freedom.

They received their yearbooks first hour. A sloppy, red cardinal on the front, apparently painted by a girl in an AP art class; glossed pages between hard covers. James looked first for Dorian's picture—painfully beautiful even in this tiny low-quality photo—then his own—*Had worse.*

Then the strangest thing happened. His yearbook was snatched from his hands. And not by Nick or Colin so they could rub it on their balls or draw a dick on it, but by Kevin Martinez, a quiet kid who was the backup point guard on the basketball team. He smiled and handed James his own yearbook and began to write.

James was stunned. He peeked at what Kevin was doing, but unless it was a very subtle dig, it appeared to be genuine. He was at a loss. He took one of his drawing pens and wrote: *Kevin, Have a cool summer. James*—and he immediately wanted it back. He wanted to cross it out and write something else, because that was too lame for words. But before he had a chance, that book was pulled from his hands as well, replaced by another. The books came and went, around and around, and he saw his own moving from hand to hand.

At the end of class his yearbook was returned, and while he didn't have time to thoroughly examine it, a

48 Scheduled asbestos abatement having been postponed since just after the Choco-Malt closing.

cursory glance revealed no dicks, dongs, splooge, or giant middle fingers. Second hour began, and it was more of the same. His book was plucked from his grasp and replaced with another. This class, though, was significant because he shared it with Dorian. He tried to watch for his yearbook as it entered the phalanx of girls, but it was like three-card monte, and eventually he gave up and set himself to waiting.

When the class ended, he went to the nearest bathroom and locked himself in the stall. He opened to the inside of the cover: Nice punch, Leo; Have a kick-ass summer, but don't kick any more ass; To James, I wish I'd got to know you better, B kewl dis SUmmER!!! From, Mike D.; Have a nice summer—Ken. Jess Gerber had drawn a heart around her own picture along with *JG*.

He flipped the pages, and there, at the bottom, was the signature he'd been looking for: To James—My weirdest friend, who just might be my most interesting one 2—Dorian.

James sat on the toilet as the bell rang, and the atmosphere around him quieted to almost nothing, and he read her words over and over and over.

The echo of the final bell was still hanging in the air when the freshmen went by screaming like the first wave of a crazed, castrated Viking horde. They ran for the front doors, which banged open with a shuttering slam so mighty it was hard to believe they remained attached. The older kids had the sense of cool to walk out, as much as they wanted to stampede their younger classmates, screeching their glee right along with them.

As they hit the sunlight, notebooks and papers flew, fluttering down in a wall of white. It reminded James of a distant cousin's wedding last summer—that explosion of party favors as they appeared from the church. He'd been pressed close to the walkway and stood as it all cascaded over him. He remembered loving the sensation and wanting them to do it again, though the party had already moved on.

10. Down the Dark Descent

The room is dark. Shadows move all around me, but when I turn to look at them, they disappear. The floor flows like water. The light changes colors—blue to black to gray to white to blue . . . and there go the shadows, but I can't actually see them. There's something in front of me. I can't really see it, but I can feel it in the partial dark, like it's a magnet that attracts whatever my insides are made of. I feel pulled toward it, but I don't want to go. I try to press my feet into the ground, but I don't feel any ground, and I'm still being pulled—pulled towards it—and I can sorta make out an outline. I can sorta see places where the darkness shifts—and a whisper . . . something.

Someone is speaking to me—and I know it's to me— but I can't hear them, can't make it out—but the whispering is coming from the Shape in the darkness, and I can see it now, and all at once I don't want to hear what it has to say. I don't—No! Get away! I kick back—away—and my feet find floor and I turn to run and that thing—the

Shape—screams like nothing I've heard, like the shriek of a bird and the howl of a dying pig and metal scraping against metal all in one, and I scream back. I stop and cover my ears and collapse and scream because oh my god I'm going to die. I'm going to die.

James's eyes opened to a dark bedroom. He was still seated at his desk, though he was bathtub wet with sweat. He sat up, and there was a thwuuck as his wet cheek came unstuck from the desktop.

It was then that James noticed the pen gripped tightly in his right hand. The nail of his middle finger dug into his thumb, a drop of blood pooled just under the surface. And there, on the paper, was the shape from his dream.

James washed most of the fear off in the shower and spent the rest of the morning online. He had to know. The dreams were awful and growing worse. Maybe if he knew the name, whatever name it was, then he could say it and release whoever was locked in that—*you have to say it. You have to admit it to yourself. If not out loud, man, okay, okay, I get it. Calm down, calm down. Go outside and have a smoke. C'mon, c'mon, Mom's carton. Out, out, out . . . ah. Breathe. Sun. Breathe. Smoke. Who's in the cage? Who is it? Who? You know; just say it.*

"Satan," James whispered, looking around. Nothing changed. Nothing happened. He took a long drag that seared his throat.

Right, okay. So Ezra says the story's wrong and it's not all good and evil and Satan and The Exorcist, so be cool. You gotta find out the real, true name of Satan so that you can set him free. Okay? I'm sure we can find this. Satan's real name.

Check Wikipedia.

James's morning dissolved in the acid of fruitless searching. He sat with his hands resting on the keys for a while before typing Satan into the Wikipedia search bar. His list began to grow: Satan, the Beast, Shaitan, the Adversary, the Devil, the Serpent, the Snake, the Diabolical, the Slanderer, Beelzebub, the Dragon, the Deceiver, the Great Deceiver, Prince of Darkness, Lucifer, Iblis, the Accuser, Angel of the Bottomless Pit—*Angel of the Bottomless Pit!*—Destroyer, Father of Lies, the Evil One, the Little Horn, Son of Perdition, the Wicked One. He searched for the name of the beast because that sounded familiar, but Google returned the number of the beast, and he did have to admit that actually did sound right.

Could that be it? The true name is 666? Does 666 stand for something?

James wrote all the names down and read through them, but nothing struck him. It felt like the name would be more . . . obvious, that somehow when he heard it he'd know it. Plus, none of these sounded like names, except for maybe Iblis. Iblis, James found, was Satan's original name in Islam. The jinn named Iblis had been filled with hubris and cast down by God, just like with the Christians. *This story keeps coming up everywhere. Iblis could be the real name. Maybe.* James clicked through the windows he had open on his browser, but when he reached the Wikipedia entry for Lucifer, he stopped. There it was, three lines down. Lucifer meant "light-bringer" or "Morning Star." *That's it! Morning Star. Lucifer is the true name!*

James's joy lasted roughly 1.25 seconds. It was put to death by a hard realization: they would know that already. They would know any of these.

Damn it. The answer isn't here.

James considered returning to his research, but it felt silly now. *You have no idea what to do.* He just wanted someone to tell him what it was he should do next. How was he supposed to know where to find the name? How was he supposed to . . . ? And then he remembered Dink.

James slid the hard ball of earth from his pocket and gently set it atop his bedside table. He leaned down until he was only inches from it, but just as he was about to call Dink's name, he stopped. Was this okay? Was he supposed to call Dink only for emergencies, like 911? James sat there, inclined forward, mouth slightly open, weighing the arguments, when the doorbell rang.

He knew who it was. How, he couldn't say, but he knew. He jumped up, wanting to get to the door before Mom or Dad, before he remembered she was at a sales conference in Indianapolis and he was at Saturday golf with his boss. Still, need propelled him, and James was at the door before the bell's echo left the room.

"You wanna come in?"

"I thought we could go for a walk," Ezra said. "It's a beautiful day."

James jammed his feet in his sneakers and pulled the door closed with a thunk.

"Which way?" James said.

"Your choice."

"Okay." *Who cares?* "We'll go this way."

They walked east and Ezra smiled as he went, his posture steel as usual, his hands locked behind his back.

They walked that way in silence for a few blocks. Sparse midday traffic and the smell of newly cut grass surrounded them. Children went this way on bikes, that way on skateboards, and in front yards and driveways they tumbled and wrestled and threw balls and drew with chalk and played make-believe.

He's waiting for me to speak. James realized that the times of "How did you get here?" and "What can I do for you, James?" were over. Down to serious work.

"I had this thought yesterday," James said as they turned south. "I was watching the news, and there was this story about all these messed-up people in the nuclear fallout zone in Kashmir. They're all like sick or old or crippled, y'know, 'cause like everyone who could leave already did. And I was looking at 'em, and so many of these people, they couldn't *do* anything. They were . . . helpless, y'know? Trapped. And I realized there are only two kinds of people—the strong and the weak."

Ezra's head inclined, and James thought he saw an encouraging smile there.

"That's right, isn't it? I mean, being good or bad matters;

that's not it . . . but if you're good and weak or bad and weak, what's the difference?"

Ezra nodded, and his smile was all patriarchal pride. "That does seem to be the way of things, doesn't it?"

James didn't say anything more on it. He nodded and turned away so that Ezra wouldn't see the bloom of satisfaction.

"I thought we'd try something new today," Ezra said.

"What?"

"I thought we'd visit Taloon."

James stopped midstep, turning wide eyes to Ezra. "What?"

"Taloon. Would you like to see it?"

Is this a test? "Yes?" James looked around and realized where they were. The ChocoMalt factory loomed over them like a bully, only twenty-five feet away. *It's not an accident that we came to this place.* "Why are we here?"

"You led us here, James."

Thinking back, James felt this was sort of true. He'd decided they should go east, but at every turn since, it seemed like they'd organically turned together, as if they both knew where they were going.

"You can tell it's a special place, can't you?"

"I feel something."

"It's a root," Ezra said, making his way to the mess of bricks. "That's how I think of it, at least. An interconnected organic highway. Our world, your world, probably others, and these roots run everywhere." They approached a door which had long ago been boarded over and locked. The old wood looked freshly splintered, and the lock hung limp and purposeless by the hook of its catch. "I told you before that Taloon is not in another place, per se. Geographically, well, who can say? When we are here—anywhere here—we touch Taloon, just as the ground touches the tree. But the connection is strongest at the roots. And this place"—Ezra shoved the great iron door and it swung open like a coffin lid—"is one big root."

It was somehow more barren than he'd expected but also brighter. It wasn't nearly as terrifying as it'd been that night. Sunlight oozed in through the myriad cracks and shattered windows. The gray floor was covered with shavings of orange rust, and when James looked up, he saw the metal pipes and ductwork above rotting like a corpse. *It's alive like a root.* James realized at once that this was what it really meant for a place to be haunted. The history of this building still lived in it. Everything that had once happened was still happening. Ghosts now, the workers rushed around, manned their conveyor belts, had lunch, and gossiped. This place was both dead and alive in its stillness.

Then a bird burst from its perch above and James jumped like a shotgun.

Ezra steadied him with a soft hand to the forearm as James tried to play it off.

"I suppose this is as good a place as any," Ezra said.

James stood, waiting. Was he supposed to do something? Was there going to be an incantation? Should he kneel? Sit Indian-style?

Ezra held his hands out, and after a moment, James clasped them. "Your mind and your body are one, James, but it is your mind that will drive this journey. You'll follow with me this time. The key is to see. You must truly see that there are more worlds. You must see Taloon. You must see this nothing between us and step through it."

"What nothing?"

"Sight, belief, ignorance, fear, what have you. Truly, there is nothing between our worlds. Except for awareness. Now, I think you'll find it easier to concentrate if you're not distracted by visual stimuli, so if you wouldn't mind closing your eyes." James felt Ezra's grip tighten, and he redoubled his as well.

"Listen to me, James. We are not standing in Stone Grove, Illinois, in the United States of America on the planet Earth. We are standing here. Right here. Everything moves; everything vibrates. It creates a song, just like a violin. When it vibrates in different ways, it creates different notes, and the same is true of the world around us. There are other worlds happening right here, right where you stand, but you can't hear them. You don't know how to listen to their vibrations. But I can show you."

James knew what Ezra wanted without a word, as one would by the slight pressure from a perfect dance partner's hand. James reached out as he had with Mr. Worthington, though this time he felt no control, no freedom. Instead of feeling like a visitor walking freely through a museum, James felt locked in a theater. He sensed that he could see this of Ezra and no more.

Very good, James. The voice boomed in megachurch surround, but Ezra's mouth did not move. *Now listen. Do you hear Taloon? Do you feel it? Follow me.*

Find it.

Find it.

Yes.

James felt pressure against every single centimeter of his body and then a dissipation, as if he was lowered into water—naked and flat against the surface, so that his whole body passed through at once—only there was no residual effect, no moisture, so maybe it was actually like coming out of water. It was happening, moving over him, and then it wasn't, and the room seemed to change. The air around him was charged: warm and kinetic, filled with the soft pulsation of movement, like those blue porch lights that burn up moths.

"And now we are on the other side of the record. Open your eyes."

No, we're in the factory. This isn't real. The wide-open, alien landscape before him opened in thin, horizontal strips, like holes in worn-out jeans, and in the spaces he saw the walls of the factory, the glassless windows and the rotting ductwork.

No, James. Stay here. He felt Ezra's hand on his, warm and slightly sweaty.

This isn't real.

This is Taloon. It's just as real. One is not true and the other false. You've traveled; you're just in a different place. Relax. James squeezed his hand tighter. *Relax and see.*

James looked away from the rips through which the factory tried to intrude and focused instead on the world before him, and as he did, the holes dissolved into Taloon. *My god, the Moons.* There were three Moons, each so large it threatened to fill the sky itself. They didn't vary at all in size or appearance, and all at once James realized they seemed to vibrate slightly, then to sway together into one Moon, then back into three. It wasn't that there were three of them, but rather there was one, viewed as though through the eyes of a drunk. The effect reminded James most of looking at the Moon and then crossing your eyes. He found it equally unpleasant. The mountains in the distance shimmered and stirred, rising and decreasing in size and sliding just the tiniest bit back and forth, as if looking for the exact spot. The ground wriggled beneath his feet, though James felt no movement. It looked like the land itself was made of a billion worms teeming over each other.

I'm gonna throw up. Even the quality of light seemed uncertain. A swirling gray-purple like stormy twilight shone on everything. James felt something pulling him back, as if someone had a hold of the back of his belt. He didn't like this place. Motion sickness grabbed him, denials howled in the background of his mind, and the rents appeared again, only this time he was only too happy to focus on his own world. The tugging became irresistible and James went with it, stepping back. And as he did the fissures opened completely, Taloon vanished like a puff of smoke out an open window, and James was standing in the ChocoMalt factory in Stone Grove, Illinois, on the planet Earth.

James felt a pain in his left hand and looked down to see he still held Ezra's hand in his own, squeezing as if it was his only tether to safety. He let go, and his knuckles screamed in relief and pain. The nausea passed, though he had to look down and make sure the ground was stationary as he heaved great big lungfuls.

"Amazing, isn't it?"

James rushed back through the door outside. He leaned against the brick and breathed and breathed, and in his mind there was a howling white noise. He closed his eyes and breathed. He opened his eyes and catalogued the road, the trees, the sky, and he breathed, and Ezra walked out of the factory smiling and said, "Very good, James. Very good."

James wanted to ask him if it was real, but he knew that was stupid.

It was real. It was as real as anything else is.

"I . . ." James was shaken in a way he'd never known possible. "I have to go." He felt . . . small. Insignificant. And in that sensation was a burning terror that threatened to suck the breath right out of his lungs. "I have to go," he repeated, hustling away, heading back home.

James did not look back; he didn't care if Ezra was following. He just wanted to be away from this place. He walked hard and fast, his head down, watching the weeds and crabgrass disappear beneath his feet, watching it give way to curb and asphalt, then a horn honking and a woman's voice and curb and grass once again.

That other place held him. Ghosts of that spastic Moon burned through to this world. He saw the ground moving, teeming, saw the grass of Stone Grove, saw sidewalk and smelled the metal-ozone air of Taloon all at once.

"Hey!"

The single sound cut Taloon off dead. Footfalls rushing toward him.

"Hey, faggot!"

James looked up. He recognized the one in front instantly. Kevin Schroeder—Nick's brother. Nineteen or twenty, James wasn't sure, he was a larger, nearly identical version of Nick. And there, trailing just behind him, were the twins, John and Pat Schroeder, redheaded and monstrous. It was one of the twins who'd yelled to him, but James had no idea which.

"You James Salley?" John or Pat said as the three of them filled the sidewalk all around him. The immediacy of the ass-whupping zapped James back to the moment, back to Stone Grove. His hand went to his pocket and found nothing. For a moment he wondered where Dink could be, before the image of the lifeless homunculus lying on his bedside table played across his brain like a terrible announcement.

Kevin leaned in, and James smelled cigarettes and cologne on his clothes. "Guess what, faggot?"

But James was not allowed an opportunity to guess, as whichever twin it was that was standing to his right hooked a fist into his gut. James felt his belly lock up, and he doubled over, his knees scraping the sidewalk as he made contact. The twin on the other side looped a punch down into James's temple, and it snapped his head toward the street, where James saw Nick.

Nick sat in the passenger seat of the Schroeders' old Kia, one eye and the corner of his mouth dark and red-purple. He looked back at James with no expression—seemed to be neither enjoying this beating nor particularly bothered by it. *Just someone else getting their medicine,* his gaze seemed to say; *sorry, bud, but nobody's there for me, either.*

Kevin dragged the heel of his shoe down James's scalp, turning his head so that he no longer saw Nick, only the pitiless, gray sidewalk. A kick stabbed his ribs and another punch snaked its way past his blocking forearms, splitting his top lip against his teeth. *You can control them! Make them stop! Do it!*

Please!

Stop them! You can! You can!

I can't! Please! Please stop. Please, please, please, please—

A soccer kick from one of the twins caught James on the jaw, almost exactly where he'd hit Nick, and his view of the world irised down to a pinprick, through which he saw the brothers begin to back away, and then he blinked, and though it felt as if only a second had passed, the brothers and their car were gone and a dog was barking. Close by. James craned back to see an upside-down, white Maltese screaming at him as a middle-aged woman in a purple swishy jogging suit looked on, worrying her hands.

"Are you okay?" the woman said.

James pushed himself to his feet, and the world swung and pulsed. He felt his face—some blood, definite bruising. Nothing felt damaged, though. "I'm okay."

She shook her head, and some of her silver hair came loose. "You don't look okay. Maybe I should call someone."

"I'm okay." He touched his lip and electric pain shot through him. "I'm gonna go home now."

"I really feel like I should call someone."

"I'm fine!" The words sounded like a growl in James's head, and the woman stiffened as if struck. "Sorry." The Maltese was really barking now. Shrieking, pulling against its leash as the woman stepped back. "Sorry."

But she was gone, running the other way with her elbows out, torso on a swivel as the Maltese ran ahead of her, barking happily, done as done could be with that boy on the sidewalk.

James walked home probing the bruises at his temple and jaw. He worked his tongue over the inside of his lip— iron-tinged, swollen, and split. He saw Taloon. He saw Nick in the car. He saw the sneaker coming toward his face. Over and over. Over and over.

He realized as he opened the front door that he'd

erected no narrative to explain his face, no excuse to miti-
gate his mother's inescapable overreaction, and he froze,
dreading the realization, her thin hands turning his face
to examine it, demanding to know what happened. James
wanted to cry out, "Leave me alone!" But there was no
one there. He went into the kitchen and found a note on
the table.

Hey, Lovie—
*Back from the conference. Your dad and I went to
Chili's. Call if you want us to bring you home anything.*
—Love, Mom

James's relief crashed as soon as it peaked. He felt weight
all over; something pressing down on him at a cellular level. There was a great big something there—right
there—and it crushed James Salley as he stood in his
kitchen looking at a note from his parents.

James grabbed a Coke and climbed the stairs. He
looked into his room. The ball of dirt was exactly where
he'd left it. He dropped a massive sigh of annoyance as he
drifted into the bathroom.

James turned on the light and inspected his face. Not
too bad, all things considered. He pressed the cold metal
can to his chin and lip before opening it and swallowing
a big mouthful. It burned the split in his lip something
terrible, and James tried to pour the next swallow into the
side of his mouth.

Over the next hour, James sucked on a dishrag filled with ice and filled the bathroom sink with cold water to soak his face. He stared in the mirror and inspected the discoloration of blood and flesh and replayed the beating—no, not replayed, relived. He was on the sidewalk again, feeling the knuckles on muscle and bone again, feeling teeth and lip meet, feeling his own helplessness. James watched from above as the James on the sidewalk turtled up, and he screamed at him, *Do something!* He told him that Ezra said he should be able to do anything he wanted to these guys—and he saw Ezra and Taloon and the Schroeders everywhere around him. Looking back at him. And James knew that he was small, that he was going to be crushed. He knew that he would never be what Ezra promised.

11. The Magnificent Dorian Delaney

The alarm clock emitted its two-tone electronic grind and James swatted it, wondering why on earth he'd set the alarm and coming back with the Post-it note he'd applied two days ago: *DORIAN—NPR—AROUND 10:45.*

From ten o'clock on, he kept the radio tuned to National Public Radio, 91.5, afraid he'd miss it. He was wary of misunderstandings and mishearings and general mishaps.

James sat at his desk, doing something he'd found himself doing lately. He would draw a man—a young man—and then slowly, adding a few lines and hairs and folds at a time, make the man age, make him old and ugly.

Finally, at 10:47 that morning, as James slurped a mug of microwaved coffee he'd pilfered from the extinct pot in the kitchen, he heard the man with the soft, soft public radio voice say that next they would hear the singing of a very special young girl. What followed were three minutes of weather and traffic, then reports on a recently found mass grave of Tibetan monks and on two hundred dead dolphins that washed up in Malibu, followed by a request for pledges and then back to the show.

"I'm joined this morning by Dorian Delaney. So glad to have you here, Dorian."

"Thank you." Quiet: embarrassed and proud at the same time.

"Now, I have to tell our audience—"

James could picture her there, sitting in a cushy office chair, pushed up to the desk. Phones and computers abound, her feet barely touch the ground, and the headphones they put on her cover most of her head. Ankles crossed, right over left, uncrossed, then crossed again, left over right.

"—and that was when you were how old, now?"

"Fourteen, last year."

"Fourteen. My word. And you're scheduled to perform at the Civic Opera House, is that right?"

"Well, it's not just me. A bunch of—"

Her parents must be there. James knew they were a small family, and when Dorian spoke of them it seemed to him to mirror some of the distance in his own family. Dorian was an only child, and her parents were separated. Still, they had to be there for this, didn't they? Standing off to the side or behind a glass partition, beaming with pride like cliché happy families allegedly do?

"And you're going to sing for us today. Do you want to get yourself situated?"

"Yes, thank you." Rustling. James could see her as if he was in the room, bowing her back and then that shrug, one shoulder then the next, like a cat. One head roll, inhale through the nose, smile.

"And what will you be singing?"

"'Habanera.'"

"Now is this Bizet or Carmen Jones?" The man with the soft voice chuckled, and Dorian followed suit. What the witticism had been, James had no idea. He made a mental note to look up Habanera, Beezay, and Carmen Jones.

"Bizet."

"Ah," he said, *"L'amour est un oiseau rebelle.* A beautiful aria. Please . . ."

And that was it. The man said, "Please . . ." and then waited, and for a moment or two the radio was nothing but that silence which isn't. Then she began. He didn't understand the words, and her voice seemed to reach and dip and trill so much that he thought for a moment it might be English, but no . . . French? He knew it, though, knew the song, or the aria, as they'd called it. He'd heard it before. Commercials, movies, just out in the active ether of the world.

Da da dada

Da dum doo day

Dootoo da dada . . .[49]

James felt that, in a way, he'd never heard music like this before, not alive and breathing. It was like the difference between seeing a gun on TV and holding one in

---

49 If you're unfamiliar with "Habanera" from Bizet's opera Carmen, feel free to bring it up and listen to it now. The story will be here when you're ready.

your hand for the first time. Certain things have a power which is undeniable. It was playful and challenging and seductive. Every line seemed to have a shot in it. Dum-dum-dum da-DUM-dum-dum. Every time her voice peaked, he pictured her neck straining upward, the work, as if she was mining the notes. It was such a flirty, dismissive thing. But lonely too. James thought of the time he'd seen Gail Asbury at one of the school dances. She'd been dancing with Colin, each pressing against the other, getting as close to kissing as possible without their lips ever meeting, and his hand brushed her breast and she smiled, but when that hand grabbed her ass she twirled away for a moment before spinning back into the embrace. But then there was later, when he tried to get her to go behind the bleachers with him and she said no and he called her a tease and left with LaMarcus and the power she'd had only ten minutes ago vanished and she stood under one of the basketball hoops and looked like she wanted to cry but couldn't because everyone was watching. That was what "Habanera" felt like to James when Dorian sang it, like both of those moments were happening at the same time, only a thousand times more so.

She snapped off the last note and again the nonsilent silence filled James's room, making him aware of the space around him. He wasn't in the studio with her. He was here. *But she's not there either.*

"Wow," the now-almost-whispering NPR host said as James searched for a clean shirt. "'Habanera.' Beautifully done."

James deodorized and grabbed his toothbrush.

"That was Dorian Delaney, and again, she'll be performing at the Civic Opera House in July with a coterie of young performers."

He checked his hair—*As good as it's gonna get*—and stuffed his sockless feet in shoes.

"Thank you again for being here, Dorian. It was a treat."

"Thank you for having me."

"Stay tuned for . . ."

James pedaled his bike north on Main Street, and as he crossed the tracks, he hit the rising pavement at just the right angle. He left the ground, and for a second, he held his breath and felt that good exhilarating fear and wind before bouncing back to the Earth. "Habanera" played in his head in perfect surround. It was his whole world as he rode, a sound track that his feet kept time to.

James slowed as he reached Dorian's block; the cold constriction of anxiety grabbed him from his solar plexus to his knees. Why was he going to say he was there? He'd ridden over without thinking it through at all. *What do I say?*

It doesn't matter. James began to pedal toward the house. He had to. He simply had to tell her what he'd felt when he heard her sing, how beautiful it was, the effect it'd had on him, everything.[50]

There were no cars in the driveway, and as he turned into it, he quietly stepped off his bike and laid it down

---

50 Except for the fact that his eyes had welled with tears as he listened. He had no intention of telling her that.

in the grass. Before he made it to the front door, though, he heard a sound around back. Soft music, heavy bass. James held his knock and walked around the side of the house, down the driveway, until the small backyard opened up before him. A grill from the Cold War sat on a blanket-sized patch of concrete, and on the other side of the yard, by the chain-link fence, was a small, blue kiddie pool filled with clean, clear water. Between the two was a chipped, white-and-yellow lawn chair, on which Dorian Delaney reclined in a red bikini and oversized sunglasses.

She hadn't heard his approach over the music, some dance-club techno thing that James was unfamiliar with. Her right hand dangled down by a glass of melting ice, and her left foot was turned in slightly.

Say something. If she catches you staring at her—

"Hot out."

Dorian jerked forward, knocking the glass of ice into the grass and pulling up the towel under her legs to cover herself.

"Sorry," James said, taking a step back. "Sorry, sorry."

"James?" The word was reproach and question all at once.

James felt his face fill with shame.

"Sorry, I'm . . . I just heard you on the radio and I had to come over and tell you that I love—that I loved it. It was, it was amazing. I didn't mean to—it's just that I went to the door and I heard the music—I said something, I wasn't just like staring at you and being creepy, I mean, I saw you and I said—"

"Okay."

"—and I said, 'cause it's hot."

Dorian stood up and folded the blanket over the back of the lawn chair. "Thanks," she said, picking up the glass. James noticed she purposefully stepped on the melting ice before walking away. "Do you wanna come in? It was getting too hot anyway." She switched off the radio as she went by.

James fell in behind her. The tiny lines at the back of her knees were white with suntan lotion, and the air she passed through was polluted with coconut. As she opened the door, James heard a snap-rustle and, looking off to the right, saw something large disappear around the house. He went over to the fence and looked, in the bushes, along the house into the front yard, but saw nothing.

Dorian held the door open. "What is it?"

James tried to replay what he'd seen, but it was too little, too fast. What he felt, though, was that it'd been a person; someone standing in the bushes who'd dashed off. He looked out into the neighborhood, but there was nothing. Still, he couldn't help thinking of the men from the Escalades, and he ran his hand along his thigh, feeling the outline of Dink in his pocket.

"Nothing," he said. "An animal, I guess."

Dorian told him there was lemonade in the fridge and went off to change. When she came back, he'd poured them each a glass. She wore jean short-shorts and an old, worn T-shirt at least two sizes too large. He could see the bikini strap, still there, poking out of the massive neckhole. The shirt read, *John's Pass Seafood Festival.*

"Oh, god, what happened to your face?" She reached out, and two fingers brushed that dark purple knot on his chin.

"I just, uh . . ." He'd been prepared to tell her the same story he'd told his parents, but as it started to come out he realized that a lie would be a barrier between them, a thing he had to remember and keep track of, and just then he didn't want anything between them. "Nick's brothers jumped me."

"What? Are you kidding?"

"Listen—"

"You should call the cops. You should. Like right now. I mean, what the hell's the matter with those guys? They're like in college—or y'know, should be. Oh my god, just—you should totally call the cops on them."

"Hey, uh, do you mind if we just don't talk about it?"

Dorian was frozen for a moment, mouth still open. She obviously had more to say.

"I came over because I heard you on the radio."

That did it.

"You listened." It wasn't a question.

James nodded. He sipped his lemonade and tried to keep the oversweet acid cringe from his face. "Where is everyone?" When she didn't answer, James said, "I figured you'd be here with your family listening . . ." She shook her head and her eyes went everywhere in the room except to him. She smiled and shrugged, and he got it.

His mind scrambled for a new subject—*This silence is killing you.* "I set my alarm and wrote a reminder." *That was a smile.* "I listened to it in my room. It was . . . I feel like it was special. Do you know what I mean?"

"It wasn't . . ." James couldn't help but smile; even her false modesty was weak. She knew.

"I've heard you sing before, and, y'know, you're always really good. You are. I mean, you know that. But today—I feel like I'm gonna sound stupid explaining it but, uh . . ." James looked down into his lemonade, knowing there was no chance he could put any of this into words while looking at her. "It was like being there while something was being made. It was like, like there was nothing, and then there was something, and you did that. I don't know. It made me feel really happy. Does that make sense?"

James peered up. *Oh, god, that face.* Dorian held all the symptoms of a smile on her face as she bit her bottom lip with a canine. James had never felt the urge to explode with such acute longing. He wanted to purge himself, to be free of this awful burden of bridled lust and impotent emotion. He wanted to howl, "Oh my god, Dorian! I love you! I love you, I love you, I love you!"

"My singing coach," Dorian said, "is this old Russian guy. He says he's in his early fifties, so only a little older than my dad, but he looks like he's a hundred. He has liver spots. Anyway, he says that all art is creation. He says that God is creation. That's the only thing that we know for a fact that God does is create. He says that's the way humans really pray is creating stuff." Then, in a nasally Russian accent, she added, "When we emulate the Creator, we commune with him."

James laughed. Her Russian accent sounded oddly like Speedy Gonzales without the lilt, but he knew enough to shut up.

"When we create," he said. "That kinda makes sense, doesn't it?"

"Yeah. And whenever I have to practice or perform, he says, 'Time to pray.'"

"Time to pray. That's cool."

And that damned silence again. James pressed his molars together as frustration swept through him. *Why is it always like this with her? I say something stupid and then I say something unfunny and then there are these silences. Is it me? Maybe it's her? No, dickhead, it's you. And this one is getting—*

"Do you wanna hang out and watch a movie or something?"

James could say, in all honesty, that he had never wanted to do anything so much in his entire life.

Dorian set out a bag of fat, soft chocolate chip cookies and fresh-from-the-freezer taquitos. James made a point to sit down first. There was a couch and two chairs, one of them a big, man-of-the-house recliner. Had she sat first, James would have found himself paralyzed. *Next to her? Across the room? What if she sits on the couch? Do I sit on the couch? How close?*

James sat at one far edge of the couch and, to his surprise, Dorian came and sat on the couch as well. Not next to him but not pressed against the other arm either. Definitely on the other half but closer to the middle, he noted.

When she asked what he was in the mood for, he simply said whatever she wanted. That got an eye roll, so he went with, "Something I've never seen." That was easy. As soon as she learned that he'd never seen *The Never-Ending Story*, the decision was made. As the credits began, Dorian explained this was her absolute favorite movie, even though it was for kids, and that when she was little she used to watch it almost every day.

For the next 102 minutes, the only words spoken between them were Dorian asking if he wanted the last taquito. James just shook his head. He watched, captivated. In the movie there was this giant force erasing their entire world, and it was called the Nothing. His mind grabbed hold of the Nothing and turned it over and over. This ever-growing void, this erasure that swallows everything, it sat in his gut like rot. There was nothing specific, no connection he could pinpoint, and so no logical reason to be afraid. And yet there was an undeniable feeling: the physiological symptoms of fear, a dark spot in his mind as if he'd forgotten something, and it dragged his consciousness from the room and into his dreams, into Taloon and the Pit.

When the movie was over, Dorian turned to him. Her knees were pulled up to her chest as she twisted her body on the couch so that she was facing him. "Whatta you wanna do now?"

And like that they were spending the day together. It was something James became aware of as it happened, though he already felt as if he'd missed so much. They played HORSE in her driveway on an old-fashioned garage hoop. James missed one shot so badly that it grazed the roof and rolled into a neighboring yard, where he had to go and retrieve it. Then they shared a cigarette, though James was pretty sure Dorian didn't inhale, and she kept saying how if Lem, the old Russian voice coach, saw her smoking he would flay her. They talked about going up to the public pool or watching another movie but didn't do either. At one point she showed him her room, and his heart beat with such madness that the excitement bordered on terror, but nothing happened, and they walked out as easily as they'd walked in.

The afternoon crawled on, but the sun didn't seem to move in the sky. Mack Truck AC inside; short shadows and wavy heat lines outside. Then, around three that afternoon, they decided to walk up to the Funky Bean for iced coffees. There, in the back corner that isn't by the sky-blue bathroom, over by the mock stage and the percussion instruments, Dorian said, "Did I ever say thank you?"

James immediately reminded himself what he'd decided—*Never mention it again*—and for a second he actually started to pretend he wasn't sure what she was talking about, but when he saw her eyes—furtive and dancing, now on him, then the coffee, the door, the barista, back on him and down—he stopped. "No," he said. "But you didn't have to. I knew."

She didn't look up. "What did you know?"

"Y'know, that you were . . . there was like an unspoken thank-you. You started being nice to me." *God, that sentence hurt to say.* His cheeks flushed, but then he noticed the tail of a tear on her cheek. "What?"

Sniffle, throat clear. "I was mad at you."

"What?"

"I was . . . different with you because it was, I mean, it was the right thing to do. It was polite."

"Polite?"

"I know how that sounds."

"Sounds?"

"You saved my life, and the doctors and my parents and everyone kept telling me how lucky I was that you came along, and you were so worried. I remember when they were picking me up, when they carried me out. They were shouting and trying to keep me awake, but I felt like I was only half there, like when you wake up overnight but you're still kind of in your dreams—and then

I saw you there. I was lying down and they were lifting me and I saw you, covered in blood, and you . . . you looked so scared. I remember, I didn't recognize you. I just kept thinking, somebody help him. He's hurt and he's so scared." She still had not looked up at him.

James's right leg bounced, his hands held the table, fighting the urge to jump up and run right out of the Funky Bean.

"Then, afterwards, when I understood everything, I felt like I—please don't hate me for saying this; I just want to get it out—but I felt like I had to be nice to you. I felt like I owed it to you, or at least everyone felt I owed it to you. But secretly I . . . hated you." Her chest went in, and her shoulders shook.

James could see that now she was really crying, and he wanted to reach out a hand and place it on hers but he couldn't make himself do it.

"I'm, I'm only saying this because it's not like that anymore. I mean, not just with you. With me." Two great big inhales and a long drink of vanilla Frappuccino-thingy. She looked up, but apparently whatever she saw in James's eyes was not what she'd been hoping for, because she looked back down. "Please don't be mad. I'm—I practiced saying this, but it just sounds awful. What I'm trying to say is that it wasn't about you. I was mad because I really wanted . . ." Dorian leaned down as if she was speaking to the table and whispered, "I wanted to die."

James could only watch as she cried. Her shoulders

slumped, as if those words had been holding her up.

"I'm . . . sorry?" he said.

And then she laughed. One sharp laugh caught like fire and morphed into a rolling, tumbling laugh that seemed as impossible to control as the earlier tears.

He was aware of his naïveté, but whatever it was that James didn't know, he couldn't say.

Dorian reached out and took his hand. "You don't have to be sorry. I told you this because I wanted to say thank you finally."

James had to force his coffee past a clenched throat.

"I'm glad I'm alive, and I wanted to say thank you. To officially say it." She pulled James's hand up and kissed it. The slightest moisture lingered as she set the hand back on the table, and James smiled, and it was like a giant period at the end of the sentence.

The tension dissolved, and they continued to talk, though the topic stayed near her suicide attempt. She told James that she now took an antidepressant and saw a therapist twice a week. She said the therapist, Dr. Dolsi, was a kind woman with old-money manners, and what they did was something called cognitive therapy, which was where you tried to become aware of the way your mind worked and change it. She told James that was a big part of anxiety and depression: her brain took small things and snow-balled them into end-of-the-world affairs. So she'd been learning to recognize when she was doing it. She even had a mantra: "Your brain lies to you." That's what she told herself when she caught her mind catastrophizing.

That was around the time they left the Funky Bean and began walking back to her house.

James had had no idea. It was a little terrifying, if he was honest, that there was such a depth of messed-upedness behind even those who seemed so successful. Oddly, the suicide attempt hadn't prepared him for this. This, the nuts-and-bolts reality of regulating her emotional distress, was harder. That was an action; this was her. What had he thought, though? Some melodramatic operatic reason? Surely if someone like Dorian Delaney tried to off herself, there was a good reason. *I could know her the rest of my life and I'd still be learning new things.*

It was a short walk back to her place, but that day's heavy-heavy heat was an assault. Sun and sweat coruscating, their lungs tired from pumping the humid air in and out. Dorian slumped down on her shade-covered front steps, and James followed suit.

"I still think about death a lot, though," she said, and James wondered if she ever ran out of things to say. It was wonderful, and when she got going, it relieved him of almost all pressure. It was as if a dam had opened, and while the river sometimes roared and sometimes trickled, it never stopped. "This one time—only a few months ago, so y'know, after the . . . thing at school, my mom and I were talking about the future, and I just told her, I said, 'I have this weird feeling like I won't live to be old,' and she just slapped me. No, I know, but I wasn't mad. I mean, at first, but then I was like, hey, idiot, you're totally freaking her out. I apologized and told her I didn't really think that, I was just being stupid. But I do. I don't know why. I've just never been able to picture myself as an old woman. Isn't that weird?"

"I don't know," James said. "I guess I can't picture myself as an old man either. I never thought that meant I was going to die."

"Yeah, it's probably just 'cause I'm like obsessed with it. Sometimes I—no, never mind. Too embarrassing."

"What?"

"Nothing."

"No, come on. You can't do that. You can't start like that and then not say it."

She squinted as if trying to apprehend a bluff. "You promise you won't laugh?"

"I will not laugh at you."

That canine bit down on her bottom lip again. "Sometimes," she said, "I lay in bed and pretend I'm dead. I close my eyes and cross my arms over my chest and pretend I'm in a casket. I'm dead, but I can still hear everything everyone says about me. At my wake, y'know? I'm laying there and people are coming up and . . . I can't."

"They're saying what they always really thought of you, aren't they?"

Her eyes went wide, as if he'd just recited a line from her diary.

"The ones who secretly hated you or secretly loved

you, right?"

"Do you do the same thing?"

"No." Look away, silence. Cheeks hot. *What are you doing?* "I mean, I don't do exactly that."

"What do you do?"

"It's . . . mine's way more embarrassing."

"What?" she said, smiling. "What is it?"

Too late now. "Uh, sometimes I'll pretend I'm laying in a hospital bed, like in a coma. But it's always because, like, the school was taken over by terrorists or something."

Laughing, but without a drop of mockery or cruelty. "Wait, no, wait. What?"

"It's always something where, like, terrorists take over the school and then I sneak up on one of them and steal his machine gun—"

"How?"

"How?"

"Yeah. How do you steal his machine gun?"

"I don't know."

"Yes, you do."

"I . . . well, usually the first one leads a group of us to a separate place and either I smash him over the head with something or sometimes there's something sharp and I, y'know, kill him."

"Wow."

"Okay, that's it. I'm not—"

"No, no. Come on. I wanna hear it."

James let a weary sigh out. He did not acknowledge

how much he was enjoying this or how terrifying it was to say these things out loud. "So then I have his machine gun and, and he's either tied up or dead. Then I, I lead a quiet . . . rebellion, I guess. Y'know, the kids follow and we find the next terrorist and either tie up or kill him, too. Then I give that machine gun to someone else, so we're becoming—this is really embarrassing."

"No, it's fun. Who do you give the second machine gun to?"

"I don't know. Different people."

"Oh, come on. Who'd you give it to last time?"

"Uh . . ." *Ken Lakatos. Don't you dare say that.* "I can't remember. I don't really focus on that part."

"Okay. Where am I in all this?"

"It's not like everyone is . . . I mean . . . I guess you're probably usually in the last group we find, with the main terrorist guy, the Hans Gruber."

"I don't know what that means."

"From *Die Hard*."

Nothing.

"Anyway, anyway, so we fight the terrorists and at some point, y'know, they become aware and there's a big gunfight and I save everyone and kill Hans Gruber, but I'm always injured."

"Hence the coma."

"Right."

"And when you're in the coma, everyone comes to your hospital room and tells you they love you."

"Well, everyone doesn't tell me they love me."

"But it's all good," she said. "Nobody comes and tells you they hate you?"

James tried to think of some way to turn this last bit, but there was nothing. "No."

"Yours sounds nicer. I like it." She leaned into the space between them. "What do I say at your bed?"

James opened his mouth, but no deflections came to mind. He'd muscled through the embarrassment of his fantasy, but he'd die before he revealed this.

Thankfully, she commuted it with a crooked smile. "Are all your fantasies action movies?"

"The ones that aren't porns." *What? Why did you just say that?*

Eyes wide, mouth open, Dorian didn't say a word.

Way to go, creep.

But then she laughed, again, and slapped him on the arm. "No comment," she said, springing to her feet with invisible effort. "C'mon. Let's get something to eat."

After Dorian had eaten half a turkey sandwich and James had taken down one and a half of his own, they found themselves back on the couch, in their old positions. The light in the room was more orange than yellow now as the afternoon inched along. James could hear the air-conditioning fans, could hear little kids outside and, a block or two away, an ice cream truck. They talked about their families. His: what it used to be and what it was now—absence, distance, et cetera. Hers: parents divorced, both already in serious relationships with other people who seemed like cartoon enemies of their former spouses, mom pushing when she was around, dad pushing when he was around.

Dorian said, "When I'm alone I wish there were people here, but when they're here it's awful."

James told her she said it way better than he could. He thought then that there were a bunch of different kinds of alone, but he couldn't figure out exactly what he meant, so he didn't say anything.

Dorian said, "I was talking to Lem one time—"

"Your old Russian?"

"Right. I was talking to him about this, about like feeling lonely, and he told me the greatest story. Sometimes I just tell it to myself and it makes me feel better."

"What is it?"

Dorian repositioned, readying herself for the telling with her feet tucked up so that she was sitting on them. "Okay, it's really, really old. It's from World War II, but it's like a really famous old story in Russia, I guess."

"Okay."

"Alright so, in like the '30s, in Stalingrad, Russia, there's this sad, lonely guy. He doesn't have any friends and he lives in a tiny apartment, okay? Anyway, around that time the first-ever Russian phonebook comes out.

So this lonely guy, he gets the phonebook and he starts looking through it, reading it, and he comes upon a man named Mr. Rooster—whatever's Russian for Rooster, y'know. So he has this idea. He goes to his phone and he dials the number. It rings a bit and then a man with a very deep voice picks up and he says, 'Hello?' And the lonely guy says, 'Yes, may I speak to Mr. Chicken,' and the other man says, 'There's no Mr. Chicken here. This is the Rooster residence,' and the lonely guy starts laughing and says, 'Oh, I'm so sorry,' and hangs up.

"But the thing is, he's still lonely. He thinks about the joke, about the call, and it makes him happy. So a few weeks later, he dials the number again. 'Hello. Is Mr. Chicken there?' And again, the man is very polite. 'No, I'm sorry. There's no Mr. Chicken here. This is Mr. Rooster.' And the lonely guy, he laughs whenever he thinks about the calls. They're like the only time he ever talks to another person, so he keeps doing them. Not every day or every week, y'know, but a lot. Every once in a while he'll call up Mr. Rooster and ask for Mr. Chicken, and every time Mr. Rooster is totally polite. He just says, y'know, 'No, there's no Mr. Chicken here.'

"But then World War II breaks out, and the lonely guy has to go off and fight. And it's years. He's away for years fighting and it's just, like, the worst war ever. The Germans and the Russians are slaughtering each other and starving and going through these horrible winters, but after, I don't know, like four years, the war ends and the lonely guy has survived. So he gets to go home, right? But the thing is, when he gets home he finds that Stalingrad has been almost completely destroyed. There was a battle *in* Stalingrad that lasted for years and the Germans bombed everything and buildings are leveled and whole streets have been destroyed.

"So he walks to his street and finds that his building is one of the ones still standing. He goes up to his apartment and finds it empty. Everything's pretty much been taken, but at least it's still there, waiting for him. So he sits down and he thinks, 'Okay, I survived. Now what?' There's literally nothing and nobody in the world for him. He's just sitting there, and then he sees the phone. He goes to the phone and he picks it up, and after a second he gets an idea and smiles to himself. Then he dials the number, and after a few rings someone picks up. It's the man with the deep voice, who says, 'Hello?' Then the lonely guy says, 'Hello. May I speak to Mr. Chicken?' And Mr. Rooster says, 'You son of a bitch, you're alive! Come, friend! You must come and drink with me at once!' And so . . . he did."

James was filled with this odd notion that he was some sort of programmable thing, where a series of inputs which made no sense, if entered in the right sequence, could create a response. He could feel the smile on his face. "I love it."

"I know, right? I don't get what it is, but it makes me so happy."

Neither of them said anything for a while then.

Dorian turned back to the TV and switched to a show with a bunch of stand-up comics doing little five-minute sets. James was half listening. Mostly he pictured the small, empty apartment, the phone sitting on a small table. He pictured the guy slamming down the phone and pulling on his coat, running out and forgetting to pull the door closed behind. He didn't follow him, though. James stayed in that empty apartment. He didn't want to know anything else about the story, because it was so perfect at that moment, with him running off to meet his friend for a drink.

An hour later, Dorian said her mom would probably be home soon and talked about how crazy she was. The implication that Ms. Delaney would be somewhere beyond upset to find a boy in her house was clear. It was funny to James. It'd been such a simple, chaste day. But parents never believe that—*They always assume we're so much better at this than we really are.* James stretched. He didn't want to leave. For the first time in weeks he wasn't consumed with the coming War, with nightmares of what lay ahead. He could breathe. It had been a wonderful, wonderful day, and he wanted it to last another fifteen minutes, another hour. He sat in a little wooden seat by the front door as he put his shoes on and thought that he should say something. *Do you wanna hang out tomorrow? Can I kiss you? Was this whole day some kind of pity thing? Do you like me? Even if you say yes, I'll never believe it. Can we please do today over and over and over again?* But instead he just retied his left shoe, stalling for time.

As James stood, his left elbow bumped the little glass table by the door and a small frog figurine teetered. James reached out to grab it at the same time Dorian did. He managed to snag the frog but only by barreling through her dainty hand, a thwack as their knuckles met, and she shook out the hurt as he righted the frog.

"Sorry."

She looked up at him, moving only her eyes. Once again her teeth found her bottom lip. There was half a smile, and something else . . . nervousness?

"You have to kiss it," she said, extending her hand to James.

James didn't think. He didn't analyze or stammer. He leaned forward, took her right hand in his, and kissed the knuckles of her index and middle finger. Her smell filled him, lips to her skin, slightly cool, and the hand in his felt both frail and able.

"You wanna know something embarrassing?" Dorian looked at him, but the bare toes of her right foot worried at the floor like a drill. "When I was little, my dad and I used to play a game where if you hit someone you had to kiss it better. I'm sure it started from an accidental hit one time, but it became a game, too. So, like, I'd punch him in the knee and then kiss his knee and he'd punch my shoulder and kiss my shoulder, like that. Anyway, this one time, I remember I punched him square in the, y'know, in the nuts. And I could tell he was kinda hurt and mad, so I told him I was sorry and I went to kiss it better. And he wouldn't let me. I remember—god, this is so embarrassing—I remember I started crying because he wouldn't let me kiss it, 'cause that's what we did. I'm sure he remembers it, but I've never mentioned it to him.

"Isn't that stupid? Saying it out loud it's really . . . stupid. I was always too embarrassed to mention it to him or any-one, really, 'cause it sounds weird and creepy, but it wasn't. Why should I be embarrassed? I was a little kid. It was in-nocent. I really hate how, as we get older, we keep turning everything uglier and uglier."

James felt as if anything he could say would land somewhere between meant-well-but-clumsy and tone-deaf moron, so instead he just reached out, slowly, to take her hand. Just before his fingers reached hers, though, Dorian's hand flashed up. Quick and light, it was at his face before he could do a thing, stopping, then landing a soft tap on the corner of his mouth.

Dorian stepped into the space between them. She put her hands on James's shoulders, stretched up on her tippy-toes, and kissed the corner of his mouth with delicate precision. He turned his face and caught her mouth—meeting, opening quick, nervous darting tongues. James put his hands on her hips as if he was holding her in place. *Move them up? Down? To her butt? What is expected here?* But then it was over, and James had the terrifying feeling that he'd missed it. *Wait. No. Again.*

"Call me," Dorian said, because that was the only and perfectest thing to say.

James nodded.

James walked out.

James smelled grass and charcoal briquettes and engine exhaust. He looked back as he mounted his bike, and she smiled and waved and disappeared inside. James rode home, slow and ambling, cutting figure eights in the pavement as "Habanera" played in his head.

12. The Abduction

From above, it was impossible to tell what James Salley was dreaming about. Unlike the spasming, torquing, twisted-up-in-the-sheets, covered-in-sweat mess that James became when gripped by his now-recurring nightmares, whatever dream held him this morning, it had a very different effect. The covers lay on the floor beside the bed, while his head and chest pushed up. His hands before him, massaging the empty air above the bed as if he held a ball.

Then it was like a charge burned through him and he was awake and stumbling from the bed to his desk, tearing off a half-covered sheet and violently tossing it aside. *Hurry, hurry, before it's gone.* James sketched out the face as quick as he could, and the whole time it repeated in his mind: *Eliza, Eliza, Eliza.* No doubt, this was her. He moved from generalities to specifics, feeling the image seeping out of his memory, returning to the world of dream. *Hurry up. Get it down!*

There. There it was. Without a doubt.

Eliza.

James felt the full-body release of discovery—glorious relief, along with a clean and weightless sort of joy. He told himself that he was being silly, that it wasn't a big deal—*But that's her! It's finally her.* James was drunk with the breakthrough. He jumped from his desk and whooped. He slapped his bed and paced his room, his gaze returning again and again to Eliza's face on the paper.

But it doesn't matter.

The War, remember? The War. Remember when you came up with the first story? It doesn't matter anymore because of the War and the armies and the return of the Creator, and Ezra said this world doesn't even matter anyways 'cause it's just a place for them to prove themselves. Remember?

But that's not right. That can't be right.

Maybe it doesn't have to be now? I mean, Ezra says they've been waiting for, what, a thousand years? No! More than that. Before there even was a BC/AD, right? Thousands of years they've been waiting. So what's . . . twenty or forty more? I can make the comic—I can do what I want. They can't tell me I have to do this now. I could . . . Dorian's finally . . . Why would I stop everything now? I have Eliza! She's right there. I have the first issue, I have, I have everything—

But Ezra says it has to happen now.

Why?

I don't know, but he does. They all do. They're waiting for you. They're aaaaaallllllllll waiting.

Let them wait! What about me? What about my life? I

didn't agree to any of this. I don't want Earth, I just want Dorian. I want . . . Ahh! I don't wanna lead any stupid army in any stupid war and Ezra and Dink and Mikhael and everyone everywhere can just—

James's cell rang, and when he looked over and saw Dorian's yearbook photo smiling from the screen, he lunged for it like providence.

"Hey."

"Hey."

"I figured you'd call me today, and it's totally no big deal—"

"Yeah," James said, "I was. It's just early. I didn't wanna bother you."

"It's eleven, James. I haven't slept past eight since I was in the third grade."

"Jesus."

"I know, right? Anyway, my dad and Deborah, his new girlfriend, who—oh my god, I shouldn't even start. She is the worst. She's one of those girls who thinks dumb is cute. You know what I mean? Like, I can tell she's not actually that dumb, but she thinks it's just the most adorable thing ever. Who wants someone who doesn't know anything about anything?"

"Well, your dad, apparently."

And then she was laughing, and it was amazing, just exactly what James had thought one of these conversations would be like.

"Right. Anyway, they're picking me up later and

we're gonna go to a matinee and dinner, so I just thought that if, y'know, if you wanted to like hang out today or something, we could go grab a coffee."

"Yeah." *Was that quick enough? Too quick?* "Yeah, definitely. When? Now? I mean, I can go now if you want."

"Sure, now's cool."

"Cool. Funky Bean?"

"God, it sounds awful when those words come out of a human mouth, doesn't it? This town needs a Starbucks."

"So . . . Funky Bean?"

"Yes, James, the Bean."

James cleaned up fast and was out the door so quick he was already sullying his washing and deodorizing with a fresh sheen of sweat. The sunlight filled up the world like water as the morning burned away, and all at once, a thought bloomed—*An end, an end, this is an end.* He could feel the truth of it, even if he couldn't articulate exactly what it meant. So many of those things and ideas by which James had defined James were disappearing. The sensation wasn't quite as sad or scary as James would've expected; it was actually pretty exciting. His loneliness—and that wet-heavy fear that loneliness uses to suffocate—it all felt like it was ending. All of it. Just walking here in the sun, James felt a power and freedom that he had never known in his life. He wanted to run, to do something big and open and visceral. He wanted to kiss Dorian again. Yes, that was it. Sweat crept down his back, and James dreamed of diving into water, of coming up to find Dorian, their mouths pressed together, their tongues the circuitry that connected their souls.

That was when the Escalade turned in front of him and screeched to a stop. James's mind was somewhere else and he started to apologize, but then the front and back doors sprang open. Two men, black suits, the clop-clack of hard soles on pavement. James took a single step back and felt four hands from behind take hold of his elbows and shoulders and—"Hey!"—he tried to twist away but they were too strong, and a moment later the hands in front had a hold of him too and he was pushed/pulled into the waiting Escalade. The men behind him climbed in as well, so that the spacious sports utility vehicle was about as full of humans as it could get.

James turned his head to see the men behind him. They were mannequins, or could have been for all the emotion they showed. Dead eyes and stiff jaws, varying degrees of brown hair cut close. Those hands, though— they communicated. They said, "Fight back and we'll break you."

"Listen," James said, but that was all he could get out. He felt the Escalade lurch into motion.

"He speaks!" a voice called from the back of the vehicle, and all at once, everybody in the speeding Escalade but James burst into song. Loud and basso, sonorous, they sang.

"WHEN ISRAEL WAS IN EGYPT'S LAND, LET MY PEOPLE GO . . ." Plastic zip ties affixed his hands and feet to each other. "OPPRESSED SO HARD THEY COULD NOT STAND, LET MY PEOPLE GO!" James heard the rrrriiiiiiiiip of duct tape and then felt it grip his mouth closed and wrap once around his head, pulling at the hairs on the back of his neck.

Someone leaned close and whispered into his ear, "You won't sway us with your poison words, Devil."

"GO DOWN, MOSES, WAY DOWN IN EGYPT'S LAND . . ." A bag was pulled down over his head and the Escalade went dark. Not black, though. The bag was porous enough that some light filtered through, though nothing could be discerned. "TELL OLD PHARAOH, LET MY PEOPLE GO!" The fabric was rough and scratchy against his cheeks. And that smell— *What is that?* "THUS SAITH THE LORD, BOLD MOSES SAID . . ." *Potatoes. That's it. It's a potato sack.* "IF NOT I'LL SMITE YOUR FIRSTBORN DEAD, LET MY PEOPLE GO!"

That was the next fifteen minutes of James's life. As they sang[51] he felt a fear he'd never known before. It wasn't—as fear had always been—debilitating but instead agitating. The fear was an itch, and behind it, something else. Something that felt gross inside. James held his hands in fists and waited, his teeth pressed together. He shook with fear, and his bladder felt as if it might go at any moment.

James heard the unmistakable sounds of tires coming to a stop on gravel. Seat belts released, engine off,

---

[51] "Soul of My Savior" followed by "We Three Kings" and then a second and third rendition of "Go Down, Moses."

clack, clack, clack, thump, thump, then the hands had him again, lifting/guiding him out of the Escalade as his feet scrambled for purchase on the loose rock. It was bright and warm and he could smell something . . . synthetic, like rubber, and then the quality of light changed. A door closed behind him and the sound of it reverberated across far-off walls and ceiling. *Warehouse? Factory? Did they drive me around and around and then bring me to the ChocoMalt factory?*

No, the smell's wrong.

A chair was pressed into the back of his knees, forcing him into it. The ties were cut from his hands and feet, but those extremities were immediately zip-tied to the arms and legs of the chair. He could hear movement. Footsteps far off, the shuffling of fabric nearby. He could smell the breath of the man affixing his right-wrist strap: fish and vinegar. The scrape of something metal being dragged across the floor, the clop of those hard-soled shoes just a few feet in front of him, a click, a mechanical whirring, and then the potato sack was pulled from his head.

James knew the man instantly—the severe cheekbones, chin like two knuckles, the butter-yellow hair.

The sunglasses were gone, lying on the table next to him, along with a running tape recorder and—James's greatest fear, which he now saw in its naked ridiculousness—James's backpack, open and empty, lying beside clear Baggies holding some of his more depraved drawings. The Baggies were grouped in three piles, each labeled in thick, black ink: *Perverse. Seditious. Evil.*

"Hello, Son of Perdition."

He nodded to someone off to James's right, and a moment later James felt something press against his throat—cold metal with a determined edge. Old Fish-and-Vinegar Breath leaned in once more. "One word out of line, one trick, and I open your throat." The warmth filled James's lap and ran down his left leg. The blond man watched the dark stain spread. The light tinkley drip from James's shorts to the floor below filled the silence, and for an instant James saw doubt darken the blond man's face. Then the tape was ripped from James's mouth like a punishment.

"Such a long-awaited day," the blond man said.

"Why am I—?" James began, but the pressure of the knife made him stop.

The blond man crossed himself, said a few silent words, and then turned his gaze fully to James.

"Yes?" The blond man said.

James didn't risk a sound.

"Let him speak."

The edge of the blade backed ever so slightly away from the pulsing artery.

"Why am I here?"

"You are here because you are the enemy and we are the katechon. You are the scourge, you are the Antichrist, and you are here to die."

"No." James couldn't help it. He didn't want to beg. He

wanted to stand up to them, but that would not happen. The tears started and multiplied, threatening to choke him. His whole body reacted, jerking up and shivering. He wanted to tell them he wasn't the Antichrist or that even if he was, he promised not to do anything. He wanted to beg and tell them they couldn't kill him because he was only sixteen and he wanted to know what it felt like to be forty. He wanted to tell them so many things, but instead he just cried.

This, it turned out, greatly confused the blond man. He had been raised to destroy the Antichrist, prepared his entire life for this one purpose (just as his father had been, and his father's father and his father's father's father, and so on), but this was not what he'd been told to expect. And as James continued to weep while sitting in his own urine, the blond man's brow crept down his face and his mouth twisted to the side. He tilted his head, staring at the boy.

"Uhhhh, one moment please," the blond man said, motioning for Old Fish-and-Vinegar and Pudgy Dark Hair to huddle up a few feet to the left.[52]

It was at that exact moment, just as James felt the knife leave his neck, that he remembered Dink. Try as he might, though, he couldn't reach his pocket. He shut his eyes tight and begged that his voice would be enough. "Dink," he whispered.

---

52 **Blondie:** Are we a hundred percent this is him? **Fish:** One hundred percent. **Blondie:** Hm. Well, I just want to say, this is not what I expected. **Fish:** Exactly. That's how devious he is. We expect cunning and brilliance; he plays for pity. **Blondie:** Yes, that could be it. [Fish thinks he hears the Antichrist say something. He turns and looks at him. Nothing.] **Pudgy:** Did anyone else notice that he pissed himself? **Blondie:** Paul, please be quiet. [to Fish] Yes, that's it, isn't it? This was a ruse we never even considered. Oh, the Little Horn is a devious one. Alright, back to our purpose. **Fish:** Benediction? **Blondie:** Quickly. [Lord's Prayer recited by all three.]

Old Fish-and-Vinegar looked over, squinting, before returning to the huddle.

And then James felt it. A flutter in the pocket, squirming, wriggling, darting free and clambering up him. And then the homunculus was once more perched on his shoulder by his ear.

"Dink?"

"Sssh. It's alright, kid. I'm here."

"Can you help?" James said in the mousiest whisper he could eke out.

"Course I can help. That's why I'm here." Dink swung around, taking in the room in an instant. "Okay, kid, you'll be fine. Just stall and act stupid. I mean dumber than the dumbest dumbass in history, okay? Set smart to zero. You got it? Deny and act confused. Nothing more. Can you do that?"

James nodded.

"I'll be back. Sit tight."

James felt the homunculus slide down his sleeve and watched as he jumped to the ground, landing with a roll. The little man darted across the floor, his tiny feet scampering until he came to the leg of the small metal table. He climbed with an undulating motion, arms and legs stretching then coming together like an inchworm. He scampered up onto the table, hiding behind the tape recorder just as the three men returned.

The blond man resumed his position directly in front of James. The confidence was back on his face, and the knife was back at James's throat. "Very clever, but I think it's time to begin." He planted his hands on his hips and stood there in what can only be described as a Superman pose. "I . . . am Adam," he said. "Who . . . are . . . you?"

"Listen, you have the wrong person—"

"Who are you?"

"Listen—"

"Who are you?"

"Uh, my name is James Salley. I'm—"

"That is not who you are."

"Yes—"

"Yoooouuuu," Adam screamed, devouring James's words, "are the Antichrist! The evidence against you is staggering. Are you ready for your trial to begin?"

"Trial?"

"Trial, yes. Like the Holy Inquisition. You will be questioned, and though you don't deserve it, you will be given the option of confession."

"Confession?"

"Then you will be smoted and flung back into the lake of fire from whence you came."

"Listen," James said as he searched for Dink, "I really have no idea what you guys are talking about. I'm just a kid. I go to school at—"

"The trial commences!" Adam shouted, his arms raised to the heavens.

"Amen," intoned the other two.

Adam wove his hands together behind his back and

began to pace before James like a caged tiger, quick steps giving way to tight spins. "I, Adam Thursberry Delacroix of the Chivalric Order of Christ's Knights, do hereby begin this trial of James Lovie Salley, herein known as the Son of Perdition—"

"I don't even know what that means!"

"Quiet!" Adam's pacing jerked to a halt. "There will be time for you to answer charges later. Now I have to . . ." He hovered over the tape recorder for an instant before waving it away and resuming pacing. "Oh, I guess we can edit it later. Okay, where was . . . Begin this trial of James Lovie Salley, herein known as the Son of Perdition, the Little Horn, Tool of Satan, Deceiver, or the Antichrist. It is eleven forty-seven in the morning, Central Standard Time. Amen."

"Amen," the other two crooned.

"Now," Adam said, rounding on James, "to begin. Paul, may I have the materials?"

"What?" the pudgy one said, his eyes suddenly wide.

"The materials, Paul. For the trial."

"Oh, I . . . they're in the bag, I didn't know you'd . . . this early . . . I'll get 'em."

James and Adam watched as Paul rushed over to a black attaché, riffling through it as he stumbled toward them. His hand burst triumphantly from the attaché with a few papers clutched tight. Adam did not seem to share his sense of victory, and so Paul handed him the papers and retreated to his former spot.

Adam snatched the top sheet and snapped it crisp.

"Your name is James Lovie Salley."

James stared, unsure if something was being requested of him.

"Is your name James Lovie Salley?"

"Yeah—yes."

"You live at 323 Jackson Street in Stone Grove, Illinois, do you not?"

James nodded.

"Speak up, please. For the recording."

"Yeah."

"Your mother is Eleanor Jane Salley, née Vuckman, and your *legal* father is Joshua James Salley?"

"Why do you say it like that?"

"Yes or no."

"Yes."

"And please, put aside the innocent act. I think we both know who your father really is."

"Satan is his father," Paul bellowed while standing at military attention. "He came up from Hell and begat a son of mortal woman!"

"Thank you, Paul," Adam said, turning to him, "but in the future, would you mind refraining from answering unless questions are posed to you?"

The pudgy man looked down and nodded. James wondered for a moment if maybe Paul could somehow . . . but it was as if Old Fish-and-Vinegar read his mind, and the pressure of the knife intensified, leading James's gaze away from Paul.

"Now," Adam resumed, "it may seem unimportant to you that we verify that information, but large truths hide in small details. Do you know the truth of numbers, beast?"

Adam waited for an answer.

James said, "What?"

"When we look at a person's name through the truth of numbers, it tells us things which they might like to hide. No one can hide from the numbers. That is how the Almighty speaks to us. Do you know what gematria is?"

James shook his head. He wanted to cry, but it was as if he was too paralyzed even for that. *Maybe Dink left me. I can't die. I can't.*

Adam nodded, and the knife left James's throat. A moment later, another chair was pulled up alongside James's own. Old Fish-and-Vinegar then handed Adam a clipboard and a pen, but when he went to place his knife back at James's throat, Adam held up his hand.

"I think we'll be alright without that for now. Mr. Salley understands his situation. Do stay close, though." And with that, Adam seated himself next to James, holding up the blank sheet of paper for James to see.

"Gematria," Adam began, "is an alphanumeric system by which numeric values are assigned to certain letters in the Hebrew alphabet. It has many variations, many cousins. There is an English gematria; there is isopsephy, which is according to the Greek alphabet; there are Kaballah and arithmancy and many more. And do you know what,

Little Horn? They can see you. That's right; there's no hiding from them. The numbers can always see. Look."

Adam wrote the name across the paper.

J	L	S
A	O	A
M	V	L
E	I	L
S	E	E
		Y

"Now," Adam said, his pen hovering just above the paper, "let's look at arithmancy first, shall we? There are two major schools, or methods, of arithmancy: Agrippan and Chaldean. We'll use both. So James gives us one, one, four, five, one, which equals twelve, according to the Agrippan, and one, one, four, five, three, which equals fourteen, according to the Chaldean. You see? Each letter has a numeric value. According to the Agrippan method, for instance, A, J, and S equal one and B, J, and T equal two, and so on and so on. The Chaldean table is the same for certain numbers, different for others, but here, let me just . . ." Adam filled in the rest of the name, so that the finished product looked like this:

J 1—1	L 3—3	S 1—3
A 1—1	O 6—7	A 1—1
M 4—4	V 4—6	L 3—3
E 5—5	I 9—1	L 3—3
S 1—3	E 5—5	E 5—5
		Y 7—1
12—14	27—22	20—16

"Usually in arithmancy you're going to reduce these to a single-digit number. But what if we didn't do that? What if we added them all together?" The scratch of pen on paper. How many times had that been the most comforting sound in the world to James?

$$12+14+27+22+20+16 = 111$$

"And then we multiply that by the number of sums we've added together . . ."

James realized what he was doing the second before he wrote the number. "No."

$$666$$

"The Number of the Beast," Adam said as a shiver rolled through him.[53]

---

53 Adam, like many in the order, was a sufferer of Hexakosioihexekontahexaphobia. It was thought to be genetic.

James shook his head.

"Oh, there's more. Let's look at isopsephy, shall we?"

"Pleeeaaaassssse, I don't know what you guys are talking about. This doesn't . . . I don't know why my name does that, but—"

Adam tore off the top sheet, revealing fresh white paper. "Isopsephy is an alphanumeric system of great mystery and majesty, coming from the Greeks. For this one, we don't even need your whole name. We need only . . ."

S
A
L
L
E
Y

"The value of S is two hundred. A is one, L is thirty twice, and Y is four hundred." He scribbled the equation in a long line, and James knew he couldn't hold it any longer. His stomach and esophagus contracted as one, but it was only a thin orange stream that splurted out onto his chest and lap.

$$200+1+30+30+5+400 = 666$$

"*You see?*" Adam shouted, leaping away from the chair. He tore off that sheet as well, tossing it above his head and letting it fall. "Can you see the *truth*?"

"I'm not . . . anyone. I haven't done anything!"

And now I'm gonna die.

"But the real evidence is in English gematria. English gematria is our true line to God's plan. I can tell you that. Simple. Perfect." He scribbled an off-balance six on the paper and held it up to James. "Six! Six is the key. A is six, B is twelve, C is eighteen, and on and on. M is seventy-eight, R is 108, Y is 150. You see?"

Adam hunched over his clipboard and wrote and wrote and wrote. For the first time, James began to notice the pain in his wrists and ankles. The plastic straps were chafing the skin even as they squeezed and restricted the blood flow. Again his gaze swept the room for Dink. He looked at the pile of clothing, the area around the table. Nothing.

Adam stepped up to James and held the clipboard out at arm's length, so that this was facing James:

J = 60	L = 72	S = 114
A = 6	O = 90	A = 6
M = 78	V = 132	L = 72
E = 30	I = 54	L = 72
S = 114	E = 30	E = 30
		Y = 150
288	378	444

"Look at that last number, Antichrist. It may be the most holy number there is. I admit, it gave us pause when we found it. The number 444 is the sum of the words Gospel and Cross . . . and Jesus. Did you hear that? Jesus!" Adam resumed his pacing, though now the steps were closer together, the shoulders tighter. James thought he looked like a cat ready to pounce on the brain stem of a mouse.

"But then," Adam said, "the Truth was revealed to us. Of course you would have the same numeric value as Jesus. Are you not his nemesis, his archenemy? You are his mirror image, dark where he is light and empty where he is whole. It only makes sense that you should have the same number." James saw Adam check his reaction out of the corner of his eye. On the whole, Adam seemed to be very pleased with the way this was going.

"It's like with Voldemort," Paul said. "He and Harry Potter have like the same everything. Even their wands, they have Phoenix feather cores, and they're the only ones that—"

"Paul!"

The room was silent as Adam stared at the pudgy man. James was sure he could feel Old Fish-and-Vinegar behind him staring as well.

"Sorry," Paul said, again searching for his favorite part of the floor.

Adam shook his head and looked around before finding James again. "Right, uh, 444, the mirror image of our Lord and Savior Jesus Christ. Jesus, 444. Salley, 444. Christ. Antichrist. Do you still deny it?"

"Yes." James had no more energy to shout it. "Yes," he said again.

"Oh, but we're not finished." Adam's smile and focus were Viagra-level back. He stomped over to James. "Look at the other two numbers. First, James equals 288. Now, 288 gives us nothing, but when we divide it by the holy number three, we find—"

"Wait. You can't just do that! If it gives you nothing, then that's an argument in my favor."

"The holy number divines Truth. It is a litmus by which any number must be tested. When you divide 288 by three you get ninety-six, which is a semiperfect number and a multiple of six. Six!"

"What's a semiperfect number?"

"Moooooving on! The numeric value of Lovie is 378. Again, that gives us nothing. When we divide by three, we get 126—which is nothing—buuuuuut, when we divide by three once again we get forty-two—an evil number."

"That's not . . . you can't just keep . . ."

"In Revelation it says that the Beast will hold dominion over the Earth for forty-two months. Quite a coincidence, don't you think?"

"No!" James said, feeling something other than terror at last. *You can't let them do this.* "It's not a coincidence, because you're just making stuff up! This is all bullshit! This—" James barely noticed the nod. The knife, on the other hand, he noticed the second it touched his throat.

"As I was saying, forty-two is a very, very interesting number. It's a wicked number. There are, of course, the

Jews. They have their so-called forty-two-lettered god."
And then, almost to himself, "I wouldn't be surprised if
you actually turned out to be him. Wouldn't the heebs be
surprised to find out—?"

"Jackie Robinson."

They all turned to Paul.

"What?" Old Fish-and-Vinegar said.

"Jackie Robinson was number forty-two," Paul said
as he attempted to polish the floor with his shoe.

Adam stormed over to Paul and slapped the attaché out
of his hands. "What does that have to do with anything?"

"You were . . . Things that're forty-two."

"Evil things, Paul. Wicked things. You can't . . . That
was actually really racist."

"It was," Old Fish-and-Vinegar said.

"You know, Paul, just go outside."

"But—"

"No, just go."

Paul walked slowly, and James was almost positive he
heard the sniffle-suck of tears as the pudgy man let the
heavy door close behind him.

Adam turned to James. "I just want you to know that
we don't condone . . . Anything Paul may have said was
his own . . . I actually have a lot of black friends."

James was unsure of the correct response, so he just
nodded.

Adam resumed his position before James, but he
seemed uncertain. His eyes ranged about as if he'd forgotten
where he left off. He stepped to the table and shuffled

through the pages from Paul's attaché. "Okay," Adam said, wheeling once more to James, his old energy again animating his face. "Let's try this. I want you to answer each one of my questions yes or no. Can you do that?"

James nodded again.

"Okay. Are you thirsty?"

"Yes."

"Is my hair blond?"

"Yes."

"Is today Sunday?"

"Uh, yes."

"Is your name James?"

"Yes."

"Do you want to go home?"

"Yes."

"Do you live in Stone Grove?"

"Yes."

"Are you the Antichrist?"

"No."

"Come on!"

Adam marched off behind the table. He stood there, hands on his hips, chewing his bottom lip, and stared at James. Finally he let out a deep sigh and looked over at Old Fish-and-Vinegar. "Peter should have been here by now. He's bringing the holy water and the strappado. I'm going to go call him. You watch this beast—and do not move that knife. Remember how cunning he is, brother." Then Adam turned to address James. "If you say a word to him while I am away, he will kill you. Do you understand?"

James nodded and Adam turned hard on his heel and headed in the opposite direction, disappearing through a small back door. Old Fish-and-Vinegar came around to the front of the chair, standing so that he was straddling James's legs, his right hand reaching across his body and holding the knife against the side of James's neck.

There was no mistaking the truth in his eyes: this man wanted to do it. He wanted James to say something. Had there been anything left in James's bladder, it would have left.

It was then, at the very moment that James felt his insides give up, that he saw Dink's tiny hand appear, rising as he summited the back and clambered onto the shoulder of Old Fish-and-Vinegar, who, in his intense neckular focus, didn't notice the homunculus at all.

That was when Dink did it. He took one step backward, coiling down like a sprinter, and then charged the head. When he reached Old Fish-and-Vinegar's neck, he leapt up and out, landing with a wet sccchhhhluunk in the big man's ear. James felt the knife tense against his neck for an instant, but nothing more, as Dink burrowed into the ear, his little legs kicking frantically. Old Fish-and-Vinegar locked up, his eyes big white orbs of confused terror, and then Dink's feet were gone.

For a moment, nothing at all happened.

Then the knife came away from James's neck. The

big man's arm moved in broad, herky-jerky jumps, like a marionette's. He stepped back in long strides, without bending his knees. Then he bent over at the waist, ass in the air, and reached his right arm out straight, so that the tip of the knife inched toward James's wrist. The dull eyes stared at him, the pupils still and fully dilated.

"What are you doing?" James whispered.

The mouth flopped open. "Taaaaaahhhhh."

"What?"

"Tahh . . . terhhhh . . . truhhh . . . Trusssssst meeeeeee."

James closed his eyes as the blade shook and flicked near his wrist. A moment later his muscles rejoiced at their freedom, the arm flexing up even as blood rushed back into his hand, filling it with little needles. James opened his eyes and saw that the wobbly thing that had been Old Fish-and-Vinegar was holding the knife out, handle-first. James took it and cut free of his other restraints, and then he was up and stumbling toward the door, the big man's hand dragging him along. James broke free for a second and ran to the table to retrieve his phone before hurrying back to the side of Dink's puppet. When they reached the door, James was shoved to the wall behind it as New Dink/Old Fish-and-Vinegar pulled it open and leaned out to the cluster of suited men standing around Paul, pestering him for details. James watched through the hinge space between door and wall. He could tell just by the flourish of Paul's arm as he recounted the story that he was already hard at work rewriting his role in this day.

"It'sssssss time," New Dink-and-Vinegar said. "Ever . . . everyone oot back."

They practically crushed him in the stampede. James caught the door just before it took him upside the head. Paul paused, squinting at New Dink-and-Vinegar.

"You okay, Donny?"

For a moment the big man didn't say or do a thing, and James wondered if somehow he was broken or frozen or something. But then he lurched forward so that his head almost hit Paul's, burrowing into his personal space. "Go."

And Paul did. He was at the back door a second later, and then the big man's hands were searching for James again, pulling him outside and pushing him toward the Escalade. He herded James up in through the passenger door and followed him. Then he pointed at the keys. "Go."

James started to protest. Driver's ed had not gone well. He was scared and watched the ground directly in front of the car instead of looking out ahead, and when he felt it drift a little to the left or right, he panicked. Then James looked up at the warehouse door standing open and realized that more than anything he'd ever wanted in his life, he did not want to see someone come out of there. Whatever that meant, he was not going to be right here when someone emerged.

The engine cleared its throat and growled. James pressed hard on the brake—*C'mon, you can do this*—and felt the engine lurch as the vehicle slipped into reverse; then he turned to look out the back window, took his foot off the brake, and slammed it on the gas.

James and the man stood in an undeveloped tract a half mile outside of town as the sinking sun and a light drizzle melted the too-hot day into heavy redness. The entire stretch where they stood was supposed to be townhouses a couple years ago, but it'd all stopped. Investors gone, loans gone, developers gone, workers gone. Mostly it was just paved dirt and a few wooden skeletons. Kids came out here to have bonfires and drink cases of Busch.

At this particular moment, James was sitting on a decorative boulder and New Dink-and-Vinegar was standing in a roughly three-foot-deep grave. James had been trying to talk to him for the last thirty minutes, trying to get information from Dink or Old Fish-and-Vinegar. But Dink said to wait until they were done. That was twenty-five minutes ago. Since then he hadn't said a word.

The trip had been a terror that should never be recounted. James was utterly lost for at least twenty minutes. He sped, then went too slow. At stop signs, he idled through or slammed on the brakes or sometimes missed them altogether. The SUV had drifted as he tried to read a street sign and scraped three parked cars. Eventually he'd managed to figure out that they were pretty much straight west, and then it was just a matter of staying on Washington Avenue without drawing any attention. It did not help when New Dink-and-Vinegar began to convulse in the passenger seat.

The big man tossed the shovel out of the grave and lay down. James watched as the man's head began to shake and blood ran out of his nose like in that video he'd seen on the Internet of that politician in the '80s who shot himself at his press conference. Then, like a child gushed from a water-park slide, Dink burst from the opposite ear of Old Fish-and-Vinegar, feetfirst and riding a wave of blood.

Dink climbed from the grave soaking wet, and the dirt stuck to him and turned dark. "You mind covering him up?" he said.

"I thought . . . I was hoping he could tell me more about . . ."

"He can't tell you anything, kid. He can never tell anybody anything ever again."

The thought filled James with a long, cold dread. His eyelids twitched in hard syncopation despite his efforts to stop them. He didn't want Dink to see, so he gathered up the shovel and began loading the soil back into the ground.

You hated him. James threw the first three shovelfuls of dirt on Old Fish-and-Vinegar's face. *He wanted to murder you. He was . . .* James shoveled faster. He wanted the man gone. Hidden and gone and gone.

Dink climbed up James's leg as soon as the last dirt was in the grave. "Wipe off the shovel and throw it in the woods there by the automobile."

James did as he was told. Dink climbed to his shoulder, and James turned away from the setting sun and began to walk home. His shadow before him was twenty feet tall and darker than mud.

"I'm going to stay with you here, kid."

James turned to see the homunculus sitting on his shoulder looking back at him.

Dink nodded as if it was settled and then looked off ahead. "They'll be scared now. I understand you're freaked out, but you're actually much safer now. They're not a muscle operation; they're a sneak-and-peek operation. Now that they know that we know—and they lost one of theirs—they're going to be mighty wary. Plus, I'll be here now. All the time, kid."

James walked along the street as North America turned away from the sun. The rain came suddenly, falling fast in fat, warm drops, and he turned his head up to it, listening to the sounds of the rain pelting the leaves and asphalt, the sound of far-off traffic and his own breath. In and out and in and out.

"It'll be okay, kid."

James tried to take in what Dink said, but nothing could get past Old Fish-and-Vinegar in his shallow grave, the way the dirt clung to the rivers of blood on his mouth and chin. It felt as if James was processing the moment over and over again.

He stopped walking. "I need to see Ezra. I need to talk to him."

"Okay, we'll find him."

"Where?"

"Where do you usually find him?"

"I don't. He usually—"

And that was when James heard the familiar squeak-squeak, growing louder with each oscillation.

Dink didn't say a word. He watched James's face and turned to follow the gaze as Ezra came along the next perpendicular street on that massive bicycle of his, executing a wide turn onto their street, riding easy through the pouring rain. His face was grave and set—the grown-up come to sort things out—as he coasted to a stop before the boy and his homunculus.

"Where were you?" James closed his arms across himself. The question screamed now; how had he not asked it before? Every time he'd needed or wanted Ezra, he'd shown up. So what happened this time? James strung the horror of the last two hours out before him, preparing to hang it all on Ezra's neck.

"You're alright, James." Ezra swung off the bicycle. He took a step toward James, who mirrored it. Ezra stopped. "You're alright."

"Why didn't you come?"

"Why didn't you kill them?"

"What?"

"Why did you stay there, James? Why were you so afraid? Why won't you grasp who and what you are?"

"You knew I was there—that, that they were holding

a knife to my throat. And you didn't do anything. You were just gonna let them do it."

Dink sat down hard on James's shoulder. "Nice move, Coach."

Ezra ignored Dink and leaned in to James, imploring, "James, who is it you're mad at? Me or yourself?"

"You! Is that a joke? I'm mad at you! They, they, they were gonna kill me."

"Then why didn't you stop them? Why won't you become who you're supposed to be?"

James's mouth hung open. He'd been about to scream *I can't*, but he suspected—no, he knew, in that deep, hidden place where we put the truths we can't swallow yet—that he could have. He could have stopped them but didn't. Just like he didn't with the Schroeder brothers. Too terrified in the moment. Too scared.

But it's Ezra making you do all this. This is all his fault. And like that, the anger was back.

"So this was a test, huh?"

"Everything is a test, James."

James felt the urge to jump on Ezra, to punch his face until his arms gave out. He pictured Ezra toppling back, refusing to fight, smiling through blood as he was hit, cooing sweet words of encouragement.

James pushed past Ezra without a valediction and charged off, walking like each step was a stomp on the face of the Earth, equal in its guilt with everything and everyone else. James couldn't listen to another word; he was a house on fire, and this anger consumed everything.

Crossing Main Street, James saw Mr. Llewellyn hustling through the rain toward his car, his arms laden with a Vinny's pizza and two white bags of food. A flame burst in James's head, a scream directed right at the science teacher. The thin, balding man stopped and rose up on his toes, bowing his back, and in the same movement, he slammed his armful of food on the wet sidewalk and let loose a howl from the bottom of his guts. As James cleared Main Street, Mr. Llewellyn was staring down at the mess of food like he didn't recognize it.

James did not slow. He stomped the earth. The fear and uncertainty inside boiling in to righteous anger—transformed. When he turned left at Frankfurt Street he realized where he was heading, and in the realization he wanted to scream. He walked faster. Faster. Until he was running down Frankfurt Street, and all there was in the world was this anger, and he knew he wanted to see them dead. He wanted to kill them.

And then James was standing on the Schroeders' front lawn, soaked down to the squishy soles of his shoes, the rain like walls of water now; its percussive symphony drowned out everything else.

He reached out his mind, just as he had with Mr. Worthington, only this time he could feel that what he sent out was rigid as steel, and when he felt them he grabbed them and dragged them outside, the side door by the driveway clanging open as Kevin and John and

Pat lumbered outside on unsure legs, their eyes wild and fearful, searching. Finding James. Walking to James. Far-off thunder cracked, and then the three Schroeders stood in front of James, and he squeezed his fists to death and unraveled every bit of rage from inside and screamed.

All of it. Pus from an infected wound—shrapnel from a bomb. James leaned over and screamed louder.

Louder.

Kevin kicked John in the groin, and Pat smashed Kevin on the back of the head with two hands, and John bit Pat's stomach, and the brothers screamed, but James did not hear them. He wanted them to die. He wanted them to beg to not die. The brothers punched each other in the face and ripped hair and stomped legs and insteps, and their eyes appeared as separate entities from their autonomous bodies. Their eyes were still their own, and they reported confusion and revulsion and terror. Pat stomped down on Kevin's leg, and there was a crack as Kevin's fibula snapped; then John bit the back of Pat's head, and blood ran down his chin, and James looked away. But when he did, he saw Nick. Same as last time— watching through a window. Only this time Nick was watching through the living room window, too scared to help his brothers. Maybe. Maybe he thought they deserved it. James couldn't tell. But there was no mistaking Nick's gaze as it fell on James. It was a realization:

There are awful things in this world. There is evil.

Evil.

James stopped. The brothers stopped. James looked down, and everyone looked back at him. Scared. Pleading. Weak.

The hate could not hold. James turned and ran. He ran until the pain of running was stronger than the pain of not.

Just after sundown in Stone Grove, Illinois, James Salley sat on the catwalk of the town's only operational water tower and stared down at the setting for all of his life so far. The summer storm had passed, and James sat up there where the wind was stronger and louder, and he looked out over Stone Grove. He didn't see the town, though. What he saw was the Schroeder brothers tearing each other apart on their front lawn. What he saw was Old Fish-and-Vinegar's dead eyes and dead skin and the dirt caking up his blood and Mr. Llewellyn's perplexed gaze at his own hands.

Who am I? Am I becoming something, or was I always this?

Am I the bad guy? Screw what Ezra says. Am I the bad guy? This is what he's asking me to do, what they're asking me to do—bring more of this to the world. Do to the whole world what I did to the Schroeders. And why?

Does it matter? It's going to happen.

You don't know that.

Yes, you do.

How can you let them make this place worse?

Maybe it'll make it better. Eventually. Like Ezra said.

A horn blew, and gates clanged and lowered, and a freight train came rushing through the town without a pause. The sound of the train populated Stone Grove, and it made James wonder what time it was, which led him to wonder how long he'd been there and why no one had called or texted to check in, and in that moment he remembered—*Dorian.*

James's hand was clumsy in its panic to remove the phone. *Off. They turned it off.* James powered on and waited.

Black to company's logo.

Status bar.

Home screen.

The number 7 was superimposed over the message icon.

Tap.

Where u at?

Hello?

Ok so it's been like 30 min and I can't stay much longer. Called u. No answer.

Gotta go. Kinda pissed.

OK! CALLED AGAIN! R U OK??????????????

> THIS IS FREAKING ME OUT! I'm at the play and I just left u another VM. Did u lose ur phone?

> So I don't wanna go by ur house or anything and get you in trouble but this is super weird. I sent you an email. WHATS UP?????

James closed the app and saw that he had four voice mails as well. He started the first one, but a few seconds into Dorian's cheery "Hey. You're not here. Waaaiiiiting," James closed it and called her.

She picked up on the first ring. "Hey, what's up? Where have you been?"

And that was the exact moment that James realized he'd prepared no alibi, no excuse. Where had he been? Why hadn't he called or texted? He had nothing. The only thing that felt stone certain was that there was no way he could tell her. *"Oh, yeah, sorry. I was on my way but then I got abducted by these crazy Catholics who're out to kill me because I'm the Antichrist. I'm not actually the Antichrist—but only 'cause there really isn't an Antichrist per se—but I guess I am who they want to kill; they're right about that. See, a couple of weeks ago the new school librarian told me that I'm the One. I'm gonna bring about that big war they talk about in the Bible, except it's not quite how they describe it. Anyway, I am super sorry. These guys were total dicks and they turned my phone off. Can you believe that? How was the play?"*

What he actually said, though, was, "Uuuuhhhh . . ."

"What?"

"I'm sorry," he said, thankful at least for one truthful path. "I'm so sorry. I hope I didn't screw up your day or anything."

"No, it was just really weird. I started to worry that something had happened to you, which is an awful thing for me because I have one of those imaginations that just always go to the absolute worst possible thing and then sorta like obsesses on it. Y'know?"

"Yeah," he said, though he felt fairly certain that he had no idea what it was like to think like Dorian, to be Dorian. "Sorry. That sucks."

"So where were you?"

"I uh . . ." *Oh my god, come up with something! Why are you so stupid? Think! Something! Anything!* "Sorry. Something just came up and I couldn't call." *Something came up and I couldn't call? That's it?*

"Right. What?"

C'mon, c'mon. Think! "I . . ." *There has to be some—* "I can't tell you." James felt the oxygen leave his body, replaced by tangible defeat.

"You can't tell me?" That tone James was having such a hard time placing? That would be incredulity. "I just, like, spent the whole day freaked out because we made a date, and not only didn't you—" It was quiet for a second, then James heard hot breath rushing directly from Dorian's nostrils to the phone.

"I—"

"Whatever. It's not a big deal. I gotta go, though."

"Dorian, listen, I'm gonna—"

"I really gotta go. I'll talk to ya."

The phone went silent. James let it drop onto his lap and leaned forward against the water tower's railing, his chin resting on his wrist. There was a plane going by and the wind rushing and the highway just outside of town, and as James closed his eyes, the world sounded like a monstrous machine ready to chew him up. And on the backs of his eyes he saw Old Fish-and-Vinegar's dead stare and Ezra's challenging gaze and Adam's hate and Dorian's coldness, and they melted together until they were one face. Watching him. Coming for him.

13. The Name

James tried so hard not to sleep. He refused even to sit on his bed, instead pulling over the chair from his desk to watch TV from. He purposefully covered the bed in debris—comic books and DVDs and candy and chips and empty soda bottles and wrappers—so that he wouldn't unconsciously relax on it.

James stopped at the J&J Food Mart on the way home and bought a couple bottles of Frappuccino and Mountain Dew, along with Chili Cheese Fritos and Cool Ranch Doritos and Snickers and Skittles and Pixy Stix, which he poured into the Mountain Dew.

At two o'clock that morning he even made a pot of coffee, something he had theretofore never attempted. It did not taste good, but he found that if he mixed equal parts milk, sugar, and coffee in a mug, then it wasn't bad.

James slapped himself and pinched himself and snuck outside twice with Mom's cigarettes, and once he even held one to his knuckle for a second until the searing burn reminded him just how delicate he was. But still, even with all of that, even with the candy and the coffee and the pop and the cigarettes and the self-mutilation, James fell asleep ten minutes into the first Matrix movie, at exactly 3:02:07 that morning.

And that's when it happened.

I smell matches and mold. Here. Here, in front of it. That Thing—inside—it rages and flexes against its prison. It begs me to come closer. Closer! Closer! The air is wet; the walls look like the bottom of the ocean. Cold, dead, hard, ugly, alien. Closer. Closer. Closer. Stop! Stop being so afraid! This will never end until you stop being afraid! Fear is the mind-killer! I run to the sarcophagus. I throw my arms around it. What? What do you want? Then I hear the whisper, and I press my head against it—Tell me!—and the next word explodes inside my head, and I see it written on the Moon and in the swirls of puddles and out of Dorian's mouth and on the sides of buildings and everywhere ever and always forever.

Its name. It tells me its name.

Morning didn't help. His adrenaline made it feel like there was someone else in his skin with him. He shook. He missed the toilet and peed on the floor, and he dropped a can of Coke trying to open it.

James slipped out the back door with one of Mom's cigarettes, a book of matches, and Dink. The morning was already a furnace, but he started walking anyway, and as soon as he turned the corner, he lit the cigarette. That was when he heard the squeak-squeak.

Ezra came around the corner a block ahead wearing a soft Hallmark smile. He rode toward James, passed him by, and then circled back, and as James walked down the sidewalk, Ezra rode in slow, looping waves next to him on the street.

"Calmer?" Ezra said, somehow managing to keep the condescension from it. "I am sorry, James. I know you were frightened. Understand, this is my first Apocalypse too, and though it may seem that I'm asking too much of you, that I'm impatient, I am very proud of how far you've come. I wouldn't have thought a boy of your age would be capable of all you've done."[54] Ezra paused, riding in a loop up ahead, then behind before falling in alongside again. "Are you ready to proceed?"

James knew exactly what he meant. In one sentence it seemed as if Ezra had said everything he'd been building up to since that first night. *Are you ready to proceed? Are you ready to leave all this?*

He had the name. All he had to do was say it and Ezra would take him away right now. That he knew. They would go to Taloon right now—no good-byes—and they would get Morning Star and the War would truly begin.

A river of *no* ran through him. *Never see Dorian again*? It wasn't Mom or Dad or any kind of future that flashed through his mind first, but *Dorian*.

---

54 This is true. Ezra had, in fact, argued that the One should not be approached until his nineteenth birthday. However, less patient minds prevailed.

No.

James stopped and turned to Ezra. The bicycle came to a stop with a deep, sharp squeak.

"I wanna stop—or at least, I wanna slow things down." James stood straight.

He looked into Ezra's eyes. He saw something flash for a second, as if Ezra's whole face went dark, but before James could identify or verify, it was gone, and again that smile was comfort itself. His head inclined toward James, his eyes lowered. "No," Ezra said.

"It's my call."

James felt the force of Ezra's gaze and his hand went into his pocket, where he took hold of Dink. He felt the little man squeeze back, letting him know he was there. It was amazing how quickly they'd arrived at a sort of short-hand understanding.

"James, you need to remember who you—"

"No! Okay, we need to slow it down. Finally Dorian is . . . and the comic and lots of stuff is different now and . . . no. Listen, I'm not ready for this all to end. I can't just say, okay, today I walk away."

Ezra stopped.

James was a step past before he realized and halted as well. He looked back at Ezra, whose eyes tightened as they searched James's face. "Today?"

"What?"

"You said 'today.'"

Oh, crap.

"James, the only way you could walk away today would be if you knew the name."

James always sucked at this game. He tried to hold Ezra's gaze, but a twitch started in his lying, weak guts and rolled up to one of his eyes. He looked down and dropped the cigarette.

"Oh, James, this is wonderful. After all this time . . . I'd almost—oh, but to see Morning Star again. James, we should go to—"

"No."

The rage was plain this time, and Ezra made no attempt to hide it. He seemed to grow in stature astride his bicycle, looking down at James, who could feel the fury coming off him in sheets. It's awful to have to rely on someone else, but there's no way around it. James could see the thoughts swirling in Ezra's mind, could catch them as easy as bubbles floating by. Why did it have to be this kid?

It matters only that I'm the One, not that I'm me.

Ezra dragged his fingers through his hair. He dropped the kickstand and leaned against the bike and his eeeaaassssy smile was back.

"You know, James, you can want to be one of them as bad as you like. You can wish for it and wait for it, fine, but that changes nothing. It will never happen. Do you understand? It will never happen. They're . . . they're mice. They're scared little creatures running from one safe, dry place to another. And here you stand, a giant, mightier than all of them put together, if only you'd embrace it, and you sit around and pine. You hope and wish that you could be one of them. You know what I say to that?" He spat on the grass between them. "Embrace, accept. You are a god trying to live amongst your worshippers, and the sooner you understand that the better. And it doesn't mean you can't have what you want. You know that. There's so much work to be done here, and you can make that little girl do whatever you like—or anyone else for that matter. Fear, James! Fear is directing you. You have to shrug it off and go boldly forward. Boldly forward!"

They stared.

"I just need some time," James said.

Ezra only shook his head, though James didn't see it as he turned away and began the short walk home. But from over his shoulder he heard Ezra speak. Five words, low, almost to himself.

"It's time to grow up."

James called Dorian. She hadn't answered the first time, and James didn't leave a voice mail so he'd have an excuse to call back. Again, this time, no answer. "Hi. This is Dorian . . ."

"Hey, Dorian. Could you gimme a call when you get this?"

He'd texted earlier too. More of the same. He still

hadn't planned what he'd say if she did call him back.

James collapsed onto his bed as Ezra's words boomed and reverberated, an accusation and an appeal. Across the room he could see the first panel of the first issue of *Fearless*: the cabin on the cliff—the ink outline half colored in orange-and-red pencil—and there was Eliza—truly her—staring back at him. *You should go work on it. You should call her again*—and with that internal disagreement, the last of his drive dripped out.

He'd slept so little lately, barely a few forced hours a night, and now it felt as if that debt was being called in. He didn't even kick off his shoes. Instead, James simply lay there, the noon sun an orange pulse against his closed eyes as he pondered the endless forking paths before him. One anxious thought burned supreme: that his future both was preordained and had myriad trajectories he could choose—though in each one he saw Ezra and the Pit and death, death, Death.

James lurched from his bed with a silent scream on his lips—eyes wide, searching the darkness—before he realized he'd been dreaming and choked it down. For a moment the room was alien and he was sure he was somewhere else, but then the desk and the table and the alarm clock came into focus. He was home. The clock read 9:53 p.m.

The faces swam back into his vision, and James

swung his legs off the bed and turned on the light as quick as he could. As soon as the illumination filled the room, though, James's whole body caught—there was Dink, only inches away, crouched and staring at him.

"You okay?" Dink said.

James could only swallow and nod.

"You were having a dream that scared you?"

Again, James's only response was a nod. He saw the revulsion in Dorian's eyes, saw that child's eviscerated face, and shuddered.

"What's it like?"

"What?"

"Your dreams?" Dink said, crossing the bedside table and sitting on the corner closest to James, his feet dangling off the side. "It's a thing I'm always curious about."

"Why?"

"Just because your dreams are so different from anything we experience."

"How do you know that if you don't know what ours are like?"

"I've spent enough time here that I have an idea. I just always like to hear about them."

"Oh." James kicked the tangled sheet off his leg and rubbed his eyes. "What's it like for you?"

"Us? Well, we don't need to sleep. That's simply not a feature we were designed with. We do sometimes, for enjoyment, though you have to go to a special place. And it's dangerous."

"It's dangerous?"

"If we just lay down and tried to sleep in Taloon, nothing would happen. We'd just . . . be. But if we go to the Great Field of Dreaming and lie down and stay very still and calm, then eventually we'll slip into what is our closest version of your sleep. We . . . we stop experiencing Taloon. Instead we see this world. It's a magical place, but it's . . . treacherous. You fall asleep there and the show is so much better than the junk and labor of your life, so you just stay. Forever."

"Really?"

"And every inhabitant of Taloon completely gets it. Everyone wants to succumb, because it's bliss. It's like your consciousness has been shipped to this world and set on the wind and it's just . . . flitting from place to place. Sometimes you'll see whole cities or deserts, and sometimes you'll zoom up real close and watch two humans mate or the impact of lightning, or you'll relive the same meeting over and over again, or you'll follow an antelope around for its entire life in just a few moments or watch generations of ants building their civilizations. You have . . . no control."

"I guess that's pretty much what it's like when we dream."

"But there's a very important difference. I've spoken with enough humans to know that, yeah, sometimes your dreams take you to Taloon, just like ours take us here, but you also get a lot of other dreams, ones that take you to other places, places that aren't Taloon."

"So lots of people go to Taloon in their dreams? It's not just me?"

"Everyone does. In fact, I'm sure you did long ago, before all this started; you just didn't realize it. How could you? Everyone assumes dreams are just dreams. Everyone assumes they're real personal and internal. What's really interesting is how transparent it all is to an outsider. When you see an artist bring something from their dreams, something from Taloon, and use it in their work, and then see all the other humans respond so strongly to it, it's clear why. 'Cause it's familiar to everyone 'cause everyone has visited Taloon. But, because you're inside of it and unaware of the interaction between our worlds, you can't see it.

"Last time I was here—I think it was 1987 in your American time. Or 1997? I can't remember. But I saw this television program about honeybees. The image struck me. A wall of bees, and when one fluttered, this subconscious signal was transmitted to the other bees, who then fluttered, so that one bee created a perfectly harmonious wave. The humans who were monitoring this were explaining how it worked, and I started laughing, because the things they can see in other species they're blind to in themselves. If you could ask one of those honeybees why they just fluttered, I'm sure they'd say, 'I don't know. I just felt the urge.' Same thing. Humans can't spot reactions to connections if they don't know the connections are there."

James was up and at his desk, sliding papers aside until he came up with the right one. "Here," he said.

"Look. I did that."

James laid out the paper and Dink walked onto it, looking down as James pointed at the tear-shaped alien artifact he'd drawn.

Dink turned his gaze up to James, who could feel the little man's tension like heat. "What is that?" Dink said.

"That's . . . in the Pit. Behind the walls, there are thousands, maybe hundreds of thousands or millions of them. They . . . they shake and, and scream."

James stopped. Dink looked as if someone had just run a ragged edge through his guts. His little dark eyes left James and settled on the drawing. One knee went down, then both, and his tiny hands reached out and touched James's version of the golden lamps. Dink ran his fingers along the edges. Each finger was only slightly thicker than the lines of ink they traced.

Dink continued to stare. James felt that he should leave Dink alone or get rid of the drawing or apologize or just say something, anything, but only one thing came forward.

"Everyone was looking at me," James said, and Dink turned to him. "In the dream. They uh, they all hated me. Everyone. Millions and millions of people—or were people. They were dead. They were crying and they were asking me why and screaming at me and I . . . uh. . . ." Eyes hot and full at the memory: the hate-filled pleading in his ears, Dorian's face, Mom's. "I'm sorry, Dink."

Dink padded across the table and leapt down. He crossed the floor, climbed the dresser, and ripped out three pieces of tissue from their pastel box. The sheets were bigger than him, and he folded them repeatedly before sticking them under his arm and using his other arm to do a sort of controlled fall down the dresser, catching himself for an instant at every handle. Then it was back across the floor and climbing up the bedside table, again with only his one arm.

The sheer oddness of the homunculus's Herculean task chased away some of the total terror recall of the dream. James wiped his eyes and cheeks and blew his nose and wiped again and blew again.

"Sorry," James said, but Dink just waved a hand at it. "Those are your friends in those things, aren't they? It's the ones who listened to Morning Star?"

The little shoulders rose and fell once, and Dink sat and folded his tiny legs. "Yes."

"I'm sorry."

"Did you put them there?"

"No."

"Then don't apologize."

"Sorry. I mean, y'know . . . you know."

"Yes."

It was quiet then, and James watched the little man and wondered where his mind was. James's own had finally excavated a truth he'd sensed the mass of for a while. "I don't wanna do it."

There. He'd said it. What he'd never quite been able to say to Ezra. Thanks but no thanks. I don't want it.

"Then don't."

It took longer than it should have for those two words to be translated from sound into words and meaning. *Then don't? Then don't. No, that's not right.* "I can't just . . ."

"Just what?" Dink said. "You can't just say no? Of course you can. You have free will. It can't be taken away, only gifted. You can say no. Understand, I'm not saying it would be easy, or even that you'd survive, but you could say no."

"But what would . . . ?"

"What would happen? I have no idea."

"What do you want?"

"What do I want? I want Morning Star and all the others to be free. I want the death or freedom of the War. But I swore myself to you, and I won't lie. You can always say no. To anything. It's the simplest act and one of the first freedoms forgotten."

The thought detonated in his psyche, crumbling walls built and reinforced many times over, and for a manic, powerful instant he saw Taloon and Earth as if he were a god looking down, the two worlds nothing but different-colored gasses floating through each other; and to those within it seems so tangible and definite, but above it's absurd that they can't see each other, that they believe so hard in their own oneness. It was disorienting, and James reached out to steady himself.

The house shrank around him. The ceiling pressed into his head; the walls wrapped around him like a blanket.

"I have to get out of here for a while," he said as he stood. *You could say no. They would never allow it. Ezra—Mikhael—they would come for you—come for you, come for you; the Catholics in the Escalades, the men in suits are coming, coming; what would you do about them?*

Dink leapt from the table onto the side of James's shorts. But as he began to make his way into the pocket, James stopped him. "I think I need to be alone."

"I understand. But I'm your protector and we don't know who's out there. Plus, I'm very good at alone. Many people have been alone with me and never even known it." And with that he was gone.

James opened his door and looked out—every light off, every door closed. As James went by his parents' room, he heard the unmistakable sounds of sleep: two breathers, just below snoring, out of rhythm. A movie played through in super-duper fast-forward: cliché college B-roll, they meet, they love, they make love, pregnant and scared, married and excited, scrambling for jobs and money, getting by, panic attacks . . . random people, biological miracles, no magical properties are infused with the names Mom and Dad. For a moment he considered sneaking in, this urge, to kiss them both on the head, to be close and smell them sleeping like they were his babies. It came and hit and passed, and a minute later he gently pressed the front door closed so that it wouldn't make a sound.

THIS IS NOT THE END

Thirty minutes later James found himself back at Haley Pond. The Moon was big and close and full, and the pond bounced the image right back at the sky, only distorted some—a child making a silly face to a grown-up. James sat, his ass farther up the incline, his now-shoe-less-and-sockless feet digging into the wet grass, feeling the pleasant rumple of the dirt below. Wet leaves glimmered like ornaments as the wind tripped by in quintuple time. James sat and sat. Dink was gone, run off somewhere but, James was sure, within sight. The traffic slowed and spread and disappeared. Night turned into overnight; lights went dark; quiet filled the air. James's butt numbed, and he rolled over on his belly and watched ants navigate monster blades of grass.

The wind died, and James watched the surface of the pond lose its ripples—still and silent, the water laid in its earthen bowl like a pause. James remembered the night when he'd been here before, sitting on the other side of the pond, the urge to dive in, the fear that someone might see; and like that he was on his feet, almost laughing he felt so full. To be alive is to be free and unpredictable. To be alive is to be a god. The thought that he'd once been afraid someone might see seemed like a memory of a child's nighttime fears. He peeled off his jeans and boxers, toppled over and extricated both feet as he writhed on the grass, ecstatic at the sensation of the naked grass on his naked flesh. The back now, the chest, as he pulled off his shirt, scrambling up to his knees and then feet, running, stumbling, down to the pond, last step, the right foot pressed down and out! Arms out, chest out, back bowed, a laugh of disbelief crowed just as he burst through the surface.

Cold! He laughed underwater and drank an accidental mouthful before coming up and shaking his head free like a dog. He dove under again, swimming toward the other side, now corkscrewing, now limp and floating. All nerves activated. He felt the water press his chest, felt it run over his bare ass and between his cheeks, and felt its cold buoyancy against his crotch. It was an alien sensation, one that screamed of freedom and power, and once again he spun through the water, feeling it touch and brush all of him.

Then there was purchase below—ground, mud, the other side—he knew he should probably get out, the fear of getting caught just inching back now, but the greed of pleasure drowned it out as he turned and buried both feet in the mud, pushing back off the other way. He swam hard, ripping through water and kicking for distance, the muscles in his arms and chest stretching and contracting, stretching and contracting, and when he reached the other side he swam up the inclined edge, his feet switching from kicking to running, and shot himself up onto the grass once more. It was only a moment, though, that he lay there breathing. Repose was death; action was the only truth now. James scrambled up with both hands and feet, and he ran. He ran as fast as his legs would stretch out before him, as fast as he could with his wet feet on this wet grass. Along the edge of the pond, the swimming and running starting to set fire to the air in his lungs, he pushed harder—harder!—arms like uneven pistons, leaning out so far he could fall on any step, catching himself. James raced around the pond, and the air rushed the water off his uncovered form, and when he reached the place where his clothes lay in a pile, he dove headfirst and slid across the grass, rolling at the end, coming to a stop on his back. He heaved, and it felt like he was breathing in the whole sky and blowing out the night clouds.

Within a minute, his breathing slowed. Within another minute, the feeling had passed and existed only as a memory. The following minute, he pulled his jeans back on, just in case. That was when the idea struck. James put his shirt and shoes on and jammed his socks in his back pocket, and then he headed off toward the ChocoMalt factory.

James found the door that he and Ezra had used now boarded up with fresh wood. He walked along the building, running his hand along the fifty-year-old brick as the disregarded grass pushed its way under his jeans and brushed his ankles. He didn't want to take his hand away; he could feel the energy of the place in his fingertips, like it was covered in a film of static electricity. There was a hum too, low and steady, though it was something James heard not with his ears but with his insides, with the cavity that held his heart. Maybe it wasn't *life* or *energy* or any other word we have, but James was sure whatever animating magic powered him and Mom and Dorian and stray dogs and old evergreen trees and everything else pulsing with life also resided in this building.

James turned the corner and came upon the broken window he'd looked through the first time he visited this place. Now, though, everything was different. He was different, the place was different, and perhaps most importantly, the light of the full Moon poured through the broken windows like a crashing wave. The massive open space was a carnival of unnatural color. The soft-blue glow of the Moon painted the burnt-orange rust everywhere like underwater Day-Glo, and the remaining exoskeletons and machines and stairs threw deep-black shadows in angled patterns across the floor. It was as if the room contained small black holes.

Using a found chunk of brick, he broke away the remaining glass from the frame and then carefully climbed in. There was a scratch as he swung his left leg inside, and when he looked down, he saw a snag and a small spot of blood.

He remembered the shape he thought he'd seen, and for a second that animating fear was back, directing him—*Out! Now!* He felt a few muscles pull against bones and joints in subconscious allegiance, but James did not move.

He took a breath way, way down into his belly, and as he released that breath, it was as if the fear rode the exhale out. And as it left him he took a step forward, walking to the center of the room, toward the metal exoskeletons which had once supported multi-ton machines and vats, to the wide-open floor where the otherworldly blue glow was brightest, where the tingling in his gut felt strongest. He stopped and stood and breathed, and with each exhale it felt as if this place was breathing in, and when he inhaled it felt as if he was drawing in the factory's exhalations.

He didn't need Ezra; he knew it. *You can hear it. You can feel the path.*

James closed his eyes. James *felt*. He reached out with his mind and—*There*—he felt Taloon, right there. He pushed. It was so natural. He couldn't believe the ease of it, as if he was simply following the path Ezra had cleared for him. It was just like stepping through a waterfall.

James opened his eyes.

This time he was ready for it, and still, the shifting landscape filled him with a whole-body queasiness. His brain seemed to be screaming to the rest of his body; it did not accept this as truth, and that doubling of his consciousness was a sickening roller coaster.

The Moons still hung over the same mountain range he'd seen last time. Is it the same time of day as when I was last here? No, it can't be. James turned, and the landscape shrugged and stuck, as if it were settling into its track. Again he felt the wave of nausea, again what he saw began to shred, and through it he could see the factory. No. James bit back the bile rising in his throat and tried to calm the sensation that the world was spinning. He focused on the land, on the place far off where it met the sky.

The rips mended. Smells filled him.

Water. Salt water. There, on the horizon. An ocean? A sea? It could be something else altogether, something James had never before thought of or seen. Then, at the very moment the thought crossed his mind, the smell turned. It combined and burst: salt water, burning wood, rot, mold.

James pinched his nose shut and swung his gaze around 180 degrees. Once again the landscape seemed to start to move with him before snapping back to position. The other direction, James found, was very different. Way, way off in the distance things were protruding into the sky. James was pretty sure that at least some of them were mountains, but others appeared too thin and flat. Buildings? Towers? James wondered if that was where Mikhael was, where he'd find the Pit.

A prison in the sea. Ezra's words slipped back into James's mind like a friendly nudge. *A prison in the sea.* The smells recombined and intensified. James knew those smells: *The Pit. That's where I'll find him.*

He didn't move, though. He told himself he should at least walk toward the sea, at least look, but even as the conversation played out in his head, he knew he wouldn't. The thought—just the thought—of finally going there, of actually being in that place, hobbled him. As scared as he'd always been in his dreams, as sure as he was that it was waiting for him, it was still on the edge of impossible for him to believe. *How can it be real?*

It isn't.

Like that, Taloon was gone. James stood in the middle of the empty floor of the ChocoMalt factory, a thin layer of sweat covering every millimeter from the top of his scalp to the bottom of his heels. The idea didn't arrive in linear form; it exploded, fully formed. *None of this is real—You're crazy. You're schizophrenic or something—This isn't real—It's all been a hallucination—You're crazy, you're going crazy—Schizophrenia—Hallucinations—Ezra, Dink, the Escalades, them taking you: none of it really happened. None of it. Not them grabbing you or the interrogation or the escape or the man . . .*

The man who smelled like fish and vinegar.

He was real.

James knew that. He saw the man lying in his makeshift grave, blood pouring from his nose, and a quiver of revulsion and guilt racked his spine. The moment passed. For an instant he'd believed it—convinced himself—and it'd been a moment of such terror and relief that, feeling it pass, he was filled up with an urge to collapse and cry right then, simply out of exhaustion.

James reached into his pocket. He bit his lip and pictured his hand coming out with a small ball of dry dirt. He'd squeeze it and it would disintegrate. *Because that's all it is. Dirt. That's all it ever was.* He tried so hard to believe the words.

When he brought out his hand, he held it up and let it fall open. There, still as a ball of dried dirt, was Dink, his legs pulled up to his chest as he sat. Then he blinked. It was an odd mannerism in a homunculus with no discernable eyelids. James wondered if his own psyche could have created a little detail like that.

"What is it?" Dink asked.

But James couldn't answer. He shut his eyes hard and wished—with more power and lust and humility than he'd ever wished for anything—to just be fifteen again, to be someone else, to have time and freedom and a full life without this horrible purpose. He wished to be with Dorian right now, not speaking, just leaning into each other, his hands on her skin. A kiss.

James opened his eyes.

14. The Quest

James made a decision. Whether it was the night before or while he slept that his mind solidified this choice seemingly without him, he couldn't say. The idea of doing it—the moment of actually doing it—was terrifying to imagine but somehow a thousand times better than the constricting anxiety of doing nothing, of lying through omission.

No, this was better. It was.

He was going to tell Dorian everything. Every word of it, from that first morning with the Escalade and the blond man filming him by the tracks, to Ezra and Dink, to them grabbing him, to Old Fish-and-Vinegar in his shallow grave. He was going to tell the story, and if she said he was crazy he'd tell her he understood, and if she screamed at him for lying, he didn't know what he'd do. He supposed he should just show her Dink. But what if Dink refused to un-dirt at the final moment? What if he had some kind of code about no one else seeing? Who knew?

Stop it. Worry about all that later. Just go there now. Go and tell her.

James picked up his phone and dialed her number for the eighth time in the last two days, figuring he would at least leave her a voice mail letting her know he was coming over, but when he put the phone to his ear, there was no ringing. There was nothing. Except . . . there, in the silence. Something. Not breathing, just an awareness. Someone.

"Hello?"

"Hello, James."

"Ezra?"

Dink stood on the dresser.

"It's time, James."

" . . . Can you just stop? I need to think."

"There is nothing to think about."

"I'm, I'm not sure I'm ready right now. Okay?"

"James, you must act now. You must be strong. You must not be a slave to fear and weakness. Do you hear me? Now is the time, while everything is aligned. Who knows what could happen if you delay?"

"I thought you said I was safe."

"You're as safe as we can make you, but the longer you delay, the greater your peril."

James swallowed. He looked at Dink, who peered back like a statue, and he tried to think of things to say, ways to stall Ezra, but his mind filled only with core sensation memories, floating for a moment before popping like bubbles: Dorian laughing, his mother crying in the kitchen years ago, the smell of orange Danish, the Schroeder brothers screaming, the heat as the first Fearless story thrashed in his brain, swimming in Haley Pond, kissing Dorian, the kids cheering for him—pop, pop, pop. All gone. No words. "I need time."

"James—"

"No. I'm not ready." James hit the button and slammed the phone down. He stared at it, waiting for it to ring, for Ezra's muffled voice to issue from the receiver, before finally looking up to Dink. The homunculus said nothing, and James stared into his inscrutable dark eyes, certain that they were alive with judgment. The silence pinched and prodded. "Stop looking at me."

Dink craned toward the window.

"I'm sorry," James said. "I know I should be one of the strong. I'm gonna be. I swear. I just need time."

And then Dink turned back to him. He stepped to the edge of the dresser and said, "The strong?"

"Yeah. Y'know, like there are only two kinds of people—strong and weak."

"Don't say things like that. They make you sound like an asshole."

"What does that mean?"

"Only two kinds of people—the strong and the weak? That's garbage. That's a child's philosophy. Only someone who's never been in battle, never really been in trouble, would say that. I've seen monsters sob, and I've seen little crying nothings lop off heads. Everyone gets crushed at some point—and it's those ones who consider themselves the strong that shit their pants and fold when it finally happens. Do you understand, kid? Don't be strong. Be honest and adaptable. Honest and adaptable are worth a hundred strongs."

"Honest and adaptable."

"Hell yeah."

Honest and adaptable. "Okay." *Honest and adaptable.* "Come on. We're going to Dorian's."

Dink hitched a ride as James walked out. Down the stairs, he had the door open before he heard the throat clear and, turning, saw his parents.

They were sitting on the couch, dressed and ready for the day. Mom smiled, and Dad noticed him and shut off the TV as he sat up. James thought Dad looked tired: baggier under the eyes, hair a little thinner, and his mid-section was starting to develop a paunch of its own. He smiled, and even that looked tired.

"Hey, buddy."

"Hey, Dad, what's up?"

But it was Mom who spoke. She looked as impeccable as ever, with her tiny shoulders and black hair both pulled back. "You know your father and I have been going to couples therapy, of course. Well—"

"Are you guys getting a divorce?"

"No," she blurted, throwing out her thin-boned hands as if to stop it. "God, no."

"No way," Dad said.

"Of course not."

"Yeah, nope. We're good, buddy."

"Yes. Good. Very good."

"Good to go," Dad said, putting his arm around Mom.

And then there was silence for a second or two, into which Mom said, "Of course, there is work to be done."

"Sure," Dad said. "Sure."

"Anyway, we've decided we need to do more family activities." Mom said it to James, but as she did, she turned to Dad and nodded, and he nodded right back. "So today we both made sure we had nothing else on our schedules, and the three of us are going to go and have a great day. I was thinking we could go to the zoo, but your father has also mentioned there's a minor-league baseball game today and he says they're very fun, though I've never been to one, so I'm not sure."

"You've been, right, James? We've been, haven't we?"

"I . . ."

"To a Cougars game?" Dad said before turning to Mom. "They're much more laid-back than a big-league game."

Mom took a deep breath and spoke as if reciting. "I'm more comfortable with things I know and places I've been, which is about control. That's what I'm feeling right now. I'm scared to go to the baseball game because it's different." Deep breath. "But it's okay to feel scared like that, and everything's new until it isn't, so sure, let's go to the baseball game."

Dad smiled. "You're amazing," he said, and they leaned in and kissed quickly and silently.

"I can't."

"What do you mean you can't?" She looked as if someone had asked her to try something new.

"I just, I have something to do. I have to go see someone."

Dad leaned forward. "Who?"

Mom said, "Well, you can reschedule with them. Your father and I have cleared our schedules for today."

"How about tomorrow?" James said. "We can do something tomorrow?"

"Can't tomorrow. Got golf in the morning, and then I gotta put together the end-of-month reports."

"Yes, Josh, we're all busy. Thank you. Now listen, James, we planned today special. It's important."

"I know. And I get it, but there's something I gotta go do. I just . . . I can't."

Dad turned the TV back on, sulking at his wife's rebuke, and she turned from her son to her husband and back, growing more and more upset. "And what if I say that . . ." Deep breath. "James, I'm sorry, but you can't go out now. As your parent, I have to sometimes make tough decisions and do what is right for you. Maybe not always what is fun or popular but what is in your best inter—"

Josh and Ellie Salley sat on their living room sofa with unfocused gazes, their bodies on pause from the last instant they'd been in control. It was easy now, reaching out, and James, unable to stand another second, had pushed out, into them both, and there, inside of them, he was struck by how little he knew of these two. The parts they held for themselves, the parts they gave to others, to each other, the vastness they held back from him. For a second it reminded him of his anger toward Ezra, the anger of being lied to, but that wasn't what it was. What he truly felt was sadness and a new kind of loneliness. He wondered if he would ever really know these people. He wondered if he wanted to.

"Just relax," James said. "Sit here on the couch and watch movies today. Have a nice day." Then he walked to the door and opened it once more before turning back. "Don't worry about me while I'm gone."

James extracted his bike from the garage and pedaled off with religious determination. He reached the end of the block before he slowed down. *Be cool. You're gonna show up sweating like a monster.* He pedaled in slow, easy depressions, coasting between each one, dying with impatience as he forced himself to just *be cool.*

Traffic was light, even for Stone Grove, and James coasted across Main Street with barely a glance each way, continuing down Jackson, cutting waves in the street, letting the air cool the sides of his head, trying to forestall even the lightest sweat, flushing, or funk. *Did I put on deodorant?* He curled his head into his body, burying it in his armpit and sucking great lungfuls through his nose. *Okay. Seems okay. Okay.*

James tried to create some kind of script as he rode. "Hey, Dorian." "Hi." "Hi, Dory."

What if she won't see you?

She will. Just tell her you want to tell her where you were.

What if she's not home?

You wait.

"So I know this sounds crazy. I'm not crazy, okay? Just because crazy things have happened to me doesn't mean I'm crazy."

That's good. Start with something like that.

James turned north onto Orange Street with a weird, new anxiety multiplying within. His cheeks felt hot and his lungs felt cold and he kicked the pedals harder, forgetting completely about being cool. He rode fast and thought of nothing. No plans, no worries. Somewhere deep inside, he knew she would believe him. He would use only words that came straight from the story, and he wouldn't try to make it sound better or prettier, and she would see he was telling the truth. He could already see her visage softening into worry and camaraderie. They'd figure it out together. A team; like *Fearless*.

He leaned hard into the turn onto Adams Avenue, heedless and blinded by a giant lilac shrub. He squinted and tensed, but the street was empty and he continued like a rocket toward Dorian's, coasting around the bend in the road and up her drive, dragging his feet to a full stop. James stepped off the bike and let it clatter to the asphalt, but as he reached the door he noticed it was slightly ajar, and the image, innocuous as it was, sent a shock of belief through him.

Something's wrong.

Summer. Hot. Lots of people left their front doors

open in Stone Grove to let a little air in. There was no reason the sight should have been alarming. And yet.

James reached out and pushed the door open. He leaned forward and placed one foot inside. "Dorian?" All the way inside now, the feeling building to a scream— *Something is wrong!* Through the living room— "Hello?"—and into the kitchen. "Dorian!"

Nothing. He felt Dink clamber onto his shoulder, holding onto his shirt.

"Dorian!"

And then he was at the door to her room, panic holding his hand in place. *Why? What are you afraid of?* The image exploded from his memory—Dorian stretched out on that bathroom floor, washed in her own blood. Turning the knob took a conscious command—head to shoulder to elbow to hand—and the door opened with a single soft creak.

Everything as it should be. The room appeared wholly undisturbed, exactly as it had the one time he'd seen it previously. His eyes searched—nothing. He'd pulled the door halfway shut before he saw it. On the floor: Dorian's gray water bottle from the Hair Bee. It was nothing. Nothing. But there it was, lying on its side with a tiny puddle of water on the wood floor below and another drip falling. It felt to James like a portent of some terrible violence. He tried to shake the thought out of his head as he backed out of the room—*Doesn't make any sense*— until his back touched the far hallway wall. Every part of his conscious mind reported that everything was fine, that there was no reason at all to believe anything was wrong. *Everything's fine. Everything—*

James rushed out of the house, across the walkway until he was standing in the middle of Dorian's front yard. *You have to find her. It's just . . . wrong. Something's wrong, very wrong.*

"Calm."

James turned to the voice, but no one was there.

"Calm down. Shhh. It's okay," the voice said, and then James saw Dink on his shoulder, his hands up and imploring. "Breathe."

James realized all at once that he'd been spinning in place, looking everywhere and nowhere. "I . . ."

"Breathe. Don't speak. Breathe. In through your nose. Out through your mouth."

James continued to drag large empty breaths through his mouth.

"In through your nose."

James heard him and did it, and it was as if the gears finally caught and the machine was running again. Everything else continued to pinball through him, but he no longer felt that he was about to suffocate, and with that relief, his body relaxed—and that was when he saw them.

Across the street, two boys knelt in a yard, drawing. Matching sandy blond hair, maybe ten and seven, heads down as their arms described furious circles on the ground. As James watched, the motions continued without the slightest change of pattern or speed.

His ears reported that Dink was once again speaking to him, but James couldn't tear his focus from the boys—that voice in his head again. *Something's wrong.*

The boys both drew with chalk, absorbed, neither one looked up or paused, even as James stepped onto their driveway. The littler one, he noticed, wasn't even drawing. His hand followed the same shape again and again but uselessly dragged the chalk through the grass off the edge of the driveway.

Wrong. Wrong. Wrong.

"Hey."

Nothing.

Dink was silent now. James saw him in his periphery, rigged, watching the boys—*He can feel it too.*

James stepped closer. "Hey, can I ask you guys something?"

And in unison the boys snapped their heads up, full open faces turned to James. "We didn't see anything," they said in one voice. Dull eyes looked through him, the hands never stopping. Then back down, the tops of their heads, sandy hair and arms frantically spinning.

James's gut went tight and cold.

"Who told you to say that?"

Blank stares up again. A two-boy chorus. "We didn't see anything."

James felt Dink slump on his shoulder, settling into a four-point crouch. James looked at the homunculus, then followed the gaze of those little dark eyes to what the elder boy was drawing over and over on the sidewalk.

Two eyes. Crude. The eye on the left was almost completely filled in by iris, though, while the right eye held only a pinprick.

And seeing it, James realized he knew. He already knew.

His phone rang, and he dug it out of his pocket to see Dorian's name and smiling face.

"Hey, Dorian, where—?"

"James?" Whispered panic. Trembling. "Help. Please. He took me. We're at the factory. I—*no! Get away from—"*

"Dorian? *Dorian!"* But the double beep announced the end of the call. James called her back, but after four rings, her voice mail picked up.

It was Dink who finally spoke. "He's taken the girl."

"Dorian."

"He's taken Dorian."

"To Taloon."

"Yes."

"To force me there."

"Yes."

James lifted his bike from the ground. "He can't make me do anything. You said so. I can choose."

"I doubt it'll be that easy." For a moment neither spoke, and James searched for possibilities, for obstacles, for what could be waiting for him, and he had to admit he was naked and lost. "James, look at me." James turned, and the little man leaned against his jaw so he could look as fully into James's eyes as possible. "You don't have to go there. Asmodis can't make you follow him."

James felt his back curl, his shoulders drooping as the breath left him. *There, Dink, you're wrong.* James knew he had to follow her, and the certainty of this must have played all over his face, because Dink didn't question it again. He squatted into his runner's stance and gripped James's shirt like reins. "Alright, then. Let's get the hell out of here."

James rode over lawns and zigzagged through intersections, declaring himself trump of all stop-sign disputes. He shot through Orange Street, skidding to avoid a collision with a rusty Ford Fiesta, then continued down Oak. In his mind, Dorian screamed for him; she tried to fight off Ezra's hands as he dragged her through; her eyes took in Taloon and were white pools of fear, nothing but tears, and she balled up and whimpered and pleaded for someone, anyone, to save her. James turned hard and rode between houses, over lawns, through the community center parking lot, and then he was flying past George Washington High School, and already it felt like a relic, like a home to a part of his life long-since lost.

He heard the two-note metallic chime of the train signal, saw the flashing lights as the arms descended up ahead, and he slowed, but just as he did his world was filled with the shrieking of tires, and turning he saw the Escalade leaping forward from the parking lot to his left. It swept out, barely missing his back tire, and spun up over the opposite curb on the grass, frozen and perpendicular to the road for a moment.

"Go!" Dink shouted in his ear.

Then he was up and pedaling, racing parallel to the tracks as the Escalade righted itself behind him. James saw the freight train approaching—middle track, westbound, staring him right in the face. *It's too close.*

"Faster, James!"

James heard the engine whine behind him as someone stomped it into the red. The train was terrifying and undeniable, but looking back was worse, and so he charged forward as fast as he could. His shoes gripped the pedals. He pumped and yanked on the handles, using any and every part of himself to make the damn bike go faster. *Faster!*

Fifteen feet from Main Street James looked back and saw the Escalade closing, growing larger. He swerved left hard, preparing for the tight right turn, and heard the Escalade's tires squeal for an instant. *Go, go, go!*

The train looked as big as a house and moved like nature itself. He saw the conductor in the thin glass eye at the top, and when their eyes met, there could be no mistaking James's intention. The train's horn exploded, filling the air with painful sound so that James couldn't even hear himself screaming as he ripped the bike to the right, closing his eyes, the train only feet away as he bump-da-bump-bumped across, and then there was only pavement under the tires and James opened his eyes and swung his head around just in time to see the Escalade make it halfway across the tracks before the nose of the train met its driver's side door. There was a sound like a metal punch as the train continued through, crumpling the Escalade, whose front tires popped out the front bottom as the back end was whipped around by the force. Catching on the end of the track, the vehicle tipped up and over and out of the train's way.

James coasted, staring behind him at the torn metal, a shock of hair and blood visible through a shattered window, and he wondered why it didn't explode, or if it was going to, and if they were dead and if maybe he should do something. He heard a woman shriek and the train's brakes, and he could not look away, which is why he didn't notice when a second Escalade blocked the road in front of him and stopped.

James collided with the hood and pitched up and over the handlebars of his bike. He heard metal give as he landed on the hood, and then there was a sickening upside-down sensation as he slipped off, landing squarely on his forehead.

Doors opened. A sharp, deep-down, first-time-in-his-life pain had a hold of James's right hand, and when he looked down, he saw the first two fingers pointing in new and creative directions. The view, however, was obscured by what felt like sweat running over his brow into his eyes. When his left hand went to his head, it came back with a horrifying smear.

"Grab him!"

It was Adam's voice. James wasn't surprised he remembered it. He figured you probably remembered things like that forever. Then hands had him—hateful, rough hands that felt like they could snap sixteen-year-old bones like kindling. They lifted him, and he saw Adam and another man, both holding short black machine guns with long magazines.

The man next to Adam looked back to the tracks, where a loud squeak announced the train's continued braking. "Oh, Lord, what has he done?"

The man holding him leaned in close and said, "Where's Donny?"

"Later," Adam said. "Get him in the car." It seemed like Adam saw what was happening a fraction of a second before anyone else, but if that was the case, it didn't make much difference. His eyes bloomed with panic, and a single whispered word slipped from his mouth: "Demon."

James felt it then, felt Dink's feet against his clavicle as the homunculus pushed off, launched himself, flying toward Adam, completely extended like a flying squirrel. Adam seemed about to raise his gun, but there was barely time for his fingers to clutch the barrel, and then Dink was on him. He smacked against Adam's chest and climbed up him like fire. The man next to Adam let out a squeal, turning and stepping away from him. Adam released the gun when Dink reached his throat. He grabbed at the homunculus, but it was too late. Dink stretched out his arms as if to deliver a great big hug, and then he plunged his little arms into Adam's throat. All four of them screamed then, James included, and Dink squeezed his evil little hug as tight as he could and twisted like a crocodile, and voila, he was holding Adam's Adam's apple.

There was a gurgle and a spitting sound, and before Adam could fall, Dink threw away the hunk of blood and gristle and flung himself on the other one. Adam screamed as Dink attacked his eyes, his hands attempting to pull the homunculus from his face.

James heard the soft trickle of water on stone and, looking down, realized the man holding him had lost the adult functioning of his bladder. He noticed the hands on him now: shaking, loose.

The other one managed to grab Dink finally, but the homunculus reached back and in one fluid motion peeled off a fingernail, which elicited a horrid, warbling scream. The man dropped Dink, who caught himself on his shirt. It was then that Dink froze, and instead of climbing the man again, he turned to James. His gaze was clear: *Do not wait to be rescued.*

Fear is the mind-killer.

Run.

James twisted his body as hard as he could. He posted his legs, torquing through them, and brought his right elbow around in a purposeful arc until it slammed home, colliding with soft meat and pelvic bone. He flung his head back and felt the dull thwack as it connected with face—nose gave, teeth cut his head, hands released—and then he was running.

His breathing and feet were the only sounds—until he heard the other feet, the harder soles. James looked back and saw the man who'd been holding him—black hair, bloody nose—closing in. He ran much faster than James, and it was impossible to imagine any future in which he didn't catch him within the next thirty feet or so. James blinked through blood, wiped away blood, and saw Moon's Pub just up ahead to his right. He made for the back door with fear as fuel, feeling like he was burning off reserves he'd never known he had.

Please don't be locked.

James ripped open the back door and looked over his shoulder; the man was only ten feet or so behind him.

The bar was much, much darker than the world outside, so it somehow managed to feel both safer and more ominous. He cleared the back room and stumbled into the main room, kicking over two stools as he emerged.

The bartender, a young guy with a Mohawk, saw him first and said, "Hey, kid, you can't be in here."

"Help me! Please! There's a man after me and he's—"

But then the Catholic appeared, and while two men stood up, presumably to do as James had requested, the large, black semiautomatic pistol in the bloody man's hand dissuaded them. They slowly eased back into their seats.

The Catholic spit blood on the floor. "Demon."

"Okay, look, look, I'm not who you think—"

"Shut up!" He held the gun out, adrenaline spike

and bloodlust rocking it with tremors. James backed up, and the Catholic closed the gap. "You will leave this world tonight, demon."

He took another step and leveled the gun straight at James's face. James folded into himself and squinted. He wanted to close his eyes but couldn't bear to look away.

This is—

A hand flashed up and pushed the barrel off and to the right just as the gun discharged. There was a crack and a pop and a little puff of smoke, and the hand turned into an arm and a back as a man thrust himself from the table next to the Catholic. He pinned the gun hand against the bar and head-butted the Catholic—once, twice—and the blood covered both of them as the man twisted the gun hand away from the bar; and when he did, James could see that it was Mr. Zoller, the bus driver, and then Mr. Zoller put his right bicep under the gun hand and snapped the Catholic's wrist and there was a scream and the gun dropped, and James turned and ran out the front door of Moon's Pub.

He ran, and he looked back, and he ran. *Nothing.* He ran past Jackson Street, then doubled back through yards. He stopped between Mr. Taylor's house and the Huangs' house and examined his fingers. There was an awful pressure in them, as if the knuckles were overinflated. He was sure—through no diagnostic or medical knowledge—that he would feel better once they were put to right. The very idea, however, of even touching them filled him with queasy giggles.

Dink had once told James that it wasn't pain that paralyzed people but fear of it. The memory rushed in, bolstering him. *Not pain. Fear of pain. Not pain. Fear of pain. Fear of pain.*

The memory also served to make James clinically aware of the fact that he was alone, that Dink was gone— *The longer you wait, the harder it'll be.*

The truth of the thought zapped his nervous system, and the next moment, without another thought, James grabbed the two fingers and pulled on them, hard. He screamed. He felt knuckle and joint slip together once more and released the fingers and collapsed to his knees in the grass.

Tears filled his eyes as he looked around to check if anyone was there. It was hard to see. The summer sun filled the atmosphere with orange particles of light and hid the rest in shadow.

There was no one.

He chuckled as he stood. *Sometimes it's just pain*, he thought.

James found that he was able to move the fingers, but when he made a fist it felt like there were shims in his knuckles.

Up! Go!

He could see the great abandoned place peeking through the trees, sitting like a careless king. A stitch grabbed his ribs as the breath of overexertion shredded his throat. His chest heaved with fatigue, and he sped up to keep it at bay; he heard only his own desperate breathing and the thwap-thwap of his feet meeting the earth. Then the houses were gone and the way opened and the trees turned into high weeds and crabgrass. James raced across the neglected field that abutted the factory. Just to the south he saw the giant main gates, all brick and wrought iron, closed forever. But they touched nothing. The barriers which had once been connected to them were long gone. James stumbled and almost fell, righting himself as he sidestepped bottles and trash, closing the final ten feet to the building and coming to rest against the ancient brick.

He closed his eyes and let his head fall against the wall. *He was here. I can still feel him.* Then he was moving again, afraid if he stopped he'd pass out right where he stood. To the corner of the building and turning, running for the window he'd climbed through last time, when another presented itself. Ground level, glass long gone, and the board covering it was wet and rotting and split, the bottom corner missing altogether. James turned his shoulder into it, and all but the top left corner came free; then he was up and climbing over the sill.

The little room he dropped into had obviously once been a bathroom, though all the fixtures and pipes were long gone. He found the door hard to budge. A few painful shoulder thrusts cleared it enough for him to squeeze out, and then he was back on the main floor again, though this time he was looking for some way up.

He could feel Ezra still. *Up!*

James saw the stairs off in the back, hidden in the shadows. They were broad stone steps that doubled back on themselves, wide and efficient like high school steps. He stopped at the second floor, but it was empty. It was low-ceilinged, probably an office once. There were no desks now, though; only pillars placed at even intervals and the hard orange glow through the open windows.

Go!

James climbed the stairs—past three and four with barely a glance—and his legs rebelled against the ascent. He stopped at the fifth floor and spun, searching. There had to be some way to—

And then he saw it. In the far corner: metal rungs and rails, the ladder was built into the wall and looked sturdy as a foundation. It disappeared into the ceiling, where it met a closed, square door.

James rushed to the ladder and scrambled up it. His fingers screamed against every requested action, but he ignored them—*Up*—and when he reached the ceiling, he flung the trapdoor open and saw nothing above but the bright sky and the dilapidated ChocoMalt water tower rising over one side; James could make out the words perfectly up close: CHOCOMALT EATS REAGAN'S DICK!!!

Then he was pulling himself up onto the roof, the flat surface covered with the dirt and stone of deterioration. James looked around as if he'd find his old librarian there, waiting. But there was nothing.

No, not nothing. There were footprints. Two sets, one large and one small, heading away from the ladder. James walked slow, picturing the two of them as he stared at the imprints. *That's her. Those are her feet.* The footprints led to the parapet at the north edge of the roof, and for a moment he thought that maybe—but no. He looked over the side and saw nothing below. It was just the footprints. He turned back to them. *This is it. They just stop here.* But James knew why. He knew where they'd gone.

There was something else on the ground, dark in the shadow of the parapet. Letters. James crouched. What was it written in? James touched the words and brought his finger up, and in the sunlight he could see it for what it was.

Red-brown. Iron smell.

Two words: IT'S TIME

The words set his hands to shaking. James closed his eyes and squeezed his fists.

Breathe.

One deep breath in through his nose. Held. Machine-gunned out his mouth. Another deep breath in.

Dorian, up on her tippy-toes, her lips on mine, softly, her gentle breath.

James opened his eyes, and in one great exhale, he saw all the fear rushing out of him. He knew it'd be back, but he felt the change nonetheless. He looked out at Stone Grove, Illinois, and he Pushed; and he felt himself pass through.

15. The War

James's ears reported that he was in Taloon before the rest of him did. The wind was strong, and just after the sound registered, he felt it against his skin and smelled the fragrance of salt water that it carried. He didn't want to open his eyes; he could already picture the maddening shaking of the ground, the wavering of the mountains, the Moon— bigger than it had any right to be, filling the whole sky— moving and crossing itself like three-card monte.

It'll be better this time. It will. Slowly, James opened his eyes.

It was not better.

The familiar landscape met him—the quality of light, the Moons coalescing and splitting, the mountain range of waves—and a terrible hopelessness overtook him. He was sure—there, in that moment—that he had gone as far as he could carry himself. All this time, fighting his own fears and disbelief, fighting Stone Grove and the dreams, and today—her house and the men in the

Escalades and the bar and the blood and all of it—that was his limit. He'd had the strength to push through to Taloon, to chase Ezra this far, but standing here now, faced with the alien desolation of this place, with the prospect of *more*, despair fell from the sky and crushed him on the spot. His legs went and he plopped down on his ass like a clown doing a pratfall.

I can't.

You can't what?

I can't do this.

Do what?

I can't go on.

Not go on. *You're not here to go on. What are you here to do?*

Dorian. I have to find her. I have to bring her back.

Okay. If you're not gonna do that, then just say so.

James shut his eyes tight against the frustration tears building. Stopping now wasn't an option. Turning away wasn't an option. James knew he had to reach Dorian or die, but the idea of just standing left him awash in fatigue and self-pity. He reached into his pocket . . . but there was nothing there. He remembered Dink's leap, and it hit him once more that he was utterly alone, and he wished that someone—anyone—would come and be with him.

Just like that, two men—or men-like things—stood before James. They'd appeared so suddenly that James was too surprised to be shocked. Or maybe he was just too tired. But he looked up at the two with his mouth hanging open and, while he had no way of knowing them or anything about them, he felt absolutely certain they meant him no harm. He had no way of articulating the feeling; to him it just sort of felt as if they radiated an energy of good-naturedness, the way that children sometimes do.

The one on the right was the taller of the two, though he was a few inches shorter than James. He was thin, a gangle of bones and sinew with barely any shoulders to speak of. His head was long and thin as well, and his eyes seemed to be connected by a single hooded brow that, on another face, could easily have given off the impression of malevolence. The other one was short and stocky, like a brick wall made animate, and he only came up to James's chest. Two big, white eyes dominated his wide face, and a mess of black hair adorned him.

"Hello?"

"'Hello,' he says," said the short one.

"What's wrong with that?" said the tall one.

"Oh, nothing. One just expects more, I guess. He being who he is and all."

"'Hello' is a perfectly acceptable way for anyone to begin, regardless of station."

"I suppose," said the short one, though he was clearly unconvinced.

"Think of it this way," said the tall one. "His actual salutation was bringing us here, the stated 'Hello' was merely a follow-up."

"Oh, that's good," said the short one. "Yes, that makes

much more sense."

The two of them turned once more to James and waited.

He looked up into the two smiling, expectant faces and felt the passing seconds fill up with their anticipation. *I don't know what . . .* "Hello," James said again.

"Oh, this is not a good sign at all," said the short one.

"No," said the tall one, "I should say not."

"He seems a bit dull."

"I hope he's not defective."

James found the effort of following the two of them cosmically tiring. As with Ezra, there was the urge to ask a thousand questions at once, all while feeling like a child, slow to grasp that which is clear to everyone else.

"*Hello*," the short one shouted, leaning over him. "*What can we do for you?*"

"Well, Munk, I don't think that's going to help anything."

"How do you know? Now that I think of it, no one ever said anything about the War Bringer other than that he would bring war, right?"

"Right."

James put his hands up, hoping they would just stop, just be quiet for a moment, but they seemed to be settling into a regular rhythm now.

"Perhaps that's all he can do. Perhaps he has the ability to begin the War but nothing else."

"I doubt that highly," said the tall one.

"But what do we know?"

"We know that he is the War Bringer."

"And what else?"

"Nothing."

"Yes, nothing."

"Hm."

"Yes, hm indeed."

James was sure his head would split clear down the center if he heard any more from them. He covered his ears and registered only a dull report of their bickering, but when he looked down, the teeming soil offered no respite. So he looked up, and there—there again!—was the Moon, like an awful nauseating parlor trick, it slipped in and out of focus, trembling in the sky; James felt his bile rising once more.

Stop it!

And the Moon did just that. Just as the thought formed and burst in his mind, the Moon stopped and stuck, stark and strong and settled; it hung in the twilight sky just as perfect as the one he was used to, only larger.

The two man-like things turned slowly. They looked at the Moon for a very, very long time. Then they looked at each other. Then back to the Moon and finally to each other once more.

"Did he do that?" the short one asked.

"I'm fairly certain he did."

"Oh."

"Yes, 'oh,' indeed."

Slowly, they turned back to James.

"Hello," the short one said.

James felt immeasurably better. The settling of the

Moon had done extraordinary things for his internal machinations. Yes, the ground continued to move and the mountains in the distance remained a writhing snake in his periphery, but the stationary Moon seemed to root the world around him into some kind of order.

With a grunt, James pushed himself back up to his feet. "I'm James."

"Oh, yes," said the tall one, "James the War Bringer."

"Just James."

"Yes, just James. Pleased to make your acquaintance, James. I am Nack, and this"—he made a grand flourish toward the short, fat one—"is Munk. We are very pleased to be making your acquaintance."

"Yes, we are," said the short one called Munk. "This is really quite something."

"And—I'm sorry," James said. "Who are you?"

"I . . . am . . . Munk. This . . ."

"No, no, I got that. You're Munk; he's Nack. Got it. But who are you? What are you doing here?"

"That is a difficult question," said Nack.

"Two difficult questions," added Munk.

"Yes, indeed," Nack replied. "I suppose there are a few answers to those questions. Let's go backward, shall we? We are here because this is where we belong. Munk and I are out and about, ranging, spying, plotting, and planning, as we do."

"Not holed up like the others," Munk said. "Out and about."

"And we were doing as we do—if I may be honest, a bit more recreating and biding our time, as we usually do—waiting, waiting, always waiting, for you. We make do; we get by—but no longer. Here you are. And there is the second answer to your second question. We'd found a perfectly flat rock and had been flipping it, seeing which side it would land on and mapping the results, when we felt your presence and, more than that, your exquisite need for company."

"And that was that," Munk said.

"Yes, and then we were here."

"You were just here?" James said.

"Yes," the two said in unison.

James nodded, feeling slow again, but then a thought struck him. "Who are you spying for—or supposed to be spying for?"

"Ah," Nack exhaled and cast his gaze up as if broaching a difficult subject, "I don't know how familiar you are with the, shall we say, politics of the area."

"Let's say not very. All I've been told is there're two sides and everyone's waiting to go to war because it's supposed to bring the Creator back. Or not."

"Pretty much it," Munk said.

"Yes, I'd say that about sums it up," Nack said with a professorial nod. "Anyway, Munk and I were advisors to the higher-ups of these two factions. And so as hostilities built and as the followers of Morning Star were rounded up and incarcerated, leaving those remaining free members to lead a bit of a guerilla resistance, both sides felt it best to have, shall we say, resources in the field."

"That's us," Munk said.

"We were sent out—one of us from Morning Star, one from Metatron—to be their eyes and ears out here in desolation, in the holes and hovels."

"Which of you is with which?"

James's question was met with silence. Munk and Nack looked at each other as two who'd been dreading this very question. They grimaced, then Munk shrugged and looked off toward the Moon, as if he'd just discovered it.

Nack turned up his hands to James. "I must admit, this is a bit embarrassing, but we can't actually remember."

"What?"

"Yes," Nack continued, "you see, we've been out here for so long, and it's just been the two of us. We found each other quickly; I do remember that."

"As do I," Munk said, returning to the conversation.

"And we've been over and over it, but neither of us can remember whose side we originally belonged to. Stories, memories, whose were whose originally. After a time it can be difficult to say. I know for a while we were keeping joint notes, figuring that whenever someone showed up we'd figure it out, and that way either of us would be able to give an accurate report on whichever side. Unfortunately, though, no one ever showed up and asked for a report. Not only that, but whoever is out there has been smart enough to steer clear of us, and so it became apparent that we would have nothing to report even if someone actually did show up."

"That was a tough realization," Munk added.

"Yes. Well, since then we've just sort of been biding our time."

"Waiting for today."

"Yes, waiting for today."

They smiled at James, the kind of smile that pulls one out of the viewer by force. James sensed they were waiting, but for what? He was at an overwhelming loss. He found he had to take a deep, clearing breath and rewind, back to the beginning of this conversation, then earlier, earlier. This place felt like it was filling his mind, rearranging things. *Why are you here? The Pit—No—the Name, the War—No, Dorian. Dorian, Dorian, Dorian . . . Ezra has Dorian.*

"I'm looking for Ezra."

"Hm," Nack said, his face scrunching up into a question. "I don't—"

"Think we know him," Munk continued as they turned toward each other. "At least not by that name."

"No, not by that name. Though we may know him by something else."

What did Dink call him? Azmo? Azotis? Asmodis? Asmodis! "Asmodis! He, uh, he also goes by Asmodis."

"That sounds . . ."

"Familiar."

"Yes, familiar, but I can't place it."

"No, nor can I."

"Still, he sounds important."

"Must be important, if we know the name."

"Yes, that's a very good point."

They turned back to James. "Asmodis sounds important," Nack said, "and if he's important, then they'll know about him at Selliphais."

"Exactly," Munk added with a definitive nod.

"Selliphais?"

"Yes," Nack said, pointing off behind and to the right of James, where the mountains and shapes rose in the distance. "Selliphais is the great metropolis—"

"The last metropolis," Munk said.

"Yes, well, great by virtue of being last."

"And first."

"Yes, and first, but now the last. There used to be many, many communities and groupings and what have you, but that was in a very different time. Now Selliphais is all that is left. But or, rather, *because* it is the last, if you are looking for someone, then that is where you want to go."

James looked off in the direction Nack had pointed. The distant air seemed to quiver like heat off asphalt, and it was hard to judge distance or tell what rose from the ground that far away. Without looking back to them, James asked, "How long will it take to walk there?"

Munk and Nack looked at each other as if they'd been asked a trick question.

"A while," Munk said.

"A great while," Nack added.

Fear is the mind-killer. James made his hands into fists and then let them go, but the tension remained. He saw the Moon hanging majestically in the sky and blew out a deep breath. He pictured Dorian, saw her scared and waiting and begging to be saved, and the rage flooded in and drowned his uncertainty.

"Alright, then. Let's get going."

James began the walk to Selliphais. He didn't know how far away it was or how long it would take him, but he put foot in front of foot and kept his eyes up. Munk and Nack hurried after him.

"Is this Asmodis integral to your war bringing?"

"By the way, great job with the Moon. I like this much better than the way it was."

"Yes, not to pry, but how did you do that?"

James made no response. One foot in front of the other, he continued toward Selliphais, toward Dorian and Ezra.

The three of them walked for hours and hours, and as the time passed, the main thing that became apparent to James was that the time didn't pass. The quality of light remained unchanged. Shadows did not move. The ground on which they were walking shifted slowly, becoming spotted with rocklike structures and large stretches that reminded James of forest floors covered in pine needles, though there were no trees. Off to their right were the mountains. James watched them roll, and it seemed as if they were egging the little band of travelers along. But still, the Moon did not move. It didn't crest or decline; it simply hung just where James had left it.

One foot in front of the other. Over and over. Munk and Nack hung just behind and had not spoken since James failed to answer their first questions. The questions remained, though, and James could not deny, even to himself, that he had stopped the Moon and placed it where it now rested. James peeked up at it out of the corner of his eye. He remembered slowly coming to terms with his powers back in Stone Grove, but this was different. He could feel that. Back there, in his world, he felt the energy as it ran from him to others, from person to person. But here it was different. Here, James felt this power burning and extending like sunshine, like it could extend out and touch everyone and everything.

Before he could follow this path, though, something reached out and snatched his attention. In the distance he saw a dark shape with a flickering light inside it, like a fire in a pointy cave. He turned to Munk and Nack and pointed to the light.

"Is that Selliphais?"

They nodded in unison and James nodded back and kept walking. It appeared small and short. He'd expected so much more.

Some time later, the three happened upon a crudely paved road made of raw stones that rolled and pitched, set at different levels as if by a drunken craftsman. The stones were held together by what looked like dirty mortar. It appeared to be a sludge of sand and rocks and dead vegetation. The stones themselves were only a gathering of semiflat rocks, difficult to traverse, but still it felt good to have this assurance that he was heading in the right direction. They'd been walking for so, so long and his legs were so, so tired, his feet so, so sore, that this road coming when it did was like tangible encouragement.

There is a way. Someone has done it before.

Twice, missteps sent James's foot to its side, sent his weight off and down, but luckily neither resulted in injury. Still, the proximity of disaster set him on edge. What if he'd broken his ankle? What if he couldn't walk? What then? He considered just walking along the side of the road, but this road seemed to have been built for a reason, as the ground along both sides reminded James of images he'd seen of the Moon: every other step a little hill, random holes and valleys everywhere, and still that ground like pine needles sliding underfoot. *No. As bad as the road is, it's definitely better than that.*

After that, James was much more conscious of each step. He watched the ground as he walked, carefully placing each step. This had three major effects:

1) He did not suffer an injury.

2) His pace declined.

3) Boredom snuck in and left a window open, through which the exhaustion James had long kept at bay was able to enter.

In a very short time, James felt certain he would fall asleep. He wondered if they were working up an incline, as their pace appeared to be slowing even more. He became positive that the next step would be his last, that he would simply pitch over asleep the next time his foot touched down. Still, he walked. Sweat oiled his skin as his eyelids droooooped.

"Hey," James said, craning toward Munk, who was walking behind. Munk and Nack had not spoken a single word since their questions had gone unanswered at the beginning of their journey, but James couldn't ignore his tired, bored mind another moment. "How do you think I did that with the Moon?"

Munk pointed to himself to verify that it was he who was being addressed, and when James nodded, he said, "Welllll . . ." He looked over to Nack like an unprepared student. "I, uh, I just assumed—"

"We. We assumed."

"Yes, I should say, we assumed it was because you are the War Bringer. Is that not why?"

"I don't know."

"What do you mean you don't know," Nack said,

drawing even with James. "Of course that's why."

"But why would that make me able to do things like that?"

"Because you're the War Bringer," Munk said, coming up on James's other side.

"Yeah, he said that, but I still don't get it."

"I'm sorry—how can you not *get it*?" Nack said. "You can do that because you are the One. You are bringing the War. Don't you see? The War is everything. Everything. Our whole world is a staging area. We are frozen, and we await one thing: the War. It's simple math. The War is everything. You are the one who will create it; ergo, you can create anything."

"That doesn't make any sense." James sped up as the annoyance worked through him, feeding his blood and waking him once more.

"I have to admit," Munk said, "I'd never thought it through quite like that."

"Okay, okay," James said, "we'll get back to that. Can I ask you guys another question? It seems like you're looking forward to the War."

"Oh, yes," they said as one.

"Very much so," Nack added.

"But why? You don't even know which side you're on."

Munk was silent then. He crossed his arms tight and looked off to the mountains.

Nack went behind James and put his arm around Munk. He whispered something to him, but James couldn't hear it.

"James," Nack said, turning to him, "you are very powerful, and if you choose to destroy me for my insolence, then that's what you'll do, but I must tell you I think it's incredibly rude and, frankly, cruel for you to throw in our faces that which we told you in the strictest confidence and which is obviously a very sensitive subject."

These two were such odd little things, and he'd been so focused on Ezra and Dorian, that until now he'd never really considered them fully. They were obviously much older than him—and they knew more than he did. But there was something unmistakably soft and naïve about them. James realized he'd felt a bit better since the moment they'd arrived, and a quick shock of shame ran through him.

James stopped, and when Munk and Nack noticed, they did the same.

"I'm sorry," James said. "I am really, really sorry. I wasn't thinking and . . . I'm sorry if I hurt your feelings."

Munk turned back and unwound his arms. He nodded his acceptance.

"Thank you," Nack said as the three of them recommenced.

"What I'd meant was, aren't you afraid? I mean, it's a war."

"No, James, we are not afraid. The War will be glorious, and we will win."

The fact that they couldn't remember which side was

whose made it to the top of James's throat, but he killed it.

"It's the reason we exist," Nack continued. "We have waited and waited and waited—"

"And waited!"

"But no more. This War will bring answers and peace. It will bring an end. Our world is frozen in a single moment. It does not move forward; it does not mature. All of existence waits on this one thing."

"Exactly!"

"And now it's here. The War means an end to paralysis and stagnation. It will bring peace—finally, peace! We can all go back to living together, as we used to. Everything can go back to the way it used to be."

"Or better!"

"Right, or better."

"Doesn't that sound wonderful?" Munk said.

But James didn't answer. He nodded, because what he wanted to say was that he was pretty sure that's not how wars worked, but it's never comfortable to dismiss what others are wholly invested in. He felt the eyes of his companions upon him and figured he should say something, but before a response could coalesce, they reached the top of the hill.

James stopped. "What is this?"

"Oh, this?" Munk said. "This is the Great Field. I haven't been here in . . . How long has it been since we were last here?"

"I couldn't say. Maybe . . ."

But James was no longer listening. He felt like he was floating out through his eyes, tasting what lay before him with his vision. He'd only felt this once before, a year earlier, when a van Gogh/Gauguin exhibit had come to the Art Institute and he'd taken the train in on a Saturday and waited in line for an hour and pressed through crowds and listened to boring tour guides, all so he could stand in front of van Gogh's paintings. He hadn't thought he'd care about *Starry Night* as much as some of the others, having seen it so often in life. But there, in front of it, he realized he'd never actually seen it before. James stood directly in front of it, then super close, then a bit away; he sat for a while, then looked at it from the right, then the left. Fifty-two minutes he watched that painting, until he felt that he'd physically affected it by the act of looking, that it had imprinted its own living self on him, that he'd somehow consumed it with his gaze, and he was positive he would never forget it. Ever.

That was how he felt as he stood at the top of this hill in Taloon. The field began just below where the three of them stood. On both sides of the road it sprouted, starting sparsely, until, by the bottom of the hill, the ground was a living sea of color. Lush, green grass with blades as wide as butter knives stood shining like cellophane and swaying in a perpetual breeze that blew in the direction the travelers were walking. Among the grass were wild patches of color: red and orange and yellow and purple. Massive, dazzling flowers burst up, standing taller than

James and dotting as far as he could see. The field spread out in all directions, and in the distance the splashes of color looked like van Gogh's heavy swirls. James heard the grass sssssssshhhhhhh-ing like a far-off ocean. The smell reminded James of lilac and citrus, so fresh it made his stomach growl as well. "Beautiful."

"Yes," Nack said, "isn't it? Obviously, some parts of Taloon are more developed than others."

James hadn't even noticed. Nothing was shifting or sliding. It was all just so.

"This was one of Metatron and Morning Star's favorite places," Nack said. "They took great care in it."

Just then, though, something caught James's eye, something to the right and a little ways off the hill. It was a huge bed of flowers, a liquid crimson like he'd never seen. James stepped from the road, slowly, one foot at a time, and began to descend the hill toward the flowers.

"Uh, excuse me, James," Munk said, "but where are you going?"

His pace quickened with the descent, he was running now, to keep from falling and also to reach the flowers . . . faster . . . faster! It was as if a supernova of flowers exploded from the ground, this deep-red mass, James felt it pulling him—Stop—what was it? He knew that smell, knew that feeling. *Inside those flowers is . . . is . . . Home! That's it. Home! Real home, before all this!* He ran, reaching out his legs and pulling the ground past him. Behind him he heard the echo of someone chasing him, of someone calling after him, but who could pay attention to that? The flowers were a bed; they were sleep itself—*No*—and James knew that if he could just reach them, then he could throw himself into them and they would swallow him up like a blanket—oh, he could feel it already: diving under a giant comforter in a too-cold room, only your face exposed to the cold as the rest of you is blissfully wrapped in your little cocoon—and then he'd wake up, and he'd be home—real home, not the bullshit horror lie that had been invading his mind. *Stop! This is not real!* He'll wake up and Mom and Dad will be there, and Dorian will be home and wonderful, and he'll wake up and it'll be his birthday—*Yes! Do it! Please!*

But then he stopped. Or rather, his feet stopped and he toppled over them. He caught himself, and his hands sank into the soft ground. His face came to rest only inches from the edge of the flowers, and one great crimson blossom hovered less than an inch from the bridge of his nose. Here, close up, the smell was different. James detected a subtler smell underneath the others, high and sickly sweet, like rot.

What stopped you?

James felt his pulse at the edge of his jaw like a threat. *What happened?* He'd given in. Some part of him had been screaming, trying to stop him, but even that last stronghold had given way. He'd accepted it. Somewhere deep down he knew the flowers were death or oblivion, that they were the great erasing, but he'd accepted it all the same. Then why wasn't he lying among the flowers now?

The answer hung at the edges of his mind, just in the periphery, but James did not want to look. He was aware, all at once, that it'd been there for a while. There was a feeling, a churning poison soup within him, which he'd ascribed to his rage over Dorian and his fear of this place, but that he now realized was actually something more. It'd started as soon as he arrived in Taloon but managed to hide amongst all the other trauma.

It was the Pull. Undeniable, now that he recognized it. He turned and looked back the way they'd come and felt the knot within release, if only a fraction. How had he missed it? It was so conspicuous now that he was aware of it. It wanted him to turn around and go back. It wanted him to go to the Pit.

That's what stopped him.

Someone shook up the can of shame within and popped the top. He'd been willing to quit, to chuck himself into the rapture of fantastical nothingness, and why? Because he was tired and scared and hurt.

James looked back at Munk and Nack, who seemed more confused than concerned. *It wasn't me who stopped me.* James figured at first that it was his subconscious, but he could feel the difference now, feel what a lie that was. It wasn't his subconscious; it was *their* subconscious—it was the multiconsciousness. It was the terrible purpose put inside him by the consciousness of others. James, however, didn't care about that at the moment. No, his thoughts veered in one particular direction.

It took less than a day for me to fail her. James crushed the soft ground between his fingers and stared into the Great Field of Dreaming, and there, only ten feet or so from where he knelt, was a leg. It was a sleeper. James was sure the instant he saw it. He stood then and searched, remembering what Dink had said. A little ways off to the left he saw an arm, thin and long, its hand clenched in a fist. Dink said they went in there to dream of our world but some got lost forever, and he felt the cold swirl of fear in his belly. *Almost.*

But you didn't. You're still here, and Ezra and Dorian are still in Selliphais.

I don't care.

Stand up.

Please—I'm so tired.

Stand. Up.

Please . . .

What about Dorian?

If you took all the sighs that James had ever sighed, from every bedtime and bath time and homework assignment and forced vegetable and disappointment and broken heart, they would not equal the sigh he gave up to the world as he pushed himself to his feet and turned to face Munk and Nack. James walked by them without a word, kicking through the tall grass and flowers, across the field and back to the road, with the pair of them following, quiet as a courtroom.

THIS IS NOT THE END

Later, James could not deny that the blisters on his feet had burst. The road remained a treacherous orgy of misshapen stones, and whenever the way beside it cleared they walked next to the road, but for the most part they were required to traverse its pockmarked surface. Selliphais loomed in the distance, short and squat and still resembling a campfire burning in a dark, dark cave, but now the flame burned brighter and the cave looked like ink-soaked coal.

The three of them had not spoken since the incident at the Great Field of Dreaming, which was perfectly alright with James. His near dream-suicide did wonders for his energy, and he found that the terror of the memory kept sleepiness at bay quite nicely.

So they walked. James watched his steps carefully, but the odd angles of pressure created blisters in places James had never before experienced. A little one grew up on the side of his second toe, while one was born and burst high on the back of his foot by his Achilles heel. An especially egregious blister flexed on his right heel. He could feel the shift and liquid of it with each step. Then his right foot lost its purchase on one rock and slid to the side, tearing open the blister, and for an instant his entire foot felt like something else altogether. There was warmth and relief and moisture, but the pain followed, and he felt an odd sensation—happy that it was gone, but sort of missing it, and scared to walk on the paper trail of dead skin, the dirty liquid of healing, and the raw, naked birth-skin below. Of course, he didn't say any of that at the moment it actually happened. He said, "Ghah! Fuuuaaah!" Then he sat down hard at the edge of the road and pulled off his shoe and sock.

James stared at the mess that was his foot with an amazed revulsion. It was pink, marbled with red, and slick to the touch. James pulled off the matching shoe and sock and saw an appendage very much the same.

"Are you alright?" one of his companions asked, though James didn't look up to see who.

"Do I look—?" James caught himself. "No. I'm not. How much farther is this place?"

"Oh, far. Very, very far."

James dropped his head in his hands and let his breath leak out like surrender. *Now what? Crawl?* He ground his knuckles into his closed eyes until starbursts played across the black screen. *I'm so tired, so tired.*

James was sure that he would cry any moment, and so he continued pressing hard circles into his eyes.

"Why would somebody build a shitty . . . stupid . . . shitty road like this?"

"Does the road not please you, James?"

James's head came up as soon as he heard the words. Munk's wide face smiled down at him.

"What did you say?"

"Does the road not please you?"

James fought off the weight of the thought—half un-believable and half so-damn-obvious it made him want to cry. He looked down the road toward Selliphais, and he saw the way as clear of stones altogether, and in its place smooth white concrete, broken every four feet or so by clean lines . . . and so it was.

A small, proud smile crept up on James, along with an urge to smack his forehead rather hard. *Of course, moron.*

"Oooooohhhhh," Munk and Nack sang in unison as they looked at a perfect re-creation of the sidewalk which lined the south side of Jackson Street in Stone Grove, Illinois.

James looked back to his feet. This, somehow, seemed more daunting. It was not the flexing and molding of a world whose existence he wasn't even aware of a month ago, a world which often felt like a dreamscape anyway. No, this was the manipulation of his own, cherished, very-very-real self. A cold swell of fear took root in his bowels, but James said his mantra—quietly, slowly—to himself. He spread both of his feet out before him and saw them healed . . . and so it was.

Then he laughed. His feet hadn't healed, per se. He had not felt any healing, as he'd expected, any kind of warmth or knitting together of skin. Rather, they were torn up, and then they were not.

He made his hand into a fist, flexing and unflexing, savoring the bliss that comes from the fresh absence of pain. The previously dislocated fingers felt newborn.

James kicked his shoes and socks aside and stood up.

He stepped back onto the road—or rather, onto the sidewalk for the first time—and peered at Selliphais. Dorian. Ezra. Selliphais looked to James as if it might be another day or two away, though who could tell what a day was here? Who could say how long they'd been walking already?

Time to go. "Come on," James said, taking a single step. But then he stopped, right foot forward, left back, as though he'd been dipped in ice. Slowly—so, so slowly—he turned until he was facing Munk and Nack. His mouth open, brow down, James could tell he was wearing the realization on his face. "We don't have to walk, do we?"

Munk and Nack looked at each other for a moment. James's tone could not be misconstrued, and so it was not wholly without trepidation that Nack said, "Well . . . no."

"We thought you wanted to walk," Munk said.

"For some reason."

"Yes, we assumed you knew better than us."

"Being the War Bringer."

"Right."

"Though it seemed very difficult."

"And you did seem very unhappy."

The annoyance burning through him was doused by his relief. There was a part of him that very much wanted to scream, to rant and stomp and berate his two fellow travelers, but it wasn't as strong as the gratitude he felt in knowing he wouldn't have to walk anymore. "I was alone when I arrived here," James said. "But I didn't want to be. I wanted someone to come and help me. Did you feel that?"

"Yes," Munk said. "Sort of."

"Yes, exactly. Sort of."

"What does 'Sort of' mean?" James said.

"I'm not totally sure," Nack said. "I'd never felt anything like it before. I felt almost like I was . . . plucked."

"Yes, that's a very good word for it. I was with Nack and we were playing a game, and then all at once I heard you and felt you, and it was almost like you reached out and closed your hand around me—"

"Us."

"Us. Yes, of course, us. Like it closed around us and deposited us here or, rather, back there, with you."

"So you didn't walk or fly or anything like that to reach me?"

"Well, as Munk said, it didn't feel as if we had much say in the method of transportation. But even if we had, no, we would not have walked. We don't enjoy walking as much as you do."

"I don't—" James closed his eyes. He took a deep breath; he did not strangle his companions. "How do you get around?"

"Hm." Nack twisted his mouth, as if the question itself confused him. He looked to Munk, whose shoulders described an almost imperceptible shrug. "I don't know exactly . . ."

"You just *be* somewhere else."

"Yes, I suppose that's as good a way as any to say it. You are here—"

"Or anywhere."

"Yes, or anywhere, and then you simply choose to be somewhere else."

"Yes, that's it."

James nodded toward Selliphais. "So all we have to do is decide to be there and we'll be there?"

"Mm-hm," his fellow travelers said in unison.

"Okay." James closed his eyes. He was pretty sure it wasn't necessary, but he felt better doing so. "C'mon." He pictured the short little building they called a tower, the pointy dark cave-looking thingy with the fire in its mouth, and he felt something not wholly unlike the sensation he'd experienced when he passed from his world to this one. It was less so, but it was definitely a sensation of atmosphere change, of transformation. Then James opened his eyes, and what he saw sucked the air from his lungs.

He stood at the edge of a suicide cliff, with Munk and Nack close behind. He'd visited the Grand Canyon once, when he was seven, and in his memory it was a transformative sight of endless depth. How could any *thing* be so *much*? He remembered looking down into the Canyon, feeling enormity that existed outside of himself. Now the feeling returned and was jacked up by the perversity of what lay before him. It couldn't be called a gorge, because there was no other side. The cliff dropped off, maybe as deep as the Canyon, maybe deeper. Vertigo swam up inside James, and he took a step back from the edge; but his eyes never left the tower. It was . . .

impossible. What James had taken for some squat building or cave was actually the top. The tower itself began
thousands and thousands of feet down. It was, simply
put, the tallest structure he'd ever seen, in life or dreams.
It was obscene and powerful—terrifying in its immensity.
It rose, blacker than any structure he'd ever seen, up and
up and up, to two cruel pinnacles, like an iron crown,
and between them burned the dim, red flame James had
seen from the road.

James felt power; he felt he was in the presence of
the impossible, of the magical and magnificent, and his
silence in the face of that seemed, at that moment, like an
affront, like space that demanded to be filled.

"Holy crap."

Then he heard someone clear their throat.

James turned to see a small group forming. All
around, as far as a couple hundred yards back from the
cliff's edge, the ground swelled into little points. It looked
to James as if the land had been somehow formed into
tents. From these, manlike beings were emerging. They
walked toward James and his companions, slowly, unsure
but gaining confidence as their numbers swelled.

They were so different from each other. That was
what really struck James. Humans, for the most part,
have such slight differences. Their colors basically range
across beiges and browns, including only hints of other
hues, while their heights and weights stick to a basic scale.
The thinnest and fattest people on Earth did not have

half the differences of some of the beings walking toward them now. There were men who were eight or nine feet tall, with skin that appeared scaled or armored. There were short things, round as balls, who moved without any legs that James could make out. A few could have easily passed for regular humans, while others appeared to be only distant cousins of humans, the way that apes are. Some were definitely male, a few female, others impossible to distinguish.

A tall, powerful-looking man stepped from the crowd. His dark brown eyes opened wide as his black hair blew over his shoulders. "Are you he?"

"He is," Munk and Nack called back at once.

The man stepped closer, looking at James the way James had looked at Starry Night. James felt the tingling blush of being examined. He tried to meet the man's eyes, but doing so only intensified the blush.

When the man had crept up to less than a foot from the three of them, still gazing into James's face like a long-lost love, he whispered, "Are you really he? The War Bringer?"

"Yes," James said. He could feel every set of eyes gazing at him, every ear straining to hear his words. If comic books had taught him anything, it was the importance of moments like this. "Yes," he said, louder now. "I am James, the War Bringer. I came here because I am looking for Ezra, who you call Asmodis."

But they were barely listening to that last bit. They

were visibly giddy, bouncing from foot to foot like people waiting in line for a bathroom. Smiles turned faces and spread with whispers, and heads ducked back into domiciles, presumably to share the info with others hidden within.

The tall man seemed to swell before James. He held his hands out, as if to present an invisible gift, and said, "I am Gabrael. I am honored that you have appeared to us here first."

"Well, actually," Nack began.

Gabrael's hand slashed the air and James's companion was silent. "I'm sorry," Gabrael said, addressing James. "One moment please." He turned sharply, facing Munk and Nack. "Munk, it has been a long time. Many of us thought you long-since lost. It is a good omen that you have returned to us along with the War Bringer."

"Really?" Munk said.

"Hm," Nack added, before turning to Munk. "I always sort of assumed . . ."

"Yes, me too. But it does seem familiar . . ."

"Uri!" Gabrael shouted. "Remi!"

Two masses detached from the crowd and made their way over. Uri was a squat being whose arms hung so far forward that it seemed as if he might be more comfortable on all fours, and his face had the pinched triangular shape of a jackal's, while Remi looked like George Mikan. "Take hold of the enemy spy, if you will."

Almost as soon as the words were out, they were upon Nack. They grasped an arm and a leg apiece and held him, dangling only a few inches above the ground. Then they began to walk backward slowly, like movers negotiating a thin hallway.

"Now," Gabrael said, turning back to James, "we will feast and rejoice, and then you may watch us drill. If I may say so myself, we are very, very good at drilling. We have been at it for a very long time. And tomorrow you shall descend to the tower so that you may—"

"Whoa, whoa, whoa, hang on," James said. "Stop."

But Uri and Remi continued to creep away, with Nack in tow.

"You two, there—stop!"

Uri and Remi froze, along with Munk and Gabrael and the entirety of the crowd and the mountains in the distance.

James let out a deep breath, and the mountains began once more to roll and the crowd resumed buzzing, though the tone had shifted. A note of fear rang in the new chord.

"Let him go."

Uri and Remi looked from their prisoner to James and then to Gabrael.

Gabrael cleared his throat and tried to force a smile, an unquestioned leader unused to politics. "Uh, I'm sorry; this, uh . . . You must understand, he is an enemy of all. He is a spy for the adversary."

"I don't care. He's my friend."

"If you would only—"

"Let. Him. Go."

This time the two holding Nack released him without checking with Gabrael, whose eyes flashed with indignant rage before he was able to film them over. He motioned away with his head and Uri and Remi appeared only too happy to retreat into the crowd. Nack, on the other hand, was enjoying his moment all alone. A big, chocolate-cake smile spread over his face as he puffed out his chest and looked over the crowd. It was impossible to miss the pride pouring out of him.

Gabrael looked down, each hand working the other as if in a fight. "War Bringer, if you would—"

"My name is James, and I'm not interested in feasts or dancing or anything else. I need to find Ezra, and I'm thinking I'm gonna need to talk to Mikhael to do that. I'm also thinking that Mikhael is in that big ugly tower right there, so if it's all the same to you, me and my friends are gonna get going. Okay?"

James realized Gabrael's joy at meeting him had lasted all of one minute. The eyes that looked at him now were full of outrage and disappointment and reproach. James wondered if this was what it was like when people met their idols and found out they were assholes.

"Very well," Gabrael said, without separating his jaws.

"Now, is there anything you need me to do? Or do you, like, need to tell anyone that I'm coming?"

Gabrael extended his arm like a host directing a party to their table. His gaze was angry and petty, and James could tell someone was going to pay for the way this had gone. He had a feeling it would be Uri and Remi. James looked back to where Gabrael was directing him, down, down, down to the bottom of the tower, where, he assumed, he'd find the front door.

"No need," Gabrael said. "He's expecting you."

James, Munk, and Nack stood at the base of the tower. They craned their necks to look up, but it was so tall even that wouldn't do, so they wrenched their spines backward as well, looking uuuuuuuup to the top, where the edifice seemed to disappear into the sky. The only evidence that it really ended was the dull red glow. And there, before them, a small door stood open, displaying only darkness.

James turned to his companions. "I guess—"

"Yes," Nack said, "we should probably wait here."

"Yes," Munk said, "definitely."

"Metatron does not see ones such as us."

"Uh-uh."

James wanted to hug them. He felt he should thank them and say good-bye, but the idea of another good-bye created a deep sucking space in his chest, and instead he said, "Don't leave, okay?" There was a jab of shame, the realization of what a child he sounded like just then, but he didn't care. "Wait for me."

"Of course," Munk said, and his smile added that it had been unnecessary to ask.

"Of course we'll be here."

"Right here."

"Okay," James said. "I'll be back."

James crossed to the tower quickly, afraid that if he slowed or gave it any thought he would stop, rush back to Munk and Nack and try to find some alternative to what he knew he had to do. And then he was there, at the door, breath like a paddleball off his shallow lungs, and still he could see nothing of the darkness within. It wasn't even that dark; it was more like standing amidst fog at night, the small traces of light diffused by the air itself. James looked back, and when they saw him, Munk and Nack smiled and waved. James turned to the door and stepped through.

The atmosphere was different inside. It looked and acted like fog but felt as dry as old sand. James swiped his hand through the air, but there was no reaction. Nothing was altered; the only movement was his.

And then he was falling. Or at least it felt like he was falling: the sensation of dropping, his guts bumping against the ceiling, and that ticklish tingle under the balls—but by the time he girded himself, it was over. Again he was still. But now light lay over everything, and he could see he was in a small and bare circular room. James saw an open window off to his right and stumbled to it, his mind momentarily offline as his senses held caucus behind the scenes. His popped ears, his groin, the calculations of his brain all reported the same thing: he dropped. Why then did his eyes claim that out the window he could see the gigantic, whole-sky Moon, the rolling hills in the distance, and the camp of Gabrael and his followers? Some still stood about, and he noticed a few hands raised, fingers pointing up at him as he gazed out the window. He backed away, into the center of the room, and the ache in his belly screeched. The Pull, the Pull, back to the Pit, it was there all the time, reminding, cajoling. There were things to do here. He could feel that, could feel Taloon wrapping itself around him like a blanket. And when he tried to push back, Taloon seemed to drop away for an instant and his old life filled his mind. *The smell of Dorian, the pen in his hand, diving into the pond at night, Dorian's room, Dorian gone . . . Ezra.*

James saw a hallway to his left. He eased over to it, wary of the window as if there were snipers outside. Then he was into the hallway, and the light from outside melted behind him. The hallway was dim but not dark. It looked, in fact, to be illuminated by hanging torches, like a castle, but all James could see was the flickering warm light itself; no source.

He thought at first that there was another doorway at the end of the hall, but as he approached, he saw that it wasn't a doorway at all. It appeared to James like a blank, black screen. It was a perfect circle and only a bit smaller than James. It looked like a mirror someone had painted black. Except—no—there was no black like that. It was blacker than anything he'd ever seen. It was an absence of light so powerful that it implied depth, as if you could fall into it.

Then a voice came from the circle. It was high-pitched and nasally but soft and full of sly humor. James felt his insides swirl and lock; had he lived a thousand years in the belly of a sarlacc, he would never mistake it for a moment: Mom.

"We are Bahamut."

The perversion of her voice—that voice which had cooed over sick-bed honey tea and called him down to dinner—in this thing, it created a physiological rebellion. He thought for a moment that he would retch, but all that came up was anger. "Don't."

"We thought it would be pleasant to hear a voice from your world."

"Then pick another."

"Very well. Is this preferable?" Bahamut said, and it was a moment before James was able to place the voice: Barack Obama.

"Yes."

"Good."

"I'm here to see Mikhael."

"Who are you?'

"I'm . . . James."

"No."

"What?"

"No."

"What do you mean no?"

"Who are you?"

"I told you; I'm James. James Salley. I'm the War Bringer."

"You are James Lovie Salley in another world. We know this. Here you are called the War Bringer, though you have not yet brought War. These are just words. In another world, you would be called something else. That is not the answer. Who are you?"

"I'm the One."

"Do you wish to hear Barack Obama laugh?"

"I don't know what you want me to say."

"Who are you?"

For a moment James considered asking it to switch back to his mother's voice. He wanted to tell her what was happening. Maybe she'd know what to tell this thing. But that would just be a lie, too, he thought, feeling his exhaustion ride this frustration back in. His eyes went hot and full.

"I don't know."

"Come closer," the thing called Bahamut said. "Let us see."

The thought occurred to James that he could turn and run, down the hallway and back down the tower—somehow—and then out to Munk and Nack. But the very act of thinking it illustrated the impossibility. The way was burned. The only exit was through. For the first time he felt the freedom only the truly desperate ever know, and he took two steps toward Bahamut, toward that darkness, pure and deep.

"Who am I?"

"Place your hands on us," it said, "and we shall find out together."

James stepped forward and felt a rush of terror— *What if I'm rotten? What if I'm the Nothing?*—but then his hands touched the mirror and he felt his feet pulled from the ground. It was as if the surface of the mirror became a liquid, a whirlpool pulling him in and down, until he could feel that he was gone, wholly within the thing called Bahamut, floating in nothing.

I'm falling, again. And then I . . . I slip out of myself. I picture edamame slipping out of its shell, and I laugh, because this can't be possible: I'm so free. Nothing holds me— but when I look down I see myself . . . falling—I see myself walking through my life, hiding from Nick, running away. I see my drawings and the shameful ones I tear up into tiny pieces and throw out in multiple trash cans so they can't be pieced together. I see me running away and hiding. This isn't me. It is, but it isn't. I'm outside of myself, seeing myself as a separate thing, a being, a human child who creates his own world in ways that make sense only to him. I watch as I kiss Dorian, but I don't feel the slightest rise in my cheeks. That's something someone else would feel. I'm just thought now— and the fear is gone! I'm free . . . no, not free.

There's the Pull, stronger than anything, and I'm moving away, leaving myself just as I discover Dorian gone, watching myself racing away on my bike, and then that me is gone, and I'm flying—but not—no, not flying, just being. I am mobile thought, hovering over Taloon, above the tower where I fell into Bahamut. Then I'm moving again, a cosmic rocket across the sky, and there's the sea—the Pit!—and I'm gone, up and circling the Moon, but there's nothing else, no space, nothing, like the unfinished edge of a painting. A tug in my belly—but you don't have a belly anymore. I laugh, descending at Mach 3, down, down to where I first appeared in this world—but instead of hitting the ground there's the sensation of passing through the surface of water and I'm still going, but now it's up and up from the roof of the ChocoMalt factory, and I look back to see Stone Grove turn into Illinois and landscapes become lines and shapes. I scream. I have no mouth, no lungs, but I scream—my very I screams, "What's happening?"

Bahamut's voice, the soothing layering of multiple Barack Obamas, replies, "We are riding the rail which cannot be seen."

Up! I reach the edge of space. Blue and black melt together—and then I'm speeding down once more, aflame like a craft on reentry, and just as impact should evaporate or wake me, I am elsewhere. Where? I can't say. Another realm?

"Another plane," Bahamut whispers.

The ground is flat and lined, colors hopping—and I realize it's a chessboard, but then I've zipped into a tree and I come out in a quiet clearing in the woods, and all around are small pools. They're larger than puddles but smaller than ponds, and one screams to me and I dive into it, and then I feel as if I'm hanging from the ceiling, alive somehow in an upside-down world, and there before me are women.

Beautiful women made of light, gowns like milk and smoke procreated, dancing, swaying, on what I'm pretty sure are clouds—but I've let go, dropped straight through the clouds and come out once again in the void, floating in the nothing.

All around me then, a dazzling carnival light explosion, and different planes begin to cycle by, each different. I see one world made wholly of fire, but then a section of flame turns to me, and I realize it can see me and all the fire is not the fire I know at all.

Then I see my world again, but it expands as I shrink, as I disappear into a particle of water in the ocean, and within it there is a massive realm of hundreds of planets circling a trio of suns. Next I see two realms tied to each other like a double helix, and when the life in one falls asleep it awakens in the other, and so on, so that each lives when the other dreams. From that one came my world—My home! Yes, I feel it again! That one is mine!—but I'm pulled away, and once again I float at the edge of space, but then up and out, too fast for even the imagination.

I float by the Sun and see the tendrils of fire leap off it, each one a world ender. But then away again. To the edge of the solar system, so that the perfect dance of matter around the Sun plays out before me.

"Who are you?" says Bahamut.

Pop! The galaxy exists all around me, and I can see plainly that our solar system is lost in the cluster of others—millions of stars like the Sun tumble like dust in a windstorm. Pop! Our galaxy roils in space. It is a beach, and every star is a grain of sand; and everywhere I look there are other beaches. Galaxies on top of galaxies on top of galaxies. I fly. I move faster than the idea of light, and past me rush the other galaxies, and I see that while each sun in our galaxy was a grain of sand on a beach, so each galaxy is a grain of sand on the beach of all this. I ache. This is too much. It's all . . . crushing me. But I only speed up—faster and faster—until I reach the edge of the universe.

The light diffuses, the lines coalesce and tighten, and then I'm passing through it, the same passing-through-liquid as before, and then I'm free of it. It was so overwhelming, so massive and awful in its unknowable enormity—No! I look, and there, everywhere, are universes. More than there were stars or galaxies, there are universes, millions on top of billions. Then, all at once, the lights start. Little at first, then growing brighter, and I can see that each light is another realm, and within the billions of universes are billions of planes of existence—and I scream.

Again I hear Bahamut: "Who are you?"

"I'm nothing!" I scream. I howl. "I'm nothing! I'm nothing! I'm nothing!"

James opened his eyes to find himself kneeling in a dim, circular room. He wasn't hurt or sweating or out of breath or anything. In fact, other than a slight tremor working his lower mandible, he felt fine. Except for that feeling dissipating in his head—an echo of terror, like waking up from a nightmare you can't remember.

This room was much like the one he'd just left. He looked

behind and saw Bahamut, black and vacant and silent.

"You have passed through, War Bringer," a voice said.

James lifted his head and saw, sitting by a small, open window, the most perfect and beautiful man he'd ever seen. The man was bald, with large eyes and a pronounced triangle of a nose. He was larger than Gabrael, maybe ten feet tall, and as James looked at him, he suddenly understood how some people could look like royalty. This man felt as if he were owed your allegiance, just by virtue of his existence.

"What did he tell you?"

"What?" James said.

"Bahamut. What did he tell you?"

James searched his brain. For a second he couldn't remember who Bahamut was or what he'd been told, so entranced was he with the powerful giant. "That I'm nothing."

"Pay him no mind. You are everything."

A pause ensued, and so James said, "Thanks."

"For instance," the giant added, returning his attention out the window, "I've been sitting here for quite some time, admiring your handiwork. The Moon, if I may say so, a grand improvement."

"Thanks. It was kinda bugging me."

"Oh, I understand. It has *bugged*, as you say, all of us for quite some time. It was Morning Star who placed it. Shoddy work. A difficult task, of course, but still."

James pushed himself up to his feet. "You're Mikhael."

"I am!" The giant leapt from his seat and rushed across the floor to James. He took both of James's hands in his own—an eclipse that made James seem like an amputee—and looked into James's eyes as if they were more than just eyes. James could feel Mikhael pouring himself out, could feel the intended conversation, but if there were specifics, James wasn't getting them. What he did get was the desperate hope and joy of Mikhael's wild gaze. He knew a dam was about to burst, and all of Mikhael's dreams and plans would come crashing out with the weight of the millennia he had waited. The hands, big as snowshoes, gripped tighter, as something like ecstasy passed over Mikhael's face.

"Please allow me to welcome you to Taloon. In the Creator's absence, I am the most appropriate, as I have the honor of being Taloon's senior resident—along with Morning Star, of course." Mikhael pulled James closer, leaning down and filling the gap between them with conspiratorial energy, a sense that something momentous was at hand.

There's something else. This isn't why you're here, is it? Something . . .

"I have waited so long for this day," Mikhael said. "And now that it is here, I feel—"

"Dorian!"

Mikhael's brow darted down, his nose puckered, and his lips folded up, drawing all his features to the center of his face.

"I'm looking for Dor—for Ezra," James said. "Asmodis."

Mikhael released James's hands and strode a few paces away. He considered James as one would an engine that's just begun emitting blue smoke. "Why?"

"I need to find him."

"So you say. But why? Surely you can't believe he is your friend? Your ally? Look," Mikhael said, leaping to the window and thrusting his arm out to the Moon. "Look what you can do. You don't need him. You don't need anyone."

James opened his mouth to speak, but Mikhael helicoptered his arms and continued, his voice rising, "This world has long been formed by impressions, by thoughts and perceptions and whims. When the Creator gave license to Morning Star and me, he gave us a blank canvas and said, 'Here. Create. Do what you will.' And we did. To the best of our ability, we strung this world together, painting with our minds until it breathed and ran with beasts and life and beauty. But surely you can tell it's an unfinished world. It has none of the perfection of your world—that world which was obviously made by the deft hand of the one and true Creator. Your world speaks with such complexity and simplicity. It is billions of moving pieces but all moving according to those magical rules—physics.

"Oh, you're surprised I know so much? Don't be! As I said, I adore your world. It is an exquisite work of art, while Taloon, alas, is but the sketchings of an amateur. It was designed not in the stone that the Creator works in but instead carved in smoke upon the air.

"Just look at the Moon you found when you arrived. It had been one of our greatest triumphs to that point. Morning Star was so proud of it, but a fixed position was never truly determined. And of course, nothing as regal as the orbits governed by gravity that you see in your world.

"Morning Star always secretly blamed me, I think, for not truly believing in the spot in the sky we'd agreed upon. The accusation was that while intellectually I may have gone along, in that deep, honest place inside where all great creation comes from, I had reservations. The others, when they arrived, slowly at first and then all at once, they noticed the Moon's lack of conviction as well, and it grated on them. They spoke of it, checking always to see where the Moon was now, where now. Morning Star was somewhere beyond upset, sure that now that so much consciousness believed the Moon to be unstable it would be impossible to right it. And, until you came, that seemed correct. But look. Look! Just like that you've set it to right. Amazing? Impossible? No, no I've long thought on this, wondering what you would be like. Who you would be. And then, sitting here looking at our new and majestic Moon, it occurred to me. You are what we made you.

"So you see, you don't need Ezra, as you call him. I understand, he was there with you on the other side. I'm sure he filled your head with all kinds of doggerel. Of course he did. Flimflam. Oh, if there's one thing that really enrages me it is the way they have co-opted you, co-opted your image. They believe you are theirs. This is absurd. They believe you are on their side, the one who will free Morning Star, but they fail to see that freeing Morning Star completes the prophecy and begins the War, thereby bringing about the return of the Creator, which, of course, means you are actually on our side. Not only are you on our side—to use such crude terminology— you *are* our side. You are the culmination of us. And when the Creator sees what we've become, when It sees how we've crushed Its enemies—those who would doubt and offend—It will return to us. It will fold us all in Its loving embrace. And I, for one, cannot wait."

"Wait," James said, "wait, wait." James rubbed his tight-shut eyes. He tried to slow everything down, quiet everything. But as he managed to quiet Mikhael and clear away his voice, it was not Ezra who filled the space but Bahamut. James heard the words again. He heard them again and again and again, like a staggered chorus.

James looked to Mikhael.

The giant leaned forward, askew, like a runner backing into the starting block. He eyed James. It was obvious that he wanted to continue, that he had so much more to say. But in that moment Mikhael's speech felt like a wormed hook, and as he made to open his mouth again, James held up a hand and stifled him.

Breathe. The more he talks the further you get from the truth—your truth. Back to Stone Grove. Why are you here? Ezra. Right. Ezra. Find Ezra. Find Dorian. Bring Dorian home. What about Ezra? Get out of here. Get away from this, this . . . What is he? And before James knew it, he felt his inquisitiveness reaching out once again, splashing down in the mind of this giant. He felt Mikhael rebel, but James's consciousness locked on like a mongoose. *Relax. Breathe.* James saw the Pit. He saw Mikhael alone in this tower, aflame with pain, screaming to the void. He saw Mikhael's blind, jealous hatred for James's realm, saw the way he tied it to his abandonment. Back, back, further— it was as if a balloon popped, and all of it came forth at once. James saw the two minds weaving this world; he saw fighting and denial; and then, beyond all that, there was a small kernel of shame baked hard as stone.

James and Mikhael disentangled, as if emerging from pools of each other, and each sucked a deep breath.

"That," Mikhael said, "I did not expect."

James shook. His belly went tight. "You're the wizard."

"Pardon me?" Mikhael said as he returned to his seat by the window.

"It was always just the two of you." Mikhael's massive face was as tight and blank as marble. "That's what Morning Star was going to tell them."

"No!" Mikhael seemed to use his arms and legs to crush the chair in which he'd been sitting, but upon its destruction it immediately disappeared and he was stand-ing. "The Creator had been there. We both felt it. It was only later that Morning Star began to deny that. The belief used to run deep in us both."

"Belief?"

"We felt the Creator! Do you think someone could mistake that? I assure you they could not. We felt It as we built, and It filled us with purpose and love and fearlessness. But then Morning Star changed—forgot—but the truth will be out. When the War is concluded, the Creator will return and we will all fall into the bosom of love."

Oh my god. The realization filled James's mind like a cave-in, and he wanted to drop to his knees and cry. "You made it all up." It wasn't an accusation or a question; James said it in the same tepid tone with which one repeats the news that a loved one is dead.

"I did no such thing!" Mikhael bellowed. "I felt the Creator come to me . . ."

But James wasn't listening anymore.

"The, the prophecy, the War . . . all of it . . . *it's a lie?*"

"No, it will bring about the return of the Creator! The Creator has promised me! We shall be reunited!"

It wasn't a lie, he realized. Mikhael truly believed the story he'd invented. The narrative infected him, James thought, remembering what Ezra had said. To continue talking to this one was like arguing with the piss-smelling whisperer who was always at the train station. *But then why is this all happening? If it's not true, then how can this all be real?*

One thought burned through the question: *DorianEzra . . . DorianEzra . . . DorianEzra . . .*

Where are they? And then, with barely a thought,

James's consciousness reached out, searching for Ezra. Like sonar it spread and raced. James felt himself here in the tower and spreading over Taloon all at once, the sensation as natural as reaching out his arm. *Why didn't you think of this before?* But James knew, somehow, he wouldn't have been able to. The clutter of his mind upon arriving, the assault on all his senses—it was too much. But now . . . things were different. The questions receded, the fear softened. James turned and looked back at Bahamut. Passing through had changed him, somehow. He tried to diagnose himself, to search through the halls of his mind, but he could find nothing out of place. No, it was instead as if everything had been cleaned, as if the layers of dust and cobweb that he now realized were his own little fears and petty self-absorbed obsessions, had been cleared away. But there was something else there. An idea? A directive? Something he *should* know, but for some reason he couldn't quite bring it up. It was close, though. He could tell he was close to uncovering it or remembering it or piecing it together. It didn't matter how—he knew it was there—*right there*—just beyond the reach of his fingers, and so he stretched. And stretched.

But then he saw Ezra, and the hidden thought rushed off. He saw Ezra for only an instant—gathered with others, waiting—but he knew exactly where he was.

James turned his attention back to Mikhael, who was watching the young man, transfixed and cautious, as someone would look at a dog they didn't trust.

"This won't work," James said.

"What won't work?"

"You know where Ezra is, don't you?"

"Know? No, I don't know where he is. I could guess, though. And were I to, I would guess he awaits you at the Pit."

"You're all trying to get me there."

"Of course we are. That is where you will fulfill your destiny. Surely you feel the urge—the need—to fulfill your destiny."

"What if I say no?"

"No?"

"No."

Mikhael brought his hands up and looked down at James, something like bemusement on his massive face. He almost smiled as he tilted his head. "But you would never do that. That's not who you are."

"You don't know me."

"Oh, but I think I do. I know you are not one who will drop his weight, knowing someone else will have to bear it."

"What's that supposed to mean?"

"Think about it, James. You are the product of all this belief. The belief is not a belief in the James of 323 Jackson Street of Stone Grove of Illinois of the United States of America of Earth. Right? Think about it. The belief is in the War Bringer, the One who will bring about a final reckoning. The belief is in the human who will release the Adversary and begin the War that will bring about the return of the Creator. In one guise or another, this is the belief. This is the belief which has resulted in your very existence and purpose—your destiny.

"No, if you fail to live out your destiny, what do you think will happen? I'll tell you. Have you figured it out already? But, of course, it's so simple. The War did not happen. Therefore, he was not the War Bringer. He was not the One, the Antichrist or whatever we—as believers—choose to call him. So the belief recycles, it builds, and soon another comes forth.

"You see? There's no other way that it could be. So if you were to refuse to fulfill your destiny, you would be stopping nothing. You would only be throwing your yoke onto the shoulders of another. And then, of course, the question is what would become of you. Who would you be? Where would you go and what would you do? And until when? And when the next One comes along, mightn't they be a little upset with you? Who knows?"

"Have there been others?"

Mikhael waved a hand and pressed on. "And if you seek Ezra, as it seems, because you are cross with him and want vengeance, well . . . very well. You will have it. He is a mote of nothingness under your foot. Crush him. Crush him with us. Yes?"

James did not nod or speak or respond. Oddly, he actually felt rather calm at the moment. He was not sure what would happen when he arrived, but he knew that he must move forward, must go to the Pit. And since the decision was made, there was no point in worrying. It would be what it would be.

Within nothing, everything. It rang through his head like a favorite old song.

Mikhael smiled. "Rufa!" he called. "Raffi!"

James turned to see two beings stepping through Bahamut. They looked identical, with thin, birdlike legs that grew into mighty torsos, and arms wide and flat, as if they were both wings and arms at once. Their eyes were wide, their mouths small, and their hair and beards grew thick and long, down to their waists. The one on the left looked over his shoulder as he emerged, mumbling, "Yeah, yeah, Bahamut. *Your mother's* an automaton propelled only by fear," before he turned to his twin and grumbled, "Hate that stupid thing."

"Warriors!"

They snapped to attention, looking from Mikhael to James and back again.

"War is at hand! Gather everyone; gather mounts and beasts! We ride to War!"

And with that they were gone, dashing off through Bahamut, and once again it was just James and Mikhael.

"We shall ride across the sky, as befits an army such as ours. You will ride at the front, with me, and when we—"

"Y'know," James said, "I think I'll just meet you there."

"What?"

But James had no way of knowing what Mikhael said or did next. He knew where he had to be, and as that single syllable left Mikhael's mouth, James simply saw Ezra, saw the Pit he'd feared so in his dreams, and he Pushed. There was no sensation. No anything. It was not a motion at all, James could see now. The sensation of passing through had probably been in his head as well.

I am nothing.

James stood at the edge of the water. The smell of salt water was back and strong, and for a moment it carried James to a beach somewhere in his earliest memories, and his mother stood in the waves, hair matted to her head, laughing, as he stood on the hard, wet sand, too scared to go out. The memory rushed in and filled him and then dissolved. He tried to bring it back up—had no idea when it was from—but all that he could call back now was a memory of the memory. The moment was gone.

This water, though, was nothing like the memory had been. The smell of salt and matches swirled the atmosphere, but there were no waves. This water lay against the shore like carpet. It was an unnerving sight, though it took James a few seconds to puzzle out why.

It's too big to be this still. The water disappeared in the distance, the way it did in oceans or Lake Michigan. But when there's that much water, it's supposed to move. This water was still as Haley Pond. James was looking out over the sea when he first saw it, and an electrothunderclap of fear blitzed his whole system. He felt it in his fingertips, in the follicles at the back of his scalp, in his knees and balls and even behind his eyes. Everything tingled. *There it is.*

The Pit.

It was out in the water, maybe fifty yards or so away, and James flashed back to the dreams, to the smells, to the shimmering walls. Four figures stood next to the Pit, facing him, the sky behind them a melting cloud of pink. James didn't recognize three of the figures, but there was no mistaking the man on the left.

How long would James have stood on the banks, afraid and unsure how to proceed, had Ezra not waved? That wave, so full of old camaraderie and warmth, the gesture of a visiting friend, set off a mindless explosion of rage in James and then he was in front of them, ten feet or so from the Pit. The water was different here. It flowed in, cascading over the sides as if the Pit were a vortex or waterfall of some kind. From all directions the water streamed toward it, and there, at its edge, was Ezra and his comrades. James barely looked at Ezra's companions, even though two of them were monstrously large. He had eyes for only the interim librarian of George Washington High School, and staring at him, he remembered all the talks and lectures and admonitions, and the words came out unbidden.

"It's all a lie."

"What is?" Ezra said with a slight incline of the head.

"The Creator, the prophecy, all of it. Mikhael made it all up."

"No, James."

"It is. I looked inside him. I saw it."

Ezra smiled that same patient teacher's smile James had seen so many times. "You don't understand, James. Even if that's true, even if it started as a lie, it's true now. We've all made it true. Look at who you are and what you can do. James, look at where you're standing right now."

Ezra's hand fell open toward the Pit. James's gaze followed, and his surroundings turned to white noise. The world was only James and the giant Pit. Standing here, James could not deny it: something down there wanted him. It called him. He felt, in fact, as if the air itself was pressing him down into the Pit. But more than that, he felt his own desire. *He* wanted it—more than anything he had ever wanted in his life.

No! Dorian. You're here for Dorian.

James looked up from the Pit and saw the pleased expression catch on Ezra's face.

"Where's Dorian?"

Ezra smiled, just as he had that first time they talked on the porch—and his eyes were like a hug, and his smile was trust itself. But now it was different. James could see it was only a glamour. It was a fresh coat of paint, nothing more. His eyes told Ezra as much, and he waited for the librarian to arrange his face back to its normal countenance.

"I am sorry, James, things had to go the way they did."

"Where is she?"

"She's at the Diplomat Motel."

The unexpected answer short-circuited his planned

response ("I swear to god, if you don't tell me where she is right now I'll kill you!"). Instead he said, "What?"

"The Diplomat. On Washington."

What?

"It's the white motor court with the colonnades. The sign out front advertises that they have HBO."

"But you . . . you took her. She called me."

Ezra smiled gently, a teacher instructing a child slow to catch on. He opened his mouth, and out came Dorian's voice. *"James?* Help. Please. He took me. We're at the factory. I—*no! Get away from*—" And then it was his own voice again, soft and comforting. "I apologize if I frightened you, James. It was necessary to get you here. I would never hurt someone who is important to you. You should know that, but I understand in your current, keyed-up state you're not thinking clearly. I mean it, though—I apologize. It was a rotten trick. Dorian is sound asleep, I assure you. Safely, pharmacologically asleep at the Diplomat Hotel, room 208, peacefully awaiting your return. You see? You don't have to choose. You can have her if you like. Free Morning Star and return to your world. If you want her by your side as you rally the world, then make it so. Surely you've realized by now that you can have whomever you wish."

"I—"

"Enough!" It was the giant on the right side of the group. He was as tall as Gabrael but thicker, with skin that appeared pale and hard as marble. "You release

Morning Star!"

Ezra leaned in and said, "Quiet, you—"

"No! Molok will not be quiet! Molok says boy go down and free Morning Star! Now!"

The giant called Molok took a single step toward James, who felt a snap inside, and all of the rage and confusion churning since Dorian's disappearance, everything which had been waiting for Ezra, was free. When Molok moved toward him, James felt that familiar rush of fear, then shame, which exploded into a single thought.

And then Molok was gone. Or so it seemed for a moment, before all eyes noticed it: a tiny, insectile spec. Eyes strained and focused, and there, roughly the size of a fly—hard to make out against the shimmering water— was Molok, his mouth open, screaming something too small for the world to hear and running a frantic, multi-directional geometry.

"Wow."

James turned to Ezra, but he wasn't the one who'd spoken. Ezra was frozen, his hands up as if to ward off an attack, staring at the tiny scampering Molok, who had finally settled on a direction.

It was the being to Ezra's side who was speaking now. "Not bad, kid."

And then James knew him. He knew that voice and he knew those eyes, and a small warm joy of recognition pushed through everything for a moment. "Dink."

James looked him over and felt, oddly, that this was

exactly what he'd assumed Dink would look like. He was smaller than the others, with legs like bows and arms like cables. His face was dirty and his mouth was pulled back in a playful and mocking grin, like a big brother.

"And this," Dink said, motioning to the one on his other side, "is Astoreth."

"It's an honor," she said. She was larger than both Ezra and Dink, and her shoulders pulled back and protruded, as if her bones might burst from the skin at any moment. She nodded to Molok, who was now trying to scale the mountainous side of her foot. "I apologize for my companion's impertinence."

James found it hard to look away from the violent bones of her face, from the small dark eyes, but when he finally did pull his gaze down, he found himself transfixed by the outlined musculature of her chest.

No. The Pit. You must!

"I—"

The wail of an army exploded from far away and washed over them. Ezra and James and Dink and Astoreth (and presumably Molok) turned and looked, and from over the mountains came the army of Metatron, as thick as a swarm of bees. They blotted out the sky, riding across the air. Some appeared to run across the sky, while others looked to be swimming or leaping, and still others rode on animals and things which James could not identify. The cry grew louder and louder, until their shouts drowned out all other noises, all atmosphere. It was a blanket of life, thrashing across the sky, undulating like a flying carpet and then angling down, toward them, toward the Pit.

James and the others said nothing. They watched, and in moments the mass was close enough to identify. At the front edges, he recognized Gabrael and Raffi and Uri. In the center, descending to their position, was Mikhael, resplendent in gold and light, as if reflecting a sun only he could see. Mikhael floated, gossamer fabric trailing. On each side of him came Munk and Nack, as if they were his escorts, though more unimpressive escorts it would be hard to find. Each rode half-crescent chariots that required every last bit of their focus and strength to control. Luckily, the descent was quick, and within moments Munk, Mikhael, and Nack were on the ground. The remaining army followed like a tail coming to rest.

Munk and Nack jumped from their chariots as if scalded, happy to be rid of them. They crossed to James, waving madly.

"We thought," Munk said, "that you would come back down."

"We waited," Nack added as they reached James, bowing slightly to him and the others.

"Nack!" Astoreth said. "We thought you were gone."

"No, no, just, uh, hard at work."

"Yes," Munk said before turning to James once more. "This has been a very eventful day."

Mikhael stepped forward then. His army did not advance a fraction of an inch, but he closed the distance between himself and the Pit, and James could feel the others shrink back in his presence.

This is it. It's really happening. And with that, James's whole self came alive in oneness and purpose, tingling with static energy. He could feel all of them, in him; the waiting, the anticipation, and in horror he realized this was his reaching out reversed. Their want, their need, their faith—it filled him like a hand in a glove; its power directed him. It felt . . . wonderful and true. He was a tool with a singular purpose, nothing more.

Dorian was a character in a book. Ezra was nobody. His family was a dream. All there was in the world was the cage, the prison, the Pit. He wanted to feel the seals open, the urge as exquisite as if it were his own prison. *This is all. All!* James was filled with the whole-body-and-soul want—*need*—of addiction, of I'll-kill-everyone-I-ever-met-just-to-make-this-happen.

Mikhael said, "It is time."

And Ezra nodded as they held each other's eyes. "Yes, it is."

James watched himself turn and march toward the Pit. *You don't have to listen to them. You don't have to listen to the urge.*

But I want this!

What about Dorian?

Later!

What about Mom and Dad? What about . . . ? What about . . . ?

Later! Later! Later! I neeeeeeed this.

James stepped toward the Pit, and as he did, he saw the form begin to appear, ascending a step at a time, just as it had in his dream. It was massive and wet, and in its movements were violence and malevolence. He could feel his own fear as it swelled into the world outside of himself. The sky darkened and the army grew quiet, losing its pep-rally ballsiness, moving closer to each other for the safety of the tribe. Then Leviathan was clear of the Pit, its clawed feet piercing the water as it stalked toward James.

You are nothing.

Its breath was a long, damp purge of death-stink. It stared down at James, eyes like a dumb and savage animal.

You're the fear. Not him. You're your own fear. You're everything. You're everything.

"You are the One," Leviathan said, its fat, wet tongue sneaking through its lipless mouth.

"I am."

"Only the One may enter."

James nodded. He felt the collective tension infecting him, felt the anxiety of those waiting on history. They could feel its imminence—and that was when the thought occurred to James. "Uh, I think I want my friends to come down with me."

"What?"

"What?"

"No, that's not how it works," Ezra said. "Only the One may enter."

"Right," James said. "But I bet I can change it if I want. Right?"

"No," Ezra said. "No."

"Uh, hey, Leviathan. I'm gonna bring a couple people down with me."

"Yes," Leviathan said. "The One will bring a couple people down with him. Yes."

James looked from Dink to Munk and Nack, and he felt a swell of gratitude that no words had been necessary. The three of them were at his side a moment later.

"Wait!"

James turned to see Mikhael, his hands up to halt the proceedings. But then, as if he hadn't expected everyone to look, hadn't planned what to say next, the words sped out in a sheepish mumble. "I wanna go."

"Alright," James said. "Come on."

James made his way to the mouth of the Pit, seeing Mikhael and Ezra following—and the Pull was different. No, not different. It was the same, but now James could see it. It was as if he'd been fighting an invisible tension, but now he saw the fisherman's line, and while being able to follow it did not make it disappear, it did allow him the freedom of thought. He placed his right foot on the top step and began the descent. The steps were thinner than in the dream—or maybe just thinner than he remembered. James looked down and watched the steps widen into a comfortable size before resuming his decline. The drop-off was just as he remembered. It mimicked fog swirling, and the bottom seemed to call out. No, what really drew the eyes were the walls, shimmering and liquid. How had he not realized what they were? He walked, listening to the steps behind him, and saw them as if from above. He saw the Pull and tested its tension against the urge to turn and run. He felt like a horse being driven on by a master it hates.

James stopped. To his right, beyond the flowing wall, he saw one of the gold teardrops. He inspected it, shimmering though obscured, like viewing light through frosted purple glass. He saw the glint of another, and as he looked at each one, his periphery caught the one next to it, then the ones just below and above, until the numbers overwhelmed and his sight adjusted. Blinking lights, swirling and innumerable in the descent, like trying to observe individual blades of grass. Just as in his dreams, they trembled with anticipation, shaking with life and begging pleeeeeaaaaaassssssse—

And there was the Pull again. James submitted to it, rushing, taking the stairs two at a time—before remembering for the final time the foolishness of such things in this place. James chose, and then he was at the bottom of the Pit, in a dark antechamber. He could barely see the bottom stair for the darkness, though he could hear the others standing nearby and saw scratches of silhouettes here and there. Faint, disobliging light hung suspended miles above at the mouth of the Pit.

The only other illumination was the pale blue glow

coming from off to the side, from what James could now see was a hallway. He felt the Pull and made for it without another thought.

James felt someone slip up next to him just as he entered the hallway.

"It's weird," James said, "having you standing next to me and not on my shoulder."

"I imagine," Dink said. Then, in a one-note whisper that James could barely hear, "I wonder, have you decided who you're going to be yet?"

James turned and found Dink's taunting smile in the dim hall. He looked back, but the others didn't seem to have heard. The hallway was snaking now, but James could see the tail of their group coming around the last bend. Ezra and Mikhael walked with purpose, and both looked as if they wanted to rush to James, as if they'd been left out of the cool kids' conversation, but they were separated from him by Munk and Nack, who were walking at all angles, pirouetting around each other as they looked up and down, taking in the arched dark-water walls that made the hallway. James wanted to ask what he should do. He wanted to tell Dink he felt trapped, driven as much by them as by his own desire to see the task done.

And as he thought this, it came gushing back, all the fears he'd had in Stone Grove. He saw Dorian singing, spine arched, head back, and he could see the music, could see the breath in patterns—and the bus driver, the one who saved him. What was his name? Was he really going to make him fight? After he saved him?

James saw his parents and the Schroeder brothers and Mr. Llewellyn; he saw *Guernica*.

You can't bring this to the world.

It's already there. You can't stop it.

No! You can't do this! But then the Puuuuullllllll. *Go! Let Morning Star go! Let everything go.* James could tell himself whatever he liked, but he knew one truth in his heart: he was powerless. And when he looked back to Dink, he saw that the smile was gone, and where it had been was concern, the worry and defense of a parent.

But if there was anything else to be said, any advice or support, it was too late.

The hallway took a final twist and opened, and just like that James Salley found himself standing in the chamber he'd seen so often in his dreams and the bliss of mindless and singular purpose rang through him.

He'd never really seen the entirety of the room in the dreams, though, never had eyes for anything but the solitary cell. Now he could not help but take it in. The walls rose on all sides, seamlessly up and up, and converged without line or crease in a majestic half-circle ceiling—like a church. As the others filed in behind him, James noticed that while the walls did shimmer, something was different. *Ice. The walls are ice.* He turned to look at Mikhael and found him taking in the room as well, though with an expression akin to pride.

A scream issued from the sarcophagus. It fired

through all of them, feeling like a personal assault on their brains. James clasped his hands over his ears and saw the others do the same. But it did nothing. The next scream ripped through them just the same. James saw Munk and Nack looking at each other with undisguised terror as he turned back to the sarcophagus. The scream was a prisoner's howl. *Let me out,* it said. *Look at me! Look at me!*

James took a step toward the sarcophagus, and it shook. He could feel the thing inside spinning with madness, throwing itself against the walls, begging and dying and demanding. A whisper of a scream slipped out, though James couldn't make out what it said. What he couldn't miss, though, was the pain, the pleading. It was like hearing the echo of a mother wailing over her dead child.

James looked back over his shoulder. All of them glanced from James to the sarcophagus and back again. All except Dink. His eyes never left James's, and in them James saw imploring. *What does he want me to do?*

He wants you to open it! He wants freedom! He wants the War! He said so!

That's not what that look feels like.

James returned his gaze to the sarcophagus. It was massive, maybe a foot or two taller than Mikhael, and covered in what looked to James like a stone version of alligator or snake skin. There was a lock set dead center on what would be the head: a rectangular plate with a tiny, perfect black circle in the middle. There was another lock at what would be the ankles and, between the two, five others evenly spaced up the center of the sarcophagus.

James took a final step, standing so close to the monstrous prison that he could feel the life within, the same way you can feel a person through their clothes. Its breath was in the air; its pulse sounded against his skin.

Say the name. It's your destiny. It's who you are.

Wait, wait. What was that look from Dink? What does he want you to do?

No, right now you need to say the na—

No! Wait! What was it Dink wanted you to do? Remember.

I don't remember.

Remember.

I don't remember!

Remember!

Stop!

I can't, I can't, I can't, I can't . . .

Just say the name.

I want—

Say the name—

I want . . .

And then the chamber was alive with sound. It was a moment before James recognized it: "Habanera." From *Carmen*. Her voice.

Mikhael and Ezra spun on their heels, looking up and around.

"What is . . . ?"

"Why is there this . . . ?"

Munk and Nack, ever amenable, shrugged, clasped hands, and began to dance. Dink, James saw with only a moment's glance, wore the beginnings of a smile.

And in that instant the thought which James had long been trying to access was revealed—all at once, in its entirety, like a magician tearing aside the curtain—and James felt a momentary rush of foolishness for not seeing it sooner. But that emotion was gone almost as soon as it came, overtaken by the weight of what it meant. His knees went loose, and a cold rock filled up his belly.

I missed it. That was it, and I missed it. With Dorian and Mom and Dad.

The last time already happened.

Unbidden and unstoppable, tears rushed from him. He did not cry out or sob, but the tears did run down his cheeks in healthy rivers.

Munk and Nack stopped dancing.

"James?" Munk said.

"Are you alright?" Nack said.

James cleared his throat and drew a shirtsleeve across his face, smearing his tears over to his ear and neck.

"I don't like it down here," James said.

Mikhael and Ezra both opened their mouths to protest.

James said, "Let's go."

And so they were gone.

Or rather, they were somewhere else. For a moment, they were sure they were back on Earth—but only for a moment. There was no mistaking the Great Field, magnificent as it was in tall, green grass and bursts of primary-color flowers.

James stood, as he had in the chamber, only a foot or so from the sarcophagus, and all around him stood the armies of Metatron and Morning Star. The freed army of Morning Star stood behind the sarcophagus, hundreds of thousands—maybe millions deep. James turned and saw Mikhael's army, even more massive and numbered, disappearing over the hills in the distance. The armies buzzed; questions, directionless movements, confusion built into the burbling whoosh of a river. *What happened? and Where are we? Why are we here? morphed as the word spread back: The War Bringer, Morning Star—here, now.*

James saw Astoreth and tiny, tiny Molok at the head of one army, looking at first confused, both at their new location and at the return of their comrades. But that was gone almost as soon as it was born. Each had caught sight of the sarcophagus; each had eyes only for it.

On the other side of James was his little troupe of explorers from the Pit and, behind them, Gabrael and Uri and Raffi and a mass of creatures too wild and disparate to comprehend. James found himself especially drawn to one who looked to him sort of like a blue elephant walking upright—*This is it. This is life now.*

James turned toward Selliphais, and as he did the tower appeared in the distance, rising and rising, until it filled a corner of the sky. Then the sky itself near the tower began to change. A star of impossible brilliance blinked into existence, and its yellow light melted into the rest of the sky, and blues and yellows swirled and swirled, and James smiled, in spite of the pain. He was fully there and nowhere else, and in that instant he was at peace, or at least resigned.

And then they were all back, alive in his mind: Dorian and Mom and Dad and even Ken Lakatos and Jess and Nick and the smell of the ChocoMalt factory and swimming in Haley Pond, the mud between his toes, and James closed his eyes and touched two fingers to his lips, feeling the kiss again, ripping open because he would never feel it again. Dying inside as all the residents of Taloon looked on. They watched as the young man with his eyes closed was borne upwards, the very ground on which he stood swelling up, carrying him as a gentle wave would, until he was above them all.

Then James opened his eyes, and when he spoke, his voice came from the sky above and the ground below; it was carried by the grass and the stones and the wind.

"The connection between this world and mine . . . is closed."

And as it was said, so it was. The denizens of Taloon could feel the truth of the words as soon as they were spoken. The sky grew denser, the air filled with a buffet of new smells, and even the ground became more corporeal. In the distance, at the Great Field of Dreaming, the heads of dreamers began to pop up here and there, their faces awash in the sour looks of those rudely awakened from a rich nap.

"They will have no more to do with you, and you will have no more to do with them."

"The War must happen in your world!" Mikhael called up to James. "The Creato—"

But when James looked down to him, Mikhael found that he could speak no more. His hands went to his mouth, then his throat, scrambling and massaging, but they could squeeze out no sound.

"We'll do all that later." James looked out to the gathering once more. "Believe me, you're all gonna wanna talk to Mikhael later."

James let the ground descend slowly, until he was once more standing before the sarcophagus. He remembered the terror he'd felt so recently, standing here—even just dreaming of standing here—and he felt that it was a different person altogether. Then James leaned close, so that his lips were almost brushing the lock set into the belly, and whispered the name.

"Jennifer."

The seven locks released with a sound like soda cans opening. They fell away as James stepped back, and then the sarcophagus split straight down the middle, and from the millennia-old prison stepped Morning Star, Jennifer.

She was beautiful and terrifying at once. The force of grace and violence emanating from her so overwhelmed James that it was a moment before he recognized her face—*Eliza*.

He wanted to say something to her, to explain. It was

obvious that she was bewildered, having had thousands of years to prepare for battle and only a few moments to prepare herself for whatever this was. She was still assessing; that much was obvious. The pent-up rage seeped out, and now she seemed mostly confused. Her mouth twisted at the corner, as if to say, *This isn't how it's supposed to happen.*

"Stop it!" Ezra stomped toward him. "Stop it! Stop it! *Stopit!*" Then Ezra was at him. "Undo all of this right now!" he shouted, all of his composure having abandoned him.

James's mind reached out, rearranging Ezra as he railed, so that the librarian of George Washington High School grew into an obese cocker spaniel—"Open the connection between the worlds, James!"—before morphing into a screaming carrot—"I'm warning you!"—and then a small, rabbit-eared, 1980s, black-and-white television set, the image of his howling visage crackling—"You cannot do this, boy!"—and then an inflated, purple, Violet Beauregarde version of himself—"I swear it. Look at me. If you do this, I will make you suffer. I will find a way, James. You know me. I will find a way there, and I will get them. I will get them all!"—and then it wasn't funny anymore, and he was just Ezra again. "That little girl. Your mother and your father, James. I will get to all of them. I will create new tortures—things never dreamed of. I will. Look at me. Believe me. This doesn't have to happen like this. You can still have it all, James." The composure was back. The old eyes, doing their best to shed the hard-cold of a moment before; back to warmth, back to reassuring. Back to a friend. "Please, James. You can have everything."

James watched those eyes change, watched them work their subtle magic, and then he stepped into the space between himself and Ezra.

"Nobody gets everything." And with that, James let his gaze fall on the sarcophagus.

Ezra began to shout, "N—"

But he was already gone. The sarcophagus was shut tight once more. James went to it and leaned in close. He whispered a word into the locks, which sealed themselves with seven small pops. Whatever word it was that James said, no one would ever know. James himself would never say.

And in the next moment, Ezra was gone. As was the sarcophagus, vanished back to its icy rest under the sea.

James turned and walked away from all of them, to a clearing between the two armies, twenty feet or so from where Jennifer now stood, regal and beautiful and confused. James stared at her, and for a moment he reprimanded himself for how poorly he'd drawn her; but that didn't matter. He was beyond that now. The limitations of his hands, of his words, the boxes and restrictions and books: all gone. James smiled at her. He nodded, and she returned the gesture as a stiff imitation.

He wondered if this severing of their worlds was permanent. Would it die with him? Would he die? Would he age here? Would there be another War Bringer?

The thought brought with it a wind of freedom. *I am nothing.*

Let there be another War Bringer. Let them do whatever they want. I'll hold it closed for as long as I can.

For an instant James saw all of them, back there, living, and he smiled, thinking that Ezra was right. He did feel like a god.

Time to pray.

James sat down, landing gently in the throne which had not been there the instant before. He peered out at the gathered masses, standing around like actors who've forgotten their lines.

"Okay," James said, and as he did the very ground behind him rose, weaving itself into the walls of his castle. "Whatta you wanna do now?"

Acknowledgments

This novel has been a long undertaking, and along the way I've received invaluable support and help from so many people, a great number who aren't even aware of the aid they gave. There are too many of you to name and so many of the moments were gone before they could be catalogued, but those moments of inspiration were lent, and for what it's worth, I'm thankful.

A huge thank-you, of course, to my agent, Alex Slater. I feel insanely lucky to have found someone who's so passionate about the work, and I'm looking forward to the long, messy road ahead.

To Emily Steele: editing is always a little scary, but working with you has been both instructive and gentle, and this book is a finer machine because of your hand in it.

Thank you to those of you who read the book during its earlier stages—your advice and questions and ideas were monumental—especially Geoff Hyatt, Jeanne Jordan, Richelle Jordan, Adam Motin, and Rob Duffer.

Thank you to Gina Frangello and Joe Meno, who've been friends and mentors time and again, and to Mark Davidov, who told me the old story of Mr. Chicken and Mr. Rooster years ago, while sharing a drink in George's Cocktail Lounge. I miss those evenings.

For the support and encouragement, Mom, Dad, Graham, and Lela: you're always there; don't ever think it's not appreciated.

And finally, thank you, Ricki, for the million invisible things, and Ben and Charlie, for being you.

MEDALLION™

For more information
about other great titles from
Medallion, visit

medallionpress.com

Read On Vacation

Medallion Press has created
Read on Vacation for e-book
lovers who read on the go.

See more at:
medallionmediagroup.com/readonvacation

CRIXEO™

WHERE LIFE AND ART INTERSECT.

A digital playground for the
inspired and creative mind.

crixeo.com